Tear

MW00949484

PRAISES FOR TEARS OF FREEDOM

One of the hardest concepts to convey when one writes of an historical era is the pathos of the moment – what individuals and what families had had to endure in the early years of our republic. *Tears of freedom* follows the O'Flaherty family, their origins in Ireland, their coming to America, and their experiences in this "new world." As the book unfolds (starting with an unusual but helpful description of the cast of characters), the reader begins to witness the struggle of this Irish family, from the arrest that causes the family being sent to America to the end of the War of 1812 and their struggle to survive the harsh realities of that traumatic time. It reveals the pathos of that time that would otherwise be lost or forgotten by subsequent generations. To understand their tears is to understand their times. To understand their history is to understand our own. *Tears of Freedom* is a reminder that the story of our early republic is not just a series of events but, rather, the story of the people of that time struggling to survive events beyond their control.

John Douglas Hall

Historical Performer (James Madison)

What a motion picture – rather, a TV Mini-Series – this would make, packing Irish history into the adventures of an endearing Danny O'Flaherty!!!"

Michael Robinson, author of *A Squeaky Kneeler.*

A forgotten, if not unknown, world history lesson told through a page turning family saga spanning multiple generations and multiple continents. O'Flaherty – Walker delivers the great Irish emigration story with all the fundamental transgressions of extreme, if not horrific, cultural disorder while simultaneously bringing the personal and poetic Irish culture and experience to light…where it very much belongs.

Kevin M. White, PH.D.

Vice President and Director of Athletics Duke University.

TEARS OF FREEDOM

The Scots-Irish Suffering That Produced the American Culture

By

DANNY O'FLAHERTY

And

TED G. WALKER - DANNY G. WALKER

MTW Publishing Co.
www.mtwpublishing.com

REGISTERED LIBRARY OF CONGRESS

TXu-2-040-944
-1st Edition-

TEARS OF FREEDOM

Presented to

____

By

____

CONTENTS

DRAMATIS PERSONAE

COLEMAN O'FLAHERTY *

Was born in Western Ireland whose ancestors were known as the "O'Flaherty Clan." He had been a fisherman, but the British Penal Laws had forbidden the sale of fish to foreign nations by those of the Catholic faith. He was married to Delia and they were the parents of six children. He was later arrested because his employer was accused of not paying debt on a farm where he and his family resided and worked. His wife, Delia and two of his children were shipped to America as indentured slaves. The three remaining children then born were surreptitiously placed with distant relatives to avoid the children being placed in orphan homes.

DELIA O'FLAHERTY *

The wife of Coleman O'Flaherty and mother to six children. Revered by her children, a loving, gregarious Irish woman who brought joy to her family and joined with her husband in always providing hope for her children.

PATRICK O'FLAHERTY *

First child of Coleman and Delia O'Flaherty. Was arrested with his parents and was sent to America as an indentured slave. Grew to manhood as a prisoner of the Crown of England. He was eventually released along with other family members because of his younger brother Dan O'Flaherty's association with General James Olgelthorpe.

BARBARA O'FLAHERTY *

Second child born to Delia and Coleman O'Flaherty. She was over eight years of age when the parents were arrested and shipped to America as indentured slaves.

DAN O'FLAHERTY *

Dan O'Flaherty was the third child born to Delia and Coleman O'Flaherty. He was a young lad living with his family at the O'Flaherty farm when four of his family members were arrested, indentured as slaves and shipped to America. Dan was placed under the care of Eamonn O'Flaherty a relative who eventually agreed to place him in the care of General and Margarita O'Shea. General O'Shea was, prior to being injured, was the most renowned Commander of the Special Forces in Spain and trained Dan to become a military leader. Dan was captured by the British Army in the Jacobite War thereby becoming a prisoner of war under the Command of General James Oglethorpe who had begun the development of Georgia as an American Colony. Spain occupied Florida and became involved in expanding its territory by invading Georgia and the South of Carolina. General Oglethorpe assigned Dan to provide the defense for that region. The Spanish were defeated, and Dan was given freedom. He became knowledgeable of George Washington through General Oglethorpe. At the beginning of the Revolutionary War, General Washington enlisted the "Blue Celts" (which was a group of soldiers Dan had organized as special Force soldiers) who became the personal security force for General George Washington's and his family. Dan rose in the ranks to become a General in the Revolutionary Army.

SIOBHANN O'FLAHERTY *

The fourth child born to Coleman and Delia O'Flaherty. She was one of the two youngest children who was rescued by Bridget O'Flaherty, a distant cousin by marriage, just as the slave ship sailed for America with her parents, brother Patrick and sister Barbara. She was raised in Ireland by Bridget and Donal O'Flaherty under the close watch care of Eamonn O'Flaherty.

SHIBEAL O'FLAHERTY *

Was the fifth child born to the Delia and Coleman O'Flaherty family. Shibeal was a small child when her family was arrested. Before the family was shipped to America a cousin named Bridget appeared and rescued her and her sister Siobhann from being placed in an orphanage. After the family was rejoined in America, she became a spy for the Revolutionary forces in New York along with her sister, Maureen.

MAUREEN O'FLAHERTY *

Known as the sixth child born to Coleman and Delia O'Flaherty while they were imprisoned as indentured slaves in America. Dan selected her to become involved in the First American Revolutionary War to spy on the British troops in New York City. She proved herself to be a gallant and most remarkable asset for the American victory over the British. Married Matthew Collier's son, Weston Collier at the close of the Revolutionary War.

MARY (O'MALLEY) O'FLAHERTY *

Daughter of Gregory O'Malley who became the wife of Dan O'Flaherty and mother of Cathal Brendon O'Flaherty, Dan "Two Dan" O'Flaherty and Bridget O'Flaherty.

CATHAL BRENDON O'FLAHERTY *

The first son born to Dan and Mary O'Flaherty.

DAN "TWO DAN" O'FLAHERTY *

One of the twins born to Dan and Mary O'Flaherty. He was a male child and in Dan's absence, the Chief of the Cherokees, Attakullakulla named him after his father as "Two Dan" O'Flaherty.

BRIDGET O'FLAHERTY *

One of the twins born to Dan and Mary O'Flaherty while the family was living with the Cherokee Indians during the Revolutionary War. Her brother was named "Two Dan" by the Cherokee Chief Attakullakulla.

EAMONN O'FLAHERTY *

A distant relative of Coleman O'Flaherty who was a giant of a man and a ship owner. He was fortunately in the right place when the sheriff came to arrest Bryan O'Flaherty (and all the Catholic employees) having accused them of failing to pay debt. While the British military was in the process of arresting the land owner and his employees, Delia Coleman asked Eamonn O'Flaherty to take possession of Dan and care for him until they had time to explain their case to the judge. The courts refused to hear the O'Flaherty pleas and four of the O'Flaherty's became slaves bound for the slave camps of America. Eamonn took care of Dan who became protégé and eventually the adoptive son of General Phillip and Margarita O'Shea of Spain.

BRIDGET O'FLAHERTY *

She was the wife of Donal O'Flaherty and the daughter in law of Eamonn O'Flaherty. Bridget was granted possession of Siobhain and Shibeal O'Flaherty by their mother just prior to the slave ship sailing to America with Coleman, Delia, Patrick and Barbara aboard as indentured slaves. She became the surrogate mother to Siobhain and Shibeal.

DONAL O'FLAHERTY *

Son of Eamonn O'Flaherty whose wife Bridget O'Flaherty rescued the two youngest children of Coleman and Delia O'Flaherty before they were placed in an orphan's home.

BRYAN O'FLAHERTY *

A distant relative of Coleman O'Flaherty who purchased property that had been in and out of the clan's possession for centuries. He mortgaged the property to an English money lender named St. Lord George who wrongfully used the property as collateral to increase a personal loan. Lord St. George failed to pay the Mortgage. The lender filed suit to foreclose the lien on the land and the collateral of which the workers were included. The O'Flaherty family and the other employees who were of the Catholic faith were enslaved and shipped to the slave's owners in America.

MICHAEL O'FLAHERTY *

A cousin to Coleman O'Flaherty who provided much needed employment to Coleman O'Flaherty's family on the farm owned by Bryan O'Flaherty. He was also enslaved and sent to America along with other members of the O'Flaherty family.

STEPHEN NEE *

A very knowledgeable caretaker who worked on the O'Flaherty farm. He provided Coleman O'Flaherty the necessary information to learn to farm and produce dairy products which was the basis of their survival as slaves in America.

LORD ST. GEORGE *

Lord St. George a presumed banker who loaned money on land mortgages but who in fact was an English fraud by taking solidly based mortgages and inflating the amount of the mortgage to a lender and failing to pay the mortgage payments even though he had collected the funds he had collected from the land owner.

SAMMY GILL *

He served as quarter master aboard a cargo ship owned by Eamonn O'Flaherty.

GENERAL PHILLIP O'SHEA *

The most recognized and qualified field and special Force Generals in the Spanish military. Husband to Marguerita O'Shea who was a member of the royal family of Spain. General O'Shea became injured by accident and retired from military service. He and his wife were very close friends to Eamonn O'Flaherty who had served Spain as a mercenary soldier under the command of General O'Shea. The O'Shea's ultimately adopted Dan as their son.

MARGARITA O'SHEA *

She was the wife of General Phillip O'Shea who was injured in an accident while in the Army of Spain. She and her husband were reclusive after the accident and prevailed upon their friend Eamonn O'Flaherty to allow them to provide care and training for Dan O'Flaherty. Dan ultimately became their adoptive son.

DR. MARK CASTILLE *

The physician who treated General O'Shea after the accident in the privacy of the O'Shea home.

GREGORY O'MALLEY *

The clan leader of the O'Malley's who resided on Clare Island in western Ireland. He was the owner of cargo ships used to ship goods to foreign countries. Most of his efforts were built around helping Catholic believers merchandise their goods. He was a very close friend to Eamonn O'Flaherty and father to Mary O'Malley, the wife of Dan O'Flaherty.

BONNIE PRINCE CHARLIE *

Son of James II, former King of England who was dethroned by King George II of The House of Hanover who were those that assumed authority after the protestant victories over the Catholics. He was the leader of the final Jacobite War and was defeated.

GENERAL CHAMBERLAIN *

English General in the Jacobite War.

GENERAL JAMES OGLETHORPE *

The father of the Colony of Georgia in America. He saved Dan O'Flaherty's life at the close of the Jacobite War and took him prisoner to America when Dan O'Flaherty defeated Spain's takeover of the Colony of Georgia and South Carolina. He became a close friend to Dan O'Flaherty and his adoptive family the O'Sheas, who was instrumental in ending England's Seven Year War with Spain.

JOHNNY CASEY *

An able-bodied seaman on the ship owned by Eamonn O'Flaherty. The Casey family provided the coffin to bury Eamonn after he was mortally wounded in the Jacobite War.

KING GEORGE II *

Successor to the throne of England after dethroning the Catholic King James II. King George was of German ancestry of the House of Hanover.

KING GEORGE III *

The defeated King of England. Son of King George II.

ALFREDO de LEON *

Defeated Spanish Lieutenant known as the champion swordsman of Spain who was defeated by Dan O'Flaherty in a duel.

JOHN MILLEDGE, JUNIOR *

John was the son of the wealthiest Scotsman in the Colony of Georgia. When his father died, John became involved in a unit of soldiers organized by General Oglethorpe known as the Rangers. At the end of the Seven Year War, Dan O'Flaherty took what remained of the Ranger Unit and formed a militia group known as the "Blue Celts." At the end of the American Revolutionary War, John Milledge, Jr., was promoted to Brigadier General for the efforts he put forth to protect the lives of General George Washington and his family.

COLONEL FELIX CASTILLO *

Commander of the Spanish troops stationed in Florida during the Seven Year War. He served under the Command of General Phillip O'Shea and was instrumental in bringing a peace agreement between England and Spain.

SAM O'KEEFE *

Harbor Master during the period Eamonn O'Flaherty was involved in shipping cargo from Ireland to Spain. He became an advisor to Dan O'Flaherty after his adopted parents were lost at sea.

SAM O'KEEFE, JUNIOR *

Succeeded his father as Harbor Master in La Coruna, Spain.

MATTHEW COLLIER *

Known as the best lawyer in Europe and confidant to those who held positions of royalty. Began as a soldier of Spain under the command of General Phillip O'Shea. The General placed him in the study of law to which he excelled. He was the attorney for the O'Shea family. He represented Dan O'Flaherty's interest against the Crown after the deaths of General and Mrs. O'Shea. He also became involved in Dan's efforts to set up a spy ring in New York to benefit the Revolutionary Army. He enlisted the help of his son, Weston to organize and command the efforts to know all that could be learned from spying on the British headquarters in New York.

WESTON COLLIER *

Son of Matthew Collier who organized and commanded the most effective spy operation during the Revolutionary War. He ultimately became an American and married Maureen O'Flaherty, sister to Dan O'Flaherty.

GRACE O'MALLEY *

Chieftain of the O'Malley family in the 1500's. Her mission was to keep Irish independent from England.

COLONEL FREDRICO de LONGORIA *

Chief of Security for General Phillip O'Shea. He personally trained Weston Collier, Maureen O'Flaherty and Shibeal O'Flaherty to become the most affective group of spies of the Revolutionary War.

LAWRENCE WASHINGTON *

The half-brother to General George Washington who became concerned for his younger brother as a teenager because of the attempts of his mother to cause her son to be emotionally harmed because of her obdurate overbearing inflexible traits. He received permission to move his young brother into his home that came to be known as Mount Vernon. At his death, Lawrence gave his estate to his younger brother, General George Washington.

GENERAL GEORGE WASHINGTON *

Chosen by the Colonies of America to lead the Continental Army against the greatest military force on earth at that time known as the British Army. He became known as the "Father of America." and ultimately became the President of the United States of America.

MARTHA WASHINGTON *

Wife of General George Washington.

TOM ROWE *

A carpenter selected by Dan and Coleman O'Flaherty to build two homes prior to the beginning of the war whish was postponed until after the war.

ANDREW JACKSON *

A person Dan met when he was a teenager when he was working as a blacksmith prior to the American Revolutionary War and who ultimately became President of the United States of America in 1829.

CHIEF ATTA KULLAKULLA *

Cherokee Chief known as "First Beloved Man" who cared for the O'Flaherty family while Dan was involved in the Revolutionary War,

THOMAS HICKEY *

One of General Washington's most trusted men to guard his personal security who was later convicted of treason for agreeing to participate in the assassination of General George Washington.

GENERAL CORNWALLIS *

Field General in the British Army who served under General Clinton in the Southern Region of the Revolutionary War.

MAJOR PATRICK FERGUSON *

British Commander of the Southern military serving under the command of General Cornwallis.

GOVERNOR BERNARDO GALVEZ *

A patriot who was highly regarded by General George Washington. Spanish Governor of Louisiana and Cuba. Selected by General George Washington to stand at his right hand at the formal surrender of the British Army.

OLIVER POLLOCK *

An Irishman in whom God trusted to use his vast fortunes to keep the Continental Army functioning.

GENERAL DON O'RILEY *

Commander of the Spanish Army of Cuba and New Orleans.

BENJAMIN CLEVELAND *

Patriot.

JAMES JOHNSTON *

Patriot.

WILLIAM CAMPBELL *

Patriot.

JOHN SERIER *

Patriot.

JOSEPH McDOWELL *

Patriot.

BANASTRE TARLETON *

Known as the most despised officer in the British Army who died known as a traitor to those who befriended him the most.

GENERAL NATHANIEL GREENE *

Commanding General of the Southern Department of the Continental Forces.

GENERAL DANIEL MORGAN *

Known as one of the fiercest fighters in the war. He was captured at the beginning of the war and freed by the British by negotiation and became an indispensable leader in disassembling the Cornwallis Army by the Special Force tactics.

COLONEL "LIGHT HORSE HARRY" LEE *

Commander of the rifle units under the command of General Nathaniel Greene. Commander of the Continental Army in the South.

GENERAL BENEDICT ARNOLD *

Traitor to America who lived out his life in shame in Europe after the Revolutionary War.

GENERAL LAFAYETTE *

A young General from France who became one of the great contributors to the cause for the surrender of Cornwallis during the Revolutionary War.

GENERAL CLIFTON *

Commanding General of the British Army of the American Revolution.

LORD NORTH *

Prime Minister of England during the Revolutionary War who resigned when Great Britain was defeated.

COLONEL GRADY JACKSON *

Commander of the occupation forces in New York after the surrender of Cornwallis. He was cousin to Andrew Jackson and an indispensable reason for the freeing of Maureen and Shibeal O'Flaherty who were being shipped to England to be hung as spies.

CAPTAIN BENJAMIN O'ROURKE *

Commander of the Revolutionary occupational troops in New York after the surrender of the British Army.

OLIVIA PEEL *

The name used by Maureen O'Flaherty when operating as a spy against the British Army in New York.

KATHERINE THORPE *

The name used by Shibeal O'Flaherty when she acted as a spy for America during the war.

DARK LADY *

Leader of an Indian tribe Grand Priestess of Maureen and Weston's wedding.

NED SHARKEY *

An attorney representing the Priestly family who abandoned property in Georgia to return to England after the defeat of the British Army.

BENNY McGEE *

Owner of a place to eat in northwest North Carolina near the blacksmith shop where Andrew Jackson worked.

MR. PRIESTLY *

A loyalist that resided near Savannah Georgia, who returned to England after the Revolutionary War and sold his home to Dan O'Flaherty's parents.

CAPTAIN ESTEBAN LONGORIA *

Son of Colonel Longoria. Served Spain as a trainer of Bridget O'Flaherty for covert spying activities in New York City.

ROBERT LIVINGSTON *

The Chancellor Grand Master of Masons in the City of New York.

JOHN MORTON *

Marshal of the parade for George Washington's inaugural as President of the United States of America.

COLONEL ALEXANDER DE HERNANDEZ *

Administrator of the training academy in Spain for special Force trainees.

EMILY EMERSON *

A name chosen by Bridget O'Flaherty while she worked as a Nanny in the home of Robert Milton Montgomery, a loyalist who planned to destroy the United States financial system.

MRS. ANNE MONTGOMERY *

Wife of loyalist, Robert Milton Montgomery.

ROBERT JR., CHARLOTTE, WILLIAM, and SARAH MONTGOMERY *

The four children born to Robert and Anne Montgomery.

MR. STEWART *

President of the second largest bank in New York owned by Robert Montgomery.

MR. TAYLOR *

Cashier of the bank owned by Mr. Robert Montgomery.

THEODORE WALPOLE *

One of the co-conspirators with Robert Montgomery who planned to destroy the financial system of the United States of America.

ALEXANDER HAMILTON *

Secretary of the Treasury and founder of the money system of the United States of America.

PRIME MINISTER WILLIAM PITT *

Prime Minister of England who worked with British General Charles Cornwallis to emancipate the Irish Catholics from the tyranny of the Penal Laws.

TOBIAS LEAR *

Personal secretary to President George Washington.

GEORGE RAWLINS *

Overseer of President Washington's property known as Mr. Vernon.

DR. JAMES CRAIK *

President George Washington's personal physician.

DR. GUSTAVUS BROWN *

One of the doctors who provided medical care to President Washington during his final illness.

CAROLINE, MOLLY and CHARLOTTE *

House maids who were present when President George Washington died.

CHRISTOPHER SHEELS *

Personal valet to President Washington who was present when the President died.

TENISKWATAWA and TECUMSEH *

Indian Chiefs who formed a confederation of numerous tribes for blocking American expansion in the northwest.

JULIUS PRATT *

Historian.

MARY BELLE HARRISON BROWN *

An orphan child whose parents died of smallpox who was rescued by a trapper in the Mississippi River bottom land.

TRAPPER JOHN *

A trapper who lived in the south Louisiana swamps with his wife and two children who died of smallpox during an epidemic. Also, the trapper who found Mary Belle after her parents had died of smallpox.

CALE BROWN *

Trading Post owner in a settlement on the Mississippi River known as Natchez and who became the adoptive father of Mary Belle.

MOLLY BROWN *

Wife of Cale Brown who became the adoptive mother of Mary Belle.

HARRIS (HARRY) BROWN *

Son of Cale and Molly brown. His mother died during child birth. His father was murdered.

BEN HAMMOCK *

Bank president in Natchez settlement.

JEREMIAH SWOOPER *

Funeral director for Cale Brown's funeral.

JAMES O'NEIL *

Commanding Officer of the Tennessee Militia located in Memphis, Tennessee.

SAM POLLOCK *

Half white and half Cherokee hired by Mary Belle at the trading post.

ROBERT FULTON *

Engineer and inventor of the first steamboat that was commercially successful.

BESSIE WALKER *

Mother of Billy Jeff and Mildred. Husband died and left them destitute. Mary Belle hired her as trading post manager.

NED CULLIGAN *

Merchant in New Orleans who sold trading goods to Mary Belle wholesale.

CAROLYN SUE AND DELTON WARNER *

Wife and husband who were being robbed on the bank of the Mississippi River as Mary Belle stopped her steamboat for trade.

J.W. HENRY *

Half trapper, half fisherman customer of Mary Belle's trading post.

JAMES MADISON *

President of the United States when war was declared in 1812.

BENJAMIN HAWKINS *

Federal Indian agent who aided the 6th Military District under General Thomas Pickney during the War of 1812.

GENERAL JOHN COFFEE *

One of the Generals serving with General Andrew Jackson to defeat the Creek Indian force at Horse Shoe Bend.

GENERAL EDWARD PAKENHAM *

British General that attacked New Orleans in late 1814. He was defeated.

ACKNOWLEDGEMENT

During the period of time when I was attempting to recover from severe concussions that I received from two separate automobile accidents in 2015 and 2016, I became extremely depressed because of the loss of memory. I had performed on stage for more than forty years as an Irish folk singer. I became very depressed as my abilities shifted from a very active entertainer's life to a life of nothingness.

For years prior, a neighbor named Ted G. Walker and I had written music together, many songs of which were recorded. Of the work we did, the songs we wrote pertaining to patriotism were the ones we liked the most. My doctor strongly suggested I discover a way to give my brain exercise.

One day during one of my darkest hours, Mr. Walker and I were visiting when he suggested we begin exercising my memory by recalling my family history. After months of effort, we had developed the O'Flaherty family story beginning in the 18th Century. I had knowledge of Irish history having been educated in Gaelic language, which was the basis for developing Tears of Freedom. I began to become encouraged and hopeful as I recalled my family history. The Walkers and I had made a journey to Ireland in 2013 which provided a basis for their understanding of the culture.

I owe special appreciation and gratitude to my co-authors, Ted and Danny Walker for their working with me to tell the story. This story gave me encouragement during a time in my life when I could no longer sing the ballads of Ireland from memory. Many of our days were spent together writing Tears of Freedom as Mary Walker typed our words. As the late Danny Doyle would often say, "She has the patience of a lion." A simple thank you seems inefficient for the long hours she spent working with us. To my wife, Lisa, my soul mate, and best friend who keeps me on my feet and shows me the light. Mo Ghrá thú.

Additionally, I want to thank Karen May who devoted her time and expertise to edit and organize the story. My gratitude for her effort is so deeply appreciated. Also, a great artist named, Jake Sager contributed to the artwork. Jake is a devout Christian and a wonderful man who gave his great talent to the project. He is such a beautiful soul.

Special thanks to my countless friends and fans who have always supported me. I am forever grateful to each and every one of you. **Go raibh míle maith agaibh!**

Danny O'Flaherty

DEDICATION

When attempting to define any nation, the definition eventually describes the character of those who inhabit the borders of a piece of land that has a name given to it by former generations. Since the United States of America became one nation, other countries have marveled at the people who have become one nation, under God, with liberty and justice for all.

In the beginning of America's history, the word freedom became a term used by every American with a different meaning by everyone who spoke the term. Because of the diversity of cultures and religious beliefs, America remains that miraculous experiment that continues to perfect its identity each day the sun rises.

This book is dedicated to the culture of the Scots-Irish who entered the borders of America as slaves of Great Britain and eventually became the vast majority of those who paid with their lives for the opportunity to become free men. Their contribution to this nation has long since been forgotten, but the gift of their efforts, sacrifice and fortitude speak each day that Americans remain free of tyranny.

The importance of these words are to renew the gratitude in the heart of every American who knows, but for the willingness to pay the supreme cost by the Scots-Irish, America would have remained a group of foreign colonies of political powers. God Bless those precious souls whose spirits continue to protect this great land.

PREFACE

All American history is the result of many seemingly unrelated events that began as thoughts of a few inhabitants of land owned by British rulers and some of the supporters of the Crown that had been granted land in America for development.

Great Britain controlled portions of what would become known as America and Australia as well as a vast number of other territories known as the British Empire. The development of America in the Sixteenth Century was for the most part simple and self-serving. The rich land owners wanted their land developed for profit. To accomplish their desires cheap labor was the most vital element.

The Protestant religious faith became the dominant faith in the European portion of the British Empire. In an effort to annihilate the followers of the Catholic faith, the Crown established what would become known as the Penal Laws. Because of the Penal Laws in Ireland and Scotland a huge portion of the Catholic population was enslaved and shipped to the Colonies of America. Almost two thirds of the Catholic faith in Scotland and Ireland were enslaved or died because of starvation during this period. The land occupied by the Catholic believers in Scotland and Ireland was then seized by the Crown of England to either be held by the Crown or occupied by the supporters of the Crown.

In America these events ultimately concluded in the Declaration of Independence by the Colonies on July 4, 1776. The dominant motive of those who rebelled against England was to be free from the tyrannical dominance of the British Crown.

The motives for each individual decision to sacrifice their blood, their treasure and their honor to cause the hope of freedom to become reality was grounded in the heart of each individual who had suffered from years of abuse by a family of monarchs whose origin began in Germany.

The Revolutionary Army was for the most part a collection of former Irish and Scottish slaves and the alliance of other foreign nations.

"Tears of Freedom" focuses on one Irish family named O'Flaherty. The O'Flaherty family ancestry was known for hundreds of years as the Clan of O'Flaherty who occupied the western portion of Ireland west of the Shannon River.

On March 5, 1722, Dan O'Flaherty was born and began his life surrounded with members of a loving family and unimaginable adversity. His ancestors were warriors who had faced life's most turbulent horrors and all the while maintaining a gentle and kind spirit that would lead him to become one of the great leaders of America's Independence.

Very few men if any gave as much to the foundation of America as did Dan O'Flaherty. He was separated from his family at a young age, placed in the hands of strangers which led to his becoming a military genius and one of General George Washington's most trusted Generals.

This is the story of a survivor of the American Revolutionary War whose family took the risk, paid the price for America to become known as the birthplace of freedom and lived to enjoy the fruits of God's love.

FOREWORD

Seumas MacManus has written in The Story of the Irish Race Chapter LIII, pages 454-455, "When fire and sword had signally failed to suppress the Irish race, new means to that end must be found. So, the fertile mind of the conqueror invented the Penal Laws.

Professor Lecky, a Protestant of British blood and ardent British sympathy, says (in his History of Ireland in the 18th Century) that the object of the Penal Laws was threefold:

(1) To deprive the Catholics of all civil life
(2) To reduce them to a condition of most extreme and brutal ignorance
(3) To dissociate them from the soil.

He might, with absolute justice, have substituted *Irish* for *Catholics*---and added, (4) To extirpate the Race.

"There is no instance," says Dr. Samuel Johnson, "Even in the Ten Persecutions, of such severity as that which the Protestants of Ireland exercised against the Catholics."

Like good wine the Penal Code improved with age. It was only in the 18th century that it attained the marvelous perfection which caused Edmund Burke to describe it as "a machine of wise and elaborate contrivance, as well fitted for the oppression, impoverishment, and degradation of a people, and the debasement in them of human nature itself, as ever proceeded from the perverted ingenuity of man"—and the French jurist Montesquieu to say of it that it was, "conceived by demons, written in blood, and registered in Hell." *

Some of our family members endured the atrocities of the British Kingdom and lived to tell the story of the cruelty enacted into law to destroy the Irish culture. This book is the story of one such family. It is written as fiction based upon historical fact. The horrible events that surrounded the lives of the O'Flaherty family were common to every Irish Catholic in the 18th Century. The suffering experienced by the Irish Roman Catholics spawned a culture that eventually became a part of the core culture of the United States of America.

The Irish culture has for almost 800 years practiced the belief of the equality of worth of all people. As the Irish settled into the landscape of America, the implant of the Irish traits gave rise to the distinct Irish identities that began to flourish by the outbursts of distrust of formal authority, signifying to everyone the understanding of the personal boundaries of individualism, while making certain everyone received a share of "fair play." Simultaneously, very few of the Irish culture gave special significance to those of wealth; their respect was reserved for those who stood firm in the fundamental belief in God and loyalty. Before the Revolutionary War began, the Irish heart was founded upon the belief in God, the family loyalty and the freedom to be guaranteed by the laws of the United States of America regardless of the cost. To those beliefs; the Irish have given their pledged their allegiance.

*The Story of the Irish Race Seumas MacManus – Chapter LIII, The later Penal Laws, Pages 454-455.

CHAPTER ONE

FAMILY

As the morning began to break, Delia O'Flaherty knew something very special from God Himself had come into her life. She could tell by the first sound he would be a different sort that life itself would have difficulty trying to tame. The breaking of dawn allowed her to see her special gift for the first time as he set his hazel blue eyes upon the face of the one human being that he would worship all the days of his life. As she beheld her private miracle, he touched her face as the first tear of gratitude moved from her eyes down her soft delicate skin. She knew there would be many more tears to follow as she watched him become the man among men that she knew he would be. That first quiet moment with her private treasure would remain with her for the rest of her days.

She kissed his fingers and his red cheeks. She moved her hands to his feet to make sure he had the right number of toes. Sure enough it was what she already knew; he was divinely perfect just as her heart had already whispered to her.

The ordeal of his birth had been lengthy. The other members of the family were still resting as he began to enjoy having his blessed mother to himself without interference. Delia was well prepared to provide his first taste of mother's milk, but he seemed to enjoy being very content with being privately held by his mother.

Delia's heart and mind began to wonder as to the name of her perfect gift. In the privacy of her heart she had always thought of distinction regarding the young man in the Bible named Daniel. There was something unique as to the method Daniel chose to confront life when he was not in control of his own choices. She saw Daniel as a noble and stately individual with a note of breeding and aristocratic character. He was admired by all who knew him, and many became impressed with his refinement and the stature that his life achieved in all his ways. She began to allow her heart to whisper to her, *Daniel, Dan, Daniel, Dan.* Each time she heard his name she knew that name would be on the lips of those who said his name to him and about him with great admiring respect.

Her eyes began to focus on her Dan as she spoke his name ever so softly in his ear for the first time. He had heard the voice for the first time that he would spend most of his life seeking to hear just one more time.

In the early 1700's, Ireland was not the place to welcome the first day of one's life, especially having arrived from the womb of an Irish Catholic young lady. The facts of life would prove that not to be the best choice because of the scorn and humiliation that had been perpetrated by the English Crown.

Just as Delia had begun allowing her heart to feel free to chisel this one precious moment in stone, the cold wind of reality reminded her of her surroundings. She felt an urge to be hungry. She reminded herself, t*here is no food.* As opposed to giving her precious time to worry, however, she decided to get back to holding her love in her arms and smiling at life and its methods of causing harm to come with each sunrise.

Dan had begun to open his eyes appearing to want a closer view of just exactly what his mother had gotten him into. But, as his mother had always done to each day God had given them, she would put a little sugar on the day, and call it a good day of blessings. As the sun began to shine, Delia began to see the very strong possibility that her Dan would have a touch of red in his hair. She thought to herself, *it was the Almighty who had put the red berry on top of a perfect son.* Even though Dan had not been on this earth 24 hours, he already knew his mother could cause the worst to become better, as she applied the true love of an Irish woman's heart to a child that God Himself had sent to her for care.

Dan had felt so much warmth and comfort; he would try one more wink of sleep before he became acquainted with the other members of his family. Dan was the third child to be born to Coleman O'Flaherty and wife, Delia. The years had not been kind to those of the Catholic faith who lived in Ireland in the 1700's. War, poverty, starvation, and persecution seemed to be the norm for each family who inhabited the island referred to as the Emerald Isle. Each inhabitant knew within themselves their lives were destined to be spent in a land somewhere else, because of the Penal Laws that had been passed to attempt to exterminate the Irish Catholics. The question was, when and where would they be shipped to be imprisoned or become indentured slaves.

Mid-morning had come as Delia and her Dan had just completed a two-hour nap. Delia heard the whispers of two little visitors, Patrick and Barbara, who were very curious as to who was lying with their mother, where they were accustomed to sleeping. Their father had gone earlier to get some more dry turf from the bog, because the other fishermen reported a north-western front by night fall. It was now March 5, 1722 and an already icy winter was going to be around for at least three more weeks.

Delia was facing the wall with Dan lying on her left arm as she turned her head and saw the two older children quietly tiptoeing toward the bed of fleece covered straw. Delia turned on her back and placed Dan on her right arm with a soft blanket over his face. They wanted to see their brother. Delia gently removed the blanket from his face to give them a good look at their new playmate.

When they saw him, their eyes lit up as Irish smiles covered their faces. Delia reached with her arm and pulled them closer. An Irish heart bowed before God's throne in humble gratitude for choosing her to be the mother of three souls that she could lead toward removing fear from their lives by introducing them to Jesus Christ.

Delia was reminded of the real world as she looked into the hungry eyes of the two older children. There was no fish to boil, no meat to cook. She thought of boiling some nettles with a few grains of corn. The salt was down to the last few grains, so she had to be very careful not to use it all. She arose and sat on the side of the bed and looking again with an adoring smile at her Dan who was ready to join into that wonderful game called, life. Delia's mind was racing frantically, *what to do? what to do?* She then felt the warmth of her mother's milk wetting her gown top. She laid back down and turned to her left side and welcomed her little man to a taste of heaven. Dan loved the taste of his mother's gift. Delia could feel his tug on her as he got a good taste of his first breakfast. She held him up to her shoulder and patted his back very gently and all a sudden, a burp created room for more than his share of the morning breakfast. Delia again gave him another joy of food that had been prepared for his first homecoming.

Delia laid him back in the fleece for a nap and turned to welcome Patrick and Barbara in the gentlest voice, *I know he already likes you.* Within a while Delia was letting them hold their baby brother. Delia was endowed with enough love to cause each child to know she had enough love to go around. Delia knew each of her children were special gifts from God, her mind turned to her husband for he should be returning soon with the turf. She went to her knees and said, *Holy Father, we have done our best, it is time for us to lean on you to provide us with today's food as you have always done when we are desperate.* She then sat down and held him close as tears poured from her heart in the sincerest Gaelic tones while she softly sang a lullaby of the ages;

Ho-bha-in, Ho-bha-in

Ho-bha-in, mo leana

Ho-bha-in, dun do shuile

Tit do cod ladh mo leana.

As she was quietly uttering a prayer, she heard a noise from outside their small cottage. She then heard a cough that was familiar. Coleman had returned with the warmth for his family. He came to the door whistling a familiar Gaelic tune. She knew in her heart her answered prayers had arrived. She pulled the door back and there stood the most precious man she had ever known with an extra heavy load of turf, a sack under his right arm and that infectious Irish smile that had taken her heart prisoner at the first sight of his face years before. He said, "Delia, you won't believe what happened. As I was returning from the bog, two fishermen were returning to shore and their currach was loaded with fish they had caught just ahead of the next storm." As Delia listened she bowed her head, again thanking God for allowing her family to have food for another day.

Coleman O'Flaherty was more than ready to hold his new son. He warmed by the fire first and asked Delia how she was feeling. Delia told him she had great joy in her heart for the gift heaven had sent them. She began wondering when this precious baby would be baptized. Coleman went to the bed and gazed upon his son with the pride of a man who knew he had been perfectly blessed.

He said, "Delia, your mother has had her involvement in his hair and I think I see a little curl." As Coleman held his son, he said, "Delia, have you thought of the name?" Delia turned quickly toward him and asked, "What do you think of Daniel?" His father laughed loudly and said, "Just what we needed, a Dan to sing our songs and tell our tales, you have done well. His legs are long and strong. His eyes are straight and true, and Delia, look at those arms and hands. He has the frame of a great warrior. He will make us proud."

A certain joy arose in Delia's heart as she listened to the words of the man she loved express praise for her to have given him a true source of great pride.

Delia busily prepared the meal. She knew her husband was starving. As they were eating she began telling him of a roof leak that had developed near her bed. He told her he had saved some thatch and would repair the roof before the storm.

Coleman O'Flaherty had not told his wife of the possible opportunity of a place to work on a farm for fear of getting her hopes too high. She had suffered all the disappointment he could ask of her. After the meal he rested a while and warmed himself before working on the roof leak. The wind had begun to increase, which told him the rain would quickly follow.

Delia went to lie down after she cleaned the kitchen. Much to her surprise, Dan was awake looking around with apparent hope his mother would return for a visit and here she was ready to cause his life to become important again. She gave him a big kiss as she made sure his diaper cloth was free of moisture. She snuggled beside him to begin again the mothering of which he felt so deserving. She looked deep into his eyes to try and discover the wonderful life he would be bringing to the earth. She whispered, *Daniel, Daniel, you are so loved.* She knew it was time for his second meal and she was ready for him to begin growing. Coleman could be heard close by working the new thatch into the existing roof. In about two hours his work was completed and ready for the test the northwestern wind and rain would give.

Dan was sleeping soundly. Delia had moved her concerns from Dan to survival, even though she was hesitant about mentioning Coleman's future plans for the family. The anxiety of having another child forced her to inquire; with a trembling voice, asks Coleman whether he had talked to any of the large property owners about some possibility of work of any kind. Coleman had been waiting for Delia to ask that question to be able to share with her a conversation he had with one of the overseers of a large farm. He said, with a smile, "Delia, I have talked to my cousin, Michael O'Flaherty, who is in charge of the labor of a large farm near Oughterard. I told him of our plight of having to repair the currach and the fishing lines becoming worn with no money to make the necessary repairs. I told him I was giving up trying to feed my family by fishing. He told me to come by in the spring for a talk about what I could do. I am planning on visiting with him a week from Tuesday with the help of God." Delia's heart leaped with joy; because she knew the farm he was talking about and knew the workers could live in the farm cottages. Delia was too filled with hope to speak a word. She reached and touched Coleman's weather-beaten hand as a tear of gratitude ran down her cheek.

Something to hope for had not made a visit to their meager lives in many years. Delia's thoughts came alive thinking about a life without having to think about Coleman drowning in the icy Atlantic Ocean. The thought of him being nearby her and the children, if the need arose, was a precious gift.

The weather conditions no longer mattered because her wonderfully kind heart would always have the presence of those she loved at a glance. Sickness was the enemy, but she knew she would be in a place where good food was being produced and that would be the medicine her family needed. The howl of the north wind no longer bothered her because her heart was set with unfettered hope toward a better day.

The day for Coleman to visit with his cousin was at hand and he had more than ten miles to go. He left before daybreak to travel the distance and to make sure he took a shortcut through the mountains and not to be late for the meeting because it meant everything to his family. When he arrived, he went to the shelter where the other workers had gathered to begin the day's work. Coleman's cousin saw him and beckoned him toward the table where he was sitting. Michael O'Flaherty was glad to see his cousin because he knew how dependable he was as a worker. Coleman asked about

Michael's family, especially his uncle, whom he had not seen in several years. Michael told him everyone was doing as good as could be expected after having endured such a cold winter. Michael then asks Coleman if he was prepared to move to the farm with his family. He told him the farming had not begun because winter continued to hold on, but he told him of the dairy cattle that needed care as well as the other animals. Michael said, "I have a person at the barn who knows all you need to know about farm stock. His name is Stephen Nee, he is about our age and he knows answers to any question you might ask."

Coleman asks the name of the landowner. Michael responded saying, "Bryan O'Flaherty who is an O'Flaherty, but is not a close relative of ours. From what I understand, he has borrowed money to purchase the farm, and I manage the farm for him." Michael then asks Coleman when he would like to begin working. Coleman was speechless. He said, "Michael, Delia gave birth to our third child about two weeks ago. We are ready to move at any time." Michael said, "That is good. Today is Monday. Let's say a week from Thursday morning will be your first work day. In the meantime, you can move into one of the empty cottages. I can tell the moving of your family is going to put a burden on you. I want you to use one of the farm wagons and a horse to transport your family back here." Coleman could not believe what he was hearing. He said, "Michael, you are a blessing from heaven." Michael said, "Take your time and be gentle with your new son, and I will see you a week from Thursday."

When Coleman rode up to the cottage, Delia peaked out the door. She could not believe her eyes. Coleman jumped from the wagon and grabbed his darling Delia and held her ever so close. Patrick and Barbara could see their father from the cottage door. They had truly missed him because their mother had told them a big secret, which was, they might be traveling somewhere else to live. It was obvious to Delia that Coleman had taken the job Michael had offered him. Coleman asks Delia, "How would you like to live where you can drink all the milk you want and have honey for your bread?" Delia took Coleman's hand and began doing an old Irish jig. The children had never seen them so happy. When all at once, they heard Dan raising his voice because he heard the laughter and wanted to be part of the fun.

The cold, the abuse, the humiliation, the fact of being neither Catholic nor hunger mattered at that moment because a blessing from God had set their feet on higher ground. Neither Coleman nor Delia had ever been away from the west coast of Ireland, and here they were traveling in a rich man's wagon with his horse pulling it, headed away from starvation and fear toward good food and joy.

When they arrived at the farm Michael was glad to see Delia again. They had known one another as children. Michael had always been, not only a cousin to Coleman, but the three of them had known a good friendship toward one another. Michael held Daniel and remarked about the size of his arms and hands, by saying, "Delia, you will have to take great care of this one. He is a warrior for sure and probably a clan leader." Delia listened closely to Michael's words because she knew in her heart Dan was destined to become a great leader. They thanked Michael for the opportunity he had given them. Michael said, "Coleman, let me remind you, Stephen Nee knows all there is to know about farm stock. I hope you will learn all he can teach you about what he knows. He is a very knowledgeable person." Coleman was beginning to understand that Michael had some things on his mind that might be very beneficial to him and his family in the future.

Delia had a good feeling about the new environment her family was becoming involved with, especially the farm stock. None of her ancestors had ever been involved with farming. Their only involvement was they had owned two cows at one time, but with the passage of the Penal Laws, it was evident the Crown intended to exterminate all Catholics in Ireland. Depending on the district where the person lived determined the severity of the application of the Penal Laws. In the 1700's, the British Empire had become known as one of the most politically, sadistic empires in the history of the world. When the Protestants came to complete political power those who were Catholics practiced their faith at the peril of their own lives. Most vicious legal penalties designed by parliament seemed to target the leaders of the Catholic Church. For example, if anyone were to house a Catholic Bishop, the penalty could be so severe, as to require the forfeiting of all property owned or leased. The estates that had existed for hundreds of years by a particular bloodline were subject to being forfeited to the Crown for aiding and abetting a priest of the Catholic faith who was trying to avoid imprisonment.

Wrong doing and injustice toward the Celtic people had gone on for many decades, but the irrepressible Celtic spirit had endured and attempted to ultimately conquer all aggressors. Delia and Coleman with their little children were no different than the same story of suffering by the Irish for centuries that had been repeated. The difference this time was, life was not going to swallow up Coleman and Delia for attempting to hope and have faith that the perils of persecution could be conquered.

Delia was enjoying her new cottage. Dan seemed ready to fit into all the families' stirrings. Thursday had come, and Coleman was ready to tell Stephen Nee that he was there to do whatever he was told. He began by telling Mr. Nee he was well acquainted with farm tools, especially a shovel and pitch fork, and was ready to apply his knowledge in any way he was told. Coleman said, "Stephen, if there is a bog nearby; and if you have a good slean handy, I'll cut a few sods for all of us to burn for the rest of the winter."

CHAPTER TWO

SUDDEN CHANGES

Many days had passed since that first day Coleman began his new job. Delia had become almost accustomed to not worrying about the next meal. The children were healthy and robust. Michael had told Coleman and Delia to involve the older children in the work by cleaning out the stalls and feeding the stock. Dan was becoming six years old and had two younger sisters, Siobhann and Shibeal. The family was well provided for in every way. Coleman had become very close to Stephen Nee. Michael was right about Stephen. He was without a doubt the most knowledgeable farmer Coleman had ever met. Coleman had learned his move to Oughterard was significantly better for his family than remaining in Creggan waiting for the weather to become good and the fish to bite. Coleman liked what he was doing. The environment was better for Delia who had become acquainted with some more mothers like herself, trying to raise a family. As Dan had grown, the hope she had for him began to be apparent. She told herself, *she was right about his potential.* He was a child that despite him being much larger than the children his age was very careful not to hurt his playmates. Delia delighted in him. She could not keep from smiling every time she looked at him. Dan was most proud of the mother God had placed in charge of his life. Dan got bigger by the day; farm life suited him perfectly. Delia enjoyed the time she had with him and hoped it would never end.

Michael had begun to talk to Coleman about the farm and the hopes he had for them both. The owner of the farm, Bryan O'Flaherty, while not being a close relative of Michael and Coleman, treated both men with respect and expressed his appreciation for their efforts to make the farm profitable. Michael had learned that Bryan had borrowed twenty thousand pounds to purchase the property, which was previously owned by the O'Flaherty family, but had been sold to other occupiers' years before. The property was originally O'Flaherty property, but because of many different political changes, the land would pass into another owners' possession and eventually the land would be repurchased by an O'Flaherty. To purchase the land, Bryan borrowed the money from Lord St. George, who was known for his ability to loan large amounts of money, based upon real estate mortgages.

Bryan had signed a note to purchase the property but did not realize that Lord St. George had borrowed thirty thousand pounds and pledged Bryan's note as part of the collateral. Michael expressed his concern, hoping they could make enough money to pay the note. On Dan's sixth birthday, a visitor arrived at the farm to purchase some corn and other food to load his ship for a voyage. Michael and Coleman knew of him as a distant relative. His name was Eamonn Laidir O'Flaherty. (1) He was the grandson of Edmond Mac Morogha Na Maor and Morogh Na Mart O'Flaithbertaigh, sons of Morogh Na Maor O'Flaithbertaigh, who was the last leader of the O'Flaherty clan. He had fought in the Irish Confederate War. Edmond was hung for the slaughter of civilians in County Clare in 1641. His son, Edmond O'Flaherty, fought for James II during the Williamite War in Ireland. At war's end he sought to purchase land previously owned by the O'Flaherty family. The land was then owned by the Blake family of Galway. Edmond's son was Eamonn Laidir O'Flaherty. He was an enormous sized man with the strength to go with it. (At his death, his bones were of such an enormous size they were placed on display.) (1) His strength was the talk of Connamara. He had the demeanor of a clan leader whose presence demanded respect from all whom he met. However, he had an unusual gentleness to his personality; he adored young children, especially those that had the capability of becoming great warriors. He had married three times, one marriage of which was to Julia Martin, a cousin of Richard Martin who was also a neighbor whom Eamonn hated because Captain Martin had fought against him in the First Jacobite War. The pair frequently fought on horseback with swords. Eamonn was the most feared warrior in the region of Connemara.

Coleman and Michael were overjoyed to meet their cousin. Coleman sent for Delia to come meet Eamonn. She quickly wiped the children's faces and hurried to the barn area. She was astonished at the size of Eamonn. Before they reached the barn, Dan saw this giant of a man and went running toward him, completely unafraid. He playfully grabbed one of Eamonn's legs and tried to throw him down. Eamonn took to Dan immediately. He picked him up over his head and began to swing him around in play. Dan was beside himself and couldn't stop cracking up with laughter. Coleman introduced him to his wife, Delia. She detected the special gift in Eamonn's demeanor that was gentle and kind.

Eamonn said, "Dan, when I get ready to go back home, I want you to go with me." Dan asks, "Where do you live?" Eamonn said, "By the sea. I have a ship and I have lots of horses for you to ride." Dan asks, "Can my mother go too?" Eamonn laughed and said, "We will have to talk to her about that."

As they were visiting they heard sounds of horses' hoofs headed in their direction. From the distance it appeared to be a company of military soldiers. As they rode closer they were sure it was a company of British soldiers being led by the Sheriff and one Deputy.

When they arrived at the barn area, the Sheriff asks, "Is this the Bryan O'Flaherty farm?" Michael asks, "For what purpose do you wish to speak to Mr. O'Flaherty?" The Sheriff answered, "To place him under arrest for the refusal to pay his debt." Michael knew enough to inquire further by asking, who has sued to collect the debt?

The Sheriff replied, "The bank has foreclosed the note owed by Lord St. George. My purpose here is to arrest Bryan O'Flaherty. Again, do you know his whereabouts?" Michael said, "He is in his home, I will take you to him."

The Sheriff told the remainder of the workers to stay where they were until he returned. Delia quickly looked at Eamonn and with pleading eyes she whispered to him, "Please take Dan with you". She softly said, "We will visit you when this is over." Dan knew something of great sadness had come to their lives. He reached for Eamonn's giant hand as tears began to roll down his cheeks and said, "I want to go with you." Only God knew the purpose of the bond that had formed so quickly between Dan and Eamonn's hearts. Delia knew it was the warrior bond of kindred spirits. Eamonn lifted Dan into one of the wagons and they drove away as the soldiers searched for Bryan O'Flaherty. Because of Eamonn's size, no one objected to Eamonn leaving.

When the Sheriff's troops arrived at the house one of the soldiers used a stone to beat on the door. When the door opened, Bryan knew a sad chapter of their lives was about to unfold. The Sheriff asked, "Are you Bryan O'Flaherty?" Bryan responded, "Yes, I am. May I ask what is the nature of your inquiry?" The Sheriff said, "Mr. O'Flaherty, by court order you are now under arrest for the nonpayment of debt." Bryan said, "You have made a mistake, I have paid my debt to Lord St. George."

The Sheriff said, "The court has decided this matter. I am here for the purpose of arresting you. The order also includes your workers because they are now indentured slaves as ordered by the court." The soldiers put chains and handcuffs on Bryan and Michael and led them to the barn. The Sheriff informed the farm workers they were now indentured slaves and would be sold to the highest bidder for a term of years. Also, all children under the age of eight years would become wards of the court. Coleman and Delia looked at one another as tears began to come forth. Their world had ended. Both fell to their knees and began praying as they held one another's hands. All the other workers joined with them. Coleman stood and prayed aloud, "Holy Father, we are a helpless few who have learned all the matters of this earth, both large and small, are under your control. Here we, as sheep of Your pasture, kneel before You are trembling with fear because the joy of our lives has been taken from us. We know from experience You have a plan for our lives, greater than we can see. Be with us now as we enter the paths of enduring obedient faith, while we lift our souls up for Your divine care because it is in You that we trust. In the name of Jesus, the Son of God, we pray, Amen."

Delia asks Coleman, "Where will we go?" Coleman said, "We will go somewhere to work, as we have been doing. They will not kill us because they need us to fill their quota." Delia asks Coleman, "Did I do right sending Dan with Eamonn?" Coleman said, "You will be blessed for making that decision."

The Sheriff brought all the other workers to the barn area. He then said, "We are going to take you to a place where other indentured debtors are being held." As they marched along those who were sick began to walk slower and slower. One of the mounted guards had a long whip which he began using to cause the prisoners to increase their pace. This was nothing new to these prisoners. They had become accustomed to abuse and pain. Their only protection was the guards were to be paid by the number of prisoners they delivered. It would be a financial loss to them if they killed or injured any of them.

The journey to the port took almost one day. Coleman and Delia were distraught with fear because of concern for their family. Delia didn't know Eamonn; he was just standing there as the threat had come to their lives. She began thinking; *her precious Dan in the hands of a stranger, God have mercy,* as confused thoughts of panic were racing through her mind.

Meanwhile, Eamonn and Dan had made their way home to Cloonadrawen, Ballinakill, very close to the harbor. Dan was barely three weeks old when the family moved from the seacoast to Oughterard. When he and Eamonn arrived, Dan said, "I have never seen so much water." Eamonn told the quarter master, Sonny Gill, to take Dan to the ship and prepare to take on the food for the journey to Spain. The season to trade the fish, leather, wool, salt and other goods, was upon them, because the market was right to make money for their cargo. Eamonn spoke fluent Spanish which gave him a distinct advantage over his Irish competitors.

Dan held on to yesterday as long as he could and fell asleep at about 9:30 p.m. The crewmen completed loading the ship at 1:30 a.m. When he awoke the ship had just cleared Ballinakill Harbor. Dan had become adjusted to drinking a glass of warm milk when he first awoke in the morning, thanks to his mother. He had slept in the same quarters as Eamonn. When he found his way to the galley, the ship's crew was not aware that Eamonn had hired a new shipmate. Just as Dan walked in, he saw Eamonn and walked over to sit by him. Eamonn said, "Dan, I want you to meet the crew." Eamonn then told the crew, "Dan is a close relative of mine and we are going to teach him to become a seaman." Eamonn looked around for Lupe Flores who spoke fluent Spanish. Eamonn asks, "Where is Lupe? Tell him I need to see him." When Dan was seated, Eamonn asked him what he wanted to eat. Dan asks, "What do you have to eat? I am ready for some water." Eamonn asked Dan if he liked bread and fish. As they were eating, Dan asks Eamonn what his duty would be on the ship. Eamonn told Dan to spend the day getting acquainted with the crew and learning Spanish. Eamonn said, "There is one other thing I want you to learn." Dan asks, "What is it?" Eamonn said, "I want you to sharpen my knives and my sword. I want you to learn how to handle a sharp knife without cutting yourself." Dan asks, "Who can show me how to sharpen a knife?" Eamonn said, "Lupe Flores." Just as his name was spoken, Lupe came to the table and said, "Captain, how can I help you?" Eamonn said, "Lupe, I want you to meet Dan, who is my relative." Lupe said, "Good to have you aboard." Eamonn said, "Lupe, when we get back home, I want Dan to know Spanish, and how to sharpen a knife without cutting himself." Lupe smiled and said, "Muy Bien." Eamonn smiled, "That is a good word for a start." Dan asks, "What does it mean?" Lupe answered, "Very good." Dan said, "Muy Bien." Lupe said, "You are doing very good."

Coleman and Delia had finished their forced march from the farm to the designated port from which the indentured slaves would be shipped to the Colony of Carolina in America. Those who had forced them to march had no mercy for any condition or illness the prisoners were suffering. Coleman and Delia, with the help of Bryan and Michael, had made the journey with four of the children. Patrick had been a great help to his parents. When they arrived at the port, they were told they had to register their names and the names of their children, as well as their ages at the time they boarded the ship. Since the main purpose for the indentured slaves was free labor, the framers of the law determined a young person of eight years of age could work, therefore, all children above the age of eight remained with their family and the younger children were made wards of the court, which meant being placed in an orphanage. The heartbreak of their lives was in the process of occurring before their eyes and they were completely helpless. Absolutely no mercy of any kind prevailed in connection with these families whose lives were being considered with the dignity of stray animals.

Delia and Coleman had always been in Ireland and had been blessed with the closeness of those who knew love and mercy and it was beyond their capability to understand those who had no mercy. As they were waiting for the tide, a late winter storm blew across the bay. They were herded into a shelter to wait until the storm had past.

Previously, during the time Eamonn was preparing his ship for the trip to Spain, a son of Eamonn came by with his wife Bridget, to meet a relative his father had brought home with him. During the visit Eamonn told Donal and Bridget of the peril the family had suffered. Bridget was most interested in the peril because she was barren. After Eamonn left for Spain and Donal had returned to his duty as a fisherman, Bridget made her way to Galway and was in the crowd as the slave ship to transport the O'Flahertys prepared to leave after the storm had past.

Delia took the three girls with her to the potty area before the ship sailed. As Delia and the three children entered the covered area a woman, unknown by Delia, stepped from behind the curtain and said, "I am Eamonn's daughter-in-law, Bridget. I have come to take care of the two young girls. Please leave them with me so they will not be placed in an asylum." Delia said, "I knew God would send an angel and here you are." Delia said, "Barbara, this is Bridget. She has come to take care of your sisters. She will keep them until we come back." Delia turned and held Bridget as a gift from God. As they shared the tears of separation she whispered, *"the four-year-old is*

Siobhann and the two-year-old is Shibeal. Delia returned with Barbara to get back in line with Coleman who asked her, "Where are the other girls?" Delia answered, "In God's care." As they walked the gangplank to depart, even though great sorrow surrounded their hearts, they had just experienced a touch of grateful joy. They were the only two who boarded the ship named, "The Georgia," with smiles on their faces and some degree of joy in their hearts.

Delia and Coleman were just plain, simple, God fearing folk who had never planned ill will against any human being on earth but, they were being herded as animals up a gangplank of a slave ship being sent to a place neither of them would recognize even if they were told the name of the country. There they were with the two of their five children, their third child in the care of a person who had agreed to help them in an emergency, the younger two handed to a stranger, named, Bridget, as they boarded the ship to leave Ireland. All they had left was God's mercy. They prayed for Eamonn to do for Dan as he would for his own and Bridget and Donal to do the same for the young girls.

The grace of God had placed Dan in the hands of a very fine man. Donal and Bridget had a cottage behind Eamonn's cottage that was closer to the harbor. The proximity gave Dan the opportunity to observe his sister's growth to an age when they could remember one another. Eamonn and Bridget knew the importance of the bond developing between them. Dan loved being the big brother and was very careful while playing with his sisters.

As God's grace is, Eamonn began showing a special interest to Dan because the child had exhibited unusual characteristics of intelligence and physical ability. Eamonn secretly told himself, *Dan is superior to my own sons in all ways.* Eamonn was very knowledgeable about the sea and shipping of cargo, but he knew there was a limit to the information he could furnish a child at Dan's age.

He did a good business with ports located in Spain. Being a Catholic, he had to be very careful with whom he did business. When Dan had reached the age of seven, Eamonn took a load of cargo to a port in A Coruna, Spain.

When Eamonn had unloaded the cargo, he decided to take Dan for a walk around the city to make him familiar with the methods of commerce and why it was so important to know and understand different cultures. There was a person in particular Eamonn wanted Dan to meet. Her name was Margarita O'Shea, who had been married to a very close friend, whose name was, General Phillip O'Shea whom Eamonn presumed to have been killed in battle while fighting a war for Spain.

Eamonn and Phillip had become friends many years prior when Eamonn had been hired by Spain as a mercenary soldier. Phillip, at that time was rising in the ranks of the Army of Spain and was a Colonel when they first met. Phillip was so impressed with Eamonn's strength and abilities as a warrior, he asked him to become a regular soldier in the Army of Spain. Eamonn refused, with gratitude for being considered as a capable soldier. Phillip and Eamonn continued with their relationship which both enjoyed. Phillip had risen to the rank of Brigadier General in charge of a unit of tough combat soldiers known as the Special Force troops of the military service. As their victories increased, Phillip's prominence and prestige increased along with the financial favors granted to him by the King of Spain. One of the gratuities deeded to him was a palatial estate located southwest of the

Port of A Coruna. The grounds were magnificent and beautifully manicured with over 500 hundred acres of trees. Margarita and Phillip had no children. Before the presumed death of General O'Shea, they were named among the elite of Spain's social register. Because of General O'Shea's prominence in the military, he was requested to attend a manufacturer's demonstration of a new weapon by his commanding General of the Army of Spain. General O'Shea accommodated his request.

As General O'Shea was observing the use of the new weapons he was standing close to a new type eight-inch cannon. When the weapon was fired, it backfired, striking the General's face, chest, arms and legs. Medical assistants arrived in time to stop some of the bleeding and he was taken to a field hospital for care. The doctors in attendance immediately determined he would lose an arm and the lower part of a leg. His face was completely disfigured, and he was on the brink of death.

His wife, Margarita, had attended the demonstration with him. The Doctors informed her there was nothing more they could do for him. Margarita requested that he be taken to their home, which was done. When they arrived, she asked the family Doctor to come to their home. Doctor Mark Castille, who was a close friend, arrived thereafter. Margarita took him to the library and asked him to be seated. She began by saying, "I know there is little, if any, hope to save his life, but if he can remain alive, I do not care about his appearance, I want him to be with me until there is no breath to support his existence. Margarita continued, "He has asked me to report him as being deceased. I may do that in the next few days, but that does not affect what I am asking you to do now, which is, I want you to do everything you can to cause him to remain alive as long as possible." Doctor Castille said, "I will do my best and may God be with the three of us." Doctor Mark Castille was the only person Margarita allowed to care for Phillip, and he did so night and day for weeks.

Within two months, Phillip awoke one morning and expressed some hunger for something besides broth, which was cause for a celebration between Margarita and Doctor Castille. Even though Phillip had decided to proceed with the announcement of his death, in view of his improvement Margarita asked Phillip if he was continuing to want the announcement of his death. Phillip further insisted that she follow through with his request. Margarita did as he requested. As expected, the nation of Spain went into mourning. Margarita announced there would be a private ceremony for the burial. Margarita began building a building behind the main house. She called it a library in Phillip's honor. The truth was, she began building a facility for Phillip's recovery. Phillip was an avid reader, a brilliant scholar, as well as a soldier that would be a compliment to any nation's military forces.

After the library was completed and a long-term plan for Phillip's healthcare was established, Margarita began to read books to him, especially those he loved so much. Each day they were together made them feel young again. They enjoyed being with one another more every day. After a while, Phillip began to realize his limitations, and dwelled on the fact of him being a disfigured nuisance to Margarita. Even though he had every reason to be happy, he began to become more and more melancholy each day because he was a man that had to have goals to accomplish. One day, he told Margarita he felt like he had become a burden to her life. She broke down crying and said,

"Phillip, as long as you are here with me, I have a beautiful life. When you are gone, my life will be gone also."

Phillip said, "Margarita, God bless you, I will try to never leave you, but I feel so useless. I wish there was something I could do." When Phillip said that, her mind became transfixed on the image of Eamonn's face. She was thinking how marvelous it would be if Eamonn knew that Phillip was alive and could help Phillip to feel useful again. Margarita began to very carefully bring Phillip up to date on all the events surrounding the lives of Eamonn and his family.

A few years before the accident, Eamonn had contacted Phillip at a time when both were not involved in a war. Eamonn talked to Phillip about the purchase of a merchant ship which he had found for sale, which was in excellent condition and available at a good price. When Eamonn arrived to discuss the purchase of the ship, Phillip was overjoyed to see him. Their bond was based upon two men who had shared the risk of death together. Eamonn trusted Phillip's judgment and felt comfortable asking him for his advice to purchase the ship to transport cargo he had available. As he began telling Phillip about the ship's availability, he got excited about the prospect of being in business for himself. Phillip asks Eamonn the cost of the vessel. Eamonn responded saying, "Five thousand pounds." Eamonn told him, "The ship was in dry dock three months ago and the sails were replaced six months ago." Phillip asks, "Who is the owner?" Eamonn answered, "A man by the name of Gregory O'Malley." Phillip said, "Eamonn tell Mr. O'Malley you want the ship." Eamonn said, "Phillip there is a problem." Phillip asks, "What is the problem?" Eamonn responded, "I do not have any money." Phillip replied, "Yes, you do. Tell Mr. O'Malley you will buy the ship." Eamonn was spellbound by the thought of owning a ship, and then he told Phillip, "I will do my best to see that you don't lose any money." Phillip replied, "Eamonn, my friend, I won't lose any money because you don't owe me any money." Eamonn said, "Oh, No! I did not come here to ask for charity." Phillip replied, "It is not charity, you risked your life for Spain and Spain is rewarding you for your effort." Eamonn was bewildered. Phillip said, "Eamonn, Spain has rewarded me for the victories we have won. I am sharing those rewards with you." Eamonn said, "Phillip, you have made my heart more joyful than it has ever been, thank you."

Margarita recalled those days of joy when Eamonn bought the ship and how the ship had given his family a way to have a prosperous life. She knew Eamonn's love for Phillip and she felt it would be only right for him to know Phillip was still alive. She also wanted to talk to Eamonn about allowing Phillip to have a purpose for his life by doing something to use his knowledge. Margarita wrote a message to Eamonn, "Come to Spain as soon as possible." When Eamonn received the message, he responded with all haste. The ship was ready for voyage within twenty-four hours. Eamonn's mind began to run wild trying to imagine why Margarita would want him to come to Spain. The trip, even though only five days, lasted so long it was as if it would never end. There was a carriage waiting for Eamonn when the ship docked. Eamonn took Dan along on the voyage to meet Margarita. Dan was wondering what this trip was all about.

Margarita met the carriage and was so happy to see Eamonn again. Eamonn introduced her to Dan and told her how Dan had come to live with him after the arrest of his parents. Dan began to take in the beauty of the home. He was mindful of those who would never see such beauty in their lives. He was grateful to have had the opportunity to behold the grandeur of such a magnificent home. Margarita had a meal prepared in such a way as to cause her guest to feel perfectly at home, if that was possible for them in such luxurious surroundings. She had prepared a meal fit for an Irish stomach. She remembered Eamonn was not bashful about his appetite.

She began to pay attention to Dan as she watched him observing every fixture and painting in the beautiful dining room. Margarita wanted to know about their voyage and all the details of Dan's learning to sail such a huge ship. Dan told her he was enjoying all there was to learn about sailing and how to sharpen a knife and a sword. As the conversation moved on into important matters, Margarita revealed to Eamonn the fact that Phillip was alive and after all things being considered was doing wonderful. She told Eamonn his face was terribly disfigured, and he had lost an arm and the lower part of one leg. She explained to Eamonn the reason she announced his death was because it was his request. He knew he would never recover and almost didn't many times. She continued revealing for almost two years, Doctor Castille fought infection and disappointing setbacks, but Phillip continued to keep living. She said, "The reason I have asked you to come is I know you would have eventually gotten word to Phillip you were still alive if you had been the one that had been injured. Therefore, I felt it only fair to let you know; the Doctor and I are the only ones to know he is still alive. At this point, I don't think he is ready to see anyone but you and hopefully Dan. I have talked to him about talking to you and he agreed. I have constructed a screening device for your visit. Phillip will visit with you and Dan, but he is not ready to reveal himself to you at this time. I think you will find Phillip has not been damaged mentally, at all. Being himself and being unable to function physically is the problem. He has become depressed and he needs a purpose to live. When he said that to me, an image of your face came into my mind, that is why I have asked you to come. I know he has a desire to be a contributor."

As Eamonn and Margarita continued visiting, both were trying to think of someone for Phillip to want to share his knowledge with, to avoid becoming more depressed. Eamonn stood up and began to walk toward the window when all a sudden it struck him of the great value Dan and Phillip could be to the lives of one another. He turned and began walking back toward Margarita and as he looked at her face a huge smile began to appear. Margarita detected from Eamonn's eagerness he was ready to share a thought. Eamonn said, "My Lady, tell me your thought because I'm thinking you and I are sharing the same thought."

As they shared their thoughts of General O'Shea imparting his knowledge, experience and wisdom to a child, Margarita became more excited with each word. When the outline of the plan began to become more developed, Margarita spoke her desire to visit with Phillip first before their meeting with him. Margarita wanted to be very cautious with her approach to Phillip about agreeing to teach a young Irish child that had no education, other than Eamonn's instructions about sailing a cargo ship.

CHAPTER THREE

PERSONAL EDUCATION

Margarita had never been happier in her life because she knew the decision Dan and Eamonn were considering would be the greatest news she could ever tell Phillip. Margarita said, "I need to go tell Phillip and get him prepared for your visit. Both of us will want to take our time with this life-giving decision, so give us some time to consider all there is to being surrogate parents. I have prepared some food for you in the dining room while I visit with him. Dan, there is one thing I need to ask you as a favor to me." Dan asks, "And what would that be, My Lady?" Margarita asks, "Would you mind if I have an interest in your future also by telling you a few things I think will become important for you later?" Dan said, "My Lady, anything you think that would be beneficial to all of us I would like to know." Eamonn said, "My Lady, you will find Dan very receptive to anything you think will be right for him."

Margarita was smiling as she said, "You make yourself at home while I visit with Phillip and hopefully I can present this matter in the proper way. He will be so excited about visiting with you." Eamonn said, "We will be right here when you are ready." Margarita closed the door as they walked to the dining room and found dishes of fruit and cheese and some other food with which to indulge themselves. Dan found the painted portraits to be very interesting. He had never seen the portrait of another person. The portrait of General Phillip O'Shea gave Dan more of a reality of the person he would be meeting. Without having any foundation to know what to expect, Dan was becoming more excited by the minute.

After about an hour, Margarita came into the dining room with a picture-perfect smile on her face and said, "I want both of you to know how grateful we are for you to be considering this for us. We will remember it forever." Eamonn said, "My Lady, this is such an honor and gift to us." Margarita said, "Eamonn, you must understand we are asking you to allow us to use the educating of Dan to hopefully improve Phillip's health. I pray you will agree to allow us this great privilege. Dan is very mature, even though he is not yet ten years of age. He will become very valuable to all people as he grows older." Eamonn was the most joy filled person on earth. His friend, the man he grieved for every day for two years, was alive. Eamonn was being asked to allow Dan to study at the feet of a man of great stature to give the man back his life. Eamonn's spirit was totally contrite and broken that an opportunity such as this had come to his family's door.

They walked together to the house in the back and entered a room that appeared to be a library. Books by the hundreds were on the shelves all around the room. Dan did not know there were so many books in the world.

There was an opening in the center of the room where a screen had been constructed. There were chairs for them to be seated. Margarita said, "Phillip, we have returned." Phillip said in a jovial tone, "My friend Eamonn, I have returned from being dead for two years." Phillip said, "Eamonn, Eamonn, Eamonn my friend, you will never know the joy you have brought to me. As you know, it is difficult for a warrior to lose all his abilities to defend himself, but when you walked in the room I felt a huge relief in my spirit because your presence brought me peace of mind, because with you around, I feel completely defended." Eamonn began by saying, "General, we have missed you. To see you now, I know my prayers have not been a waste. You have been on my mind every day during these days of your absence." Phillip said, "I am sure Margarita has told you the extent of my injuries." Eamonn replied, "Yes sir, she has." Phillip spoke from his heart by saying, "Eamonn my face is torn to shreds, one arm is gone and the lower part of one leg, but my warrior spirit has remained the same. Because of that, I feel well enough to get up and do a few things, that is why I agreed to allow Margarita to contact you. I knew you would help if you could."

Eamonn said, "General, to be of service to you and your wife for the rest of my life would be as if I had been given more in life than I could ever deserve." Phillip said, "Eamonn, you sweet, sweet soul. Your spirit is life itself to me. Before we begin to shed tears, let's talk about Dan. What Margarita tells me, because of the peril of some of your relatives, you have become the caretaker of a young man who appears to have the potential to become a person who can bless the lives of others, if he is properly trained." Eamonn said, "General, I have four natural born sons of my own and they are about to be grown men. None of them have the natural strength I have; none of them have the ability to learn as this young man. That is why I consider it the greatest honor we could ever be given if you would consider giving him part of your time to teach him the ways of life I will never be able to teach him. I had a thought of putting him in a monastery, but I feel he is more like us in his spirit. I don't think he would fit around a church. I could teach him to be a sailor, but I think he has more potential than that. To me Dan is a young man every man would want to have as a son." Phillip asks, "What is your thinking about how we should handle this situation?" Eamonn said, "General, I live over six hundred miles from here. I must slip by the British government when I can to get a load of cargo which is a risky business. If I leave him, he must have a place to stay." Phillip asks, "Are you opposed to him staying with us?" Eamonn said, "General that is the only thing I would consider. I know he is a hard worker and can be of help around your place to earn his keep." Phillip said, "Say no more, Eamonn. Dan will reside with us."

Phillip said, "Dan, I want to make sure you are agreeable to what we have been discussing about your future. Is the agreement Eamonn and I have made agreeable with you?" Dan replied, "General O'Shea, because of the British government, I am an orphan. My parents had been taken away from me and I had no place to live, no food to eat, until Uncle Eamonn agreed to rescue me. I believe the most Holy God through the love of Jesus Christ, His Son, has brought Uncle Eamonn, yourself and your dear wife, into my life for a Holy purpose. For that gift, I have given my life over to Himself, Eamonn, and now you and your wife. I am willing to do whatever I can to show my gratitude for this great honor that has come to me." When Dan had completed his statement, the three were utterly amazed at the wisdom of this young man. Each of them knew they had been entrusted with a Holy Treasure. They knew by Dan's life being entrusted to them, it was their duty to fulfill their obligation to God by teaching and training this young man to the best of their ability.

Phillip said, "Dan, I have a feeling you and I will enjoy the days we have ahead of us. What do you think about getting started now?" Dan said, "Whatever you think, sir." The first question Phillip asks was, "Where are you going?" Dan said, "I thought it was here." Phillip said, "A man does not know how to get where he is going until he knows where he is at any given time. If you will look on the wall to the left of the first book shelf, you will find a map of the known world, go ahead and look at the map. Remember, the earth is as round as a ball, but the map shows the different countries on a flat surface. Perhaps the first lesson should be the names of all those countries which would require you to know how to read. Are you ready to learn how to read?" Dan said, "Yes sir."

Margarita said, "Phillip, Eamonn and I going to the house to get a room ready for Dan to stay with us. I think about another hour of class work should be enough for today." Phillip said, "That sounds like a good start." Dan said, "Thank you, my Lady."

When Eamonn and Margarita got to the house, they went to a bedroom next to her own. She got some sheets and pillowcases and got the room ready for Dan. Eamonn was chuckling to himself wondering *what Dan would think of his new quarters because he had never slept on a mattress.* When they had completed preparing the bedroom, Eamonn asks if there was anything else he could do to help her. Margarita said, "Eamonn, I wouldn't know where to start. No one has been here but the Doctor in nearly two years. I have not paid any attention to the yard or the garden. My life has been dedicated to getting Phillip well enough to have a life. If you don't mind, I would appreciate it if you looked around to see if the garden needs care." Eamonn said, "My Lady, I have ten members of my crew at the docks now. When we arrived, I saw several things that needed attending. Would you allow me to get my crew of pure Irish blood to your house in the morning and get this place back like it should be? I will make a vow to you that no word concerning your life will ever leave this property." Margarita said, "I trust you, Eamonn, do whatever needs to be done."

At sunrise the next morning eleven Irish souls were busy changing a rundown mansion into a well-kept palace. There were some tree limbs that had fallen, two years of unraked leaves and other matters that needed attention. Margarita was having the time of her life learning how to cook Irish food, some of which was for the first time. After a week the grounds, the lawn and every repair of the home was completed. Margarita was transformed into a new person. She appeared to be a lady who had hope again, because a huge load had been lifted from her shoulders.

At the end of the week Eamonn told Margarita he needed to get back to Ireland. Margarita said, "I know Phillip and Dan want to see you before you go, let me go tell them." Within a short time, she returned and said, "They are anxious to see you now." Eamonn walked in as Dan jumped up and ran to see him. Dan said, "Uncle, this is going to be good." Eamonn said, "I hope for God's blessings to be on the both of you until we meet again." Phillip said, "Eamonn, I looked at the grounds last evening. You are a precious friend, may the son of God never allow you to be weakened, thank you so much for bringing the appearance of life back to us. You will be pleased to know Dan is everything any good man would want to have in a son. He is moving along much faster than I would have expected of anyone. He is a natural born student. I think when he has finished developing, we will all be surprised. Again, thank you for everything; we will be anxiously waiting for your return." Eamonn told them farewell and he was on his way to his homeland.

As time progressed Dan began to sense a feeling of closeness to General O'Shea and his wife. He had been given the trust of complete freedom to do or say whatever he desired. The tension of life had begun to melt away. While he was but a small child, Delia had taught him to dance the Irish jig at which she was very accomplished. Dan remembered his mother's sweet voice and the moments of pleasure he had learned. One day while he was on the ground by himself he began whistling the tune of a song his mother had taught him. He did not realize Margarita was watching him through the window of her home. Dan whistled and danced, and Margarita was impressed with the skill and agility he displayed. As they were eating the evening meal, Margarita revealed to him, in a complementary manner, she had seen him doing the Irish jig. Dan was embarrassed for a moment and then said, "I didn't know you knew what to name what I was doing." Margarita replied, "Dan, you must know by now you are in a province of Spain that is almost entirely Irish immigrants or native-born citizens. In fact, there is history of the Milesians who invaded Ireland about 500 BC from Spain which the O'Flaherty clan derived from and settled in the west of Ireland. So, you see, Dan, you're back where you ancestors started from."

There are many of our citizens who know how to do the Irish jig." Dan said, "Thank you, that makes me feel more at home." Margarita said, "Dan, will you do the jig for Phillip?" Dan said, "My Lady, there needs to be a day when the General will come out of hiding, on his own accord. It would be good for him to come out of seclusion.

If he continues, what will he do when I have gone to fulfill my purpose in life?" Margarita had never considered there would be an end to the life she now loved so much. Margarita said, "Dan, you are so right. I am going to persuade him to consider giving up isolation to see you do the jig." Dan said, "I would love to bring you and him some joy for all you have done for me."

Margarita set her course toward getting Phillip to come from behind his prison. She thought to herself, *Dan has brought more to our lives than we could ever repay.* Dan was becoming a gift for which they could have never hoped, because they had no understanding a child could bring so much joy. The next morning as Margarita prepared Phillip's meal, she put a red rose in a vase on his tray. She gently opened the door because she was serving his breakfast earlier than usual. Phillip, with a loud voice said, "Margarita, I have been waiting for you. I want to tell you this little experiment, of which we find ourselves involved, has begun to cause me to feel worthwhile again. There is something very special about this young man that has caused me to want to become involved not only with his education, but with his life. I sincerely want to be a part of the adventure of his life. I think we all are going to be absolutely amazed by his many outstanding accomplishments. By the way, where is he? We need to get started." She said, "At this time, he is in the kitchen waiting for me to return, but darling, there is something we need to discuss first." Phillip could feel, *something of great importance about to unfold.* She said, "Yesterday I was in the living room and Dan was in the courtyard. The window was opened, and I could hear him whistling an Irish song as he danced the jig. "Phillip, it is something you must see." Phillip said, "Tell him I am ready to start the day with a lively Irish jig." Margarita said, "He will only do the jig on one condition, which is, you must come out of your prison, so you can see the whole thing." Phillip said, "You go tell him I said, to get himself over here now and I will be ready to watch his performance without a prison cell to hide my scars."

Margarita rushed to the house and said, "Oh Dan! Wonderful news, he is waiting on your performance to begin his day." Dan jumped up and ran to the front door of the library. As he walked in the General was standing on his one good leg with a military stiffness ready to salute. Dan began whistling, Phillip sat down as he watched Dan with one of his toes pointed down to begin the jig with the music of an old Irish tune that stirred the memory of his mother holding his hand as she taught him the trademark of the Irish culture.

When Dan had completed the dance, Phillip said, "Bravo, bravo, Dan I had no idea you were as athletic as you are. Margarita, I want you to gather all the information necessary to enroll him into a private military academy to learn sword fighting and the use of military weapons. A friend of mine has an academy which is known as the Premier Academy of Spain. This is a revelation that is completely unexpected. Margarita, do you remember who has a stable of Spanish War Horses for him to learn to ride?" Margarita said, "I will locate the right person as soon as I can." Dan's young mind was in a whirl. He had no idea what turn his life had taken because of his mother teaching him something as simple as the Irish jig.

Margarita went back to the main house to plan how to get Dan enrolled with the right professional people. The question was what relationship she would use to see to it Dan received the best of training. She decided she would be his mother's sister, making her Dan's Aunt, if Dan approved.

When she asks Dan if she could introduce herself as his aunt, Dan responded by saying, "I would prefer you telling them you are my adoptive mother." When Margarita heard Dan's feelings for her from his heart, she sat down and buried her face in her hands as tears began to roll from her eyes. There was a long silence. She finally said, "Dan, for me to be considered worthy to be called your mother would be the highest honor of my life. Would you mind if we go now to talk to Phillip about this matter?"

As they entered Phillip's quarters, he could tell matters of a serious nature had come to their minds. Margarita said, "Phillip, there is something the three of us need to discuss." Phillip asks, "What has happened?" Margarita said, "A short time ago, Dan and I were discussing the relationship we would have with Dan when I entered him into the Academy. I told him I would tell them I am his mother's sister, so as to give him status to receive the best training possible. Dan says he prefers to be known as our adoptive son. I told him it would be beyond my fondest dream if he was known as my son. I have come to ask you your opinion of how we should introduce him." Phillip said, "Margarita, could you love him more if you had given birth to him?" Margarita said, "I love him as my son." Phillip asks, "Margarita, would it be pleasing to you if he were known as our son?" Margarita said with a broad smile, "If you agree to share him with me, I will allow you to be his adoptive father." They turned to Dan and Phillip asks Dan, "Would you agree to be our son?" Dan said, "Sir, for me being an Irish orphan to be asked to be considered to be a son of General Phillip and Margarita O'Shea has to be one of heaven's greatest gifts. I pledge to you I will strive to never bring dishonor or shame to your most excellent name." The three embraced with hearts of love that had grown from a path of tears.

It had been a good while since Eamonn had brought freight from Ireland. Phillip began to get concerned. Phillip asked Dan to ask Margarita to allow him to hook up the carriage to go to the port to determine when Eamonn was due to dock, and if so, what date he would arrive. Dan enjoyed his ride to the port with Margarita, so she could enjoy a change of scenery. When they arrived at the port, Dan went to the docks to check the departure and arrival schedules. Dan had learned enough about reading to recognize Eamonn's name. He read the words, "Due Tuesday." Dan went to the carriage and told Margarita, "Eamonn is due Tuesday." Dan felt so big; he had never felt that smart in his life. He jumped back in the carriage and they went away to downtown. Margarita asks Dan, "What are you doing?" Dan said, "I'm taking you for a ride. You need some sights to see and new air to breathe." Margarita began to loosen up as the horse galloped along on such a beautiful day. Dan was smiling from ear to ear; as he felt in control of providing joy for someone he loved to cause her day to be made better.

After about an hour of riding and looking at the scenery, they decided to get back to enjoying this day of their life with General O'Shea. When they arrived, Dan put the horses in the barn and went to the General's quarters. Dan walked inside as Margarita was telling Phillip about her day. She told him about her unexpected ride to town and about Eamonn's arrival on Tuesday, which made Phillip very happy. The day was so full of wonderful memories that everyone needed some good rest.

The next morning, Margarita decided to take Dan to the military academy. Phillip was in full approval with what she was doing. Dan was ready for his great adventure to begin. When they arrived, she began explaining to Dan the importance of there being a purpose for her showing such an interest in his military training. Dan realized if he was to be nothing but an Irish peasant he would not be allowed to walk in the paths of the prestigious hierarchy as just another orphan, simply because he had talent. Someone would have to provide him access to the opportunity, and it seemed that the O'Sheas were willing to do so by becoming his adoptive parents. Dan said, "My Lady, thank you for allowing me to become your son." Margarita smiled. It was as if Dan knew her thoughts, and his gentle words made her explanation so much easier. Dan was becoming keenly aware of the economics of supply and demand and how even though there were minor differences in each culture, the ultimate goal was to earn money. He had been made aware of the effect of having money from his peasant surroundings of birth. There was a decision for everyone to make. If the government was a system that allowed the freedom of choice of remaining a peasant or seeking ways to improve the living standards of the family, Dan knew from experience being a peasant was not the choice he would make. Dan was becoming more and more aware of the blessings he had been given by Almighty God by not only being allowed to eat food every day, but to be placed in the best of circumstances, financially and socially.

One morning when Dan arrived to begin the day of learning, the General began by saying, "Dan, when I was your age I did not have the opportunities you have ahead of you. The military was one of the two options I had. The other was to work in the fields as a peasant farmer. I chose the military and that turned out to be a good decision. There was something I recognized immediately and that was, the conventional method of military combat was for the opposing forces to line up in an open field and march toward one another firing their weapons. I saw that method of warfare was not for me, because that is a good way to get killed.

I began applying myself to learn some different methods of combat. I learned through the ages that the most successful leaders determine their success by the number of soldiers who survived a battle. I learned the best tactic to defeat the enemy is surprise with an adequate force to accomplish the victory. That is the method I used to win the victories we won. There is nothing better in warfare than having the correct information as to the enemies' location and the size force he has to defend your attack. As my experience increased, so did our victories. As our victories increased, so did my responsibility. When I was appointed General, I was given a division of the finest combat soldiers in the world. Most of our fighting was done at night, which gave us the advantage of surprise. I intend to teach you and train you to become the best military combat expert I possibly can.

My hope will be you will never have to use the knowledge I give you, but if you are called upon, you will not only be ready, you will be the best soldier on the field. As the training proceeds, if you have any questions or disagreement, please speak up. It is very important you learn and know all there is to know about all the other subjects, but you must remember the entire country of Ireland is under siege. We do not know how long it will last. Should you be called upon, I will have the satisfaction of knowing you are the best."

After the military training had begun, Phillip knew Dan would become a great soldier. One morning, Dan awoke, and his thoughts had shifted to concern for Eamonn. He wanted to be at the dock when the ship landed the next day. He asked the General if he would object to him being at the dock when the ship arrived. The General had only one qualification which was, bring him to see me as soon as he arrives. Dan awoke early; he had previously arranged to take the carriage to the dock.

At about 4 o'clock a.m., Dan saw the light of a ship coming into the harbor. Dan's heart began to race, thinking, *hoping maybe it was Eamonn.* As the ship drifted slowly to the dock he could see it was Eamonn's ship. One of the ship's crew recognized Dan and threw him a rope. Dan stiffened his legs and leaned back to slow the ship for docking. When the ship stopped, the news Dan was waiting had been told to Eamonn. Within minutes, Eamonn hollered, "What are you doing up so early? You are supposed to be getting ready for school." Dan hollered back, "I took the day off." Eamonn laughed as the gang plank landed on the dock. As soon as it landed, Dan made his way to the deck of the ship. Eamonn grabbed him to throw him up in the air, as he had always done, but something had changed. Dan was almost six inches taller and was weighing almost one hundred pounds. Eamonn was taken by surprise that Dan had grown so big, so quickly. Dan could see Eamonn had marks on his head and face. Dan asks, "Did you have trouble?" Eamonn said, "It is getting harder and harder to ship the cargo out of Ireland. I am thinking, *there may be a warrant for me if I return to Ballynakill.* Dan said, "The General is ready to see you. I know he can help figure out a way to keep you from harm." Dan drove the carriage up to the front walk very quietly so as not to awake

Lady O'Shea; however, she was standing at the front door waiting for them to arrive. Regardless of how Eamonn smelled after several days at sea, she wanted to feel his massive arms around her to give her that sense of protection that only Eamonn gave to her.

Eamonn had brought a gift with him that was wrapped and stored in the carriage. Margarita told Eamonn of the progress her two men had made. She reported Dan possessed an astonishing learning skill. She told Eamonn of Phillip's progress of no longer needing a screen to hide behind to visit with his best friends. Eamonn was so pleased with Dan's progress. He knew Dan was special, but the evaluation Margarita had given verified what he expected to be the truth. Eamonn asks, "When do you think the General will be awake?" Margarita said, "He has been awake for some time waiting for you." Eamonn asks to be excused to retrieve the gift from the carriage. When Eamonn returned, he was ready for a visit with the General.

The General was prepared to welcome his friend personally. Eamonn took his hand with a warm greeting. The General saw Eamonn had brought something with him. The General asks, "What do we have here?" Eamonn enlisted Dan's help to remove the covering from the gift. When it was uncovered, the General, Margarita and Dan were amazed at the apparatus. Eamonn said, "I have built you this for traveling we will be doing." The General asks, "Traveling, traveling, are we going to be traveling?" Eamonn said, "General, circumstances in Ireland have gotten worse. I am not sure, but I think there may be a warrant out for my arrest. I would like to talk to you about that. Right now, let me see what you think about this toy I have made for you. You can see it is built like a chair. You can sit in it; you can also see it has four wheels which means it will roll. Look, you can also see it has two wooden hooks up over the back of the chair. Those are to fit over, my shoulders. The thing is very handy. You can sit, you can roll, and you can be carried. You will notice I have put a belt to strap you in when you are being carried. Please inspect it very closely. You will notice the wood is very sturdy. When you feel brave, I would like for you to come sit in the chair for me to show you how it works."

The General had the utmost confidence in Eamonn. He said, "Let's try it." The General sat down. Eamonn strapped him in and turned to place the back of his massive shoulders under the plow handle shaped hooks. He then stood up with the General in the cart and began walking him around the room. Laughter began to break loose that had not been heard in the O'Shea mansion in many years. Eamonn squatted down, turned around and began rolling the General around the room again and again. The laughter again erupted. Tears were streaming down Margarita's face as she witnessed life returning to her beloved soldier which she thought would never occur. Dan was ready for his turn to transport the General. He squatted, placed his shoulders under the hooks, stood straight up and began his turn around the room. Again, laughter and joy filled the room.

When the celebration and demonstration was complete Margarita said, "It is time for a hearty breakfast, suppose we eat in the main house?" Since the General had not entered the main house in years, there was occasion for another celebration. Again, laughter and happiness poured out and off to the main house they went with the General comfortably riding in his cart, as his best most trusted friend provided the power.

As they were completing their breakfast Phillip said, "Eamonn, I need to know more about your trouble in Cloonadrawen." Eamonn said, "General, I am not sure you are aware of the British Empire's plan to exterminate all the Catholics in Ireland, but if they continue at the present rate they will succeed. While you have been recovering, the plan to exterminate every Catholic in Ireland has become more intense. Three years ago, some of us were making a living shipping dried fish, beef, and some salt pork to other countries. When the British government learned of our business a new law was passed which abolished the shipment of meat products to foreign nations, but as you know, the Irish people are very resourceful. We then began to sell the hides of the animals for leather, and then another amendment was added to the Penal Laws to prevent any leather goods from being sold and shipped to foreign markets. The penalty in some cases for any violations has been death or being sent to a penal colony in a foreign nation." The General was stunned at the degree of savagery the British Empire had adopted into law. Eamonn said, "Further, some of the people are being sent as indentured slaves to foreign nations for raising questions about the amount of rent they have to pay for housing." Phillip asks, "What do you think is the purpose?" Eamonn responded, "Land, the land is being used by the Crown to purchase loyalty from the Kings sacred few supporters who are willing to support the schemes of royal greed that is rampant in the empire. The Crown is involved in seizing all land held by Catholics to bribe supporters of the Crown, which requires the elimination of the Catholic land owners."

The General asks Eamonn if he had thought about the alternative to the present calamity without risk of personal harm. Eamonn said, "There may be an opportunity to resume shipping, perhaps from a safer location." Phillip inquired, "Where would that be?"

Eamonn hesitated for a moment and then said, "I hope you won't think I am trying to get you involved in another war, but there is an area not far from Ballynakill Harbor that has been occupied by the O'Malley family for many years. Some of the inhabitants are from the Cordelier Province here in Spain. The trade between the two ports is well known but the British are seemingly disinterested in the connection. Do you remember some of your friends who trade with the O'Malleys' whom we purchased a ship from years ago? I feel certain they would be interested in renewing business arrangements with the O'Sheas. If that can be done, we can avoid the English interference all together." Phillip became intrigued with the possibility of establishing a trade relationship because it is so desperately needed. As Phillip pondered the desperation of all these innocent people, he told Eamonn they needed time to think through a good strategy.

Phillip then asked Eamonn to sit down for a moment to listen to something the three of them had to tell him. The General told Eamonn of the decision they had made concerning the adoption of Dan as their son. Eamonn asks the General, "Is that what you agreed to do?" General O'Shea said, "Eamonn, Dan has become our son as well as the answer to our prayers for him, for you and for us. Dan has brought a life to us that we would have never experienced if he had not wanted to be with us. When Dan came into our lives, darkness and despair had begun to cover our eyes and our hope was fading. Dan brought his life to us to share and we have given him our lives to share. We are in hope you will agree." Eamonn said, "I will be eternally grateful that you have found happiness in sharing Dan with the O'Flaherty's. I know he will become a man that will make all of us proud."

CHAPTER FOUR

ALTERNATIVES

The discussions as to the eradication of the Catholic believers in Ireland continued. The more Eamonn revealed to Phillip the more inspired Phillip became to find a path around the tyranny until political change could be brought about. Eamonn said, "There is a way around having to use known harbors to load the trade ships." Phillip was most interested in Eamonn's comment. Phillip asks Eamonn how the arrangements with the O'Malley's could be made. Eamonn said, "I think the O'Malley's own at least three more vessels which have been converted from warships to cargo ships. I was thinking of working schedules to have the cargo ships loaded off shore with the smaller boats bringing the goods to the cargo vessel." Phillip said, "I like that idea, I can see with the right planning a larger vessel could be loaded during the night in about eight hours." Eamonn agreed. Phillip asks Eamonn, "Who do we need to contact first?" Eamonn said, "What do you think about us taking a trip to Clare Island to talk to the O'Malley family?" Phillip said, "Eamonn, one of the major concerns I have is being in the sunlight. Can you think of a covering we could use to protect my flesh from the sunlight and the salt water?" Eamonn said, "I know of some material called cotton that would shield your face."

Phillip asks, "Where can we buy some cotton material?" Margarita said, "I will take care of that for you." She also said, "Surely, you know I will be with you on the voyage." Phillip said, "I had hoped you would be."

Dan had listened to every word and was amazed how being financially capable made the plans of men more attainable. He was learning from the best teachers he could ever know because they were men who not only talked about it; they had acted upon their thoughts with success.

Margarita was very excited about the adventure. The planning of the voyage had all of them happier than they had been in years. She hurriedly contacted the doctor and received the medication he thought Phillip would need for the journey. She asks Dan to take her to town to locate some soft cotton to make bandages for Phillip's face. Phillip was aware of his total dependency on the lives of others to be allowed to function effectively on matters of importance. As he saw those he loved hurrying around preparing to do a good deed, he couldn't help but become so grateful to God to allow him to continue to participate in the affairs of life.

Within two days, they had set sail for Clare Island. The weather was welcomed with a prayer of gratitude. Dan was very attentive to the General. He was in his cart which was tightly bound to the mast pole. The fresh sea breeze blowing on the soft cotton caused a healing effect to Phillip's face. Margarita was enthralled with watching Dan perform as an able body seaman. She was so proud of him and the progress he had made in the years of them being together. She asks herself, w*hat would we have done without this young man's life becoming a part of our life,* and then she also asks, *what would we do without Eamonn?* Dan knew he had become very special to the O'Sheas. They had grown to truly love one another as a family.

Within seven days, they had arrived at Clare Island. Eamonn had sent a message to the O'Malley's prior to leaving for Spain indicating he had reached the point of intolerance with the British invaders and would no longer take their abuse. When the ship pulled into the harbor, the O'Malley's had prepared a welcome akin to the old Celtic ways. The entire O'Malley clan attended the celebration. The clan had decided to speak Spanish in honor of their revered guest but, much to their surprise, Phillip began speaking Gaelic and the mood quickly changed to a family get together. Dan was shocked as to the manner in which Phillip and Margarita were received. He felt like he was with royalty of the genuine sort.

Dan finished off the evening with a jig that brought old memories of the better days to everyone. Eamonn raised his glass to remember Grace O'Malley, the seafaring Queen of the clan in years of long ago. After the toast an old bard sang one of the most touching Gaelic songs ever written about her queen ship, Lady Grace.

The time had come for rest. Phillip had exhausted himself, but he was alive with memories he would have forever. The next morning the purpose of the voyage was on the minds of both families. They gathered at Gregory O'Malley's home. Eamonn was appointed to begin the meeting. He began by telling of the circumstances he had recently endured. Eamonn said, "It is time for all of us to realize we are nothing but lambs waiting to be slaughtered. I do not intend to continue to live my life as a slave waiting to die. Some of you probably remember Phillip O'Shea's family from County Kerry.

General O'Shea was raised in Galicia, Spain. He has lived his life as a military man until he was wounded several years ago. He was my Commanding Officer. I have contacted him to enlist his help for us to do what is necessary to allow us to continue to care for our families. I have told him of your family's spirit and willingness to try to bring about a resolution. He has thought about it and would like to make a proposal."

General O'Shea began by saying how grateful he was for the arms of welcome the O'Malley family extended to his family. He said, "Thank you all for the food and the warmth you have so graciously given to us. From what I understand, your family has some ships that were former warships which have been converted to cargo vessels. I am assuming the ships are in good condition. I would like to propose entering into a partnership with the O'Malley family to purchase an interest in the ships. My thinking is a fifty percent ownership. I would also like to propose for your family to oversee gathering all the cargo available in your area to be shipped to a foreign port for sale. I am willing to provide the purchase money for the goods. Most of the work will be done at night by smaller boats taking the cargo to the larger vessels which will be anchored off the coast. My estimate is it will take eight hours to load the cargo. The ships will then sail to Ballyferriter, County Kerry, and anchor off the coast to be loaded by smaller boats the same as before. The ship will then sail to a foreign port to market the goods. The partnership will share fifty-fifty in the profits minus the payments to those who supply the goods."

When the General was finished, Gregory O'Malley asked his family if they had any questions. There were no questions. Gregory asked those who favored the partnership to say, "Aye," which they did, and there were no objections. The partnership was approved. They then went to the O'Shea family at Ballyferriter and presented the same offer to the O'Shea family. Everyone agreed, and the partnership was approved. Within two weeks the ships were fitted for service and Eamonn was the Captain of a ship that could carry two hundred fifty-eight tons of cargo. Within six months the British occupiers were wondering how everyone was appearing so well fed.

As time passed, Dan grew in stature and maturity and developed into one of the outstanding swordsmen in Spain. He had also become a horseman second to none, and his skills became known throughout Spain. Margarita and Phillip felt glorious with each day's rising of the sun wondering what additional joy this young man would bring into their lives.

Margarita had hinted from time to time concerning their approval for him to form a relationship with a female, if he chose to do so. Dan had no interest in becoming involved with anyone other than the family God had given to him. His mind was becoming more and more skilled in the use of military weapons and horsemanship. Dan was held in the highest regard by his classmates and teachers.

Phillip continued to pour himself into causing Dan to become knowledgeable about everything including military strategies and tactics. One day the General brought up a subject that was new to Dan, which was the colonization of a new country called America. Dan had always assumed that his family had been sent to America. He quickly showed an interest in the formation of the colonies. Phillip began gathering all the information he could find to be able to share it with Dan. One of the subjects they discussed was Spain's interest in America. Phillip located some information which explained the continued conflicts between Spain and Great Britain regarding Spain's interest in a peninsula named Florida. Phillip explained that Spain had settled the area named Florida and Great Britain had settled the area north of Florida which was named Carolina. Both countries continued to try to expand their areas of ownership which resulted in a constant conflict regarding the southern part of Carolina and the eastern part of what was to become known as Georgia.

Dan was very interested in that area of the world and hoped to visit it someday. Dan's mind stayed upon his mother and his family and the days of joy he once knew. He was six years old when his mother put him in Eamonn O'Flaherty's care, at a time when everyone was arrested at the Bryan O'Flaherty's farm, because of the allegation of non-payment of debt by Bryan O'Flaherty. That was the last time Dan had seen his mother. At times the grief was more than he could bear, but with Eamonn's care, Dan grew to endure the pain of not being allowed to belong to his family. Phillip and Margarita loved Dan as their own son.

As the years passed, he began to learn more and more of the English savagery. He learned of the voyages the indentured slaves were forced to make to foreign lands, in most cases, never to return to their homeland. The thought of seeing his family again preyed heavily upon his mind. The horrific truth of how the prisoners were treated on the slave ships that took them to their destination, even told in the most delicate manner, was more than he could bear.

Dan was old enough at the time to understand what he was hearing as to how his brother and sister, as well as his parents, were treated. The hope and prayer that remained with him was their lives would be spared until they were together again. As he continued to think of the two and a half to three-month voyage, enduring unimaginable brutality, starvation, infections, sickness, and with little rest, he would shed tears of deep, deep sorrow. He remembered his father and the work he did each day to provide food for all the family. As Dan pondered each circumstance he had come to know, he began to ask himself, *who are these people who are not only bringing harm to us but are seemingly enjoying their ability to destroy and murder the innocent.* As he began to use the destruction of his own family as a compass, he began to want to know more about the personalities that were driving these tyrants who held such enormous power over the citizens of nations. Dan recognized no person could be trusted with the final authority over another human being. Throughout his studies with General O'Shea the General had emphasized the deepest most sacred gift from God to humanity is the freedom to choose the way for one to live their life.

As Dan used the availability and access to vast knowledge, it became clear to him from the history of the world that greed and power are the ultimate desires of the leaders of nations. He learned the value of allowing a person accused of a crime to be taken before a jury of his peers to determine his innocence or guilt. The Irish genetic design that filled his spirit caused him to know the difference between slavery and freedom. His prayer was to be allowed to live in a nation where personal freedom was the bed rock foundation of the law.

As Dan wondered about his family, he asks the General, "Is there a way I could find out their whereabouts?" The General suggested asking Eamonn during his next visit the name of the port from which they sailed to a location in America on a ship named, "Georgia." The General said, "From what I understand the land in Carolina is good fertile soil and has become a good investment for the Crown of England." The General tried to ease Dan's pain by stressing how valued slaves were who had farming experience. The General said, "Your mother and father are survivors. I can tell how they must be from how you are. You have that O'Flaherty blood which has endured for hundreds of years. Take my word and my prayer; someday you will see your family again. In the meantime, you know we love you as our very own son."

When Eamonn returned to port, Dan learned of his arrival. He hitched up the carriage to go to the dock to bring Eamonn to see Margarita and General O'Shea. Eamonn was very glad to see Dan. He remarked how much Dan had grown in such a short while. Margarita was prepared for her most favorite visitor of all times. The General was in the cart when Eamonn arrived. Margarita asked if everyone was ready for the evening meal. Eamonn was the first to say, "My Lady, I have thought about this all day, yes I am." As they gathered around the table, the true spirit of joy filled the room. The General was ready to give his report on his student's progress. Eamonn was so proud of the way the O'Shea's had provided so much more of everything than Eamonn would have ever been able to provide for Dan. Eamonn asks, "What has Dan been eating? He is almost as tall as me?" Margarita said, "Oh, it is just a few dishes I whipped up for a growing young man." They laughed because they knew Margarita paid special attention to Dan's food to see to it he ate only the best food available. Dan was almost the height of Eamonn and weighed more than two hundred pounds. The General had watched him cutting trees around their home and was completely amazed at the natural strength he possessed, which had not affected his agility. The General would remark to himself, *he is a natural born warrior*. The General was filled with a sense of humble satisfaction how Dan had developed under his guidance.

The General asks Eamonn how the business was progressing with the O'Malleys. A huge smile came across Eamonn's face as he said, "General, there are more Irish people eating good food in Ireland than the Crown intended. There have been some occasions when the weather was not what we had hoped for, but we managed to load and move on. The main thing is the company is making money and the O'Malleys and the O'Flahertys are happy with the bargain they made with you. As the weather improves we will need to buy some new sails. I prefer to have the work done in Spain, if that meets with your approval." The General said, "Of course."

Eamonn said "There is one other matter you need to know. There is some talk about Bonnie Prince Charlie coming to Scotland. Do you have anything to say about our position in this matter?" The news struck Phillip unexpectedly; he began to wonder, *has my purpose been to prepare Dan for this event?* Phillip had never been faced with having to risk a life he considered more valuable than his own. Phillip's mind launched into a sea of new thought because he knew the hope of victory was remote. When he had completed his analysis, he concluded the prospect of victory, even though remote, is worth the sacrifice to free innocence from the savages of Great Britain. The General said, "Eamonn, you must take Dan with you when you return to Ireland. He must be given time to organize a force to support the Scots in this great effort." Eamonn bowed his head as tears ran down his cheeks when he said, "General, I must go with him." The General said, "Eamonn, you must help him put together a fighting force like none other. He has been trained to win the battle."

A daunting spirit swept across the plains of their hearts. They had never considered the prospect of separation from one another, much less the possibility of Dan becoming killed in battle. Margarita waited until she and Phillip were alone for her to fall on her knees sobbing the tears of a heart broken mother who had her child snatched from her arms by the perils of war. Phillip needed consoling as he attempted to console Margarita. The question they asked themselves was, *did we do right by training him to be the first to step forward in every fight to give his life?* The General was finally able to speak to Margarita in a manner to give her hope. He said, "Margarita, I promise you we will be allowed to see him again. Until that day, we will trust God and the fact he is the best trained soldier in this fight. He knows how to fight, and he knows how to stay alive."

When Eamonn docked at Clare Island he told the O'Malleys of the possibility of Bonnie Prince Charlie leading the Jacobite's in the battle to regain the throne from King George II. This was the second and final battle by the Roman Catholic believers to try to overthrow the House of Hanover, who represented the Protestant believers' interest. King James VII of Scotland, (James II of England) had been dethroned long ago. In 1745, George II himself went from England to fight the French in Belgium which was viewed as an opportune time to invade England, from the north with the aid of the Irish and Scottish Highlanders. (2)

The plan of the supporters of James II (Jacobite's) was to gather various clans in Scotland by invading Scotland. (2) The plan included forming the clans into one force and then to invade England. Prince Charlie was able to rally a force of three thousand Frenchman he had brought with him which included the Irish that the clans had gathered. (2) The Irish were placed under the clan of Dan O'Flaherty O'Shea, who was known for being the best of the best.

Dan was agreeable to lead the clans in battle provided they agreed to follow his leadership as opposed to running head long into the battle without a plan of attack. He said, "The order will be to fight at night and attack by surprise." The first battle took place in 1745. The combined units of Highlanders and Irish clans were armed with swords, daggers and pistols that were cocked for firing. (2) Dan led his troop to the edge of a clearing where the British had camped for the night. In the very early morning hours Dan lead the attack against the sleeping British. They charged the tents without hesitation, slaughtered all but a few that were left wounded. A group known as Dragoons escaped. Most of the shots fired by the British missed the mark as the soldiers ran for their lives. (2)

The battles continued to be fought as Bonnie Prince Charlie prepared to invade England. As they drove south the Jacobite force increased with each victory and reached numbers that exceeded five thousand troops. (2) However, as the Jacobite's reached the outskirts of London, the officers under the command of Prince Charlie betrayed him and retreated toward Scotland.

On the retreat Dan and his troops were involved in some hard-fought battles, winning most of them. As the retreat hastily continued, Bonnie Prince Charlie saw the gap of the escape route rapidly closing. (2) He ordered Dan's Irish and Scots regiment to hold the line against General Cumberland and General Oglethorpe at Shap Fell as the dark and the rain began to affect the battle. The two Generals assumed the entire Jacobite force was involved but the darkness held the secret that Prince Charlie used the weather conditions and the darkness to slip most of his troops through without harm. (2)

At day break, even though Cumberland and Oglethorpe rose to fight Prince Charlie's troops, they were facing a group of two hundred of the fiercest fighters they had ever faced. They fought both units of British soldiers until there were six Irish soldiers wielding weapons while the others lay dead or wounded on the battlefield. At that time, the truth was revealed. The Prince had escaped and left the gallant brave to pay for their freedom. General Cumberland and General Oglethorpe were amazed at the loss of British regulars who had fallen to their death from the grit and gall of such few who gave their all for their brother's escape. (2)

Dan and five others survived the slaughter. A discussion took place whether to kill the six men or take them prisoners. Just as they were about to kill the prisoners, General James Oglethorpe rode up and asked the Lieutenant what action was being taken against the prisoners. The Lieutenant explained the decision had been made to kill the prisoners. General Oglethorpe intervened and asked the prisoners whether they submitted to surrender. Five said no and were shot. Dan became a prisoner of war. General Oglethorpe asked to speak to Dan before he was taken to the stockade.

General Oglethorpe told Dan he had closely observed his leadership throughout the battle. The General admitted he had never witnessed such battle tactics in his many years of being a military officer. He then asked Dan where he grew up, and Dan told him, in the house of O'Shea in Spain. General Oglethorpe told Dan he had known of a General O'Shea who was perhaps the greatest General who ever fought for Spain. The General said, "Unfortunately, he was killed in a freak accident years ago." Dan said, "General Oglethorpe, General Phillip O'Shea is not dead, he is my adoptive father. He is the one who educated and trained me. He is the man who taught me the tactics and strategy you saw me demonstrate in these battles."

General Oglethorpe was taken by surprise to have found a person of Dan's character fighting for the enemy. The circumstance was beyond General Oglethorpe's capacity to understand how this meeting could be anything more or less than divine intervention. He said, "Dan, there is nowhere to leave you here. If I leave you with the military, you will be shot. I cannot allow you to return to Spain because we are at war with Spain. I have colonized a location in America I have named after King George II; we have named it Georgia. Would you agree as an officer and a gentleman to surrender yourself to my care? I do not mind if you send a message to your father and mother informing them you will be traveling with me to America as my prisoner."

All the time General Oglethorpe was talking to Dan, the General's mind was traveling at a fast pace. If he had the opportunity to select one person to accompany him to Georgia it would be Dan, with his abundant wealth of knowledge to defend against the Spanish invaders from Florida. General Oglethorpe felt he had just personally won a great victory. There would be so many opportunities for Dan to be of use in his adventure to America. He felt comfortable enough to ask Dan for his father's address to send him a personal note that Dan was in his personal care and no harm would come to him.

On the voyage back to England they discussed the necessities for the journey to America. The General asked Dan for his mailing address because he wanted to put his parents mind at ease about his safety. Dan was beginning to find all Englishmen are not the brute, savage types his family had been ruled by in Ireland. Dan could tell the General was sincere about his motives. Dan said, "General, you must be patient with me. I do not doubt your sincerity, but you are a bit unusual from the experience I have had with the Protestant British." General Oglethorpe said, "Dan I was a member of the British Parliament where I learned how Great Britain is despised by other countries because of governmental abuse, injustice and slavery. I have been involved for a number of years trying to persuade others to abolish slavery and the majority of the Penal Laws because of what you and your family have had to endure. In fact, one of the reasons I have worked so hard to establish the Colony of Georgia is to give the people of sound character an opportunity to prosper from their own efforts. There will not be slavery in Georgia. Before you judge me too harshly, even though I am your enemy, and even though you are in captivity, you might find we share some of the same views regarding equality for all men."

Dan responded, "General, you are definitely one of a kind. It appears to me that regardless of the government you serve, you have found a way to cause the lives of the helpless to escape British tyranny. That is the same opportunity I have hoped to discover. My hope is someday to be allowed to participate in a nation that recognizes the freedom you have begun in Georgia."

As they prepared to board the ship for America a messenger delivered a note to Dan. Dan wanted General Oglethorpe to know he had received the message. General Oglethorpe said, "I saw him hand it to you. See what the note says, it may be from your parents." The note was from a Lieutenant in the company commanded by Dan. The note stated, "Eamonn is critically wounded and will not survive, signed, Lieutenant O'Malley." Dan looked at General Oglethorpe straight in the eyes and said, "I am in the process of losing the dearest friend I have ever known. I would deeply appreciate being alone." General Oglethorpe said, "Do what you need to do. I most sincerely regret your grief." Dan walked to an area where farming implements were being loaded for a voyage to America. He kneeled and bowed his head in humble gratitude for Eamonn's life.

CHAPTER FIVE

WAKE

As Dan was muttering words he was sobbing, because if there was ever a man he wanted to be with when he crossed over Jordan it was Eamonn. Every good thing that had ever happened in his life could be traced back to Eamonn. A life without his presence would become a day without hope, without caring. Each step Eamonn had taken on this earth was directed toward doing something good for someone else beside himself, *my God, my Lord, what a treasure his heart has been on this earth,* Dan prayed for Eamonn's soul.

As Dan was kneeling and weeping, General Oglethorpe handed Dan a letter wherein he had been appointed by General Oglethorpe as his Emissary, to act in his behalf in all matters. Dan knew the power and authority that one document carried throughout the British Empire. His grief was put on hold for a moment as he tried to understand what the General intended for him to do with the authority he had just granted an enemy of the Crown.

Dan rose from his knees and turned to face General Oglethorpe. The General looked straight into Dan's eyes and said, "Dan, you know the letter I have given you is an act of treason against the Crown, which if misused could cost me my life. I gave you the authority because I know you are trustworthy. I feel you have been hurt enough in this life. You want to, and you need to be with your uncle and friend as his soul leaves this earth. He needs to know God has placed your life in good hands. I expect you to go to his bedside and be with him during his last hours. I trust you will attend his funeral and then sail for Savanna, Georgia when your mission is completed." Dan extended his hand to General Oglethorpe, shook his hand and bid him a safe journey to America. Then, Dan took one step back and saluted him and said, "General, your trust is well placed. I will return when this mission is completed."

Dan went to the shipping office and presented the letter given him by General Oglethorpe. The clerk said, "We have a ship leaving for Ireland in port presently and should be leaving soon." Dan was given approval for the voyage and he went to His Majesty's ship to sail to Ireland.

When the captain learned of having General Oglethorpe's Emissary on board, he invited him to have his meals in the Captain's quarters. Dan was given the opportunity to know the enemy who had stripped his family's honor and dignity and left his life as a wanderer, by denying him any sense of ever being allowed to truly belong. But, he felt the hand of God had guided each step he took and placed his life with Eamonn and the O'Sheas.

The Captain was a jovial type person who was far removed from having felt for the harm done to others by Royal edict. His life was the worship of gaining a pension to sit and drink ale as he bragged of his sea going exploits of hauling human flesh to different parts of the earth for disposal. Dan soon learned the vast difference in cultures was the complete void of concern for the peril of suffering by their fellow men and was amazed at how shallow the man truly was, completely without conscience or concern for anyone but himself. Even though orphaned, and detached from any permanent family structure, Dan had been blessed by God to care about the condition of suffering people. Dan said to himself, *I had rather be me when I see God than this poor creature that does not possess the slightest understanding of the Spirit of God being available to dwell in his life.*

The few days of travel gave Dan time to prepare to be at Eamonn's side. He felt a heavy obligation to General Oglethorpe for providing this act of human kindness. Dan was thinking, *of the blessing of being a warrior and being a prisoner of war, and yet being allowed to travel at no cost to bring comfort to someone he loved.* The only way Dan could rationalize his blessings was God's Spirit being actively engaged in General Oglethorpe's life. After the voyage Dan thanked the Captain for his courtesy and told him he would give him an outstanding report to General Oglethorpe. As Dan arrived at the harbor, where he had lived for several years with Eamonn, he recalled each day awakening to a new unending joy. Eamonn always had something very special planned, from a fishing trip, to picking berries for a good-hearted neighbor.

As he arrived at Eamonn's cottage, he was surprised to see two beautiful young ladies attending Eamonn. They did not appear to be caretakers. Dan was most interested in who they were, as he began to focus his eyes on the eyes of each of the young ladies. There was a faint memory of having seen their eyes before. He finally had to say something as his inquiring memory searched the familiarity of their eyes. Finally, Dan told them his name and noticed their expressions lit up with beautiful Irish smiles. The older of the two said, "My name is "Siobhann O'Flaherty." The younger one said, "My name is Shibeal O'Flaherty." Dan sat down to try and take in what he had just been told. While he was staring at them, Shibeal said, "You are our brother." Dan's breath became labored as he quickly began mentally recalling, *the day he remained in Spain as Eamonn agreed to allow him to stay with the O'Sheas.*

Dan held out his arms which were quickly filled with two of the most darling young ladies he had ever seen. They began to re-establish their childhood thoughts by realizing the magnitude of the blessings God had bestowed on their lives. The moment would be treasured forever in their hearts. As they began thinking of, *how improbable their being together truly was, they began to realize it had to be God's plan that made it possible.*

The mood quickly changed when Dan asked about Eamonn's condition. Siobhann said, "He has been getting worse by the hour. His fever is extremely high. As you know, no doctor will attend him because of the Penal Laws." Dan asked, "Can I see him?" Shibeal said, "He has been praying to see you, one more time." Dan pulled the curtain back and there lay the greatest man Dan's heart could have ever found to love. Dan kneeled by his bedside and could feel Eamonn's giant hand touch the top of his head. Eamonn said, "My Dan, you have come to see me off again." Dan said, "And again, I must remain onshore to complete the duty you prayed for me." Eamonn said, "Dan, you gave me life I did not know was possible until you were handed to me by your dear mother. You caused my life to have meaning I did not know would ever be." A gentle quietness eased into the room as tears of separation ran down their cheeks. Dan laid his head on Eamonn's massive arm as his soul departed with one last breath. Eamonn's face glowed with a heavenly presence as he apparently saw the approaching hand of his Savior who had come to take his sweet, sweet Spirit to the Holy Land.

The girls had heard the departing words and came to kneel by the bed. Dan felt them and reached to hold both as their tears flowed to soften the memories of such a precious soul. They could not turn loose of the only true blood belonging they had ever known.

When they arose to begin again another page of the book of life, Dan asked them, "How on this green earth have we come together again?" Dan told them his story was simple. He recalled for them how the Sheriff had come to arrest Bryan O'Flaherty, because he had not paid his debt, which was not the truth. He recalled their mother, Delia handing Eamonn his hand at age six and told him to leave quickly, which he did. He continued, "At age seven, Eamonn took me to Spain and put me in the care of his Commanding General named, Phillip O'Shea and his wife, Margarita who provided me with a life of unbelievable care and training that anyone could ever hope to be given. At age twenty or so, I was called upon to become involved with Bonnie Prince Charlie to regain the throne from George II, along with some Scottish supporters of the cause. I was captured by the British and am now a prisoner of war under the authority of British General James Oglethorpe. He is a very kind human being, contrary to every other Englishman I have ever known. He has allowed me to attend Eamonn's funeral before I am placed in a prison in America. "How have you found your way to where you are now?"

Siobhann began by saying, "We were much too young to remember, but we have been told by our adoptive parents, Donal and Bridgett O'Flaherty, our mother and father, Coleman and Delia, were shipped as indentured slaves to America. Bridgett went to the docks and asked our mother to leave us in her care because she and Donal had no children. They took us in and we have lived with them until two years ago, when our mother (Bridgett) died. Donal could not care for us so he brought us to his father, Eamonn, who has cared for us for two years. We found out Donal was killed in Scotland about two months ago. Eamonn returned home from fighting with the Jacobites. We did not know he was wounded until a fever came upon him and he has been in bed for about a month."

Dan said, "You have made my heart know how much God loves our family. We must now set about to tell the others of Eamonn's passing. Do you know someone who will go to the O'Malleys to tell them the wake will be Friday?" They said they knew of a friend who will go tell them. Dan asked, "Do you know of the place for family burials?" Shibeal said, "There is a graveyard where a number of the O'Flahertys are buried. I will take you there." Dan said, "I need to dig the grave. I want to have time to do it by myself. Please ask Eamonn's relatives to allow me to do this. It is very important to my soul."

Dan asked, "Is there anything you need before I go to the graveyard. Do you have food?" The girls assured Dan they would be fine. Dan found a shovel and a hoe and took it with him to the gravesite. As he dug the grave each shovel full of dirt reminded him of the daily burden Eamonn had cheerfully lifted from him and his entire family. Eamonn's heart had no limit to its ability to help carry a load for those he loved. Eamonn was an enormous human being in every way. His physical size was historic.

When Dan had completed the grave, he was exhausted. There were several large rocks that had to be removed. After he had dug the grave, Johnny Casey, who had served with Eamonn as an abled body seaman most of his life, had come by to give Dan a message. The Casey family was known as coffin builders and they had built the coffin for Eamonn because they had the highest respect for Eamonn's family. Johnny also told Dan he knew of a priest that was passing through in disguise and might give Eamonn a Catholic burial. Dan said, "Eamonn wouldn't want a priest, they've done enough damage to our people already. Sure, the Penal Laws have been putting the curse on us every day, but sometimes we don't know who the worst, the priest or the

English is, anyhow, Eamonn was the most spiritual man I have ever met. I'm sure St. Peter would let him in before any of those priests. I'll never forget the day I was confronted by one of the priests myself. I asked him if my name was in the Book of Life." The priest said, "I don't know." I said, "If you don't know if my name is in the Book of Life, how can you tell me you can remove my name. If you cannot remove my name, then I must be in touch with the Someone who put my name in the Book and can remove it if He so desires." Johnny said, "Dan, I have never heard you talk like that before, but since you are on the subject, I feel the same as you do. I brought the coffin for Eamonn. It was no surprise it was the finest they had ever made. It will take eight men to carry his body."

On Friday morning Dan took the coffin to a structure the fisherman had built to clean their fish. They had decided to have the box sealed and loaded on to a cart. Those who could began to gather in the afternoon. Everyone had on their mind the thought it could not be Eamonn had died, because Eamonn was such a giant in the minds and hearts of everyone in Connemara, they knew he would never die. It was just like Eamonn, it was too large a thought for anyone to absorb that Eamonn had died, the same as with all creatures created by God.

As the wake began people came to give their respects from every direction, even by sea. The O'Malleys sailed in from Clare Island. Dan was down by the fireplace putting turf on the fire and as he looked up, there standing in the doorway, was Gregory O'Malley, his wife Sara, and ten others whose lives were intertwined with the goodness that

Eamonn exhibited toward all people. As Dan greeted everyone he glanced toward those who remained in line and his eyes remained stayed upon the most beautiful blue eyes he had seen since he saw her when she was younger. He caught her eyes glancing at him with the silent undisclosed beauty that had been held in reserve for that one person that drew her from the covering of her delicate silence. When their eyes met again, both knew their hearts had been ordained to be as one forever. Their souls had become transfixed to submit the remainder of their days in the embrace of the hearts of one another. Both knew the present moment in time would last forever.

It had been years since General O'Shea, the O'Malleys and Eamonn O'Flaherty had reached an agreement to deliver some of the oppressed Irish people from bondage by providing ships to sell their goods to foreign nations. It was at that meeting Dan discovered there was more to life than what he had been taught, in that, his eyes beheld beauty nothing short of divine beyond anything he had ever beheld in his life and now again he was beholding the one he had chosen as his life's partner.

Mary's eyes became joined with his as they became closer to one another. Even without their knowledge, their hands began to reach out for the other. Dan said, "My name is Dan O'Flaherty, and what blessed name do you bear?" She said, "That of the Christ child, Jesus's Mother." Dan whispered, "Mary." He said, "Young lady that is the name I will carry in my bosom all the days I have remaining on this earth. You do not know, and I do not know whether our paths shall ever cross again, but wherever you find yourself at whatever time, you can be assured that I will be thinking of you."

When the appointed time had come for them to again touch one another, Dan, in his most elegant tone asks, "Mary, how has your life been?" Mary responded, "Incomplete." Dan said, "We share the same feeling. I assume you know we are joined forever." She said, "I am aware of that." Dan said, "Before we part, I will tell you to some extent what we need to do to be with one another."

The wake began with the exchanges of Eamonn's stories and fables that had grown with each year of his life. Gregory O'Malley stood up and told the story of how he became lost at sea in a fishing boat in a fog, and he began to talk to Himself above because the currach was no match for the swiftness of the tide. Gregory did not know Eamonn had become concerned for him and had set about hoping to find him. As the currents increased, Gregory revealed his concern and became more frantic. When, as God would have it, he heard a voice, the sound of which could not be mistaken, it was Eamonn who had come to find his friend. Gregory raised his glass as he said, "When I heard Eamonn's voice, I knew I had heard the voice of God. Eamonn came to me as I let my voice guide him toward my boat." When Eamonn came beside my boat, he said, "Gregory, where are you going?" Gregory said, "To shore as fast as I can row." To that tribute the crowd raised their voice with kind, Irish laughter. Beannacht Dia Go Eamonn (God Blessings to Eamonn.)

When the laughter and honor had subsided, the lady in her mid-years stepped forward and said, "I have to say this, and to be able to say this, I am assuming there are no English lovers at this funeral." One Irishman answered, "There better not be." The lady began her story by revealing her husband had been sent in bondage to some foreign land for a crime he did not commit." She said, "I was left with a daughter of fourteen months with no way to feed the child. A British soldier came to my cottage and told me his wife could not bear children and he wanted me to give him my daughter. He told me if I did not honor his request he would put me in prison, I told him I needed three days to think about it. During those three days of great sorrow, I told Eamonn of my trouble. Eamonn asked me to tell him the soldier's name. I told him. Now, I want to introduce this group to my daughter who is a grown young lady. After I told Eamonn what the soldier had done, no one has ever seen or heard from the soldier again. I am here for the purpose of making my gratitude for Eamonn's life known. I am sure that others of this gathering can tell their own story about the man, Eamonn, who was our protector. May God have mercy on his soul." The crowd was most solemn and reverent as each person placed their own personal value on having met such a man of his kind. After three days the voice of separation called out for Eamonn to lay his burden down and be with his Holy Father forever.

Dan saw Mary looking toward him and he felt the urgency of their meeting before having to part. He walked toward her and said,

"Mary, we must visit before our time has passed." He took her hand and they walked to an area behind a field where Eamonn's cottage was located. There was a group of trees that provided some privacy and Dan began by saying, "Mary, I must tell you this. I am a prisoner of war, I am returning to England to sail for America to meet with my captor. I have no guess as to the years of my confinement. I do know I would not be here with you except for the kindness of General James Oglethorpe whose prisoner I am. He has indicated to me he is interested in my military knowledge which means he may expect me to become a British soldier. I do not think that arrangement would be possible. However, I am sure there are other uses he may have in mind for my military skills, other than serving the Crown of England. I will find out some time this year what my status will be. There is only one question in my mind I need for you to answer, and that is, will your love for me endure the time that may be required?" Mary reached and touched Dan's hand, as she said, "You are in my heart forever." Dan said, "I have a gift for you." He reached in his coat pocket and revealed a necklace one could tell had not been designed by a jeweler. It was a cross built from a metal that would not rust, tied to a leather string he had also made. He said, "Mary, as I put this around your neck, to me it joins our hearts forever, I pray your heart allows you to feel that deep for me." Mary said, "Dan, if you will recall the day we met, there was a piece of driftwood that had floated to the Island and as we visited without your knowledge, I committed myself to you forever. It is very important you know nothing from that commitment will ever change."

They both stood up, Mary looked at Dan as she beheld his hazel blue eyes, she asks, "Would you like to kiss me?" Dan said, "Mary, only if you think it is proper." Mary said, "It is something we both need." As the waves of the Atlantic Ocean gently washed ashore, two hearts stood before God and man joined forever.

CHAPTER SIX

NEW WORLD

In 1749, Dan had buried his most trusted friend and relative, Eamonn O'Flaherty. Dan was a prisoner of war under the authority of General James Oglethorpe. His mission became traveling to America to meet General Oglethorpe to further explore the General's purpose for taking such risks to allow Dan to care for Eamonn during his hours of departure.

After the funeral, and the bonding with Mary, he set about to travel to Bristol, England to sail from there to meet General Oglethorpe in America. With the letter of passage, he had received from the General, he had been treated with the utmost courtesy throughout the voyage. As he was approaching Bristol, England from Ireland, he was severely tempted to sail on to Spain to see Phillip and Margarita, but his commitment to General Oglethorpe did not include personal indulgence in more choices than he had already been so graciously granted by the General. Dan did not want to show disrespect to the General.

The ship to America would not leave for three days. The risk was, he would be in one of England's busiest ports being used by the military to transport prisoners and soldiers to other parts of the British

Empire. After he had submitted the letter identifying him as General Oglethorpe's personal Emissary, he had time to go to an area away from the port to avoid chance recognition by some enemy that could cause problems. He found a place about two blocks from the docks that allowed him the anonymity he felt was required to remain safe. He pulled his hat over his brow and began walking the streets in the heart of enemy territory. He found a bench to sit, look, and think.

As he was enjoying the fact he was an un-discovered prisoner of war with a letter of complete authority to command anyone to submit to his will, he felt very secure he might be able to survive without being detected. In fact, he was sitting there enjoying the private amusement of his conflicting identities when a hand touched his shoulder and a voice asks, "Dan, what are you doing here?" Dan's first instinct was to run and not look back. He didn't want to know who the intruder might be, but then, which one of his enemies would call him Dan? Dan quickly realized he may be a comrade. He stood, turned and looked and there was Lupe Flores, the shipmate Eamonn had assigned to him to be his protector and teacher aboard Eamonn's ship. Lupe said, "Dan, I was wondering if you remembered me teaching you Spanish." Dan asked, "How could I ever forget, are you ready to enjoy all the fruits of your teaching?" Lupe said, with great pride, "Let me hear it." Dan said, "Muy Bien." Lupe beamed with triumph; his favorite student had remembered his teaching. Dan could not help but embrace his friend; he was ready to be in the company of some of yesterday's most wonderful memories.

Lupe began by telling Dan he had drifted since Eamonn had gone to Scotland to fight for the Jacobite's. He told Dan, he was just drifting, not headed anywhere in particular, or in any certain direction because it didn't matter to him where he was at the end of the day. Lupe whispered, "Dan", in a low tone, "What in the world are you doing in this place? Don't you know there are at least three reasons you could be arrested and hung?" Dan said, in a low tone of voice, "It has sure crossed my mind." Lupe said, "You have got to get out of here. Some of these guys you see standing around here would sell your life for a shilling. My man, this is a dangerous territory for you to be walking around like a yard bird."

Dan listened to Lupe and realized the value of the letter he had in his pocket signed by General Oglethorpe, even though he was a prisoner of war, he was the only one who would know who he really was. He also started thinking and asking himself, *who is it I know I would trust as much as General Oglethorpe has trusted me?* The answer was, *no one.* Dan asked Lupe, "Where are you sleeping tonight?" Lupe said, "Around the corner, come on." Lupe led Dan to an alleyway behind some buildings. Lupe brought him to a doorway recessed in the rear of a building and there was a blanket Lupe had managed to get from somewhere. Lupe said, "Pick you a spot and sleep good. I'll see you in the morning." Dan asked, "Lupe, where you are going?" Lupe said, "I'll see you in the morning."

As they visited the next morning, Dan brought Lupe up to date on Eamonn's death and the fact of him being a prisoner of war. He told him of his captor, General Oglethorpe, who was proving himself to be an exceptional gentleman. Dan asked Lupe what he had planned. Lupe said, "I have learned one thing in England, do not ever use the word Catholic. I have felt like a leper ever since I arrived. As far as plans go, what I do know is one thing, I am a seaman." Dan asked, "Have you ever thought of working on the shore?" Lupe said, "No one is going to hire a Spaniard on a British ship, even if I don't say Catholic. This is a white man's island. I need to get out of here." Dan asked, "Do you want to finish the job Eamonn gave you?" Lupe asked, "Which one?" Dan said, "Taking care of me!" Lupe said, "I am ready." Dan said, "Even if I go to prison for a while?" Lupe said, "I don't know about fifty years." Dan asked, 'Ten?" Lupe said, "Ten is ok."

The next day Dan booked passage for both of them to America. Since it was an English ship, they planned to remain apart from the other travelers. The weather became more beautiful the closer they came to Georgia. When they docked, Dan began asking questions as to the location of General Oglethorpe's camp. Everyone they talked to was very helpful and Dan eventually arrived at the General's doorstep. An orderly found the General and told him he had visitors. When General Oglethorpe saw Dan, he was overwhelmed that he was looking at a prisoner he had found that had kept his word to the very letter of promptness. General Oglethorpe was astonished he had come to know a man of Dan's character and honor. He rushed to Dan with opened arms and said, "Dan to say the least, I am so pleased to see you. I trust your journey was successful." Dan said, "Thanks to you sir, it was most successful."

The General asked Dan if he would like to see the progress the Colony had made in its approximate twelve-year history. Dan said, "General, I am very impressed with what I have seen so far." The General asked, "Who is the gentleman you have with you?" Dan told the General the history of his relationship with Lupe since he was six years old. Dan said, "Actually, he is the person Uncle Eamonn put in charge of me to keep me out of trouble." The General asked, "Well, did he do a good job?" Dan said, "No sir, General not so far!" They all enjoyed the humor.

The General said, "Dan, I know you have wondered why I have taken the risk I have taken to assist you through your family's grief." Dan said, "General, I have thought about it the entire time of my absence from you." The General said, "Dan, I took the risk because I saw your talents on the battlefields of Scotland. I had never seen maneuvers completed with such skill in my entire career as a military officer. You exhibited the tactics and strategies we need here in Georgia to defeat the Spanish invaders. The Carolinas and Georgia have become land the Spanish invaders want to take from us. Up until this time, the British Army has been embarrassingly unsuccessful in turning the Army of Spain away. (3) The settlers we have brought to America are not warriors; they are farmers and artisans, some are former prisoners, who have been released to go to work for themselves at farming. Because of the Spanish attacking the settlers, there has become a serious question whether our experiment in creating an environment of equality for all men will succeed or fail. I truly believe you are the person that can keep this great venture from failing."

Dan asked, "What have you done so far to combat the Spanish?" The General answered, "Dan, I have begun a unit, we are calling, the Rangers. I would like to see you take what we have begun and turn it into a real fighting force." Dan asked, "What steps have you taken to infiltrate the enemy with scouts and spies?" The General said, "I have not been able to accomplish any infiltrations, primarily because of the language difference." Dan said, "General Oglethorpe, I think Lupe and I need to go into Florida on a mission ourselves to map out a strategy before I begin spending time to train troops. Do you have an officer that would be available to begin selecting some young men who may qualify as Rangers?"

General, I don't mean this in any way to offend you, but I would personally prefer selections from the Scottish and Irish settlements. I don't like to waste time having to train men to learn to become angry. I like men who are born angry in search of a battlefield." General Oglethorpe said, "I fully agree, searching for gentlemen warriors is a waste of time."

Dan asked the General, "Have you established contact with any of the people in Florida?" General Oglethorpe responded, "There is a history of relations with the Yamasee and Creek Indians which proved valuable in the early 1700's, but later became a source of conflict."

The General continued, "In 1740, the British attacked the Fort at St. Augustine, but failed. This opened the borders of Florida to fugitive slaves. Ultimately, a primarily black settlement became a settlement of Seminoles and blacks. They had been enticed by the Spanish to set up buffer zones to act as defensive units for Spain."

Dan said, "General, I am going to need some time to organize a plan I need to properly lead the Rangers into battle. If you approve of that plan, I will proceed." The General said, "Not only do I approve of it, I offer you my sincere gratitude for accepting this responsibility. If this conflict was between the British Empire and Spain I would not ask you to be a traitor to Spain. The conflict is between farming families who are attempting to learn to independently provide for their families and Spain." Dan said, "General, I fully understand, and I agree to be of service to these people."

Dan contacted Lupe and told him the request the General had made, and he would become the Commander of the Ranger force. Lupe asked, "Where does that leave me?" Dan said, "I am going to make you a Sergeant and put you in charge of setting up a system of spies and scouts." Lupe asked, "Does this mean I am going to be in the military service on land?" Dan said, "Are you opposed to working on land?" Lupe said, "I don't know, I have never worked on shore."

Dan said, "You will like it and I will be close enough for you to continue to train me."

As they prepared to embark, the General offered maps which were crudely drawn to provide Dan with a base line to prepare him to learn all there is to know of his new battleground. General Oglethorpe also told him the Florida Peninsula was heavily populated by Spain on the eastern part of the Peninsula. He explained for the most part the western part is occupied by Indians native to the land. That comment gave Dan a thought of, *attempting to train a group of spies from an area that would be completely unexpected.* Heretofore, the battle ground was the East Florida Coast line with the British forces attacking from the north. All the Spanish forts had been constructed with that approach in mind.

Dan decided to explore as much of the western part of Florida as he could to try and build allies from the tribes of Indians who knew the territory. Lupe had loaded the pack horses and had found two of the finest bred Spanish War horses in the General's stable. From the maps, Dan learned most of the settlements were located where the fresh water rivers ran into the sea. Up until Dan arrived, the battles had taken place in those locations.

Their route of exploration began by heading due south along the east coast line toward what would later become known as Jacksonville, Florida. General Oglethorpe had constructed several defensive forts of which one was named Fort Frederica. Dan decided to follow the St. Mary's River west as far as the terrain would allow them to travel. The traveling was difficult as they meandered their way through miles and miles of swampland. Dan began to learn why most of the settlers remained on the east side of Florida which was away from where the vast swamps were located.

When they had traveled three weeks toward the southwest, Dan realized the value for his type military tactics would be along the eastern coast. He turned back due east to find his way to the coast line. Once they were to the coast, the terrain appeared possible for staging night time, quick, fierce, brutally savage attacks. They had traveled south for two days when they discovered a village that was inhabited by blacks who spoke English. Lupe began visiting with one of the tribesmen who told him they were Seminole Indians. The tribesman told Lupe their ancestors were runaway slaves from the British Colonies. Dan soon decided he would not be able to find warriors from a tribe who was allied with Spain. They traveled as far as St. Augustine where they recognized the damage to the fort that General Oglethorpe had inflicted during the siege in 1740.

After viewing the different possibilities of attack, Dan told Lupe they needed to return to Georgia. They traveled for two weeks as Dan made plans to solve the problem. When he arrived back at the settlement he met with General Oglethorpe to give him his analysis of the plan to attack the enemy.

Dan began by saying, "I can understand why the British troops have had difficulty accomplishing victory over the Spaniards. From what I can see, up to now, all the attacks have been from the established conventional methods of accepted military tactics. In other words, an organized force against a fort with organized force." General Oglethorpe agreed with Dan's analysis. Dan said, "General, this conflict will not be concluded in the usual manner of predictable military procedures. It will be accomplished by establishing small units of night fighters who are well trained to kill the enemy. I think there is a way to establish a scouting group that does nothing but locate the smaller groups of Spanish patrols around the Spanish fortified areas along the coast. In my opinion, there is only one man, who knows how to establish such a force, that I consider being vital in accomplishing victory."

General Oglethorpe said, "I assume you are going to tell me that person is your adoptive father, Phillip O'Shea." Dan said, "Yes sir, that is the person." The reason is, "I cannot be in two places at the same time, and I will be deep under cover on the battlefield. I need someone who will be training replacements. General O'Shea is the only man who can produce the quality of personnel this mission will require." General Oglethorpe asked, "How would you propose persuading a former General of the Army of Spain to commit treason against a nation that is attempting to expand its Territory?" Dan said, "General, a great deal of the problem has already been solved." The General asked, "Dan would you please explain that to me?" Dan said, "My adoptive father needs only to see what you have done here in Georgia to establish a community based on equality of all men. My father has the same interest and belief you have in this matter and will be willing to help prevent any nation that is involved in taking those God given rights from other men. General, you will be greatly surprised at how much you and General O'Shea think alike. He would give his life to a cause such as the one you have begun, to give men freedom from governmental abuse." The General asks Dan, "How do we proceed to get the General to Georgia?" Dan said, "I would propose you sending a letter to General Phillip O'Shea informing him of my capture and imprisonment. You can inform him I am under your direct authority. You can tell him I have asked you to contact him to come to America accompanied by my darling mother, Margarita, for organizing a combat unit to keep some colonials safe. You can also tell him I want and need to see him and my mother." General Oglethorpe said, "I should have the letter ready tomorrow morning." Dan said, "General, in the meantime, with your permission, of course, I would like to visit some of the settlements to locate some of the prisoners and the indentured slaves who might be able to do the kind of fighting we need done." The General said, "I will have the letter of authority prepared within the hour for you to interview whomsoever you desire."

Dan decided he and Lupe needed to take a good bath. He had noticed animals downwind from them had begun to run off as they rode through the woods. The one thing Dan was having trouble with was the number of snakes he and Lupe had seen in the swamp areas. Lupe said, "Dan, I found a snake I really like." Dan asked, "What kind was it?" Lupe said, "A dead one." Dan said, "Lupe, that kind with a cottonmouth makes me want to sleep in a tree."

After they had cleaned up, they went to the kitchen of General Oglethorpe's home and asked the cook if she had any biscuits and gravy. She told them she would have it ready in a little while. Dan and Lupe were sitting in the General's back yard waiting when Dan asks Lupe, "Can you believe I am in prison but, for some reason I just don't feel like I am a convict. I don't even feel like some brute in the British Army is going to arrest me and put me in jail because I swatted one of the royal flies. You know what Lupe, America is just different than anywhere else I have ever been. I like this place. General Oglethorpe is the best Englishman in the world. He has already made the prisons clean up their mess and took the authority away from abusive ship captains that have harmed sailors. And now, look at what he is doing for all these poor people who now own their own land. Lupe, any man who is involved in helping that many people, is a good man. I know General O'Shea will find him to be a man who will do what is right."

After they had eaten a huge breakfast cooked in the General's kitchen, they went to find the General to get the letter of authority to interview the prisoners for service. The General had the letter of authority prepared as well as the letter to General O'Shea. Dan read the General's letter to General O'Shea. The words in the letter renewed in his heart the memory of what those two blessed souls had been to his life, a tear rolled from his eyes as he told the General, "Sir, I think that will suffice." Dan said, "By the way, thank you for the breakfast." The General smiled and asked, "How is that?" Dan said, "Your cook prepared us a plate of biscuits, gravy and smoked salt bacon, and we ate until we made ourselves sleepy, thank you. I'm on my way to talk to some fellow prisoners from Ireland and Scotland, to hopefully find some good soldiers." The General said, "I pray your efforts will produce good men."

General Oglethorpe said, "Dan, may I speak to you privately for a moment." Lupe walked on out to the horses to wait for Dan. General Oglethorpe said, "Dan, this subject is rather difficult to discuss, but I know you will keep it confidential. Dan responded, "Why of course, sir." The General said, "Dan, my wife and I have been discussing the possibility of having some help from someone who could do some house work. She thinks the both of us need to slow down somewhat to allow some good person to help with the chores. If you talk to a worthy person who can help us, we would be most appreciative." Dan said, "General, are you thinking male or female help?" The General said, "Dan, we would prefer a clean female if possible." Dan said, "I will try my best to find someone satisfactory for you." Dan then turned and walked toward the horses after he had saluted the General.

Dan and Lupe were on their way to the prison, which except for the grace of God and the heart of General Oglethorpe would be where he would have spent his life. They stopped at the first facility which was the location for the debtor prisoners. Dan's family knew how serious it was to fail to pay debt in Ireland because that was the charge against Bryan O'Flaherty that destroyed their family. Dan handed the Warden the letter of authority, signed by General Oglethorpe. When the Warden read the letter, he stood up and asked, "Where would you like to begin?"

Dan asked, "Do you have the prisoners segregated by culture?" The Warden said, "Sir, they are segregated. I did not do it myself. They found one another by speaking the same language." Dan asked, "Do you happened to know where I could talk to the Scottish and the Irish prisoners?" The Warden said, "They are housed next to each other, it won't be any problem." Dan recalled the Highlanders in the Jacobite war. They and the Irish were the fiercest warriors on the field, however, General Oglethorpe and General Cumberland proved fierceness alone will not carry the day. Dan was looking for soldiers who possessed intelligence, focused anger and self-control, who could get the mission done and not get anyone injured, if possible. He naturally preferred the Irish, so he began talking to the Irish. Ever present in his mind was his brother, Patrick, his mother, Delia, his sister, Barbara, his father, Coleman O'Flaherty, and Michael O'Flaherty. Bryan O'Flaherty was the owner of the O'Flaherty farm where the O'Flaherty family was arrested because Lord St. George who, even though having been paid the mortgage payment by Bryan O'Flaherty, had failed to pay the creditors he owed. Also, because the Bryan O'Flaherty mortgage had been pledged as security for the debt of Lord St. George, Bryan O'Flaherty and his entire staff was arrested and became convicted indentured slaves. Dan completed his observation of those who seemed fit for service having found five young men about his age who seemed worth interviewing. He began to interview by extending his hand and introducing himself. The first three refused to voluntarily do service for the Crown of England. The remaining two said they did not want to learn how to kill other people.

When Dan interviewed ten prospects from the Scottish clan, he found four he knew would be good soldiers. Dan made arrangements to have them sent to General Oglethorpe's headquarters. Dan and Lupe went on to another prison that didn't contain any Gaelic speaking inmates. He then moved on to another facility that appeared to be more of a cottage type facility. Dan met the Warden, who explained his facility was primarily for families who worked as slave laborers for farmers in the general area of the present facility, as well as all the farming at the facility. Dan asked to be allowed to visit with the Gaelic speaking group first. The Warden personally escorted Dan to the prison gathering place. He began selecting those about his age to interview. When the group had gathered, Dan began by trying to save time by eliminating those who refused to serve the Crown of England. When he had completed his inquiry, three men about his same age remained to be interviewed. When the others were dismissed one of the three came to Dan's table and asked, "Sir, may I ask your name?" Dan said, "I am Dan O'Flaherty." The man asked, "Do you remember having a brother?" Dan said, "Yes, his name was Patrick." The man asked, "What was your mother and father's name?" Dan answered, "Delia and Coleman O'Flaherty." He then asked, "Would you like to see your brother?" Dan said, "More than you could ever know." The man said, "I am Patrick, your brother." Dan bowed his head in disbelief that he had heard the words he had just heard. He asked, "Are you really him?" Patrick said, "I am your brother." Dan stood up and wrapped his massive arms around the flesh of his flesh and the blood of his blood. It was more than either of them could take at one time.

Patrick said, "I remember you looking back and waving at us as Eamonn took you away the day they came to get us." Dan said, "Patrick, let me look at you. I would have never known you, we could have passed one another on the street and we would have been strangers. We must savor this moment as the sweetest taste of heaven we could ever know. The possibility of us being together would not have occurred without God's grace." Dan openly prayed, "Holy Father, we both know to some extent how large this earth is and how insignificant we are, yet, you cared enough for us to find one another after so long a time. Thank you, Father for this moment. Amen."

Dan stood up and said, "You must go with me away from this prison." Patrick asked, "What do you mean?" Dan said, "I can get you out of here." Patrick asked, "Where will we go?" Dan said, "With me." Patrick asked, "Where? What about Barbara, Mama and Daddy?" Dan almost collapsed. He asked Patrick, "Are you telling me, they are here?" Patrick said, "Yes, they are here." Dan said, "We must find them.

Where are they?" Patrick said, "Follow me." They walked about a quarter mile to a cottage and Patrick said, "Wait a minute, let me tell them."

Dan was completely beside himself to see his family. He stood in front of the cottage as Patrick entered the door. When Patrick looked at his mother, she could tell something different to what they were accustomed had come to their lives. Delia said, "Patrick, Patrick what has happened?" Patrick bowed his head and began sobbing. Coleman got up as Delia walked to Patrick. Patrick said, "Mama, Dan is outside." The words spoken by Patrick were as if they were words of another language, because no one could place the words with the message he had spoken. Delia kneeled at Patrick's feet and said, "Son, what is the matter?" Patrick looked in his mother's eyes and said, "Mama, Dan is outside waiting on us." Delia's world stopped turning as the message began to reach her conscious thought. Delia said, "You mean, our Dan?" Patrick said, "Yes ma'am." Patrick stood up and began helping his mother to her feet. Coleman began walking to the door in disbelief. He and the others stopped when they saw a huge six-foot four inch two hundred thirty-pound man who was last seen by his family when he was six years old.

Dan could not wait for all of them to linger in times past. He wanted to feel his family in his massive arms and kiss them as tears ran down their cheeks. Their hearts were bursting with a joy they had resolved would never be allowed to touch their lives again in this lifetime. All the family was feeling as if they had been reborn as they smothered one another with the love that had smoldered in their hearts for almost two decades. As Dan was kneeling in front of his mother with his arm locked around her waist and her head bowed holding her darling son close to her again, he looked at the front door and there stood a young lady he had never seen before.

Dan whispered in his mother's ear, "Mama, who is the girl?" Delia had momentarily forgotten her baby daughter. She said, "Dan, this is your baby sister, Maureen." Dan stood up and walked toward Maureen to give her a family hug. Maureen began walking toward Dan with a shock of red hair blowing in front of the most gorgeous blue eyes Dan had ever seen. He stopped as he saw Maureen tighten her fist and walked up to Dan and gave him a light punch in the stomach and said, "Betcha think you're big, don't cha?" Dan felt as though his identical spirit was standing in front of him. His face stretched into a smile as he put his arms around his baby sister and twirled her around. He could not take his eyes off her. The bond of brother and sister took place in one instant. Dan put her feet back on the ground as Maureen began to feel as though the family had not told her the whole truth about her mother's son. Dan had met a kindred spirit that just so happened to be his sister.

All the family had to sit for a moment to take in small portions of what had just occurred. Dan said, "Come here, you beautiful angel, I want you to sit on my knee." Delia sat on his knee and laid her head on his chest and reminded herself of March 5, 1722 when she had him to herself in a small cottage in Galway, Ireland. Dan said, "Mama, I saw Siobhann and Shibeal a short time ago. They have grown to become two of the most beautiful ladies you could ever hope to know. The angel that rescued them from the Crown, named Bridget, died two years ago, and they had been living with Eamonn. Eamonn died several months ago and now they are being taken care of by the Gregory O'Malley family. I told them I would send for them." Delia continued to sit on Dan's knee adoring the man she knew he would grow up to become. Coleman had not spoken a word; all he could do was ponder the life God had given a family that was no different than hundreds of thousands of Irish outcasts. Only God in His mercy had allowed him and allowed His family to see one another one more time.

Coleman said, "Dan, I don't know what you know about this new world, but from what I have seen, this land has potential to do something for the people." Dan asked, "Have you heard of General Oglethorpe?" They all nodded, they had heard of him. Dan said, "Do not be surprised how this sounds, but I am in prison under the direct authority of General Oglethorpe. He has brought me here to America to command a unit of Special Force soldiers to keep Spain from encroaching on English held land. He has a place named Georgia that has been organized to serve people like us who are willing to work. It is a grant of land by King George II to set up the colony. The purpose of the plan is for hard working people to farm land granted to them to provide for themselves while having enough acreage to raise a crop to be sold for money. The acreage is limited to fifty acres per family which includes a town plot for living and a forty-five-acre farm to raise a money crop. The General has brought cotton seeds with him which, when harvested, can be woven into cloth. The theory is, one family gets one farm, but I have noticed there is land in Carolina that is as good as the land in Georgia. I have got my eye on Carolina dirt."

Delia asked, "Dan, does this mean we can't ever go home?" Dan said, "Mama, being in Ireland is what got us sent to prison. I don't think we need to go back to Ireland until the law changes. At present, I am going to accomplish some things for General Oglethorpe to see if our lives can be made better, together."

Dan began thinking of what General Oglethorpe had talked to him about. He began thinking, *Maureen would be a good choice of help for the General's wife.* Dan told them he was going to meet with the General to arrange for them to be released from prison and he would be back to get them in a few days.

CHAPTER SEVEN

NEW ARRANGEMENTS

When Dan returned from his search for recruits, he went to visit with General Oglethorpe. When the meeting began Dan made it perfectly clear, he knew he was a prisoner of the Crown that had been placed under the General's authority and had no right to ask for any more special favors of the General, other than those the General had already granted him, but he told the General he needed one other concession of which he was not entitled.

When Dan had completed revealing the plight of the O'Flaherty family, the General had begun to tear up. He had never heard of a family that had endured so much undeserved injustice and hardship in his life and continued to be blest by God with good health and now the possibility of being together again.

Dan said, "General, do you suppose I could prevail on you to give my birth family an opportunity to be set free from prison. Sir, I also think you will agree the convicted slave's mark has been registered against them is unjust. My thinking is, if my adoptive father, General O'Shea and his wife Margarita, came to lend assistance in the conflict with Spain, I know my mother and father could work for them." Dan had tried to avoid asking the General to grant them a piece of Georgia land because of them being Catholic. The General said, "Dan, do you suppose these great people would consider farming fifty acres in Georgia, if I could free them from prison and get them a grant of land?" Dan said, "General, I will certainly ask them if they would consider it." The General said, "There is a fifty-acre plot that was abandoned two months ago which has a house located on the property. See if they would like to look at it." Dan's heart was jumping with joy. His mother was not going to believe, her family was on the brink of no longer being a slave, but was about to become the owner of fifty acres of land in America. Dan also told the General he had found a slave they could interview for his housekeeper duty.

In three days, the O'Flaherty family had been released from prison, agreed upon General Oglethorpe's order and had been transported to Georgia to see their new home. On the way to Georgia, Dan asked about Bryan O'Flaherty. Coleman said, "Bryan died about three years ago."

When the O'Flaherty family arrived in Georgia, they went directly to General Oglethorpe's office. Dan introduced his family with the exception of his two sisters, Shibeal and Siobhann who were in Ireland. The General was most complimentary of their son Dan, who had proven himself to be perhaps the most productive person England had ever placed in confinement, which was meant as a bit of English humor. Delia said to herself, *she had always known that he was very special.* The General said, "We need to be very truthful with one another,

Catholics are prohibited from being a part of this economic development experiment. I will ask you, as a favor to me, please confine your worship of God to be in a private manner. I know all things, especially regarding something as absurd as the conflicts of Protestant and Catholic, will change, but at this time, there is a conflict. I know without a doubt the O'Flaherty family will be one of the most outstanding families in the Colony." At the end of the meeting, Dan introduced his sister Maureen to Mrs. Oglethorpe and the General. He left Maureen with them as he gathered the family together to view their land.

When the meeting had concluded, Dan took them to their new home. When Delia and Coleman saw what Dan had told them, they knew they would never return to Ireland. When they had unloaded the wagon of their few belongings, Dan asked them, if a prayer would be appropriate. Coleman said, "A celebration such as this is what prayers are for." He said, "Lord, again we bow before Your throne as Your children to honor and glorify Your name. You promised us someday we would be set free. Our faith did not hold on in complete belief. We gave up hope. We didn't think we would ever see one another again, but You, Lord have kept your promise. Our lack of faith has made us ashamed, and we ask forgiveness. We now thank you O Lord, our Gracious God, for these blessings. May each breath we take honor your name, until we are called home. In Jesus name, Amen." As they began to walk the land, the more excited they became. Each of them would pick up a hand full of dirt and say to themselves, "Our dirt, not the Kings dirt, but our dirt."

The previous owners left a cook stove and a pile of wood. Coleman was anxious to see the forty-five-acre plot, so he could get started on a money crop. The General had made arrangements for the farmers to get all the cotton seed they needed for their first crop. They were expected to save the seed from their first crop for the next years planting. Dan was ready to start looking for some good farm stock to get his family on the road to becoming financially independent. Dan was amazed how little affect prison life had on their moral fiber. Their determined, self-willed, Irish character had remained in place.

The O'Flahertys did not give the English even one day of their life for punishment. They were the same people, filled with hope, joy, and as enduring, and determined as they were the day of their arrest. In this family lived the moral fiber with which to build a new nation. The elements of the blessings were far greater than any truth could ever tell, as the unblessed of the world were coming together to become a blessing to the world.

Dan made sure everyone was satisfied with their beginnings as he returned from taking them to see the forty-five acres which was not very far from the home site. He told his mother he would return with some farm stock. Delia requested a beginning of sheep, goats and a milk cow. Dan grinned as he recalled that glass of warm milk she would give him each morning for breakfast.

Dan had to be the most joyful soul in Georgia as he saw the hand of God's Holy Spirit reconnecting the O'Flaherty family members together again. He told himself, "This has to be answered prayer." Even though it was an event he would enjoy extending for his family, he had responsibilities he had to give his attention, the first of which was to organize the Ranger group to protect the settlers from the attacks from the Spanish Army. Dan directed Lupe and Patrick to Ranger headquarters while he stopped by to visit with General Oglethorpe.

While talking to the General about Maureen, he told Dan he and his wife were very pleased to have Maureen as their housekeeper. Dan was most pleased Maureen would have the opportunity to be with him while he was involved with the Rangers securing the borders of Georgia.

General Oglethorpe reminded Dan of a number of soldiers being held prisoner who had participated in the Jacobite uprising. The Warden had assigned them the duty of improving the land around the prison, by removing trees and building bridges. Dan learned the Scottish prisoners had natural skills of pioneering and were very adept at farming which made them of great use to the entire colony.

Dan asked the General if he had a facility planned to house the recruits. General Oglethorpe said, "We will begin immediately to construct a facility, with the help of the new recruits." When Dan had organized a force of more than two hundred men, he began the training that had brought General O'Shea his victories. As each man was trained, they became adjusted to night fighting. Dan explained to them, "The plans are to get rid of the enemy one man at a time."

He explained to them, especially the Scottish, "There will not be the brute force attack the Highlanders have always practiced. Our tactic is to eliminate the enemy in as quiet a manner as possible and dispose of the body. There are enough alligators in Florida to handle the body disposal problem. Each unit will be on its own and will operate strictly at night. The use of guns will be only when necessary. You will find horses, cattle, stock of all kinds around the fort walls. Our responsibility is to strip them of their main weapon which is their horses. As we become more effective with this operation, the missing soldiers, the missing animals and the lack of any evidence of a known enemy will put fear in every soldier's mind. There are scouts who have been infiltrating the populated areas for weeks and are now ready to take the attack squads to the enemy locations. Remember, the only friends we have in Florida are the ones who are with us. Everyone else is an enemy. When we get started, plan on being away from camp at least a week. All units must plan to contact one another at least once a week to keep our locations known, but separate. Remember, surprise at night, is our best weapon." With that basic plan, Dan began training the men with different methods of silent combat. The goal he set for each unit was to eliminate at least five enemy soldiers per day, per unit.

The Spanish military had always begun their attacks down the coast in southeast Georgia. That told Dan the location of the majority of the best trained military personnel who had participated in the attacks on the settlers. Dan wanted to eliminate that threat first. He began a special training for three groups to focus on that particular location first. He knew if he could put fear in the elite troops of the army, the commanders would find it very difficult to persuade other soldiers to replace them.

When he knew the men were ready, Dan personally led them to the location to begin Operation Fear. Dan taught the men how to move stealthily in the dark with the dependence completely on good scouts. Lupe had done a good job preparing the scouts for their first night attack. The first target was always the sentry had been posted around the fort location. After the sentries were eliminated, the next move would be to remove the horses from the holding pens, very quietly, and lead them to a group of mounted Rangers who would take the horses to Georgia.

Dan was very satisfied with the Scottish soldiers, whom he thought would be too aggressive to become night fighters, but he was greatly surprised. Despite their massive size, most of them became very subdued and learned the art of controlled aggression.

After a week of intense pressure, the Special Force Rangers reported back to their camp area to report the fruits of their labor. Dan had left a lookout to observe the fort the next morning to report the reaction to the missing men and animals. The scouts reported the fort was absolute chaos. Lupe reported a sentry was shot for leaving the gate open.

Dan waited three nights for the fort to settle back down before he sent the squads back to eliminate more sentries. On the fourth night, he told the squad leaders the commander of the fort would double the sentries.

At about 2:00 a.m., the squads separated, and Lupe and his scouts led them to the target. The Scots enjoyed hitting the enemy in the top of the head and then killing them. The Irish liked the knife to the throat, to prevent the possibility of noise. Dan was thinking about, *the next move of the fort commander.* He was reaching the point where no one would be placed on guard duty and that is what Dan was waiting to occur. Dan had guessed right. There were no guards to stop the Rangers from scaling the wall.

Dan had the men prepared for the night when no guards could sound the alert. The Rangers wore Indian moccasins and made no sound. Dan was prepared to take a sufficient amount of gun powder to blow up the barracks. The timing had to be perfect to roll six kegs of gun powder into the barracks with the fuse lit on each keg.

A week passed before Dan felt the men were prepared for their great adventure. Lupe had found a part of the fort wall was only twelve feet high. That was the perfect height to allow a man to stand on the shoulders of another man and reach the top of the wall and pull himself up and over the wall.

Dan trained the three teams for the exercise. The big Scots were the key to the plan. They used a net to put the kegs of gun powder in to raise them gently up and let them gently down. The fish net was the answer to the problem. Lighting the fuses was the last problem to be solved. Lupe had been inside the fort pretending to deliver goods to the kitchen. He said, "There is a latrine close by the door to the barracks." He suggested lighting the torch in the latrine and taking it a few steps away to the door of the target.

Dan liked the plan and had the men ready for the maneuver. After midnight, the three teams met at the rear of the fort. One of the tallest Scots squatted down while another stood on his shoulders. When the big Scot stood up the climber grabbed hold of the wall and lifted himself up to the top. He had taken a rope with him to throw one end of the rope back over the wall as he held the other end.

Two of the squads made it over the wall. The remaining men loaded each keg in the fish net, which was pulled to the top of the wall. One of the men stayed on the wall to lower the kegs to the ground. They completed getting the gun powder over the wall and then began carrying the kegs to the barracks door. Dan placed the fuses in each keg. Two men went in the latrine to light a torch. They brought it back to Dan. Dan put the keg in the door way, lit the fuse and kicked the keg for it to roll down the walkway of the barracks.

After he lit the last fuse, they ran back to the wall as the first keg of gun powder exploded. Then the second, and so on, until they all had exploded. The fort sentries began shooting at the Rangers. The Rangers were able to disable the sentries as they went back over the wall to meet Lupe and return to the training facility. Lupe had several scouts at the fort. The next morning the two massive gates to the fort were open. Lupe again pretended to be one of the workers and went inside the walls of the fort. He counted one hundred dead bodies and some workers were carrying others out of the ashes of the barracks. General Oglethorpe had not known of Dan's plan to blow up the barracks. He told Dan he was glad he didn't know, because he was not sure he could have approved of the tactic.

Dan said, "General, war is not for gentlemen. War is killing the enemy. Whatever it takes to destroy the enemy is what war is about. Kill or be killed, and if the enemy is not dead, he needs to be. I have looked in the face of children whose parents have been killed by these Spanish soldiers trying to steal the farmers land. My duty is to make sure there are no more orphans in America. That is my duty as an Irish American, not a gentleman."

General Oglethorpe was stunned for a moment. He had never heard the truth spoken so truthfully. His training had come to him at a much higher level of ruthless civility. He had finally heard the words of a true Irishman and he finally knew why England had not been able to defeat the Irish. The Irish understood war, while the English understood greed. General Oglethorpe said, "Dan, it is most unfortunate you have not been with me since the beginning of Georgia. I somehow feel the Spanish would not be the threat they have become if you had been here."

Dan said, "Sir, I think you will begin to see the beginning of a retreat by our enemy. We have another one of the forts scheduled for next Friday." General Oglethorpe said, "Dan, you handle the problem in any manner you think is prudent. By the way, I received a letter from your adoptive father, General O'Shea. He and his wife should be arriving in three weeks." Dan was so happy to know they really cared enough for him to make such a long voyage. He was very encouraged to have someone who understood war to become involved in removing the intruders from the soil of the settlers. He was sure General O'Shea would have his same point of view, which was, the Spanish were committing an act against the worthy poor, who need military support to defend their interest.

Dan was beginning to understand General Oglethorpe was for what was right. He had been under the impression the General was a staunch supporter of the King's rule. But, Dan now saw that General Oglethorpe was a man as himself, who raised God laws of human kindness and common ordinary respect for his fellowman above the desires of the Crown's interest. It had dawned on Dan, as he observed the way the General structured the rules and regulations of the systems to govern Georgia; the basic theme of the plan was individual independence from the rulership of any one person or group of people. His vision was to set up a society for those who yearned to be free.

After he had made his report to the General, he was missing his family. He said to himself, "There is no better way I could live this day than to be with those I love." He had found some good farm stock for his father to begin working the farm. It crossed Dan's mind, his parents did not have a good horse to ride in case of trouble. He went to the pens that had been constructed to hold the Spanish War horses and selected one for them to use. Dan asks Lupe to help him move the stock to their farm. Dan had been blessed with so many good families he felt like the most blessed man alive.

When Lupe and Dan arrived, they could tell how grateful his parents were for the home God had provided by the amount of work they had done to improve the place. The first thing Delia and Barbara had done was wash and scrub the floors. His father had begun cutting back the weeds that was beginning to be a nuisance. Dan's mother asked, "Where is Patrick?" Dan said, "He is taking care of the war, while I take a day off to just look at you, the love of my life." Delia smiled that smile Dan had missed seeing for so many years.

Delia began being inquisitive as to living with Eamonn. Dan said, "Mama, time with Eamonn was for almost two years. Delia asked, "What did you do then?" Dan said, "Eamonn had a friend in Spain who was a General in the Army of Spain. He was injured in an accident and needed to pass his knowledge of a unique type of military tactics on to someone else. At the time, he felt his life would be over in a short while.

His wife, Margarita asked Eamonn to allow him to teach, train and care for me as long as the General was physically able to do so, because they did not have heirs. I began living with them in Spain when

I was nine years of age. As we stayed together, the O'Shea's became impressed with my ability and arranged for me to expand my studies to include intense military training. The General's health kept improving to the extent of traveling to Ireland to assist the O'Malley's and the O'Flaherty's in purchasing ships to transport Irish made goods to foreign nations. The bond between the O'Shea's and me grew to the point they treated me and cared for me as they would a son. I learned to love them very much.

In 1745, Bonnie Prince Charlie tried to overthrow King George II. I was asked to join with the Jacobite's in Scotland. After almost invading England, the officers in support of Prince Charlie betrayed him and we were forced to retreat toward Scotland. I commanded a group of Special Force soldiers and held General Cumberland and General Oglethorpe back for the main Army to retreat. I was captured, and General Oglethorpe intervened to keep me from being shot as a prisoner of war. He arranged for me to go to Ireland to attend Eamonn's funeral. I was able to meet with my two sisters who were living with Eamonn after Bridget died and Donal, her husband, was killed. Eamonn died from wounds he received in Scotland.

When I arrived in America, General Oglethorpe placed me in command of a unit of combat soldiers known as the Rangers to keep Spain from invading the land the Colonists have worked. My mission now is to drive Spain as far South in Florida as I can."

The family was completely shocked to learn Dan was now supporting the Crown. Delia asked Dan, "Do you think it is right to help those who are slaughtering our people?" Dan said, "Mama, this is not Ireland, this is America, a new country. My thinking is if we take advantage of the help the British can be to build this country, some day we may have a country that is completely different from being under a system of one family Monarchs. My goal is for all of us to be free. I want to own land. I want to earn money and be able to keep it. I want to be part of a nation that looks to God for His guidance."

Delia was thinking, *I knew he was special, but I didn't know he would be this special.* Dan asked, "Mama, do I have to milk the cow to have warm milk in the morning?" Delia said, "No! I will have your milk for you when you get up." As Dan lay on his blanket on the floor, by his mother's side he had time to think of many different things that could have happened to him to keep him from ever seeing his family again. He prayed a silent prayer, *Merciful Father, You have been so good to us. Thank you for your protection. May the thoughts of our minds and the ways of our hearts please You in all that we do.*

Coleman, Dan's father, wanted to talk to Dan about Patrick qualifying for his fifty-acre plot of ground. Dan said, "I don't know all the rules, but I think there has to be a wife, but I will talk to the surveyor for the colonial farmers." Dan told his father he would take care of it, but he had to prepare for his next attack first.

The fort Lupe had scouted was a short distance closer to the Carolina border than the fort that had just been taken. Lupe had gone into the fort as a worker and didn't find it too much different than the first one. Dan's plan was to eliminate any threat that could be made on the settlers who had no military protection. Spain had shown its aggression long enough. Dan knew his tactic of fear in the heart of every Spanish soldier would take its toll on the will of the soldiers and force them to think about nothing but their personal safety.

As Dan was discussing the same tactics with Lupe they had used on the first target, he was amazed to learn the fort still had sentries patrolling the perimeters. Dan said, "Lupe, how long does it take these people to learn we mean business?" Lupe said, "Hopefully, after we get rid of this bunch, maybe someone will discover we are here to stay."

Because of the sentries marching out of the fort, Dan felt the same tactic that had worked on the first target would work on this one. Lupe led the squads to their staging area and one by one, the sentries vanished. Dan thought apparently, the evidence of what had occurred at the first target had not been communicated to the second fort. When the sentries were terminated, Lupe sent the squads back to headquarters. Lupe reported later nothing had changed. The next night, they went back to the fort and there were no sentries, which meant someone was getting the message.

Dan decided he would give this group the opportunity of just opening the gate and retreating south as everyone hoped they would. As the sun rose, the gates opened, and individual soldiers began to walk through the gates without their weapons or battle gear. They walked out and began walking down the road south to St. Augustine. When Lupe reported the news to Dan, he was relieved another massive slaughter didn't have to take place.

Dan told Lupe of a plan to cause more fear. Dan said, "Lupe, how would you like to ride a horse down the road these soldiers are walking and telling each one of them if they return for any reason, we will kill them." Dan continued, "Lupe, you know what, that sounds like too much fun. I think I'll do it myself." Dan found some cloth to cover his face and chose one of the Spanish horses he had taken from the first fort along with his sword, pistol and dagger and struck out to put fear in the enemy.

Dan wanted to kill the first soldier he approached, but after struggling with his first emotion, he decided to talk with him in his native language. Dan had selected a black covering for his face. When the horse got close to the soldier, he dismounted. Seeing the soldier was disarmed, he began to discuss his purpose for leaving the fort. The soldier was surprised to see Dan had on a mask to cover his face. Dan asked him where he was going. The soldier said, "I am headed to Spain, I am quitting the Army." Dan asked, "Why?" The soldier said, "The English have gone crazy." Dan asked, "What did they do?" The soldier said, 'They came in the fort and killed over one hundred soldiers." Dan asked, "Why?" The soldier said, "I don't know."

Dan said, "Let me tell you why those men died. They crossed the line into Georgia and killed some of our farmers. I want you to stay alive for one reason. I want you to tell your friends if you or any of your soldiers ever come back to the fort, I will personally kill you with my bare hands. Tell the others if I see a squad of any soldiers headed north, they are marching to their death."

CHAPTER EIGHT

ORGANIZED FEAR

Dan took full advantage of making sure every soldier on the road in full retreat to St. Augustine knew their enemy up close and personal. One of the officers who had joined the retreat had kept his sword. When Dan dismounted, the officer drew his sword. Dan asked his name. The officer replied, "Alfredo De Leon." Dan said, "Lieutenant, this is not something you want to do." The Lieutenant said, "Sir, I am the best sword fighter in the Army of Spain." Dan said, "That is what I am trying to tell you. You have a lot to lose." The Lieutenant smiled and said, "I will not lose, Seńor." When Dan saw the Lieutenant would not be a candidate to carry the message of fear to the other troops, he said, "Are you prepared to die? If not, say your prayers."

Before the Lieutenant could react to Dan's speed, the point of Dan's sword had gone through his throat, as his blood told the story of his death. Dan left his body where it fell for the others to see their fate, if they continued to be led blindly to their death.

Dan had made certain each soldier from the fort had the opportunity to meet their worst, most unforgiving enemy. Dan earnestly prayed the men would abandon the conflict, after he had visited with every one of the troops on the road, he hoped they would leave.

When Dan returned to headquarters, he talked to Lupe about visiting with some of the Indian tribes around the Okefenokee Swamp. Lupe asked Dan, "What do I need to talk with them about?" Dan said, "I want you to buy 700 poisonous snakes. We will provide sacks to transport the snakes." Lupe asked, "What are we going to do with that many snakes?" Dan said, "Win a military battle." Lupe asked, "How much will we pay per snake?" Dan said, "Five pence for the big ones, two pence for the smaller ones."

The three weeks of anticipation waiting on the arrival of General O'Shea and Margarita, both of whom Dan loved with his whole heart, had been a slow period of time. Dan's mind had been at full speed thinking of the many changes in the lives of all of them. He hoped General O'Shea would feel as though he could be of some use to bring about a resolution to a conflict that had gotten out of control. It was obvious to all observers England was most serious about settling America with their cultural desires, whereas Spain was seeking land to explore for gems, precious metals, and anything of value to be transported to Spain. Spain had not shown any interest in putting investments of the Crown's money into land development for settlers. England had begun to learn land and investment opportunity for private investors would eventually provide a massive tax base that would benefit the Crown.

The two different economic philosophies found a ground for conflict in Florida, Georgia and Carolina, which began a dispute which had no hope of resolution without conflict. There had to be a way to accommodate the desires of both nations. Dan knew if anyone could it would be his adoptive father who would be the architect of a Treaty that would be beneficial to all parties.

General Oglethorpe anxiously awaited their arrival also. He cleared his calendar of all other obligations, so he would be able to visit with the O'Sheas during their visit. The ship arrived timely and was met by General Oglethorpe and Dan, as well as a group of the Georgian dignitaries. Dan could not control himself. It was a day when social restraint was not in play. When he saw Margarita, he held her for the longest time as tears of joy fell from their eyes. General O'Shea was in his chair Eamonn had built for him. The General's aide was in charge of the power to roll the cart down the gang plank. Dan restrained himself until the cart was safely on the dock, at which time he approached the General and knelt on one knee and held the General's hand to his forehead. The General's face was covered with a cotton cloth, but he was most pleased to see his adoptive son again.

When Dan stood up, he replaced the aide and pushed the cart toward General Oglethorpe. When Dan brought the cart to a stop, General Oglethorpe saluted General O'Shea and expressed his personal joy to finally make the personal acquaintance of perhaps the most brilliant military mind in all of Europe. The General had prepared for the O'Sheas to reside in his home during their visit.

After the O'Sheas had settled in, they all met in the General's magnificent garden. General Oglethorpe was anxiously waiting to report the exploits of Dan to his adoptive parents. General Oglethorpe began by giving all the details of how he had met Dan on the battlefield at Shap Fell in Preston. He told the O'Sheas of having observed Dan's military tactics and maneuvers from an enemy's point of view. He told General O'Shea in his entire military career he had never witnessed anything like the maneuvers he had seen Dan perform. He said, "Dan was one of six survivors and as the British troops prepared to execute Dan, I said to myself, *what a waste of talent that would be to kill him.* After he was captured, I took authority and supervision over him, after Dan and I had an understanding, and he has exceeded all his obligations under our agreement. I would trust Dan with all my affairs both military and private. He is a brilliant and honest young man."

General O'Shea and Margarita told General Oglethorpe of their confidence in Dan; to the extent they had jointly named him as heir to their entire estate. Dan overheard what she had said and could not believe what he had heard. He knew they were fond of him, but nothing of that magnitude had ever crossed his mind. He knew the O'Sheas was considered as one of the wealthiest families in Spain.

General O'Shea said, "General Oglethorpe, the irony of this is, I have been dead for over fifteen years because of the wounds I received from the accident, but Margarita insisted that regardless of how I appeared she wanted my spirit to remain with her as long as possible. I eventually agreed, and my health began to improve. At that time, Dan came into our lives and gave us purpose, which became a precious gift from God, through the gift Dan's presence brought to us."

General Oglethorpe said, "My wife and I feel the same toward him as you do. I will say some of his tactics and strategies are not the same as I would personally perform on the battlefield, but his methods of warfare have become essential to the commitment we have made to the settlers we have persuaded to occupy the colony we have established. Dan has an unrelenting quality of protecting and maintaining the commitments he makes to other people. He has brought me to the realization of how shameful and wrong the Crown has been in becoming involved in the extermination policies in Ireland for the sake of taking the Irish land to be granted to the King's political cronies. The policy is outrageous, when I consider the number of children, such as Dan, who have died from starvation and abuse. The amazing quality of all Dan's gifts from God and his parent's teachings is his devotion to justice. Dan's gift is to do whatever is right. His heart and his loyalty are given to that purpose.

One of the primary examples is the present circumstance that he is encircled by now. Technically, Dan is a prisoner of war under my command for treason committed by the Jacobite's when Bonnie Prince Charlie attacked England with the aid of Ireland and Scotland. I had previously made commitments to the Colonists to provide them protection since the Colony of Georgia has been established; Spain has been under the policy of expanding their Crown's holdings beyond Florida into the Carolinas. I led an attack on the fort near St. Augustine and other forts to no avail. I asked Dan's help to protect our settlers. He has begun a plan to escort the Spanish troops to a safe distance from Georgia and Carolina. He has accomplished more in two months than I have in fifteen years, thanks to your training and expertise. Dan has not reported even one loss of life since he took the control of a group we have named, Rangers. The force consists of, by a large majority, Irishmen and Scotsmen. The forces that Dan has organized are becoming known as the most feared fighters in America."

General O'Shea and Margarita were delighted to hear the kind words offered to them about their son, especially since England was technically an enemy of Spain. General O'Shea began to show a sincere interest in the work General Oglethorpe was doing for people who would never have had the opportunity to rise above the poverty level by their own efforts. The one-word General O'Shea was most interested in hearing was, "equal". That word caught his attention. He began to inquire into the details about the project to which General Oglethorpe was giving his time, knowledge and efforts. He told the General he was providing a path for those who were willing to work hard and manage their affairs properly, so as to rise to a level of self-made independence for their families. General O'Shea was also aware of General Oglethorpe's dedication to improving the English prison system.

General Oglethorpe was forthright in telling General O'Shea if the Colony of Georgia is not successful, those who are being released from prison, with no hope, will be back in prison because they will be forced into criminal activity because they will not have an alternative to provide a living for their family. General Oglethorpe said, "That is why Dan's purpose is so important to the colony. Without his defense being provided for them they will have to give up and seek opportunities elsewhere."

As the visit continued, one of Dan's officers came to the General's home to talk to Dan who knew immediately something unplanned had occurred. Dan excused himself to address the problem. When Dan and the Lieutenant got to the front door of General Oglethorpe's home, the officer told Dan three of the scouts had learned of an attack being planned on the settlers. The plan was designed as an attack of revenge for the destruction of the barracks at the first fort.

They mounted their horses and rode toward Ranger headquarters. Dan said, "Lieutenant, apparently we are dealing with slow learners. We will have to improve our educational procedure for these people." Dan said, "I need to talk to Lupe." The Lieutenant told Dan he had reported in three days ago searching for a wagon. Dan grinned to himself because; *he knew Lupe had accomplished his mission.* Dan requested the Lieutenant find Lupe's location and report back to him. Within three hours the Lieutenant reported Lupe's location.

As Dan rode up to where Lupe was located, he saw a camp fire. Lupe had a wagon load of poisonous snakes he had purchased from the tribes around the Okefenoke Swamp. Dan said, "Lupe, we must act quickly, because it is reported the troops located at our next target are planning a revenge attack on the settlers soon." Lupe said, "I am ready." Dan said, "Lupe, take the wagon on to the Ranger headquarters. I am going ahead to get the men ready." Lupe said, "I will meet you at 1:00 a.m." Lupe had arranged for the scouts to meet Dan and the men at the fort. When everyone was assembled the sentries had been eliminated.

Dan began giving the men the attack procedures. He explained that each man would be given a sack of snakes that would be thrown over the walls of the fort with the opening to the sack untied. Then the men would reassemble at a distance from the forts front gate to wait for dawn. Dan predicted after sunrise, there will be gunfire from within the fort. He said, "When the guns are no longer firing, the front gates will open, and the Spanish soldiers will rush out to attack. We will be hidden, and our snipers will eliminate the first group. The next event will be a flag of surrender. We will then take the men prisoners and march them to our prison to hopefully be used to enter a peace treaty."

At dawn, the sentries began seeing the snakes crawling everywhere in the fort and began killing as many as they could find. The men in the fort began spending their time searching for the snakes they could not see. The enemy's fear caused a charge through the front gate where the snipers were poised and ready to fire. At least, thirty Spanish soldiers were shot in the first charge. Then as Dan predicted a soldier with a white flag of surrender came through the gate a short time later, as all the soldiers began to follow one another to prison. The cottonmouth moccasins had won the battle for the Rangers, who had no casualties.

The Rangers closed the gates to the fort after they had removed the ammunition, gun powder and weapons. They set fire to the fort and took the prisoners to be detained. When Dan returned to visit the General and Margarita, his plan was to take the O'Sheas to meet the O'Flahertys. The General was excited, as well as Margarita, to finally have the opportunity to meet the birth parents of Dan who had become the source of their life's joy.

The meeting of the two sets of parents who had participated in the beginning adventures of Dan's life was finally done. Each parent told of how Dan had blessed their lives, and what a joy it was to claim even one day of kinship to such a precious spirit.

Coleman told of their misfortune of being placed in prison in a foreign land with no hope of return to their homeland; and how all that suffering ended the day their son arranged to have them set free even though he was a prisoner himself. As Coleman continued, he said, "We knew even when he was three years old, he was special, but without your lives having touched his, he would never have been given the hope to cause him to grow. Because of you, he has become able to bring life to others. God bless you, for all you have done."

Margarita said, "Mr. O'Flaherty, we were blessed with the gift of helping complete what you and your wife had already begun. For sure, there was quality in his character before he met us. Dan has given us far more than we could ever give him. After the unfortunate accident that ended the General's military career, he had no life until Eamonn brought Dan to our home. Since that day, we have had life because of Dan. We are blessed by you for sharing your blessing with us."

Delia said, "We do not know the customs of any land, but our own. Our custom is, when special friends come for a visit, we eat together. If you don't mind, I would like to set the table for us to eat together." Margarita said, "Delia, I would love to help you." Delia said, "Well, come on, we can visit while the men folks talk." It wasn't long before Dan was enjoying the company of most everyone in his life he loved. The O'Sheas became well acquainted with what General Oglethorpe was arranging to assist people like the O'Flahertys to have somewhere to belong, when the prison years had ended.

The next day, the two Generals began the day getting to know one another better as both of them had begun to place a higher value on one another's character. General O'Shea began to see how he could be of great benefit to the success of the colony by causing the two warring countries to perhaps see the others point of view.

General O'Shea and Margarita decided to take an escorted carriage ride into Florida to learn more of the colony and the people.

They decided Dan could accompany them as the General's son and visitor from Spain searching for land for a residence.

They arrived at the Fort in St. Augustine in a few days. When they arrived at the fort, the sentry approached the carriage and asked for their identification. The General gave the sentry their names as the family of General Phillip O'Shea. The sentry took the message to the commanding officer of the fort. When the officer heard the message, he immediately stood up and marched to the front gate. As the officer was approaching the carriage, Phillip recognized him as a former officer in one of the battalions of which Phillip was Commander. When the officer approached the carriage, General O'Shea said, "Felix, you may not recognize me with this covering, but the good part is, I recognize you." Colonel Felix Castillo said, "General, you will have to forgive me for being astonished, but I was told you had been killed". General O'Shea said, "Some of me did die, but what is left is something for Margarita and my son to care for but, the heart of the General you once knew is still alive."

The Colonel saluted the General and reached for his hand again to touch the man he honored above all other men he had ever known. The Colonel asked, "Who is this young man?" Margarita said, "Felix, this is our adoptive son, Dan O'Flaherty O'Shea. We as a family wanted to visit America." Colonel Castillo was most overjoyed the General had come by to visit with him. He insisted they stay in the guest quarters that had been reserved for the Commanding General of Florida. Colonel Castillo insisted they have dinner together to discuss the adventures they had been involved with since they had not seen one another in many years.

When they had gathered for the evening meal, the Colonel had his wife and children attend in the General's honor. Margarita had known the Colonel's wife from years before as they stayed near one another when their husbands were away. Margarita and Lucinda had been the best of friends in their former years. The Colonel began the meal with a toast to the most gallant soldier he had ever known, General O'Shea. They visited for almost two hours. As the evening moved along, General O'Shea began to become inquisitive about the plans the King of Spain had for Florida. The Colonel said, "The best I can tell, there are no plans other than using the ports to harbor ships traveling from Mexico, Peru and other locations where gold and other precious metals are stored." The General made a comment inquiring about whether he had heard of settlers moving in to occupy the land. The Colonel said, "I think the Crown sees Florida as a big seaport, not fit for habitation."

Dan in the meantime was taking every fact he was learning as information to use in the future to take the fort out of the control of Spain. As the two officers and their wives visited, he walked out on the porch to observe the weakness of the fort for an attack. He was most aware that his presence with Colonel Castillo might be causing him to hesitate to tell the General some valuable information. When he walked back into the room, he heard General O'Shea ask the Colonel the name of the Commanding Officer of Florida. The Colonel responded, "I have that honor because none of the other officers would take the assignment. I took it because I do not like the politics of being around the Crown. I am a soldier, not a politician. I have tried to stay away from politics the same as you did."

The General said, "Felix, tell me what you know about the English Colonies." The Colonel told the General, "It looks to me the Crown of England is bringing settlers to America to build another country." He said, "General Oglethorpe has established a Colony named Georgia, which is for settlers who are farmers. Our orders are to keep England from completing their plan." The General asked, "Why is the Crown interested in disrupting a plan to allow people to take care of themselves?" The Colonel said, "I don't understand how the people can take care of themselves, what does that mean?" The General said, "Felix, have you ever wondered what happens to a prisoner who has been released from prison?" The Colonel replied, "No." The General said, "Well, let me tell you what happens. If the prisoner has no way to make a living, he resorts to crime to feed his family and then is caught and returned to prison." England's King George III has learned the expense of having all these prisoners back in prison, is too expensive. To try to solve the problem, he has granted General Oglethorpe some land to be given to the prisoners to raise food to feed their family. Colonel Castillo said, "To me, that is what should be done." General O'Shea said, "There is only one problem and that is the Spanish troops invade Georgia, killing the farmers and the solution for the poor people fails."

The Colonel asked the General, "How can this problem be solved?" The General said, "My suggestion to you is, to persuade your Commanding Officer to become interested in trading the land in Florida for England's land in Cuba. From what I have read, the ports in Cuba are deeper and the wind is not as erratic as Florida. And, Felix what would be wrong with being Commandant of an entire Caribbean Island?" The Colonel began to imagine what it would be like just having to be concerned about an attack from off shore as opposed to land and sea defenses.

The Colonel asked General O'Shea whether he would mind if he contacted his Commanding Officer and told him you are alive. The General said, "Of course not." The Colonel said, "General, do you know General Oglethorpe?" The General answered, "I have made his acquaintance." The Colonel asks, "Do you know him well enough to ask him to release the prisoners he has just taken from a small fort we had built near the border of America?" The General said, "Colonel, Spain and Great Britain have been at war for almost seven years. It is time for the two nations to get together and settle their differences. If I was in your position, I would recommend to the Crown to trade Florida for Cuba." The Colonel made up his mind to send a dispatch to his Commanding Officers of the losses Spain had suffered by the use of military tactics he had never seen or heard of before. He recommended to the Commander to bring about cease fire between the two countries, until a peace treaty could be entered separating Spain's interest from American soil.

General O'Shea complimented the Colonel for being very wise by taking a new approach to the resolution of the differences between the nations. He also told the Colonel he intended to make arrangements to meet with the Spanish Commanders of the Army to recommend the separation of the two nations by sea as a good resolution to some of their differences. After the discussion, the families agreed as to the solution of the problem and retired for the night. The next day, the families had a good breakfast, as the General told the Colonel he would meet with General Oglethorpe to talk about the release of the prisoners.

General O'Shea was very anxious to return to meet with General Oglethorpe to tell him of the possible breakthrough of a Treaty of Peace with Spain. When General O'Shea met with General Oglethorpe, they were glad to see one another. General O'Shea revealed he had gone to Fort Castile De San Marcus near St. Augustine and Dan had accompanied him on the journey to make sure he was protected. General O'Shea told the General of the relationship he has with Colonel Felix Castillo the Commanding Officer in charge of the troops in Florida. General Oglethorpe was most surprised to learn of a possible relationship that could put an end to the destruction of Georgia. General O'Shea told the General he had discussed a possible agreement to trade Florida to Great Britain for Cuba. He told General Oglethorpe the Colonel had agreed to recommend the agreement to his superior officers. General O'Shea said, "I have got to go to Spain to get the King involved in the negotiations to sign a Treaty." He told the General, "It is time for our differences to be resolved." General Oglethorpe said, "I fully agree."

General O'Shea asked the General if he could recommend passage for him and his wife as well as his son to Spain. General Oglethorpe told General O'Shea Dan had become well known because of his efforts to drive the Spanish south of Georgia. The General said, "General O'Shea for many reasons, I do not think it would be wise to run the risk of Dan being recognized which would compromise your efforts to get a Treaty signed. General, I don't think either one of our two families could handle Dan being in a Spanish prison."

General O'Shea said, "General, thank you for your good, sound advice. I was allowing my personal desires to affect my judgment. General O'Shea asked the General about passage to Spain.

The General said, "Well all I have available is an English ship which would be in trouble if it tried to land in Spain. However, there is a smaller vessel that arrived from Ireland three days ago. The ship was loaded with dried fish and leather goods. It is due to sail tomorrow." General Oglethorpe did not know the Irish ship was a ship that the O'Shea's owned and was a sure trip to Spain.

General O'Shea and Dan went to the port to meet Gregory O'Malley. When they arrived, Gregory could see and recognize the cart Eamonn had built for his friend, Phillip. Gregory arrived in port with a wary eye of suspicion and concern having landed in an English port. His thinking was, *the ports of Europe had become too risky for him to continue dealing with the Europeans, because he never knew which country was allied with the other.* He had always wanted to sail to America. He had heard of the possible opportunity for those who are willing to work, and he wanted to experience independence without government interference. The three of them were extremely glad to know they had managed, so far, to avoid death or prison. Gregory told Dan his desire to be with him when he felt the time was right.

After they had discussed the news, Gregory wanted to talk about America. Dan was the first to speak up. He said, "Gregory, it is a place only in your fondest dreams, would you believe a place like this exists. General Oglethorpe has established a place where you can buy land to raise farm products for sale." Gregory said, "You mean to tell me, a Catholic can buy land in America?" Dan said, "All you have to do is keep your mouth shut and pray in private." Gregory said, "I need to think about this. Maybe we need to start thinking about shipping our goods from America to Europe after we settle here."

While they were talking, General O'Shea was listening as he had begun to consider the possibility of moving to the new world. But, the more pressing problem was, to get Gregory to provide him passage to Spain. The General had made up his mind to do everything he could to bring an end to the conflict, between Spain and England.

CHAPTER NINE

ROYAL POLITICS

Gregory told General O'Shea he would be ready to sail to Spain on the high tide in three days. He needed to make repairs for such a long journey. When Dan and the General returned to the Oglethorpe home, he told General Oglethorpe he had made arrangements for the voyage. After he informed Margarita, she began getting prepared for a voyage she did not want to make; she wanted to remain in the world Dan's life had brought to her.

General Oglethorpe was elated they had found passage to Spain. He suggested to General O'Shea they discuss some of the details of the Treaty which he thought would be acceptable to both parties. General Oglethorpe's thinking was, *Spain would insist upon having a presence in Florida and would probably insist upon retaining the forts they had constructed with Fort Castillo De San Marcus near St. Augustine, being their main interest.* The General asked General O'Shea to be careful that no military presence for Spain be allowed in any of the forts. He again stated, "One of our obligations to our settlers is, for them to be provided a safe environment." General Oglethorpe began telling General O'Shea he had become the representative of Great Britain against Spain. General O'Shea chuckled and said, "My loyalty has always been to, what is just and right and from what I have witnessed the Colony of Georgia is an inspiration that is God ordained. In fact, if the other Colonies began to emulate the methods you have begun here, America would be a refuge for all those to have available when the heavy hand of royal blood threatens to take their land and lives from them."

General Oglethorpe began to realize General O'Shea was beginning to consider becoming a participant in the experiment of freedom that he had begun. General O'Shea said, "General, I am considering an investment in some land in America, do you know of any land available?" General Oglethorpe said, "General, I have been considering a matter that may be of interest to you." General O'Shea said, "If it is a request, I hope I can provide a solution for you." General Oglethorpe said, "I have been considering talking to the King to persuade him to grant you a tract of land of your choice in Carolina when you bring this Peace Treaty to finality. I was thinking, since you are the one who will eventually be known as the author of the Treaty, to end the Seven Year War, I am sure the southern portion of Carolina will become habitable. I intend to ask the King to grant you a sizeable portion of that land, if you think you would have interest in it."

General O'Shea's mind began to spin with the possibility of him and Dan owning a part of America and having a place to work together. General O'Shea said, "General, there is one other consideration I consider greater than any financial gift King George could grant to me and that is a pardon for my son." General Oglethorpe smiled and said, "That was going to be the next matter, I intended to discuss with you." General O'Shea felt as though he had finally become positioned to show Dan his gratitude for the life he had given to him. All the questions that had come to rest on General O'Shea's conscience of deep gratitude were now about to be resolved.

General Oglethorpe said, "General, you will be leaving in a few days headed to Spain to talk to your King and I will be going to England to talk to my King. Hopefully, by God's ever-present Grace, we will be back together in about six months."

After meeting with General Oglethorpe, General O'Shea began wanting to meet with Dan and Margarita. Early the next morning, Dan was ready for a visit. The three of them together again, was the beginning of a great day. General O'Shea began by telling them of General Oglethorpe's offer of land and a pardon for Dan, which brought great joy to the three members of a very happy family. While they were together, the General told them when all the details of the Treaty is accomplished with Spain, he wanted to consider relocating their lives together in America. He asked Dan if he intended to return to Ireland, Scotland or Spain.

Dan said he was sharing the same thoughts the General had spoken. Dan said, "There is something in me that cries out for freedom. I would be at war with any nation that does not recognize human rights as granted by God Almighty. I was not born to be under the control of a government." General O'Shea suggested, "Since the conflict is at a standstill, it might be wise to get General Oglethorpe to show you the land he has in mind for our family." Dan knew General Oglethorpe would be traveling to England to discuss the treaty, but he would inquire whether one of his staff knew the location of the land. Dan said, "By the time you return, I will know the location."

General O'Shea said, "Dan, there is one other matter we need to discuss and that is, our estate. We have never discussed financial matters before, but it has come time for you to know everything there is to know about our financial position. As you know, the King of

Spain has always been more than grateful for the service I rendered the Spanish Empire. You have noticed we do not involve ourselves in investments and risky adventures. We have accumulated a large estate in Spain. Margarita and I have discussed all the details of my death. When I die, Margarita will inherit the estate with the remainder, after her death, to be given to you. You have been the greatest gift God could have ever sent to us. Even though we are not bound by blood, there is a spiritual bond we have earned by the inextricable intertwining of our minds, hearts and souls. After we are gone, we want you to have a life of your own. I have taught you all I know about economics and accounting. If you choose to live a moderate life, you will be able to pass an estate on to your heirs. I intend to persuade Gregory to bring his family to America. This is the only place on earth an Irishman will ever find peace of mind."

When General O'Shea had completed explaining the family financial matters, he glanced at Dan who had his eyes closed as he bowed his head in gratitude. He began by saying, "Sir, under the best of circumstances, my life would have existed as an Irish orphan waiting to grow into the age for slavery. Because of Eamonn, you, and my darling mother Margarita, I have been gifted with a life you took from your heart and gave to me. I could never be worthy of such blessings. But, because of your love for me and our love for one another, you have made me worthy in your eyes. I thank you both for every thought you have had toward my training and upbringing. I will vow to you to never willingly bring shame to your most sacred heritage."

Then Dan said, "We have had an exciting morning and I am going to push you to your room for some rest. I need to make sure the troops are resting, since we have a cease fire in effect."

The next morning, General O'Shea and Margarita were in a down cast mood for having to leave Dan to the care of General Oglethorpe. But, the excitement of meeting with the King, to announce to him the fact of being alive, they were making their day have a good beginning. As the ship caught the high tide and headed for Spain, Dan stayed at the dock as long as he could to watch the mast as it disappeared over the horizon.

Dan had an urge to be with his natural mother and father to help them with the cotton crop that had begun to show signs of being a good one. His father couldn't stop talking about the quality of the soil they had been granted by General Oglethorpe. Dan's father said, "This has to be the best cotton land in the world." Dan said, "Maybe so, maybe not." His father asked, "What do you mean?" Dan said, "Since we have a few days off from the war, I would like to take both of you on a little journey to some other parts of America. We will probably be gone three or four days. You need to take some food and some clothes."

They headed out to a settlement by the Savannah River that eventually became known as Port Wentworth. There was a ferry that could take the horses and the carriage across the river. Dan had arranged with General Oglethorpe for his aide to assist Dan in locating the land General Oglethorpe was discussing with General O'Shea. After they crossed the river, they traveled in a northeasterly direction entering what would eventually be named, Hampton County, southwest of the Coosawhatchie River. The aide told Dan all the land they were traveling over is the land General Oglethorpe was talking about. As they rode along Coleman asked the driver to stop. When the carriage stopped, Coleman got out and walked about twenty steps and picked up a handful of the dirt and said, "Dan this is better dirt than the soil in Georgia."

As they rode further, Dan began imagining being involved in a farm he could not see across from one boundary to the other. He was astonished until he began thinking of, *the kind of man General Oglethorpe was and he knew he would have in mind some of the best land in Carolina for farming.*

They continued to ride through the area until dark. After they made camp for the night, Delia began reminiscing the memories she had collected from the years of tears she had shed resulting from circumstances completely beyond their control. But, here she lay on a blanket, in a new world with her son, Dan, and her devoted husband by her side. It was beyond her ability to even imagine riding along in a carriage, belonging to an English General, searching for a piece of land the King of England would grant to an adoptive father of her son, which would give her family an opportunity to care for themselves the rest of their lives. She was overwhelmed with the thought of anything that fortunate ever coming to her life. She then began thinking, *of the blessing from God to all her family through a third child of hers named, Dan.* Tears silently fell from her eyes as the joy filled a heart that had known sorrow most of the days of her life. She was beginning to learn her heart felt better when it didn't have sorrow. She thought sorrow had always been her lot in this life. She grieved constantly to see her daughters, Siobhann and Shibeal. Since everything had begun to occur in her life she thought to be impossible, she had felt faint hope she would see them again, if it was the Will of God.

She was enjoying her journey with Dan. She needed a rest from the toil of a farm. When she awoke the next morning, she was lost for a moment and then remembered; *she was in a new world that did not have the horror of being in Ireland.* She looked up and Dan had rekindled the fire from the night before. Delia had brought some smoked bacon and some soda bread. They had a feast and then began their journey back to Georgia. Their hearts were filled with hope beyond any they had ever known.

The months passed with Dan passing the time keeping the troops active and learning more about the terrain, where they would be fighting, should the fighting continue. Dan was also spending time with Lupe, visiting Indian tribes that had presented themselves as friendly. Dan made friends very quickly because he was always ready to meet the challenges of the tribe's best warriors. Dan could out run, out shoot any of them with a bow and arrow and was King of the Tomahawk throwing. Dan kept it all in fun by making sure he and none of his men made any kind of advances toward the tribe's women. The chiefs grew in great respect for Dan and his men. When the Rangers killed a wild animal for meat, they always found tribe members to share the food.

In the year 1763, Spain relinquished its claim to Florida in exchange for Great Britain's control of Havana, Cuba, which had been captured by Great Brittan during the Seven Year War. (4) When Dan received the news, he was more anxious than ever to see his adoptive parents. He knew they would be arriving any day.

Dan was asleep when General Oglethorpe summoned him to his home at approximately five o'clock, a.m., in 1763. When he entered the General's library, he could tell the General was most upset. He asked Dan to be seated and then placed his face in his hands and began to sob openly. After a few minutes, he regained control of himself and said, "Dan, I hate to be the bearer of bad news, but it seems the ship General O'Shea and Margarita sailed on to return to the Colonies has been lost. A hurricane apparently struck the ship last week and another ship located evidence of the name of the ship they were on, floating in the water." Dan stood up and asked General Oglethorpe if he could be alone. The General said, "Dan, I am so sorry. I pray you will be comforted during this dark hour." Dan left the General's home and went to the corral, saddled a horse and rode toward his mother. When he arrived, they were sleeping. He walked in the cottage and went to her bedside, kneeled, and laid his head on his mother's arm, and began to sob tears that had been stored since the day he waved goodbye to her from Eamonn's wagon. She rolled over as she had done on the first day of his life and held her precious son in her arms. She lay completely still as he whispered, *"General O'Shea and Margarita have been lost at sea."* Dan could feel the muscles in his mother become tense as they wept the tears of separation for the loss of the two souls who had stepped into her shoes when she had been placed in prison. As they lay holding one another, every precious memory of *the first years of Dan's life slowly drifted back through her mind and heart.*

When the sun arose, Dan got up from his knees and walked to the porch. Delia followed him to where Coleman was sitting drinking his coffee. Dan said, "Dad, General O'Shea and Margarita have been lost at sea on their way back to be with us." Coleman didn't say a word. He lowered his head as tears began to flow. After an hour or more of silence, Dan said, "Mama, I believe they were the angels you and Dad prayed for to take care of me." Delia said, "They were the precious gift of God my prayers and tears purchased from God

Himself. No one could have ever been more perfect to teach you the path to freedom than those two precious souls. Their lives are the sources of our gifts."

When Dan had cried his sorrow to the point of having to rest, he mounted his horse and rode back to the General's home. The General was on the porch when Dan rode up to the house. Dan was glad he was not interrupting the General's day. General Oglethorpe knew that the Peace Treaty between England and Spain had its very foundation in the heart and soul of General O'Shea and Margarita. Dan told the General he had been with his parents thanking God and expressing how grateful they were for the O'Shea's lives and how grateful he was for them reaching out to him in his most desperate hour.

The General said, "I truly understand how you feel, Dan, and I offer you my deepest sympathy for your loss." Dan said, "General, I could not have been more blessed, than their lives blessed me." The General said, "Dan, this is one other matter General O'Shea arranged for you and I suppose now is a good time to tell you. In the negotiations with Spain, he asked that King George grant you a pardon which has been done. I also initiated a conversation with him regarding the Crown honoring General O'Shea for the efforts he extended while negotiating the Peace Treaty by awarding him and his heirs a sizeable estate in the Carolinas. I have arranged with King George several options from which you can select the land of your choice. I have also been informed by the Kings Ambassador, who put the final details to the Treaty; General O'Shea was also given a sizeable grant of land of his choice in Florida. I am sure you can work out the details when you probate the estate in Spain." Dan sat listening to the

General talk, but estates, wealth; fame fortune meant nothing to him at this dark period of his loss.

The memorial service arranged by General Oglethorpe was a ceremony to behold. Dan was honored the Ribbon of Freedom by England for his work in preventing Spain from killing the settlers. Every settler in Georgia that could make the trip did so to honor a heroic family's effort to protect them from the invasion by Spain. When Dan was asked to say a word, he began by saying, "When I was a child, just another Irish Catholic orphan, and these two precious people took me in and devoted their lives to my well-being, I was given every opportunity to learn from two people who were teachers, born of God. Whatever they were willing to impart to me, I received as a gift from God Himself, because the General taught me, 'A true gift is not for keeping, it is for giving.' Whatever contribution I have had the opportunity to give to the lives of those gathered here today has been because of the gifts of life I received from my parents, Eamonn O'Flaherty, General Phillip O'Shea and my adoptive mother, Margarita O'Shea and his blessed Honor, General James Oglethorpe and my natural parents, Delia and Coleman O'Flaherty. Whatever I have done or am able to do in the future of the Colonies, I owe to God and these great people who trusted in me to take from them and share with you. Thank you for all you have done to cause America to be possible."

After the ceremonies, the General approached Dan to thank him not only for his service, but for the kind words he had said about him. Dan said, "General, the kindness of the words is not in the words but are in your heart which is the very definition of the word, kind. You are without a doubt the best friend a man could ever have." A tear fell from the General's face as he listened to Dan speak his heart in a very unaccustomed manner to his former enemy.

The General inquired of Dan's plans. Dan said, "I am aware of some of the property the O'Shea's were awarded, but I am not sure I know all of it. I need to get to Spain to read the will and have it officially probated. After that, I am dedicated to returning to America to do what I can do to help America grow. I have begun to feel I am a part of something big."

The General said, "I have received some correspondence from Pennsylvania asking, whether some of the leaders could talk to you about some problems they are having protecting their settlers." Dan said, "I would appreciate you contacting them for me. Tell them I will contact them when I return from Spain."

General Oglethorpe knew he had lost Dan's daily companionship for a period, but he knew he would return. Dan readied himself for the voyage of a life time. He was anxious to know more about Spain and the political issues that it faced.

He sailed on a Spanish ship that had begun trade with the Colonies. Georgia was beginning to compete in the world markets with cotton and cotton goods. When he arrived, he went to the palatial home where he grew up and studied under General O'Shea. He was surprised to find the home occupied by the staff the O'Sheas had hired. He asked the butler to assemble the staff.

When the staff was assembled he introduced himself as Dan O'Flaherty, the adoptive son and heir of General O'Shea and his wife, Margarita. When he said his name, the faces of the staff lit up with smiles. They all knew his name because he was who the O'Sheas talked about constantly. They were so pleased to be able to meet him.

Dan began asking questions regarding the upkeep of the mansion and all the other issues common to the ownership of property. Dan had fought battles, skirmishes and most every kind of conflict associated with warfare, but he had never fought the battle of the legal system and money. He didn't know what to expect and he didn't know where to start. He remembered a man when he was very young that worked on the docks that always helped him dock Eamonn's boat, when they would arrive from Ireland. His name was Sam O'Keefe. He asked the butler to get him to the docks to locate a harbor master named, Sam O'Keefe.

There was a small enclosure at the end of the dock that gave the harbor master a view as the ships arrived. Dan walked to the enclosure and saw a man that was much younger than he expected. Dan asked to talk to Sam O'Keefe. The man, about Dan's age, said, "I am Sam O'Keefe, Jr., but I think you want to talk to my father." Dan said, "Probably so. How can I contact him?" Sam Jr. said, "He is not able to work anymore because of his poor eyesight; however, his health is good. May I ask, what is your name?" Dan gave him his name and Sam's facial expression implied he had heard the name. Sam Jr., said, "You are Eamonn's nephew." Dan said, "To save a long explanation, yes." Sam Jr., said, "My father will be so glad to see you, he has often talked to me about you and Eamonn." Dan said, "Could I trouble you to tell me where I can find your father?" Sam Jr. gave him the route to follow, of which Dan's driver was familiar. When they located Sam's house, he was sitting under a tree wanting company. He had, for his working life, sat at the docks directing the ship traffic of the harbor. He had come to know most all of the people who mattered, politically.

Sam recalled Eamonn and Dan; they were among his favorite people. Sam asked about Eamonn, and Dan brought him up to date on the fact of Eamonn's death which he was so sorry to learn. Dan began by telling Sam of the death of the O'Sheas and he had been named as heir to their estate. He told Sam of the teachings of General O'Shea, some of which were to select only the most trustworthy advisors. Dan said, "Mr. Sam, I do not know who to trust because I have never had to hire an attorney. You are the one man I trust to help me." Mr. Sam seemed embarrassed that a man of Dan's stature and upbringing would value his advice. Mr. Sam said, "Dan, I am getting up in age and my children will be asking the same question to someone else someday. My advice would be for you to hire a man named, Matthew Collier. He is known, not only as the best lawyer in Spain, but he is known as the most honest. He has represented some of the royalty in matters of this kind." Suddenly, Dan felt inspired, because he knew Mr. Sam was an honorable man and would not mislead him. Dan embraced Mr. Sam and told him, "When this event is over, I will be back to see you."

Dan told his driver to take him to an attorney's office named, Matthew Collier. Within a short time, he was sitting in front of a small office with the name Matthew Collier on the door. Dan went in and asked to speak to Mr. Collier. Within a few moments, Mr. Collier, who seemed to be unusually friendly, came to greet Dan. Mr. Collier escorted Dan into his office. Dan began by telling him the complete history of his life with the O'Sheas even to the last meeting in America when General O'Shea had left America to meet with the Ambassador of Spain to enter a Treaty with Great Britain to end the War in 1763.

Mr. Collier began his statement by revealing to him he had represented the O'Sheas from the time he completed the study of law until the Treaty was signed with Great Britain. Dan was amazed he had never heard Mr. Collier's name mentioned in all the years of being with the O'Sheas. Mr. Collier revealed every matter concerning the O'Sheas had been handled in the strictest confidence on both sides, but Mr. Collier said, "Dan, I am very familiar with everything you have ever said or done, from the first day you walked into their home. Mrs. O'Shea and I conversed in every matter concerning your life and training. From what I understand, you have exceeded all our expectations."

Dan prided himself in being more knowledgeable than most everyone with whom he had business but could not understand how after years of being with the O'Sheas he could have missed such an important part of his knowledge of the affairs of the O'Sheas. Dan could not believe Margarita had not told him about Mr. Collier, but it was now unimportant because he had found his way to where he was supposed to be without having to guess whether he had made the correct choice.

Matthew Collier said, "I suppose you are wondering about the relationship I had with your adoptive parents." Dan said, "If it is not too much of an imposition, I would like to know the truth of the beginning of your relationship with them." Mr. Collier said, "I think you are entitled to know the whole truth from the beginning. I was born in Wales into a very poor family environment. At the age of twelve, it became necessary for me to leave because of starvation. It wasn't long before I was on a ship destined to dock in Spain. When I landed, I met a good man who was the harbor master at the port. He knew I was hungry and he asked me to go home with him. I worked for him until I was fifteen years old and joined the Spanish military. While I served in the military, I was assigned to a company of Special Force soldiers. My Commanding Officer was Phillip O'Shea. At the time we were young and able to do the Kings bidding. We were truly a tough group of men. We never considered defeat because we were the best of the best in Europe. We were involved in a battle with Portugal when I was wounded and was deemed to no longer be of military capability.

At that time, Colonel O'Shea arranged for me to get an education with a military pension. When I had completed the first degree, several of the professors told me I should study the law. Again, my friend and General Phillip O'Shea arranged for me to study law under the tutelage of the top five lawyers in Spain. After acceptance by the Academy of Law, I began law practice with the assistance of General O'Shea who desperately needed my services."

Because of his victorious exploits, General O'Shea, had become the most eligible bachelor in all of Spain. He was sought after by every woman of royal breeding in the whole of Europe. One of the most beautiful women in the world was in the line of successors to the throne of Spain, but the royal law disallowed the Princess from marrying a commoner. Because of our relations, General O'Shea gave me the problem to solve for him to be allowed to marry the Princess. After I had convinced myself there was no legal way around the law of succession, I suggested to them that the Princess abdicate the prohibition of government control of their lives and be joined in Holy wedlock with one exception. Dan asked, "What was the exception?" Mr. Collier answered, "That she retains the right to inherit the division of her royal estate in real and personal property and with the rights of her heirs to inherit her royal estate upon her death." Dan asked Mr. Collier to continue the story. Mr. Collier said, "The Princess abdicated her rights of succession to the throne and had her name changed with Holy approval to Margarita O'Shea."

Dan was speechless. He was thinking, *you mean to tell me my adoptive mother was to become the Queen of Spain?* Mr. Collier asked Dan, "Do you understand why that bit of truth is important to you?" Dan said, "No Sir!" Mr. Collier said, "The estate of Margarita and Phillip would have escheated or gone back to the Crown, whereas, you are now entitled to inherit her entire estate, but Dan, you have to understand, Spain is on the verge of bankruptcy. King Charles is doing the best he can, but the financial status of Spain is critical regardless of how right you are legally, the royal lawyers are not going to give up that much money easily."

Dan said, "Mr. Collier, meeting you is again one of those events that has happened to me all my life. No other man in this world could have known what you know and would have kept it secret. I think our meeting has at its root a divine purpose. I hope whatever it is; you will give me your prayers and guidance to live life in such a way God Himself will be proud." Mr. Collier said, "Dan, I have known your life for many years. It is not in you to do wrong or fail at what you try to do for right. You are a man of God."

CHAPTER TEN

BELONGING

At the conclusion of a hard-fought legal battle by Mr. Collier that ultimately transferred the interests in the estates of Phillip and Margarita O'Shea to Dan, the Crown lawyers finally realized Dan's claim was valid and if the Crown took the money it would be illegal. Mr. Collier made an offer to settle the entire case which was accepted. The agreement was signed, and the suit was dismissed. The entire O'Shea estate was transferred to Dan that made him one of the wealthiest men in the world.

A month before, Dan had sent a message to Gregory O'Malley, who was now Dan's partner in the shipping business, stating he would like to meet with Gregory O'Malley's family in Spain, along with his sisters, Siobhann and Shibeal, as soon as possible. After Dan had settled with Mr. Collier, he rode in his carriage to the dock to ask if the O'Malley ship was due to land. The harbor master said, "They arrived yesterday." Dan asked, "Where are they staying? Sam, Jr. answered, "They are at a lodge two blocks from here." Dan's heart sunk. He could not grasp all that had come to him without any effort required of him, other than the prayers he so fervently prayed without ceasing. The question raced through his mind, *how to best manage wealth beyond riches?* He slowed his race to the lodge to see the O'Malley family to consider the seriousness of his burden. He thought of the people whose lives were involved with his and the awesome weight of making decisions that would affect so many. His heart cried out to God for rescue to overcome the waves of doubt of his capabilities and worthiness. He stopped and looked back at the sea that had brought him to this place years before, as he thought of, *his view of the world at that time. How Eamonn had brought him to this very dock and left him with the O'Sheas to prepare him for the wars his life would be faced with until peace could again touch his soul. Now peace had come with great blessings of responsibility.* He turned again and looked toward the lodge where a heart had joined with his in years past. He was reminded of the joy that was awaiting his presence as he knocked on the door to greet those hearts to which his heart belonged. When he saw Mary, every care vanished. She had the necklace made of leather and a cross around her neck that had been placed there by Dan years before to be their bond forever. He held her and asked her, "Are you ready for forever to begin?" Mary said, "Yes." He knew whatever his lot in life became, the strength to prevail would be provided. Dan asked if everyone was ready for a ride to his house. Everyone answered their readiness. Dan arranged for two carriages to take them to their destination. When the carriage turned into the drive, Dan could feel Mary's hand tighten as she saw her house in Spain for the first time. All the O'Malleys and Dan's two sisters acted as if they were doing something wrong and were in fear of being arrested. Dan said, to all of the visitors, "Welcome to our home." These humble Irish families had lived under the threat of imprisonment or death for most of their lives. The remaining days of their lives would be involved in a long period of adjustment for them to feel free.

Dan told them to make themselves at home and if they needed any help, to ask the butler. In the meanwhile, he wanted to visit with

Mary in the garden to see if she had changed her mind about their marriage. Dan told her how he had missed her. She quietly said how she had missed him too.

He told her of his love for her and asked if she was sincere about proceeding with the commitment of their lives to one another. She said, "Dan, I have waited all my life for this moment, to stand in the presence of a man whom I not only loved, but also whom I deeply respect." Dan said, "I can arrange for a priest to come to our home and say the words." Mary said, "That would be very pleasing to me." Dan asked, "Do you know anyone in Spain you would like to invite to our ceremony?" Mary said, "My family is all I know." Dan said, "I have three friends here, I would like to ask, if you approve." Mary said, "Dan, whatever makes you happy is my greatest joy." Dan asked the butler to send a message to Mr. Sam O'Keefe, Mr. Matthew Collier and Doctor Mark Castille, inviting them to their wedding tomorrow, at four o'clock, p.m.

The chef prepared a meal the guests would never forget. He was of Irish decent and knew all the foods that whetted the Irish palate. The three honored guests were in attendance.

After the ceremony, Dan wanted the opportunity to speak to his new collective family. He began by saying a prayer of gratitude for Eamonn, General and Mrs. O'Shea, and told all they had done for him when he was placed in their care by God, Himself. He told them of the abundant joy that had come to his life by these three people, causing him to rest with the knowledge he belonged where he had been placed, because of the evil that had separated his life from his biological family. He said, "From the day my mother placed my six-year-old hand in Eamonn's, I knew I would be cared for in all ways. I also knew when Eamonn was asked by the General and Margarita to be placed in their care, I knew in my heart I belonged where God had placed me. I stand before you today, with us having been placed in one another's care for the remainder of our days, and I know you are to whom I belong as my extended family, and I will give you my oath to protect you to the best of my ability for the remainder of my days.

With that having been said, I need to share with you knowledge that has come to me that could affect where we decide to live the remainder of our days. I have been involved in protecting settlers who have left their homelands for numerous reasons and have immigrated to America. I have come to know a man named, General Oglethorpe, who is involved in providing homesteads for immigrants who are of good character and willing to work. My mother and father are in a Colony named Georgia; they were in a slave camp and General Oglethorpe had them released. They are farmers and are involved in producing cotton for the world market. Because of some agreement made with General O'Shea and the British Crown I now own property in the Colony of Carolina and Florida. This land, if worked properly will produce enough cotton to feed many families besides ourselves. I do not feel the warmth of belonging in Spain, Ireland or Scotland. I do feel I belong in America. Even though it is under British rule, I do not believe the majority of the people will tolerate much more of the dogmatic abusive conduct of a foreign monarch governing their lives. I can see in the future well enough to know America will someday separate itself from the dictators of Europe. I want to be a part of that conflict. At present, we need to evaluate our position because we are now in a position to make choices we have never had before. We need to convince ourselves, Ireland is not an option. Our lives need a rebirth in another place. I will be requesting Mr. Matthew Collier to become administrator of my property in Spain. I will be asking Mr. Sam O'Keefe to be the overseer of this home, with the understanding this will be his residence. We will maintain the same staff under the direction of the butler, Mr. Monroe." Mr. O'Keefe asked, "Can I go back to my house periodically?" Dan said, "I would expect you to do whatever you need to do to manage your affairs. Each of you will be paid each month by Mr. Collier." Dan said, "Mr. O'Keefe, you are welcome to entertain your guest at any time, the butler will work out the details for your menu. Now it is time for us to begin honoring the most beautiful, wonderful bride in all of Europe, may God Bless Our Holy Union." All the festivities were memorable. Dan wanted everyone to know Mary would be reorganizing her life to be with him in America and her family was welcome to go with them to perhaps a land of opportunity. Dan offered each member of the O'Malley family the alternative of residing in Spain as opposed to moving to America. The family had forgotten what it was like to have a choice about anything. Some of the younger adults had never known they had a choice about anything. The family went to the garden area for Gregory to talk to them about their choices. Dan and Mary went to their bedroom that had a porch extended over the first floor. They sat on the porch and listened to the birds singing, as they drank in the joys of being together after a long, long journey of being apart. They held hands and gazed at the wonderment of the monumental blessings provided to them by a God who expressed His love to them in every way imaginable.

Dan turned to Mary and said, "I have never known what it was like to be at complete peace in my entire life. Today, I want you to know your presence has brought my soul complete peace. I now feel my life is complete." As they held one another, their hearts knew, God Himself had given them a field of His greatest blessing.

The next morning when Dan awoke and went to the kitchen, he found Gregory waiting to talk with him. Gregory O'Malley the chieftain of the O'Malley clan was recognized in Ireland as a great warrior and was a descendant of the famous Grace O'Malley, who was the Queen of Umali, Chieftain of the O'Maille (O'Malley) clan, rebel, seafarer, and fearless leader, who fought against the British Empire in the 1500's. She saw her mission as that of keeping Ireland independent from the English Crown. [5] Gregory was known as a clan leader whose mission was to continue the efforts of his ancestors to restore the independence of Ireland. Ireland was once the recognized center of spiritual wisdom for the world, which once provided knowledge, yet undiscovered anywhere else in the world. Ireland was the place of the rebirth of spirituality that provided all knowledge, pertaining to the recognition of the one true and living God. All of the spiritual movements of Europe can be traced to the Irish scholars of the sixth and seventh centuries.

Dan and Gregory shared that same desire for independence and the rights as granted to man by God. Gregory was forthright with Dan by asking if America had land where his family could live and work without the interference of Great Britain. Dan said, "Gregory that was the purpose General Oglethorpe established the Colony of Georgia. The General himself is the authority over the land and I can assure you, there is not a man anywhere better than him." Gregory said, "We are tired of this endless turmoil of sneaking around as thieves to try to survive. If you think America is the place to begin, we want to follow you." Dan said, "Gregory, let me remind you, we own three ships and could own more, if we need more, to transport our goods to Europe."

Dan asked, "How long would it take for you to notify the other two ships captains to meet us here in Spain?" Gregory said, "I am sure we could get together in three weeks." Dan said, "We need to think of all the farming equipment we need to take with us. I know it will be cheaper than buying it from England." Dan and Mary decided to spend the next three weeks doing something besides waiting on the other two ships to arrive. Mary had never been to town shopping; she told Dan she wanted to go to town. Dan hitched up the carriage and they were on their way. The trip to town reminded him of his playful rides with his beloved Margarita. Mary had been living the life of a hermit, hiding out trying to keep hidden from the British soldiers. Now, she was free in a new land, free of threats and abuse. Dan said, "Mary, we have got to decide the type of clothes you like to wear. Remember, my adoptive mother was in line to be the Queen of Spain. She loved for me to take her to shop for new clothes. I have been trained by royalty to select beautiful clothes. Would you like to go to some of the shops that have the better clothing, or would you like something more moderate?" Mary said, "Dan, you know I do not have any knowledge about what we are saying or doing. You know as well as I do, I am a woman from Ireland that has no knowledge of what you want me to look like. All I know is get out of bed and hope to survive for one more day. Why don't you decide how you want me to dress, then I will tell you if I like it."

Dan knew exactly the right place. He and Margarita would visit the little store when she wanted to play or go on a picnic. When they arrived, the shop keeper remembered Dan and Margarita visiting with him from time to time.

The shopkeeper looked at Mary and remarked, "How beautiful you are." As he displayed the choices of clothes for Mary, Dan saw a dress that caught his eye. He said, "Mary come look at this one." Mary looked at the silk dress that was her size. When Mary saw the dress, she knew it was of the finest silk, and he also knew it was the dress of her dreams. She asked for a place to try it on. The shopkeeper asked his wife to assist Mary when she tried on the dress. The lady escorted Mary to the changing room. When Mary touched the dress, every female quality of her being, surfaced. She said, "I like this, how does it fit?" The lady said, "It could not be more beautiful on anyone, than it is on you."

Mary told the lady to tell Dan to come to the dressing room for his approval. Mary stepped out of the room where Dan could see her and the dress. He was stunned by what one dress had done to change his Irish maiden into a woman of distinction. Mary stood in front of the mirror and was pleased with what she saw. Dan said, "Don't hurry; I have two more I want you to try." Mary was having the time of her life. The lady said, "Mrs. Mary, you need to have your hair done." Mary had to guess what she meant by her statement. Dan said, "Mary, Margarita had a lady come to our home to have her hair washed and curled. Would you like to have her help you with your hair?" Mary agreed to allow the woman to help her. By the end of the day, they had visited five more stores and Mary began to be open to Dan and express her own desires in the selection of her clothes, which made him so happy. Mary said, "Today is the most wonderful day of my life besides yesterday and the day before."

Dan was enjoying every moment of getting acquainted with his new family and planning for the future of a nation that set forth the freedom of each person rather than tyrannical self-interest. On the way back to his home, he stopped by to visit for a moment with his lawyer, Mr. Matthew Collier. Mr. Collier told him he had plenty of time to visit if Dan needed to discuss some matters of concern. Dan told Mr. Collier Mary was with him and he could send her on to the mansion. However, he told the driver he could return in a short while to also take him home.

Mr. Collier could tell Dan had matters of grave concern on his mind that required Mr. Collier's undivided attention. Mr. Collier told his clerk to take the rest of the day off and put the closed sign on the door. As Dan began the discussion it became clear to Mr. Collier Dan was deeply committed to the American Revolution and the necessary preparation to prevail over the mightiest Army in the world. Mr. Collier knew Dan had been trained by the best Special Force General ever known in Europe. Mr. Collier was very attentive to every word Dan had to say. As the discussion continued, Mr. Collier revealed he had a son who had become qualified to practice law in the Courts of England and he had decided to move to America to practice law.

Dan became intensely interested in the world view his son might have after being educated in England. Mr. Collier told Dan his son Weston Collier had returned to Spain with full knowledge of the English tyranny that had swept the Colonies of the British Empire.

Dan asked Mr. Collier what he thought about setting up a law firm in the colony of New York. Mr. Collier told Dan his son would have a great interest in such a venture. Dan then introduced Mr. Collier to step two of his plan. Dan told Mr. Collier he wanted Weston to purchase a home in the more prominent area of New York for which Dan would provide the financial arrangements. Dan then revealed to Mr. Collier he also wanted to purchase a farm with approximately two hundred acres convenient in distance to the City of New York. He also disclosed to Mr. Collier to build a horse stable to care for at least one hundred Thoroughbred and Arabian horses. He asked Mr. Collier to build a facility that would provide a rest and entertainment area to provide for twenty-five military officers.

Dan then revealed his plan to set up a spy system to allow the loyalists' time to become convinced, by observing the spies on a daily basis, proving their loyalty to the Crown. He told Mr. Collier he was not certain who all the players will be because the stress of becoming a good infiltrator is not a game that some people enjoy playing. He said, "I hope and pray your son will have an interest in building a new nation."

Mr. Collier told Dan, "Weston is a most unusual young man. He has always enjoyed people. He has a sincere belief there is goodness in everyone, perhaps sometimes misguided but nevertheless some goodness. He told me recently some things about the cruelty the British have applied to some of their citizens that caused him to re-examine his theory of innate goodness in all men." He continued by telling Dan his son should return momentarily.

Dan took time to tell Mr. Collier how grateful he was for taking care of all the matters that had arisen in the management of the estate. Mr. Collier told Dan he had been with General O'Shea for so long, taking care of the O'Shea estate was no problem at all. Just as Mr. Collier finished his statement he heard a knock at the door. He went to the door and it was Weston, his son.

Mr. Collier told his son most all the information Dan had revealed to him. Weston was amazed that an opportunity of that nature and magnitude would be offered to someone his age and lack of experience. Weston told Dan he was uncertain whether he could perform at the level the duty would require. Dan agreed it would not be a duty that could be learned by trial and error because you only get one mistake. Dan asked Mr. Collier if he recalled the name of the Chief of Security that served with General O'Shea. Dan told them he had heard his father say many times the Colonel was the most talented person he had ever known. Mr. Collier told them his name is Colonel Fredricko De Longoria. Dan asked, "Do you think he will be available to train Weston? I am willing to make it worth his while." Mr. Collier said, "I am almost certain, if a revolution against the British does begin in America, I am positive Spain will support the Revolutionaries. It shouldn't take me long to contact him since he is another one of my military clients. I can let you know tomorrow what he has to say." Dan agreed to meet the next day, hopefully with Colonel Longoria.

Dan had stayed longer than he intended, but he knew many good things were about to begin. When he arrived at the mansion everyone had eaten the evening meal. Mary came to the kitchen to see to it her Dan did not go to bed hungry.

The next morning, he was up early to do some praying to ask God's intervention in his decision to select the right people to perform the task that was assigned to them. He had opened the door to General O'Shea's library to revisit some of the memories that had set him upon the road of becoming a warrior. Mary saw the door open and asked Dan if she could come in. Dan answered, "My lady, you can come and go into any room in our palace." Mary smiled and said,

"Dan are you real sure I am in the right place?" Dan said, "You fit this place perfect. This is where God intended for us to be." Mary said, "Dan I hope you are right because I love this home."

Dan told Mary he was expecting a message or visit from Mr. Collier today to wrap up some business before leaving for America. Mary told him she would tell him when Mr. Collier had arrived. About eleven thirty Mr. Collier, along with Weston and Colonel Longoria, had arrived. The butler walked them through the home to the library. Dan met them as they were coming toward the library entrance. Dan was very pleased the Colonel had responded to his request.

Dan asked the butler to bring lunch to the library when it was ready. Mr. Collier began the meeting by saying he had discussed the proposal with Colonel Longoria and his response was he would like to know more about the technicalities of the plan to set up a network of spies in the Colony of New York.

Dan began by telling the Colonel his knowledge of an armed rebellion is very limited but, it begins slow and builds momentum over a period of insults and disagreements before the hostility gets out of control. The Colonel agreed with Dan's analysis. Dan told the Colonel he expected the open hostility to begin in approximately two years. The Colonel agreed to Dan's calculations. Dan asked the Colonel whether he would entertain an offer to train agents in the art of espionage in behalf of the Revolutionaries before hostilities reach that point. The Colonel explained he had observed the British Empire arrogance for two decades and had felt for many years there would come a day when they would have to pay for the abuse of others. The Colonel also revealed his family had suffered some personal loses because of the British conscious indifference to human suffering.

Dan told the Colonel he would leave the financial arrangements up to Mr. Collier. He asked Weston if he had time to consider the proposal. Weston told Dan he was ready to begin. Dan told them he would stay in contact with them through Mr. Collier and he would be praying for their progress. They adjourned the meeting and went back to the main house and enjoyed a delicious meal.

Dan told them he was presently serving under General Oglethorpe in Georgia. He told the Colonel he was sure there would be others whom he would be sending for training. The Colonel told Dan he would produce a group of infiltrators that would make him proud. Dan told the Colonel General O'Shea's high regard for his ability.

By the time the other two ships arrived, Gregory had located the farm implements and other items they would need to begin a new life in America. Gregory really liked the idea of sending the cotton to Spain and other markets and shipping goods back to America. He had talked to Sam O'Keefe, Jr., telling him of the plan to ship cargo from America and ship cargo back to America on the three ships he and Dan owned. Sam Jr. told Gregory he could keep him busy, because he knew the merchants involved in shipping goods and receiving goods. They got the ships loaded in one day which included passage for some fellow travelers going to America. As they were drifting along on the open sea, Mary said, "Dan, this will be a voyage we will never forget. We will be telling our grandchildren about what we are doing right now. I have never been as excited about anything in my life. This is going to be so good for our family." Dan said, "I feel like we are headed toward our homeland. Mary, I want you and our family to be happy and safe. Mary, what do you know about what I do?" Mary said, "I have been told you are a person who protects other people, is that right?" Dan said, "That is exactly what I do, and I hope you understand, when some of our people get attacked by Indians or robbers or whomever, I will be asked to help them." Mary said, "That is wonderful." Dan said, "Sometimes it is and sometimes it is not, but the good part is, I fight at night when it is too dark for the enemy to see me."

They were having such an enjoyable time getting acquainted with one another. The three-month voyage was over too soon for them, because they had begun to have time to truly know one another's likes and dislikes. Mary was having such a good time as they pulled into the harbor, she whispered in Dan's ear, "You are going to be a daddy." Dan didn't know how to respond to her news, except stare out in space in wonder as to what being a father would be like. Mary was the happiest most recent arrival to America.

When the boat docked, Dan walked the gang plank with Mary in his arms, as he gently put her feet on American soil for the first time. General Oglethorpe had been told of Dan's arrival and he sent a carriage to meet them to bring them to his home. He was standing at the front gate as the carriage arrived. Dan was excited to introduce Mary to the General. Mary had dressed in her blue silk dress for the occasion. When the General saw Mary, he was taken by her Irish beauty and said, "Dan, this is the most gorgeous young lady. Is this one of your well-kept secrets?" As the General touched her hand, he said, "Mary, it is truly an honor and I want to be the first to welcome you to America." Mary in typical female Irish fashion took all the pomp and circumstance in stride, as she bowed her head to the General and said, "Thank you for being the one of God's servants to rescue my precious Dan. You will be forever in our prayers." Dan beamed with pride. He had no idea Mary possessed the polished qualities of culture she had displayed in greeting the General.

General Oglethorpe told Dan their bedroom was prepared for them to stay with him until other arrangements had been made. Dan told him how grateful he was for him to provide a plan for Mary to be comfortable. The General said, "Dan, there are so many things to discuss, I have decided to postpone all those matters until you have settled into some good rest." Dan agreed to the General's plan.

Dan had saved the meeting of Mary and his sister Maureen until the last of Mary's welcome to America. When they had unloaded the carriage, Maureen was there to carry their belongings to their bedroom. Dan said, "Mary this is a sister that I had not known existed until I found my family in the debtor's prison. Her name is Maureen and she is the youngest of our family."

Maureen had been a good student of Mrs. Oglethorpe teaching her proper English. As Maureen began speaking fluent English, Dan took note of how bright Maureen had to be to accomplish the language in such a short time. The two sisters-in-law adored one another immediately. Dan had a feeling that Mary would be well cared for during her pregnancy.

The next morning, Dan arose early, even before the cook had begun her day, which would include a pan of her famous biscuits for Dan. The General came to the kitchen shortly after Dan, wanting to get started on some matters of importance. As they talked, Dan felt compelled to inform the General of his becoming a God Grandparent in the very near future. The General was most happy to have another natural born American. The General began by telling Dan of a message he had received through his surveyor, who had done all the work on the subdivisions and boundaries of the Colony of Georgia. A relative of his had done the same kind of survey work in Pennsylvania that he had done in Georgia. His message to his relatives was, there had been a terrible Indian uprising in Pennsylvania in that, most of the land occupied by the settlers had been taken back from them by the Indians. The surveyor that works for the Colony of Georgia told his relative of your victory over Spain in Florida and suggested you be contacted to give them some relief. I suggested to him you would be the perfect choice. Dan said, "General, you are not aware of the farmers I brought with me, who are prepared to begin farming as soon as you approve their location." The General said, "This is wonderful news, where are they now?" Dan said, "I told one of your men to take them to where the other settlers are located." The General said, "Dan, I want to meet these people, let's eat a bite, and go get them started." The cook was ready when they walked to the table. She grinned when she put two of her biscuits on Dan's plate.

The General was glad to meet the O'Malleys and when he was told they had brought their own farm implements, he was more excited. Some of the immigrants were Scottish, and they seemed to know more of the requirements to being pioneers than the others. Gregory unloaded the cargo which was taken to the settlers who had begun to clear the land for homes to be built. The General was busy making the arrangements for the settlers to get started. Dan took Siobhann and Shibeal by to see their parents. He told them of his good fortune and for the first time in their lives, he was going to let them decide what they wanted to do.

Delia and Coleman didn't know how to respond to Dan's news and seeing their daughters, so Dan made it easy for them. He said, "Daddy, mama, you have seen the land in Carolina and you have seen this Georgia land. There is another tract of land in Florida, which we can go see when you are ready. After you have seen all the land, I want you to choose where you want to live, and we will build a house on it for you to raise your grandchildren." Coleman said, "Dan, I don't even want to see the land in Florida, because I know it can't be as good as the land in Carolina. What piece of land do you think we ought to try to work?" Dan said, "Daddy, I am thinking like you. I want to work the land that is best." Dan said, "If we take the Carolina land, there is so much of it, it will take five days to ride across it." Coleman said, "We are going to need some good help. What are we going to do?" Dan said, "Gregory O'Malley is now my father-in-law. I married his daughter, Mary. We own three ships. We can talk to him about getting as many Irish families as the three boats are able to carry and bring them to America." Coleman said, "I heard some folks are buying slaves to help farm." Dan said, "We have been slaves, and we have been prisoners, I don't want to own another man or imprison the innocent, that is not right before God and we are not going to use other people to make money for ourselves. We want what is fair and right to everyman." Coleman's face beamed with pride as he heard his son expressing the righteousness of God.

Dan said, "Mama, ya'll think about it. You and daddy, Siobhann and Shibeal will need to spend some time getting acquainted. I have got to get the O'Malleys and the others some farm stock, so they can get busy. Let me know when you are ready to ride to Carolina again. I will bring Mary by to see you. Dan had not heard from Lupe since he returned. He found him at the Ranger Headquarters and told him to gather the farm stock that was needed for the new farmers. Dan began to be concerned about Mary, while he was making his way to the General's home. When he arrived, much to his surprise, there was Mary sitting in the swing in the courtyard, reading a book. She was so glad to see him. He asked her if there was anything she needed. Mary said, "Dan, how could I ever ask for more than I already have?" Dan said, "Well, how do you like America?" Mary asked Dan "Is it as big as Ireland?" Dan said, "And more." Mary asked Dan, "How big is it really?" Dan said, "Mary, I am not sure, but I don't' think anyone really knows, but everyone agrees it is big enough for all the Irish families and every Scottish family in the world to have a place to call home." Mary said, "I didn't think any country was that big." Mary asked, "Where is my family?" Dan said, "Your father is at the docks unloading the ships and some of the others are at their land beginning to prepare to clear the land to build their homes. General Oglethorpe is getting the new settlers the correct piece of land."

Mary said, "Dan, has it occurred to you what is really going on?"" Dan asked, "In what way?" Mary said, "It seems like only a few days ago, we got on a ship and sailed to a piece of land called America. We are Irish Catholics, and in our homeland. We were prohibited from getting an education, having a profession, being a candidate for public office, being involved in trade or commerce, living in a corporate town or within five miles thereof, owning a horse worth more than five pounds, from leasing or owning land, from getting a mortgage on land, from voting, keeping arms for protection, holding a life annuity, purchasing land from a protestant, receiving a gift of land from a protestant, inheriting anything from a protestant, receiving rent for more than thirty shillings per year, from making a profit from the land of more than one third of value, being the guardian of a child, appointing a Catholic guardian of their child, attending a Catholic worship, and attending church of any kind but a protestant church, from educating a child, being taught by a Catholic teacher, and from sending a child abroad for education." Dan said, "Mary, I truly believe that part of our lives is over. I have been here for years and each year, I have observed in America, no one objects to us worshipping God in the manner we believe is right. This is a new place, new people, a new world with different attitudes toward everything, but, there is one thing I believe and that is, just because we don't have to hide all the time and sneak around to find food, that doesn't mean we can accept things as they are because we know it can and will get worse. We have got to push back and keep pushing back until we get King George III out of our lives. I will not rest until every British soldier is out of America. Somehow, I know there are others who feel the same as I do now, and others who are on their way from Ireland that think like I do. Most of us are from broken homes caused by the King of England. Our parents have been enslaved and imprisoned. We know the penalty for being disloyal to the King. My prayer is for safe passage to all those brave hearts who are crying out to be delivered from the boot heels of tyranny. May the winds be in their sails to bring them safely to this haven of the beginning of freedom for the entire world. And, may we have all found that place to lay our heads down in a sweet land of rest where we know we belong."

CHAPTER ELEVEN

TOWARD FREEDOM

After the Treaty with Spain had been signed, Dan's notoriety and fame had swept throughout the other colonies. He had become aware that some of the British officers stationed in the Carolinas had begun to seemingly go out of their way to have Dan's activities observed with a close eye.

But, Dan was busy with a series of thoughts he wanted to begin to explore. He decided a good visit with General Oglethorpe would be a good beginning, to determine which direction to direct his efforts. He arose early and to his surprise, General Oglethorpe was in the kitchen, in a mood that was not common to his usual demeanor. He began to disclose some of his concerns, regarding the Colony not developing as he had hoped. Dan said, "General, I woke up thinking of how I could bolster the process of getting more settlers to complete the development of the towns and the other common amenities, associated with a stable productive environment to become financially sound. I have a theory, and I would like to see if you agree with my thinking.

The Rangers have fallen into disarray since the Treaty has been signed. I am sure you agree, there are some very good soldiers in that group which, if we should come to need protection from whatever direction, they are highly skilled. In my opinion they need to function as a unit. With your permission, I was considering a thorough search for more soldiers to recruit to build up our military effectiveness." The General said, "Dan, you and I are thinking the same thought. Honestly, I do not know the status of the Rangers, but most of the group you had organized has moved on. There is talk some of the present Rangers are criminals, and that has caused me great concern for the settlers."

Dan said, "General, since I am going to be interviewing recruits for military purposes, I would like to expand my search to include prospective land owners for the Georgia land development. I am also thinking of paying the remaining debt owed by some of the indentured slaves to offer them an opportunity to own their own property." The General said, "Dan, I don't know how many you are planning on freeing from slavery, but that could be very expensive." Dan said, "General, when slavery is involved, no price is too high to pay a prisoner out of bondage. Jesus gave His life for us, to free us from the slavery and bondage of sin."

Dan continued, "General, I have asked Gregory O'Malley, my father-in-law, to bring as many Scottish and Irish families as he can to America." General Oglethorpe said, "Dan, you sound exactly like me talking to myself, when I was your age. Maybe that is why God has joined us together. While we are on that subject, there is one other matter you need to know. I am beginning to think of retiring and going back to England."

Dan was struck hard with the news he would be separated from a man who redeemed him from being shot and provided him a path toward freedom. Dan asked, "When do you have in mind leaving?" The General said, "Not anytime real soon." Dan said, "I am preparing to go to Pennsylvania, do you suppose I could trouble you for one more letter of passage to get me there without a problem?" The General laughed, "Dan, the way your popularity is growing, I will be asking you for a letter to travel very soon." Dan said, "I have no idea how soon I will need to recruit new personnel for the Ranger group, but, I will be trying to find farmers and get some worthy slaves released, so I will be around for a while." Dan said, "One more thing, do you want me to make other arrangements for Mary to reside?" The General said, "Dan, if you even thought of moving that precious young lady from our home, I'm afraid you and I would be headed toward a disagreement. You and Mary are what my wife and I call duplicated joys. Please, remove from your mind any concern for her being an inconvenience to us; your concern is not well founded. She will be well protected, as long as you have to be away."

Dan didn't realize the time had passed so quickly. Mary came walking into the kitchen to get a glimpse of Dan before he left. General Oglethorpe said, "It is time for me to dress for the day. I will see you again at breakfast." Dan stood up as the General left the room, and then he gave Mary the Dan smile he had created to make her day have a good beginning. He embraced her, to again reassure her of being in a place where concern for some British brute to come bursting through the door, would not, and could not happen. Dan could feel the tenseness of her body melt away, as he took time for his arms of safety to renew her reassurance. She wasn't dreaming, what she was feeling was real.

Dan asked her if she wanted orange juice or coffee. Mary said, "Milk, and warm it please, for some reason the baby seems to settle down when the milk is warmed in the morning." Dan smiled, because he knew that was a sign that his future might include a son who also liked warm milk. Dan and Mary had a most enjoyable morning together. She asked Dan what he had planned for the day. He told her he was going to the prisons, to recruit some soldiers to go to Pennsylvania to bring peace to return to the region. Mary asked, "Is that far away?" Dan said, "It is many days journey from here." Mary asked, 'When will you return?" He said, "In about three months." Mary said, "I want you to be here when the baby is born, if you can be." Dan said, "Mary, you and the baby are my number one priority. If I must ride night and day, I will do my best to be here."

Mary asked, "Dan, do you think I can get someone to take me to see my family, and your mother and father?" Dan said, "I don't think that would be a problem. You get dressed and I will have a carriage waiting." Dan saddled his horse, which was one of the prize Spanish War horses he had captured from the Spanish forts. He rode to the Ranger Headquarters to find Lupe. He was there waiting for Dan. Dan said, "Lupe, I need to go by to see mama and daddy to tell them Mary will be by for a visit. Can you get someone to take a carriage to take her visiting?" Lupe told Dan he would take care of it.

Dan felt there was no time like the present to tell the remaining Rangers he was organizing a troop to go to Pennsylvania to settle some problems that had arisen between the Colonists and the Indians. He explained he would not accept anyone who was opposed to night fighting. Dan could tell from the response some of them had not been trained to the standards he required to be considered. He asked to speak to John Milledge, Jr. Lieutenant Milledge stepped forward. Dan said, "Do you mind if I speak to you privately?" The Lieutenant answered, "No Sir." While Dan was visiting with him, he asked the Lieutenant a question, which was, "Lieutenant, if there is a war declared against King George, which side of the conflict would you support?" The Lieutenant said, "Mr. O'Flaherty, you don't know me. I know you know my father. But, I want you to know, I was born in America. I was not born in Ireland. I have heard some of the harm the King of Great Britain has done to my ancestors, and I am ready to put an end to the English rule over us." Dan said, "John, I am putting together a private group of the best warriors in this country, and the basic requirement is, every member of our team has to understand regardless of who we are fighting, whether we are fighting Indians, Spaniards or any other culture, we are together for one purpose, and that is to kill, maim and run every red coated British soldier off of American soil. I am committed to pledge my life and my fortune to that purpose. We can begin now to have a fighting force like none other. Do you want to be a Captain in that Army?" John, Jr., was more excited than he had ever been before. He had felt some of Dan's words in his heart, but he had never heard them said. Dan said," John, they have killed enough of Ireland's children and parents. Now, we have a battlefield for warriors to show them what war is all about." Dan said, "Come on, I want to go see my mama and daddy and then I want to head for the slave camps, to provide a taste of some good old American freedom to a hungry bunch of Irishmen, who will like the taste when they are set free."

When they arrived at his parents' home, Lupe was there waiting on the porch with Coleman, drinking coffee. Lupe hollered, "Who you got with you?" Dan said, "A stray I picked up between here and the barn." John was a very serious-minded young man, but even he laughed.

Dan hugged his mother and introduced John Milledge, Jr, to her and his father. They said, "Come rest awhile." Dan said, "Mama, I came by to tell you, Mary is coming for a visit with you and her family. We are going to the prison and slave camps to see if there is anyone there who wants to be set free." Dan then said, "Daddy, I am going to be tied up for a while. Why don't you get General Oglethorpe's driver to take you and mama to that land we went to see? You can ask Mary if she wants to ride with you. I didn't find the road all that bad." Delia said, "I'll ask her when she gets here, that sure sounds good to me, daddy, what do you think?" Coleman said, "I have had that land on my mind since we left it, I would love to see it again."

Dan, Lupe and Captain John rode off to the slave camps. When they arrived, he knew the warden and was free to ask him any questions about the inmates. He told the warden he needed to find some good young men of Irish or Scottish decent, to help him put down an Indian uprising. The warden said, "Two weeks ago, we received a boat load of just the kind of men you described, but they have seven years of debt to pay for their passage." Dan asked, "Could I talk to them while I am here?" The warden said, "That can be arranged."

The warden led the prisoners to a grove of trees away from the walls of the prison. Dan asked them to sit or stand while he told him his purpose. Dan told them he was putting together a force of fighting men who would be trained to fight Indians at night. He told them it would be a permanent group. He also explained to them their authority would come from the Colonies that needed their service. He then asked them, "If a war occurred between the Colonists and the English, which side would you support?" There was dead silence.

Finally, a huge robust Scotsman said, "I will not fight for England." Then, a muffled mumble began to be uttered by every one of the men that was, "I will not fight for King George!" Dan said, "And I won't either!" Then Dan said, "Has anyone here lost a family member since England has ruled Ireland?" Every hand was raised. Dan then asked, "Has anyone's relatives been put in prison, while under the British rule?" All the hands were raised. Dan said, "I became an orphan when I was six, and have just now found my family. I want the opportunity to live in a nation that will protect us from foreign invaders and will guarantee our families will stay together." Everyman said, "Me too!" An Irishman very close to Dan's size asked, "How do we pay our passage to get out of this slave camp?" Dan said, "That can be arranged." Suddenly, there was a hush fell over them as one of the prisoners prayed, "Thank you God, for our deliverance. May we walk in the path of freedom, all the days of our lives. Amen."

Dan walked with the group to the warden's office and asked him the amount of the passage to free all the men. The warden told Dan, "One thousand pounds." Dan said, "I am handing you fifteen hundred pounds, if you will deliver these men and their baggage to Ranger Headquarters near General Oglethorpe's home." Dan said, "Before we separate, I want every one of you to understand, I have not told you that you are now free men under British law. I am telling you, you are free men. You now have a chance to choose your own path you do not have to become a Ranger. You are free to go wherever you so desire. I am not a slave owner. I want you to be free. If you want to join with us, the warden will supply you with a ride. If you want to go somewhere else, go. If you do go to the Ranger Headquarters, I will see you one day this week."

Captain John Milledge Jr. was very interested in the way Dan handled his business. The one common factor of all the Irish people was, they had all learned to submit to authority, under the hand of King George. That God given will to have fire in each word of anger, and the sweetness in each word of love had been trampled out of their souls by the boot heels of the enemy of the poor.

The warden at the next prison was glad to see Dan. When Dan asked the question about the Scottish and Irish inmates he responded in the same manner as the other warden. This particular group of prisoners was dominated by Scotsmen. It numbered over fifty men. Dan asked to be allowed to visit with the prisoners privately to which the warden obliged his request. When Dan was through visiting with the men, every man joined in the Special Forces group. The warden was paid in full for their passage and delivery. Dan, Lupe and Captain John, Jr., were well pleased with the fact their numbers were over one hundred warriors. Six of the officers who had previously served with the Rangers joined up with Dan.

When Dan had put his team together, he needed clothes for each man to have a change and a suit to wear. Dan thought about having the Ranger quartermaster order some uniforms, but then he thought of the suspicion it would cause in the British command. Dan then decided to talk to some of the Irish and Scottish women who were skilled at sewing and let them get cloth and make uniforms for the men designed to fit each man individually. It didn't take much inquiry to locate some Irish and Scottish women anxious to make some extra money.

The next morning, Dan received a big surprise when he learned every man he had met at the prison remained with the group.

The next issue was the training Dan was going to put them through would be most difficult. Most of the men were half starved. Dan began the routines with good food and light exercise. As their weight began to increase, he increased the exercise.

In one month, it was a sight to behold. Dan could tell that quenched anger had begun to surface in each man, as they began to increase the value of their food intake. Dan made sure they were eating as much pork and beef as they could hold. As the group progressed, Dan became more and more convinced he had a group of warriors that would become victorious, regardless of the talents and skills of the enemy.

All that was left for Dan to do was teach them how to quietly dispose of the enemy and stay alive. Dan reminded himself of how the Scottish soldiers, in order to be the type fighters he needed, must overcome their tendency to charge head long to crush their enemy with one blow. Dan taught them by teaching them that dead is all the enemy has to be. Mangled and brutalized was completely unnecessary when all you must do is make the enemy stop breathing. Dan loved the art of throwing knives and tomahawks. He was the best of the best, with swords, and required each man to know how to win with a sword.

Dan told the men he had begun to learn that other rifles were available besides the one known as "Brown Bess." The rifle was a smooth bore which fired a single shot ball, or a cluster shot and fired multiple objects as that of a multi-ball shot gun. There were two variations of the "Brown Bess," the short land pattern, and the long pattern, the short land was shorter, less bulky, and less heavy than the long land pattern. [(6)]

Dan also told the men, "We are going to be fitted with the most modern equipment money can buy. All you have to learn is how to use it." He also told them they would begin with the "Brown Bess," and learn what there is to know about the bayonet. He told them to keep in mind, "The English and Indians sleep at night and that is when we do our hunting."

When the troops had completed the training to the level of Dan's approval, Dan was ready to begin the journey to Pennsylvania. He assigned three of the scouts to keep accurate maps of the areas they would travel through from the south to the north. He said, "There will come a day, when we will have to know this land better than our enemies."

Dan decided to go on to Pennsylvania while the troops were in their best form. He planned on taking another fifty extra Spanish War horses for spares. They were going to be headed due north to a settlement known as Charlotte, North Carolina. General Oglethorpe had supplied them with British maps of Carolina and Virginia. From what they could tell, the best route was due north all the way to Pennsylvania. Dan wanted to be most careful to map every minor detail which would, in the future be the foundation to save some American lives and become the foundation of victory over the British.

The whole company was looking forward to being on their first survey of America. They were excited to learn more about this land that was becoming so near and dear to them. General Oglethorpe said, "Dan, before you leave, there is one thing I would like to discuss with you, it shouldn't take too long."

Dan followed the General into his study and pulled his chair up next to the desk. The General began by saying, "Dan, I am about to break an oath I made years ago to a very dear friend named Lawrence Washington, whom I came to know in my early years of military service. Whether you know anything about Masonry, I don't know, but we were both members of the Masonic Lodge. In the early years of Georgia, I established a Masonic Lodge known as Solomon's Lodge No. F & A.M. which is, the first Lodge of Free Masonry in the Western Hemisphere. (3) When the lodge had its first ceremony, Lawrence Washington attended. After the ceremony, we shared many of our thoughts, and we found we had many matters of life in common.

Through the years, we have corresponded frequently. When his father died, he left a son who was his half-brother, named George Washington. The young man's mother was an unusually obdurate and was what Lawrence determined to be a threat to a very capable and talented young man. When George was fourteen, he moved in with his brother, Lawrence, in a home named Mount Vernon, which was named in honor of a British Admiral who commanded an expedition in South America. During the expedition, Lawrence was promoted to the rank of Captain. (7) After George moved into the home at the age of fourteen, Lawrence contacted me requesting me to become the executor of his estate, if he died while George was under the age of twenty-one. I agreed not only to become his guardian; I also agreed to provide a home for him. None of those conditions ever came to pass, but I have kept in close contact with George, since Lawrence died. George has always wanted to become a British officer. I did everything I knew how to do to get that commission for him, but I failed, because George was not born in England. He was born in America and the British Command would not accept him into their league of British arrogance. I advised him to continue to serve the colonies in the capacity of a military officer. George is a good soldier and has not been treated honestly by the British Command. George is an unusual man and I want you to know him. I am going to hand you a letter of introduction, I want you to deliver to him personally. If you will recall a few years ago, I told you I had received a word from Pennsylvania, inquiring about someone to defend the settlers against Indian attacks. That letter was sent to me by George Washington, my God son. I am wanting very much for you two men to meet one another."

Dan said, "I really appreciate you telling me about your connection with him. I will know how to respond to him when we meet. I am also looking forward to learning the terrain between here and Pennsylvania." The General said, "Dan, I have a feeling George will talk to you about America, and I want you to know, I think like he thinks. We agree on most everything concerning America." Dan said, "General, I do not know anything about politics. I am just a warrior." The General said, "That is exactly the reason I want the two of you to meet one another." Dan began to know there were others who were beginning to think the same as he was thinking. Dan was even more excited about the journey. He felt it was for a purpose he could not fully understand.

Dan rode to the Ranger Headquarters, where the men were ready to leave. They had on their new uniforms in a beautiful pale blue, under the flag of the Blue Celts. There was a pride in the eyes of every one of the troops that gave Dan a certainty they would be outstanding soldiers. Dan looked at Captain John and said, "Move them out, Captain." In one week, they were halfway through the

Northern part of Carolina. One afternoon, Dan decided it was time for a break. He began looking for a good place to clean up and have some fun. He located a lake not far from the road that seemed to be the right size to clean 123 Scottish and Irish soldiers. Dan began thinking, *if a revolt against King George III did break out; it would be many years before the conflict became resolved.* With that in mind, and the Indian wars confronting him, he wanted to get to know each man better. His goal was to mold the unit into the best unconventional fighting force ever to walk on a battlefield. Dan had been taught by the best warrior of Spain, and he would not shame him by walking away from a battle defeated.

After three hours of scrubbing, wrestling, rough housing and bleeding, it was time for a break. They were stretched out under some shade trees and it wasn't long before an afternoon nap had begun. When they awoke some good food was ready to be served. They thought the day was complete until William McIntosh, the biggest of the lot, quietly took a bagpipe out of his wrappings, and began to blow a tune that soon touched the Celtic heart of all those who longed for the Highlands, the lowlands, the mountains, and the valleys of home. A silence fell as Big Bill touched the chords that brought the tears to every heart. When he had closed the sounds of some memories long past, Dan said, "Big Bill, give me a jig, and let me see if I can keep up." Bill played one common to all the men. Before he blew the last note, every soldier had joined in the unity the sounds had brought forth. Dan had the opportunity to revisit those precious days of seeing his mother spread her arms to reach for him, to give him a whirl of joy in a world of violence and anguish. No matter how bad and violent it became, he had his mother to hold. As the sun began to set, and when it did, every eye lid had closed yesterday into the past as a day to remember.

After they had eaten the next morning, they set out again in search of a man named, Washington. Dan thought to himself, *surely, he would be familiar with the Indian problems in Pennsylvania and could advise him whether to become involved.*

As the troops entered Virginia, Dan and two of the scouts began to become aware of the shod hoof prints; it was obvious the tracks were made by military ridden horses. At about noon the rear guard rode up to Dan and reported a group of English soldiers on horseback were approaching. Dan slowed the pace to give the troop time to catch up. When they did, Dan quickly counted approximately fifty men. The captain leading the troops rode up beside Dan and told him to stop. Dan obliged his command. The British officer confronted Dan, by inquiring who they were, and what was their reason for traveling in the direction of Pennsylvania? Dan told him he had been summoned to the Commonwealth to provide protection of the settlers. The officer then asked him, "By what authority he had assembled the brigade?" Dan opened the envelope and showed the officer his letter of authority signed by General Oglethorpe. When the officer saw the General's signature, his attitude began to change, and he quickly turned his troop and rode away; a short while later, the men were on their way to a place named, Mount Vernon. As they rode along, the people they saw were most friendly to the troop, as if they welcomed a color besides the red coats, the British wore.

General Oglethorpe had shown Dan the map location of the Washington home on the banks of the Potomac River. He changed his path to a northeastern direction toward Maryland. Dan began to realize just how beautiful America was, as they traveled toward a settlement, which was becoming a town known as Richmond. Dan's mind stayed focused on every rise and hollow. Somehow, he knew he was on ground that would someday yield freedom or death. Before they reached Mount Vernon, they selected a camp site some distance from the Washington home.

The next morning, Dan and Captain John Jr., arose early and were on the road before all the others woke up. Within an hour, they arrived at the home and a tall man of distinction came to the door and asked, "May I help you?" Dan answered, "Well, Sir, I hope so. My name is Dan O'Flaherty O'Shea, and I was sent to your home by General James Oglethorpe." The man put forth his hand with an obvious gladness and said, "I am Colonel George Washington."

The two men stood and looked at one another with an amazed smile. Both had wondered, *whether they would ever actually meet one another.* The Colonel welcomed Dan in his home with great exuberance with the comment, "I hope you haven't eaten breakfast, Martha will be disappointed if you have." Dan asked Captain John Jr., to remain with the horses, while he visited with Colonel Washington.

CHAPTER TWELVE

UNEXPECTED PLAN

Dan could tell as he walked through the Washington's home, some deep tracks had been made on the floors. Dan had an immediate trust for Colonel Washington he had experienced in very few other men. He possessed a genuine sincerity with humility that expressed his skill at having mastered self with the utmost discipline. Even though Dan was ten years his senior, and excelled in the knowledge of war, he was most impressed with his presence. Dan thought to himself, *that is the kind of man Scots and Irish will follow all the way.*

Colonel Washington escorted Dan to the back yard, on the bank of the Potomac River. Close to the bank of the river, was a huge oak tree with a table and some chairs. It was evident many prayers had been prayed with Washington's eyes looking to the east. The Colonel said, "So, you are General Oglethorpe's guardian angel he has written me so much about?" He said, "Dan I don't think there are any descriptive words left to use to describe the magnitude of esteem the General has for you. The story I liked the most was the fort you captured with cottonmouth moccasins. After he sent me that letter, I went to the history books and learned you are the only commander who ever won a victory with snakes." As they continued visiting, they looked up, and down the lane from the backdoor, came the Colonel's beautiful wife, Martha. Dan was introduced as the Commander,

General Oglethorpe described, as defeating Spain. With that statement, Dan did blush to some extent. Martha asked, "Dan, what do you prefer for breakfast?" Dan said, "Whatever you normally feed the Colonel, will please me." She said, "Give me a few minutes." Dan said, "Please, my Lady, take your time."

Colonel Washington told Dan how much he appreciated him making such a trip. He said, "I had hoped to find time to come to Georgia, but Dan, to tell the truth, there is trouble everywhere I go." Dan said, "Colonel, you mentioned in one of your letters to General Oglethorpe, there is an Indian problem in Pennsylvania." The Colonel said, "Dan, I don't know if you know, but I am a land surveyor. Sometime back, I was asked to go to Pennsylvania by some land speculators to survey land they thought they had purchased from the Penn brothers. When we went to the land to subdivide the property, I found the land occupied by an Indian tribe. It was evident to me the tribe had been on the property for a long period. After a meeting or two with the Penn brothers, after which, we visited with some other innocent purchasers, I decided it was too complicated for me. In fact, I haven't been back, and do not intend to return. Dan said, "At first I thought you wanted General Oglethorpe to send me to Pennsylvania to prevent harm to the settlers." The Colonel said, "I am so glad you came by here first. That place is nothing but trouble. It reminds me of a spot where every thief in the country showed up to sell land that did not belong to them. At that point, Martha hollered from the back door, "It's ready." Dan enjoyed a wonderful meal and when they finished eating, at the suggestion of Colonel Washington, they went back to the tree to complete their visit.

The Colonel said, "Dan, the real reason I wanted to meet you was to share some thoughts and possibly a vision I have been having recently. There is unrest among the colonists as to the King of England regarding America as a slave camp for the Royal elitists' financial interests of Great Britain. I don't think the Crown has kept up with the number of immigrants that has flooded the shores of America, because of the royal abuse of every culture, with the exception of the chosen few. The English-German mixed breed King had come to view Australia and America as places to deposit the less sophisticated of Great Britain and profit by the labor of them as debtor slaves who work the fields of the King's friends. The law the King has approved is for the purpose of exterminating those who practice religion other than that which is approved by the Crown. Ireland and Scotland are the cultures who are suffering the most. The English law has caused the immigrants from Ireland to exceed all other cultures that come into America, most of which is the result of slave trade caused by the passage of the Penal Laws. America has become the New Ireland and Scotland because of religious persecution and slavery because of greed. Some have agreed to work for as many as seven years without pay for passage fare."

The Colonel continued telling Dan some of the information he had learned by listening to citizens of the colonies express their distaste for England. Colonel Washington said, "Dan, what I have observed is, once the Irish and Scottish come to America and get food in their stomachs, they are ready to finish the job of getting any submission to the Crown, out of their lives. They want to be free, but no one knows the kind of government to put in its place, without some Monarch or Sheik or whatever else they call themselves, telling them what to do next. As for me, and my family, I don't want anyone standing between me and God, telling and demanding me to do what they think is right. I think I can figure out what is right for me and my family without asking a Monarch, three thousand miles away from here that earned his job by his mother being bred by some King. Right now, as I see it, the knowledge and experience of the abuse and knowledge of the extermination laws the Irish and Scottish have brought to this nation will eventually develop into a revolt. My family and I are supporting those who want to reject an English Monarch from ruling our lives. There are many voices speaking out against British rule. My question to you is, what side will you support?" Dan said, "Colonel, at the age of six years, because of British law, I was taken from my mother and father's arms. My brother and sister were over the age of six years and they were shipped to the slave camps in America. I was handed to a cousin by my mother who provided for me for several years. I had two sisters younger than me that was covertly placed in the hands of some distant cousins, and because of that, probably saved their lives. Since I located my parents in a slave camp, I learned my parent had another child. I was later adopted by a Spanish General named Phillip O'Shea and his wife, Margarita. I was raised in an elite Spanish military environment. My adoptive father was a Spanish General, who had been decorated by the King of Spain, with that country's highest honors. He was the originator of the Special Forces in Spain, which was a complete deviation from conventional warfare tactics. He was injured in a most unfortunate accident at a young age and was forced to retire from military service. My adoptive mother was in the line of succession to become the Queen of Spain. She abdicated her position in the line of succession, to marry my father. She was the sister to Bernardo De Galvez, who was also a Spanish military leader who now lives in Louisiana and is a patriot and supporter of the Continental government. He became an officer in the Army of Spain at an early age. He went to Mexico to fight the Indians. He received many battlefield promotions and wounds from battlefield injuries. After he returned to Spain, we became well acquainted through my mother who loved him very much. He and I became acquainted because he enjoyed the sword and we worked together to improve our skills in the art. He was sent to France when he became fluent in the language which will serve him well when he becomes Colonial Governor of Louisiana. (12) I have graduated from the most elite military academy in Spain. I was involved in the Jacobite War in 1745 and was captured by General Oglethorpe. He took me prisoner and brought me to America to defend against the Spanish attacks on the settlers of Georgia. We organized a group of night fighters, which are named, the Rangers. He placed me in Command of that group, and we became successful in defeating the Spanish takeover of Georgia and Carolina. I have no regard at all for the tactics of conventional warfare. My training is infiltration of the enemy with scouts and spies to eliminate all that can be eliminated in the dark, by surprise, if possible.

I have put together a permanent force of Irish and Scottish fighters, which I have brought with me in case we were needed in Pennsylvania. They are camped down the road toward Richmond. While we are here, I would like for you to meet them." The Colonel said, "How about now?" Dan said, "When you are ready, I will meet you in front." Colonel Washington mounted his horse and within a short time, he was meeting a group of Scottish and Irish soldiers that impressed him as being well trained troops.

When the Colonel had completed meeting with each one of the men, he took some more time to again visit with Dan. Dan had brought Colonel Washington more relief militarily than he had received from any other source. The Colonel asked Dan, "Which way are you going?" Dan said, "Colonel, I have learned of some gunsmiths in Pennsylvania that have modified a rifle that can shoot over three hundred yards. I intended to meet them and examine their work." The Colonel said, "I have examined the rifle you are referring to and there is a problem in the reloading procedure. Also, the weapon requires extensive training to master the rifle's maximum capability."

Dan explained to the Colonel, the stoic fixed, placed soldier is a perfect target for a man at three hundred yards distance. Dan said, "Colonel the two elements of warfare that works for a Special Force unit is, surprise and fire power. If we have a weapon that can hit a target at three hundred yards, two hundred rifles can kill twenty-four hundred enemy troops every hour and never have a casualty."

When Colonel Washington heard that statement, he was taken back. He had never thought completely through of what a sniper can do to a company of soldiers who are marching in an open field. As they talked, Colonel Washington began to look at the possibilities in an entirely different manner. Colonel Washington said, "Dan I told the Continental Congress the weapons were too expensive." Dan said, "Colonel, I want you to remember these words, as the war begins to take more time than you have planned, you are going to need fresh troops. There may be a time when there are no more troops available. If that situation arises, remember this tactic, get in and out as fast as you possibly can, with the most firepower, and you will win." Colonel Washington said, "Dan, the Colonies cannot withstand a long war. They do not have the money." Dan said, "Colonel, I am going to make a statement that is only for you to hear. I want your oath on it, to never repeat what I am going to tell you." The Colonel said, "You have my word." Dan said, "When your other sources have failed, you can call on me for whatever you need, you will have the money and you will have the protection." The Colonel thought to himself, *that is the largest statement I have ever heard a man say.* Then Dan said, "When I finish in Pennsylvania, I intend to return to Georgia, if there isn't something else that happens. I want to be with General Oglethorpe, as he prepares to retire." The Colonel said, "Dan, I have never enjoyed a visit in my life, as much as I have with you. I can now see General Oglethorpe's opinion of you is well placed." Dan said, "Colonel, America is the only hope the Irish and Scottish have to remain alive with any kind of dignity. We have come to this place for one purpose and that is to give our all, to be free from the cruelty of government. The only government that is trustworthy is a government that recognizes the equality of all the citizens."

Dan rode back to Mount Vernon to tell Mrs. Washington of his appreciation for her hospitality, and again he told Colonel Washington of his gratitude for the time he was granted to visit. Dan intended to write a letter to Mr. Collier advising him of his visit with Colonel Washington and the necessity to move forward with the plan they had discussed. Dan did not realize that Mr. Collier and Weston had already made arrangements to purchase the property they had discussed because Weston had made unbelievable progress in advancing his skills as a spy.

Mr. Collier purchased a residence and was in the process of completing a Retreat Center in conjunction with the horse farm to entertain the British officers. Mr. Collier had notified him after he had left Georgia on his way to inspect the rifles and meet George Washington. He would learn of the progress when he returned to Georgia. Since Dan would not have the availability to send the dispatch to Mr. Collier, he asked Colonel Washington to send the letter for him. He told Colonel Washington, "This is a notice to my attorney in Spain of the authority I have given you to fund whatever you deem necessary." Colonel Washington said, "Dan, I like to be involved with men who know how to do what needs doing. I am proud to know we are fighting together," Dan saluted the Colonel and directed his troop toward Pennsylvania.

Dan constantly urged the map makers to use their best skills to make the maps for a later use. After visiting with some residents of Pennsylvania, he was directed to the manufacturers of what was called, "The Pennsylvania Rifles." He met with the gun makers who were anxious, to demonstrate their craft. Dan had the entire troop observe the details of the use of the weapon. He did not want to buy guns the men would not use. After they had visited with each gunsmith, he decided to delay the decision to purchase the rifles until the next day to make sure everyone had their say about the weapons. After breakfast the next morning, he wanted to have everyone in the discussion. After listening to their comments, he decided to take Lupe, Captain John Jr., and a Sergeant to fire the weapon. The gunsmiths were glad to supply a place to fire the weapons. Dan had each man fire the weapon. Each one of the men were excellent marksmen. The discussion was to purchase two hundred of the weapons, so long as no one knew of the purchase. The gunsmiths agreed. Dan asked when they would be ready, and they agreed on a date. All the men continued to be amazed at America. The size, the beauty, the freedom, even though they were under the royal thumb, no one tried to arrest them, the longer they stayed, the more each man became involved in wanting to learn more about everything in America.

Some of the men began to talk to Dan about, "How can all these different nationalities live in the same country?" Dan was baffled at how much thinking they were doing, as they each began to lay an emotional claim to America. Loving a country was an emotion none of them ever had before. Each man had begun to think about, *their families and the possibility of having land and not depending on anyone for anything.* The more they thought, *the more they began to express their desire to take the land away from England, and they were not by themselves.* As the private discussions became public, some men of respect and public stature began to openly express disagreement with the Crown being in control of their business.

As they rode along the map makers continued to describe the terrain and Indian locations for future map references. Dan decided he needed to separate himself from the troop to ride through the hidden valleys and settler locations. As he left the troop, he placed Captain Milledge in charge and told him to take their time and get acquainted with the settlers, when possible, to get a better understanding of the feel of the people toward English dominance. Dan wanted to take his time learning the locations of all the forts and camps of the enemy. He changed his clothes to have the appearance of a settler to try to go unnoticed. As he traveled west, he began to find Indian villages that had not been disturbed by the land grabbers. He became acquainted with every tribe whose land he crossed.

After he saw that Indian Territory would not be a part of the battleground, he turned back east. The further he traveled the more he saw evidence of military horse hoof prints, indicating British scouting patrols were active in the region. As he moved along, he noticed a herd of wild hogs and it reminded him he had not had fried pork in weeks. The gunsmith in Pennsylvania had let Dan buy one of the rifles to use, while the others were being manufactured. Dan thought, *this is the time for me and this new weapon to get well acquainted.* He was two hundred fifty yards from the herd which was the perfect distance for a sniper shot. He leveled down on a half-grown pig that appeared to have been getting more than her share of acorns and fired. The others scattered, but there lay Dan's prospect for fresh pork ham, ready to be butchered. He decided it was time to rest awhile, because he had meat, a clear running creek for water, and a desire to be alone with God, to remember. *all the complicated tear-filled paths that had led him to this place.* He said, to himself, *I am going to sleep clean and full tonight.* When dawn began to break, he drank some coffee and finished eating the fresh pork he had for supper, to prepare for the new day.

As he was cinching his saddle, he heard a noise coming through the brush. The camp smoke had been blowing toward the north. In about five minutes, three British soldiers rode up, and began asking him about a shot that was heard the evening before. Dan said, "That was me. I killed some camp meat for supper. There is some left if you want it." The British soldier doing the talking asked, "What kind of weapon did you use to kill the pig?" Dan said, "Mine." The British officer became brusque in his tone toward Dan. and demanded to see his weapon. Dan could tell he was again faced with the reality of being under the control of British rule. By that time, the other two men had dismounted and began walking closer to Dan getting ready to cause damage.

Dan very calmly asked, "What is this all about?" The officer asked, "Where are you from?" Dan said, "Originally, from Ireland." The officer asked, "Are you a Catholic?" Dan said, "I am." The officer ordered the two men to take Dan into custody. Dan asked, "On what charge?" The officer said, "You know a Catholic cannot possess a weapon." Dan said, "This is not Ireland. This is America." The officer said, "You are under the same King." Dan said, "I am not under any King. I am an American." When Dan said that, the officer said, "Treason, take him!" Dan drew his sword. The three soldiers drew their swords. In an effort to keep from killing them, he decided to wound them severely. He started by marking their faces. Then he decided to put some holes in their upper arms. Within ten minutes the soldiers were on their knees begging for mercy.

Dan said, "The worst part of your ignorance is, I have a letter in my pocket signed by General James Oglethorpe authorizing my passage anywhere in the Colonies. I have also been awarded the Ribbon of Freedom by your King George III for defending Georgia from attack by Spain. It appears you have two choices. You can fail to report this encounter, or you can report it and let the two Generals decide whether a Catholic like me can possess a weapon. I am going to help each one of you on your horse. From now on, it would be wise for you to not make up your mind about a person who practices the Catholic faith. It would be wiser to find out who they are. The officer asked, "Who are you?" The response was, "I am Dan

O'Flaherty O'Shea, an Irish Catholic who has come to America to create the birth place of freedom for the whole world." The brash British officer said, "When we meet again, Dan O'Flaherty O'Shea, be prepared to die." Dan said, "Sir, you need some more training by the better man before you lick your wounds." The two other soldiers had enough of Dan's training and rode off to avoid more of Dan's wrath. The officer said, "I will see you hang for this." Dan said, "It is a real shame I am not closer to home because if I were, I think I would take you home as a trophy of the most absolutely stupid beast I have ever encountered."

Dan said a silent prayer as he rode away from the hatred he had just encountered; asking God to, *show our people the way, Oh God, to take this land from these Godless creatures.* It had become time for him to head toward his darling, Mary. He had promised her to be present when the baby was born if he could. Dan was anxious to see his family again, to give them a report of some more of the America they were beginning to claim as their own. It took Dan another week to get back to Georgia. It was late evening when he arrived. As he was putting his horse in the barn, he heard a familiar voice saying, "Dan, is that you?" Dan stopped and said, "Yes, Mam, it is me." He could hear Mary giggling as she came toward him. Dan was half through unsaddling the horse and turned to run to meet her. He had never in his life experienced coming back to someone who was waiting for him to return. He had begun to know the true meaning and depth of the Gaelic words, "Le Ceile" meaning together and "Godeo" meaning forever. Dan knew no other language spoken by any other culture that could touch the depth of meaning of the two words spoken in Gaelic because it was the language of the spirits of all the centuries that spoke those same words to continue the communication with God Himself.

The O'Flahertys intended to keep the connection their families had known with the Almighty with themselves and through their children's children. Mary began telling Dan about what was feeling like another Celtic warrior. Mary said, "Dan, sometimes I think he is already mad about something. I know I haven't done anything to upset him." Dan said, "You know Mary, some of us are born to fight. It could be, he is one of us." Dan said, "When do you think it will be?" Mary said, "My mother says it should be just after the next moon change." Dan said, "About ten days?" Mary said, "That feels close, if not sooner." They went to the house hoping to see the General, but he was at the settlement attending a meeting. Dan said, "I am worn down. I bet you are too. Let's see if we can find a cool breeze somewhere and rest awhile." The last words Dan heard Mary say was, "I hope it is a boy, like his daddy."

The next morning, after breakfast, and a chat with the General to give him an update on George Washington, Dan was ready to see his parents. The General gave him a letter from Mr. Collier. The letter brought Dan up to date on the progress in New York. The weather was unusually hot when he arrived at their home. His father was on the porch sharpening a hoe. When he saw Dan, he hollered, "Look whose here!" Delia came outside ready to hold Dan in her arms again. He was so blessed to have them with him after all the years of torment and loneliness. Dan got a chair for his mother and they began talking about his journey north. Dan told them he went through several colonies and had breakfast with George Washington on the banks of the Potomac River. He also told them he felt a revolt building everywhere he went. He said, "Mama, I think the Irish people want to run the King out of America." Delia said, "I hope they do." Dan asked, "Mama, did you and daddy go back to Carolina to look at the land?" Delia said, "Yes, we did, and we are more confused now than we were when we went the first time." Dan asked, "Why?" Delia said, "There is so much of it, we don't know where to start." Dan laughed and said, "Why don't we look at it like this?" The first thing we need is a place to live." Coleman asked, "Well, where are you going to live?" Dan said, "I'm going to be living in Carolina, close to you and mama. Do you want a place with hills or do you want to live in the bottom land? I'm thinking all the land is good for farming, daddy, am I right?" Coleman said, "It's all good dirt for cotton or whatever grows the best." Dan asked, "Are we going to raise cotton?" Coleman said, "I think we need to raise the best money crop." Dan said, "I do too." Dan said, "Mama what do you think?" Delia said, "I agree."

Dan asked, "Have you met any of the new folks that have moved in lately?" Delia said, "I have met some of the ladies." Dan said, "What we need is a good carpenter to start us some houses." Coleman said, "I met a man last week that said, he knows how to build houses." Dan said, "Sounds like he is the man we need to talk to. Where does he live?" Coleman said, "Not far." Dan said, "Let's go talk to him." Coleman said, "Let me get my boots." Dan asked his father, "Do we need a horse to get there?" Coleman said, "No, we can walk."

When they found the man's cottage, his wife told them he was in the back working on the barn. They walked around to the back and met, Tom Rowe. Dan said, "Mr. Rowe, we need at least two houses built in Carolina just across the river." Mr. Rowe said, "That shouldn't be a problem, because I have bought lumber from a sawmill in South Carolina." Dan said, "Our property is located south of a settlement called Augusta, Georgia, just across the Savanah River, near a settlement called Barnwell." Mr. Rowe said, "That's where I get my lumber." Dan asked, "When can you get started?" Mr. Rowe said, "Whenever you are ready." Dan asked, "How much do you charge?" Mr. Rowe said, "Let's don't talk about the money, until you see me work." Dan said, "That suits us. The first thing I want to do is build a ferry to cross the river from Georgia. Do you think you can handle that?" Mr. Rowe said, "I'll need some good help. We will have to build it on land and slide it in the water." Dan said, "You hire all the help you need. I am going to be tied up with some other plans; you and my parents can figure it out. I will be around General Oglethorpe's place if you need me."

Dan and Coleman walked back to the cottage and told his mama to get ready to start figuring out what kind of house she wants. Dan said, "There is enough land for you to get what you want. I need to get back to Mary to see if she needs anything." He rode off toward General Oglethorpe's home. When he got within distance to see the house, he saw a group of about fifty British soldiers dismounted, standing at the front gate. As he rode closer, he could see four officers standing on the porch talking to General Oglethorpe. When Dan saw one of the officers was the officer he had disciplined while returning from Virginia and Pennsylvania, he knew there would be trouble. Dan dismounted and walked to the porch, where he then saw the other two soldiers he had also disciplined. General Oglethorpe said, "Dan, these men have come to arrest you on several charges, one of which is, Treason. I have tried to reason with them, I have told them who you are and all you have done for Great Britain, but they insist on placing you under arrest without bond." Mary was listening to the General when all the sudden she felt faint and collapsed in Dan's arms. Dan caught her as she fell and took her in the parlor of the General's home. It was obvious their child was in the process of being born. The General said, "Send someone to fetch the ladies. It is time." Maureen appeared as Dan brought Mary through the door to find a place for her to lie down.

The British officer in charge of the arrest said, "Mr. O'Flaherty you are to come with us." Dan said, "Not until the child is born." When he said that, one of the soldiers hit the back of his head with the butt of a "Brown Bess" rifle. When the soldier struck Dan in the back of the head, Maureen reached for Dan's knife. She plunged the knife into the soldiers back just under his left shoulder blade. She then twisted the blade to be sure it cut his heart. The soldier fell to the floor mortally wounded. Immediately, three other soldiers standing by seized Maureen and tied her hands and feet. They took her to the horses and tied her face down on a saddle. When Dan fell to the floor unconscious, two of the soldiers grabbed his boot heels and drug him to the front porch. One of the other soldiers walked Dan's horse to the porch and the soldiers put Dan's unconscious body, belly down, on his saddle and tied him around his neck and feet and cinched the rope tight and tied the rope to the saddle horn for the ride to the English prison in Savannah.

General Oglethorpe was outraged to the point he threatened those involved with Court Martials. The General had finally witnessed the Penal Laws of England being enforced. He had learned firsthand, the cul tural hatred that had become engrained in the minds and souls of the military. He knew no assistance would come from the local military; it would be an issue that had to be presented to Parliament and directly to King George III, in whom he knew there would be no concern forthcoming for an Irish Catholic who had fought against the Crown.

Dan regained consciousness about two miles from Savannah. His immediate concern was for Mary and their first child. He knew the outcome of any case against him in a British military court would not be in his favor. He also knew he would not be allowed to post bond or be represented by a qualified attorney. He saw only one option which was escape, before he was locked up.

He began listening to the soldier's as they were laughing and talking about their prisoners. He distinctly heard one of the Sergeant's say, "I know what the jailer is going to do with that red-headed beauty." Dan knew immediately Maureen must have involved herself in his defense. He remained appearing to be unconscious. As they approached the front of the stockade, they made a turn where Dan could clearly see Maureen tied face down on the horse next to the horse on which he was tied.

When they arrived at the fort the troops were dismissed. The officer kept the two soldiers with him that were present at the first encounter. Dan continued to appear unconscious as the blood ran from the gash in the back of his head. When one of the soldiers reached to untie the ropes from his neck, Dan quickly pulled the soldier toward him, grabbed his throat and crushed the bones, then eased him to the ground. Maureen witnessed what Dan had done and remained to appear apparently unconscious.

As the officer was making preparation to walk into the office, Dan eased up behind him and pulled his forehead back and cut the officers throat. The remaining soldier was on the opposite side of the horses, checking the cinch on his saddle, when he felt Dan twist his neck, just before his spinal cord was severed. When Dan had completed killing the three soldiers, he very patiently untied Maureen's hands and feet and whispered, *be very quiet and follow me.* Maureen sat up in the saddle as she and her brother were now free from the treachery of the three British soldiers. When they were some distance away from the fort, they applied their heels to the horses' flank.

CHAPTER THIRTEEN

FUGITIVES

When he arrived at General Oglethorpe's home, he went inside to find Mary. General Oglethorpe was the first to see him and walked swiftly to him to determine what had occurred.

Dan asked, "How is Mary doing?" The General said, "It shouldn't be too much longer." The General pointed to the front porch directing Dan to where they could talk. When they sat down, Dan said, "General, my time here is over, I have got to take my family away from here. I think the best place to be is in Florida." The General said, "Dan, I am not sure, but I think you need to go to Alabama. I have some good contacts with the Cherokee Indians that will provide you a safe haven until I can get this thing unwound." Dan said, "General, I am very sorry to have to tell you this, but I had to kill those three men. They did not have any intention for me to have a trial. They were seeking a way to kill me. The King will not forgive me twice for killing his soldiers. I am pleading with you not to get involved." The General said, "Dan there is something else you need to know, when the soldier knocked you unconscious your sister Maureen killed him with your hunting knife. I hated to multiply your problems, but I had to tell you." The General said, "Dan, you are right, the more I stir the worse it would get. The entire Parliament is protestant; they would never listen to me again."

Dan said, "I am taking my family with me as well as the men, I will be in contact with you and you can contact me if you need me. I hope you know the depth of the gratitude that I have for all you have done for me and my family. Whatever you need until you leave this earth, you know I will do whatever I can to bring your desires to a reality, you have been the best friend a man on this earth could ever know." General Oglethorpe said, "Dan, you and your family have been the reason I have delayed my retirement. With you having to go into hiding, I am thinking I will probably be returning to England. I know there is no way for the colonists to be able to negotiate with the King. It appears war is going to be the choice of both sides. I am grateful to God I do not have to openly make a decision to commit treason. My heart will remain with the colonists. I will pray for you and your family." Dan said, "General, I will be around if you need anything. My prayer is when we get the disagreements settled; we can travel to England to visit with you." Dan turned toward Maureen who had gone to Mary's bedside when he heard a sound worth hearing. He went to Mary's room and found Maureen cleaning a big boy that had all the characteristics of being his father's son. When Dan looked at Mary, she said, "I knew you would be here." Dan kneeled by her bed and said, "Thank you for loving me. My being here with you is the most important happening to ever occur in my life. God has blest us beyond our ability to realize. Thank you for being the center of the blessings God has gifted to me. We have had the opportunity to spend our time together and there cannot be a blessing greater. You need to rest. We will visit again when you awake. I need to get to know our son while you rest."

After Mary had slept for three hours, she woke up wanting to see her son. Dan brought him to her. After a feeding, Dan said, "Mary, a very serious matter has come up that requires my personal attention and I will need Maureen's help. General Oglethorpe will explain the details to you after I have gone. I must leave now."

Mary could tell Dan was talking but not telling her all he wanted her to know. She knew under the circumstances the less said, the better. Dan told his mother and Maureen to get ready to leave as soon as she and the whole family can get prepared to leave. He told Maureen she would be going with him. Dan walked outside, saddled fresh horses for him and Maureen and roped three spares to take with him and headed toward the Blue Celt Headquarters. He pulled the men together within a few minutes and told them it was time for them to leave the colonies. He told them to prepare to head west and Captain John Milledge would bring them to the correct location. He said, "At present, my main concern is Mary and our son. I am trying to keep them alive. I will deeply appreciate your protection of them until we are together again."

Dan's thoughts were to keep ready for the revolt to begin and until that time, have the opportunity of being with his family. When he was by himself, outside the incident that had just destroyed the first peace and contentment his mother and father had ever known, he began to see not much had changed from the days of living in Ireland. The only exception now is, he and Maureen were wanted for the murder of four soldiers. Dan said, to himself, *the only thing that has really changed is, we will be in a different place when the war starts.* I will still be with my family waiting for that something no one ever anticipates to start the killing of one another." While he was considering his new plans, he was thinking of having a son to teach the paths of life. But, the one thought that preyed upon his mind was the thought of his son having to be separated from his parents. His focus was bent toward a strategy of making certain no separation, but death would come to plague their holy union.

Dan's analysis of his eventual location had many possibilities that had to be considered, with Dan and Maureen being fugitives from British justice being a priority. He decided to have five of the men go with them to map out a strategy, which would provide an answer to every problem that might arise. He also needed a scout to lead his family, as he searched for a place to sustain them until the colonists made up their collective minds to oppose the King.

Dan had heard of good hunting grounds, northwest of the Carolinas. He reminded Lupe of visiting with some trappers, who told them of a trail that followed a series of valleys from the southwest to the northeast that didn't have an end to it that anyone had found. Dan said, "Lupe, we need to find that path, it sounds like a place where we can have two sides of our defense taken care of by the mountain ranges. If that is true, all we will have to do is watch both ends of the trail."

He stopped by to see Mary again to tell them the scouts would be ahead of them and would report to them periodically. Dan said, "We will leave markers for you to follow." He told the Captain, "If there is trouble, send a scout and we will be on our way". Dan said, "I intend to do plenty of visiting and getting acquainted with the Indians, as we move along." Dan, Maureen and five men took off to the northwestern line of the Carolinas. When they had been on the trail for five days, the terrain began to have some steep hills, which caused them to have to slow their pace. They traveled on for two days without seeing any evidence of British presence, which made them feel more at ease.

One late afternoon, they began to find hoof prints of horses that had been shod, which brought about caution. They followed the trail into a settlement, which would later be called, Ashville. They went to the middle of the settlement and found a blacksmith shop, which answered the question of the shod horses. They continued to be on the alert for Red Coats. Dan finally determined the British had concentrated the troops on the eastern side of the colonies, leaving the western one half unprotected. He was thinking, *the British didn't want two wars at the same time, one with the colonies and the other with the Indians.*

Dan's horse had a loose shoe that needed repair. He went to the blacksmith where he found a young man, who said his name was Andrew. Dan said, "Andrew, my name is Dan O'Flaherty. I've brought my sister with me and I'd like for you to meet her. Dan went to the horses and told Maureen he wanted her to meet Andrew. Maureen walked up to Andrew and said, "I am glad to meet you." Andrew said, "My goodness, you are so beautiful." Maureen said, "I thank you. I am glad to meet you. We have been on these horses for days and to tell the truth, I am in need of a good bath." Andrew said, "Lady, you are beautiful even if you do need a bath." Dan told him he was in search of a trail that began somewhere west of the settlement, and he asked Andrew if he had ever heard of the place. Andrew said, "I don't just know where it is, but I know how to get there, because it is on my way to where I stay."

Dan asked, "What do you mean, where you stay?" Andrew said, "The British killed my family, and another family took me in and

I work for the man's brother here at the shop. Dan could tell he had found the makings of a real friendship with a young man who had his family destroyed similar to what had happened to him.

Dan said, "Andrew, do you know anyone in the settlement who could take us to the trail?" Andrew said, "I sure do." Dan asked, "Is it you?" Andrew replied, "Yes sir." Dan asked, "When would you be ready to start home." Andrew said, "As soon as the owner returns, I can go."

In a short time, the owner returned. Andrew told him he had a little job he needed to do, and he would be back in the morning. Dan had begun to really like Andrew. He asked Andrew, "What is your full name." Andrew said, "Andrew Jackson." Dan said, "My name is Dan O'Flaherty and my home was in Ireland at one time." Andrew asked, "What happened?" Dan said, "The British invaded our land and decided to claim the land that was owned by Catholics. They began to pass laws to kill all the Catholics in Ireland. My family was placed in an indentured slave camp here in America. When I got old enough, I came to America to set them free, which I did. The British are beginning to do the same thing in America as they did in Ireland, which is, kill anyone who has something they want. Recently, they tried to cause harm to my family and I prevented them from doing so.

We are now trying to find a new place to settle, hopefully, somewhere on the trail north." Andrew said, "From what I hear, you sure better be ready for the Indians. They do not want white people on their hunting grounds." Dan said, "Andrew, we had better be on our way. Maybe I can find a way to live with them."

It had become dark by the time Andrew found the beginning of the trail. When they found a good place to camp, he told them,

"Good to meet you, hope to see you again." Dan said, "Andrew, I want you to take this money and put it away somewhere for hard times. If you ever need me just head up this trail, I will be up here somewhere." Andrew knew the money pouch was extra heavy, but he didn't know until he found a candle to light at home that Dan had given him five hundred pounds. Andrew knew he had found a friend that would be his forever.

At day break the next day, they woke up almost feeling free again. Dan said, "I don't know how far north this trail goes, but I do know we are not the only people on it, so we need to be careful until we get acquainted with some good neighbors." They had traveled a day up the trail before they saw some Indians. Everyone was nervous at first including Dan, but he didn't show any sign of being in the wrong place. As they got closer, Dan held up his hand giving them the sign of peace. They waited for Dan to approach. Dan asked Lupe, "What are they?" Lupe said, "I think Cherokee." Lupe could talk a few words. He held up his hand and asked, "Where is Chief?" The Indian waved his hand in a direction of a well decorated teepee. Lupe told him, "We have come in peace to meet your Chief." They turned north and began walking toward the Indian village; within a short time, they came to a village of about seventy tepees.

Dan had become accustomed to the Indian culture and of the formality of introductions which eventually involved different contests to test his fighting skills. Dan had never lost to any Indian on any of the contests with other tribes. He did not know if the Cherokee would be friendly after he won or not. But it was time to get to the truth of what his neighbors might be offended by, so he decided to win. Dan defeated the top two braves of the village in everything including throwing knives and tomahawks. The Chief was very familiar with the white man's weapons and wanted one for himself. Dan and the others knew what a regret that would become later.

The Chief began to put pressure on Dan for the weapons. But, Dan decided to distract him by offering him one of the Spanish War horses they had brought as a spare. The Chief became content, but Dan knew it was time to be on their way before the Chief got his mind back on the guns. Dan told the Chief how grateful he was for his hospitality and they were back on the trail. The one fact Dan had learned about Indians, each and every one of them are motivated by what belongs to someone else. If they want it, they will do whatever it takes to get it, even if it requires taking the life of the owner.

As they moved through this God ordained natural trail, Dan's mind was on the precious gift that was behind him coming up the trail. He had heard from one of the scouts the Blue Celts and the family were making steady progress. Dan estimated they were about two days ride ahead of them. He decided to slow the pace, to allow the troop to remain closer together for protection. One of the scouts reported another Indian Village about one mile ahead. Dan prepared to meet another group of Indians with the hope of soon finding a territory where he and the Indians could live in peace.

As they approached the village, it was apparent the tribe was aware that white men were in the camp, but they were not afraid, which indicated to Dan the tribe could be receptive to white men, as opposed to being frightened of strangers. Dan was taken by surprise when the Chief came out to greet him with a hand shake. Dan knew this Indian had been to town. The two of them made a good match.

Dan was six foot four inches and Chief Attakullakulla was less than five foot four. (8) Dan quickly thought to himself, *he didn't get to be Chief as a warrior, so it must be brains.* The Chief spoke some English and was very cordial.

All of the men felt at ease for a change. Dan and Lupe were able to fill in the blanks enough to make the Chief understand they were looking for a place to stay temporarily. Dan told him the number of people involved in his family and the Chief was surprised. He also told him he had two things to offer the tribe, one was protection from their enemy and two, money. The Chief was most interested in the protection. Dan told him they could kill enough animals to feed themselves and the tribe. Dan disclosed to him he would be leaving when the colonist decided to fight for their independence. He said, "We will fight for the people, not the King." The Chief agreed to talk it over with the tribe and let them know. Within three days, the Chief told Dan they could stay. Dan was relieved, because he was located in the center of the western side of the colonies. He could use the Appalachian Trail to either fight in the north or the south.

The next day at sundown, the family began arriving; Dan was overjoyed to see Mary. She and the baby had a good journey. They were cared for by Dan's mother and father. They had placed feather mattresses in the wagon which made the ride much better. Captain John Milledge, Jr, had done a good job leading the family through so many pitfalls. Dan said, "John, if we were in a war I would give you a medal. Thank you for taking care of my family for me." The Captain said, "Sir, it is an honor to be of service to you and your family." Dan introduced his family and the men to the Chief. The Chief was overjoyed to have the protection he had needed without putting his people at risk.

Dan was anxious to get time to be with his two personal blessings from God. Mary saw to it her child did not experience hunger. It was obvious he had gained weight on the journey. As the day began to wind down, Mary asked, "Dan, what would you like to name your first son?" Without hesitation, Dan said, "Cathal Brendon O'Flaherty." Mary was surprised he didn't name him Dan. Dan said, "I want him to be his own man." Mary asked, "Why did you choose Brendon for a middle name?" Dan said, "You know what Mary, there was a Saint in the sixth century named Saint Brendon, who with twenty monks sailed to Newfoundland and down the east coast of America, telling all the good news that Jesus Himself, the Son of God, had come to save us sinners from His Father's wrath on judgment day. I believe Cathal will be the voice of freedom for a new nation, once we send King George and his brutes back to Europe."

The next day Dan met with the Chief to determine the need for food for his tribe. The Chief could not help but smile. He had never experienced such a man as Dan before. While they were visiting, he told Dan he had been kidnapped as an infant from another tribe in the north. He also revealed to him he had later been sold to a Cherokee tribe who eventually titled him, "First Beloved One."

Dan shared with the Chief his experience of being taken from the arms of his mother by the English and his parents sold as indentured slaves and sent to America. When the conversation was over, the Chief reached for Dan's right hand and said, "Big Dan, my friend." Dan talked to Lupe and told him to take some of the quietest men and go get five deer for the tribe and two turkeys, if they can be found. The troop was blessed with three of the best hunters Dan had ever known. The meat was taken to the tribe, skinned and cleaned. The tribe was very pleased with the bargain the Chief had made with the white men. When Dan was talking to the Celts the next day, he told them, "It is only by God's Grace, that we are allowed to remain here on their hunting grounds. There are many reasons we can be asked to leave. The main reason would be, if one of the men made an advance toward an Indian woman that was married. We all know our being here is something we have to do. If we are forced to go further north, we will have to contend with the colder weather and less food. Where we are now is the most perfect place we can be, when the war begins. We can go south or north wherever we are needed at a fast pace. I know as time goes along, you are going to want to be involved in female companionship. I am sure also, some of the Indian maidens will want to have company with you. The only thing I am going to require of you is, if you seek female companionship, you must inform Captain Milledge. I will then talk to the Chief to get his answer before the relationship proceeds. Remember, this whole thing can blow up with one mistake. I want each of you to hold one another responsible for this order to be obeyed. I need your word that it will be." Every man gave Dan his vow to meet the requirements he had set forth.

The relationship between the two camps endured without incident other than three of the soldiers had taken the vows of Holy wedlock to Indian maidens. Dan asked the Chief about using some of his tribe as scouts. The Chief approved and told Dan the men were very familiar with the area around Pennsylvania and Virginia. Dan had begun taking groups of the men in one direction while Captain Milledge took the other troops in another direction. Dan could sense the time getting closer to the war beginning. Dan and Mary took full advantage of being with one another. Their son had more baby sitters than he needed. The Indian women brought their children to see the newborn white child. Dan and Mary felt at complete peace with the Indians in the wilderness of a new land; they had begun to claim it as their own. Dan had selected an especially gentle horse for Mary to ride through the Appalachian trails. As they rode a trail one morning, Dan told her it was as if they had been together forever, they truly loved one another with their whole hearts. Mary, Margarita and Delia were the only people who had ever seen the gentleman Dan was in his spirit. While traveling the mountain trails, Dan and Mary found a lake far back in the mountains that captured the quietness of their spirits. The fishing was good, and they claimed that one area as their own. Mary told Dan it was as if there was no one else on earth but them. As each day and night passed, the fondness of their hearts grew for one another. Dan told her one morning, "I am not sure I want to go back to all the confusion." Mary said, "Remember there will be confusion as long as there is no place for peace allowed by hate mongers." Dan said, "Mary, the time is coming soon when we will not have these opportunities to be with one another, probably for a long period of time. Remember this, even though I am away from you, I am always with you. When you reach the time, you are missing me the most, get someone to come with you to this place, my spirit will join you here." Mary closed her eyes as she prayed for, *the moment to never be forgotten.* They traveled back to camp to again see their family and continued to enjoy being with one another.

After a week of being back at the camp Dan woke up early one morning and told Mary he had to make a trip to Virginia to visit with General Washington. He took a number of the men with him with five good scouts from the tribe. The scouts knew of a route through the mountain ranges which they took toward Mount Vernon. Within three weeks, most of the journey was completed as they entered the territory where the red coats were operating. They began traveling at night to prevent a confrontation with the British troops. They reached their destination late one evening. They bivouacked for the night and Dan was on his way the next morning to visit with Colonel Washington.

He arrived just after dawn and went to the back door. He was met at the door by the cook who was preparing breakfast. She asked him in to have coffee and breakfast. She left him in the kitchen and went to talk to Mrs. Washington. She returned and told him Mrs. Washington would be down in a short while. A short time later Mrs. Washington walked in and said, "Dan O'Flaherty, what a surprise. It is unfortunate you have missed General Washington. He has gone to meet with the troops, while the Congress is working to approve the Independence documents." Dan asked, "Am I to understand we are declaring ourselves independent from England?" Martha Washington said, "From what I understand, that is what they are working toward. If they approve of the document, we will be at war with England, I am sure." Dan asked, "Did you say, General Washington?" Martha said, "Yes, he agreed to take the responsibility of the Army." Dan said, "Are you telling me, he is organizing an Army?" She said, "Yes." Dan said, "Our troops are ready Mrs. Washington, I am sorry to have disturbed you so early, but I must be leaving now." Mrs. Washington said, "Dan, I will be praying for you." Dan said, "And I for you, my Lady."

Dan knew the time had come for every Irish heart to grasp the moment and realize freedom was more possible now than ever before and could be achieved with one more final effort of grit and determination which could cause their lives to be set free, as long as they lived on this earth.

When Dan returned to the men he said, "The war has begun. We need to cover some ground very quickly to go to Pennsylvania to locate the Continental Army of the Colonies." Lupe said, "I can go find the men." Dan said, "I need to go to Pennsylvania to pay the gunsmith and pick up the rifles. I know General Washington needs us as fast as we can get to wherever he is located. Let's meet in Pennsylvania at the gunsmiths in a week." Lupe said, "I may be a day late, but wait for me."

Within a week, everyone was ready to do their best to get the British out of America. Dan said, "Our main effort will be to locate General Washington as soon as possible." In nine days, they were in Boston. General Washington was glad to see Dan and his men. He asked Dan if they could meet privately. Dan told him he was ready. General Washington said, "Dan from what I have seen this war is going to be the kind where your training will be most effective. Your rifles are the perfect weapon to keep the British from effectively maintaining an offensive. I am going to depend on you to use your finest skills to do everything you know to keep them off balance. I also want to make you aware I am going to need your financial help to keep the Army together. The contract most of them are under expires the end of the year." Dan said, "General, the conversation we had previously about this matter was not idle talk. Tell me what you need, and it will be done. The bulk of the funds are in Spain. I will give you the authority to exercise the use of the funds as you deem necessary, for whatever purpose. I consider it an honor and a privilege for the Irish and Scots to be included in this great undertaking." The General said, "Dan, this undertaking will not be concluded quickly." Dan said, "General, the Irish and Scottish are here as long as it takes to accomplish victory."

The General said, "Dan, your efforts are going to be vital when the battlefield moves from the seashores to the open country, especially in the south. We have another officer who excels in the battle tactics you apply. He is in Canada and his regiment is the most effective group we have." Dan said, "General, you will not be disappointed in our soldiers. We have good scouts and that is something the English will never have to equal ours."

After the first Americans were killed in Lexington, thousands of volunteers began to step forward to support the Minute Men. Within days, more than twenty thousand patriots responded to the call. The British had been led to believe the Americans were not trained for a military response and would not be a challenge against the most powerful and well-trained Army in the world. When some of the British officers saw the battle readiness of some of the American soldiers, they returned to England to avoid the disgrace of defeat they knew was going to occur.

Barely two months had passed since the first American fell in Lexington before the Congress had appointed George Washington, General of the Continental Army. Unfortunately, there was no turning back. That moment in time for the parties to have reconciled their differences had passed. Reports had begun to come in from the colonies reporting military encounters in many towns. The house tops in Boston were used as bleachers by the colonists to watch the British assault the Americans from the British ships anchored in the harbor trying to kill American snipers. After the houses in the town were burning, it was clear to everyone, there was no misunderstanding, the War between the Americans and England had begun.

At the beginning, King George III had sent a diplomatic type of military leader to quail the seriousness of the rebellion which he had drastically underestimated. When the quality of the Scottish and Irish American soldiers became known and reported to the King he decided he wanted a bloodline of arrogance that had proved his repugnance for the Irish. He found the one man who not only matched the King's arrogance, but also the open disdain and contempt for the Irish culture. Lord George Germaine was the perfect man to suit the King's taste for the slaughter of those souls who had escaped his grasp in Ireland and had fled to America. Lord Germaine's battle plan was simple, use the highest degree of force that Britain could muster and finish the rebellion in one battle. That approach to the rebellion pleased the King immensely. (9)

Lord Germaine began organizing an Army of over twenty thousand troops. He was unable to get the English citizens excited about killing their relatives. When the recruiting failed in England, he began recruiting Germans. He soon began to tell his Generals in America, he was sending twenty-five thousand new recruits. (9)

General Washington began to assemble a core group of volunteers, all of which were enlisted for a term, generally one year. (10) Among his officers he was faced with the pettiness of rank. Some of the officers had been promoted to exceptionally high ranks in the Colony militias, but when transferred to the Continental regular Army, it became necessary to demote them to fit the organizational requirements of General Washington's plans. Most every soldier in Washington's army had been a hard-working farmer a few days before enlistment. The problem of discipline was enormous. Every Irish mouth had the right answer to every military problem and did not need some young officer with more rank telling them any different. Fights broke out between the troops; it was one huge problem of teaching discipline to individuals to become part of a group of soldiers. On one occasion, the General himself had to become involved in stopping the damage being done by the troops to one another.

General Washington soon found himself running out of time with a large group of the men's contracts expiring in December 1775. It wasn't long before the Continental Army had dwindled down to about five thousand troops. (10) As winter set in the tempers on both sides of the lines had begun to cool. But, this time was also a period for the truth of what the savage British butchers had done to fellow American's in Lexington and Boston, as the word began to be circulated throughout the Colonies. The atrocities committed in several towns had united the hearts and souls of Americans throughout the land.

During those first few months of 1775 and into the early months of 1776, America learned by losing battles. Dan received a message by courier to report to Command Headquarters, as soon as possible. When Dan reported, he could tell something of great importance was weighing on the General's mind. The first order of business was, the General told Dan he was being promoted to Lieutenant General, with the responsibility to command troops to provide protection for his life and the lives of his family members. The

General revealed to Dan that a plot to assassinate him and his wife had been uncovered. He said, "Dan, it appears more than six hundred loyalists have been proved to be involved. The worst part is, one of my closest friends, whom I had selected to protect my personal safety is involved. His name is Thomas Hickey. (11) Some of the participants are not in the military and cannot be charged with treason because technically, the colonies have not united into one nation. Hickey will be tried for treason because he is in the military. (11) We have the others confined, but the major issue is my wife, Martha. I need for you to provide protection for her and my family."

General Washington continued, "Other issues involve the British sending a military force to the southern colonies. I have the support of several individual fighting units, but I need you to pull them together into one combined unit, under your command. There are two men I want you to contact as soon as you have my family under your protection. I also need you to setup a network of spies here in the north, to keep me informed of the British plans."

Dan said, "General, with your permission, I would like to proceed as fast as I can to Mount Vernon to secure your family. I will assure you, the men protecting your family will be the best Scottish and Irish warriors in America. Also, we have a network of infiltrators already in the British command that has been very effective. As soon as we can get them acquainted with you, I can begin some defensive preparations for the southern Colonies."

Without anyone's knowledge, Dan had set up a spy operation many months prior to the Independence document being signed. He did this in hopes of knowing in advance who the patriots were when it was time to rely on information supplied by strangers. Dan had made it a point to become knowledgeable of the New York area because the British had shown a special interest in the colony. Dan learned the colony was filled with loyalist to the British cause, because the area was the center of commerce.

As the alignment of British troops began filling the Colony of New York, Dan learned General Henry Clinton would have his headquarters in New York. Dan knew that would be the birth place of the best knowledge for General Washington to be prepared for the British movements in advance. Dan was very patient in selecting the right personnel for the Special Force Unit to be effective.

Within three days, Dan had arranged for the group of secret information providers to meet with the General. General Washington was aware of some of the work the undercover spies had provided but did not realize how deeply they had infiltrated the high command of the British Army.

Some of the spies revealed they had been knowledgeable of the tactics of some of the British officers from what they had learned of them while they were in Ireland. All those involved in the spy operation were aware of the great risks they were taking but were grateful for the opportunity to be standing with those who were willing to stand against the British.

Even though Dan was being moved to a different responsibility, he knew there was an element missing in the timing and quality of information being given to General Washington. The majority of the information was being received two weeks from the time it was sent. Dan felt someone had to step in that could provide valid information timely. Dan was considering Maureen and Shibeal as the missing elements to the establishment of a group of spies that could infiltrate the high command of the British headquarters. He knew both sisters knew how to survive. One had been born in a prison camp and the other had survived the tyranny of Great Britain's control of Ireland. He felt if they were placed in the right training environment they could learn the methods of a survival and covertness, they would become the answer to the vital link of gathering correct current information. Both young ladies were gorgeous to look upon while possessing the cunning and knowledge of manipulation to be the exact perfect pair to cripple the British efforts. The only problem left was to make sure his mother understood the risks her daughters would be taking.

When Dan felt comfortable the transition of the spies had been made to General Washington, he took the remainder of his force to Mount Vernon. They rode without stopping. Dan was grateful to have arrived before harm had come to Mrs. Washington. It was mid-morning, when they arrived at Mount Vernon. Dan knocked on the door. A servant recognized him and went to tell Mrs. Washington. When Mrs. Washington came to the door, she recognized Dan and told him to come in and tell her the news. Dan told her the General had sent her his love and wanted her to know her prayers for him and the Colonies were being answered.

Dan informed Mrs. Washington all the information regarding the personal safety of the General's family and of his being appointed to provide security for her. Mrs. Washington was most appreciative to Dan for the personal interest he had shown to the General and the assistance he was providing for the war effort. Dan introduced Mrs. Washington to Captain John Milledge, who would be in charge to provide the security for the entire family. Dan explained to Mrs.

Washington, the General had assigned him to other responsibilities which needed his attention. However, he explained, Captain Milledge would remain in charge of the security until all precautions had been taken. He then told her Captain Milledge would then re-join the troop to accomplish the mission General Washington had assigned to him. Mrs. Washington again told Dan how appreciative she was for the care.

CHAPTER FOURTEEN

SOUTHERN CAMPAIGNS

When Dan returned to General Washington's camp, he was informed the General was most anxious to see him. As he approached the General's location a group of officers had gathered for a meeting. Dan stood under a tree waiting for the meeting to conclude. He did not want to interrupt. When General Washington stood up he saw Dan waiting to give him a report as to the safety of his family. The General immediately dismissed the group of officers as he walked toward Dan. The first question out of his mouth was, "Is Martha and the family well?" Dan responded, "General, you have a remarkable family. They are missing you and want to see you when you can get away for a day or two."

The conversation shifted to the responsibility Dan was having placed on him. The Southern Colonies would require a leader who knew the territory and the people to unify a force to defeat General Cornwallis's main force, as well as the Loyalist Militia, commanded by Major Patrick Ferguson.

The General said, "Dan, you know the south better than any officer on the general staff. What I think we need is a person who can keep our commanders in the south from entering an aggressive conflict with a better prepared British Army. We must fight a defensive war until they make a mistake. I want you to organize and train the Militia to become night and day combat soldiers, always with a way to escape, if something goes wrong. Major Ferguson is one of Lord Cornwallis's top officers. If you can organize and defeat him, the morale of our troops will change the moment they sense victory. I want you to take as many of the men of your regiment as you can with you to train the militia. There is a particular man I want you to visit for me. Your Uncle Bernardo Galvez is going to be a key in the defeat of the British Army in the south. He has now become the Governor of Louisiana and Cuba. Dan, you have become the revolution's most vital link to Spain, who has become our ally."

Dan said, "General, I was fighting against Spain in Florida for England in 1762, while my adoptive uncle was fighting the Apache Indian in Mexico, and now he and I are fighting against England with him representing Spain and me representing America. I hope and pray to get to meet with him when I get back south."

General Washington asked, "Dan, have you ever met a merchant named Oliver Pollock?" Dan said, "I have heard General Oglethorpe mention his name several times, all of which was very complimentary." Dan said, "From what I have gathered from General Oglethorpe, he is a very fine man that can be trusted. Another man I heard the General discuss was Don O'Reilly, who is now the Governor of New Orleans." General Washington said, "Dan, those three men can determine the difference of victory or defeat in the south. I would strongly suggest you go with all deliberate speed in their direction. They will help you set up the spies and scouts you will need to defeat Cornwallis. Remember the British are strangers to this land. Their reputations are known by every Scottish and Irish family in this country. With very few exceptions, every one of those families are our allies. It is your responsibility to provide them an Army to give them hope. The Army will have credibility when the right men have applied their support and prayers to cause it to become an Army. Remember this, we need a victory to rebuild the belief that victory is possible. If you can select a battlefield of which you are familiar and a brash opponent who thinks he knows how to win, you will defeat him, and that will cause the British Generals to know we are prepared to give our all for freedom." Dan said, "General, I am on my way to New Orleans to see my uncle to get his help to put together some regular Army troops as well as the militia." General Washington said, "Dan, be sure and contact Benjamin Cleveland, James Johnston, William Campbell, John Sevier, Joseph McDowell and Isaac Shelby. These men are ready to fight."

With the correct information and direction given him by the commanding General, Dan set his course for New Orleans to locate his uncle by adoption, who had become appointed the Governor of Louisiana and Cuba. Dan sent a courier selected from the Blue Celts to go to the Indian Village in East Tennessee. The purpose was to deliver a letter to Mary and the family and to have Maureen and Shibeal go with an escort of three Blue Celts to meet him in New Orleans at the Governor of Louisiana's Mansion. After several weeks of traveling the backroads, he arrived in New Orleans which was in a vast area of swampland alongside the Mississippi River owned by France. New Orleans was later purchased by the United States of America known as the Louisiana Purchase. From the outset of his term as Governor, Galvez established an anti-British policy, by maintaining a trading relationship with France, and by setting up a smuggling operation to aid the rebels.

The British had blockaded eleven of the ports of the Thirteen Colonies but had left the port of New Orleans and the Mississippi River open to transport. This was important because the Colonist needed supplies. (12) Oliver Pollock, an Irishman, who grew up in County Tyrone in Ireland, had arrived in America in 1760 and settled in Pennsylvania. He eventually moved to New Orleans and through the President of the Jesuit College in Havana, Cuba became acquainted with Don Alejandro O'Reilly the Governor General of Cuba, who was also an Irishman. Oliver Pollock and Don O'Reilly became close friends and Governor O'Reilly became the source of great assistance to the Patriots. O'Reilly became one of Spain's most famous Generals and was in command of 2,600 troops. (13) When Spain entered a Peace Treaty with France, the land known as Louisiana was granted to the French but, because of the population of New Orleans being partially French, and partially Spanish, disagreements developed between the co-occupiers. As the Spanish increased in population, the food supplies dwindled. Oliver Pollock knowing of the crisis brought a shipload of grain and flour from Pennsylvania to give aid to the people. At the same time, the price of wheat had taken a monumental increase in price, which would have made Oliver Pollock a fortune. But rather than raise the prices, he lowered the prices with much gratitude being given to him from Governor Galvez and Governor O'Reilly. His generosity caused his fortunes to escalate to enormous amounts. He then became one of the largest personal contributors to the American Revolutionaries. All the while his fortunes were escalating; the bond between himself and the Governors drew closer. (13) The situation was the perfect circumstance for Dan to arrive and apply his talents.

When he arrived, he went to the office of Governor Galvez. When asked by the guard, "Whom may I say is calling?" Dan said, "Tell the Governor his nephew has come for a visit." Dan could hear the whispering as the guard repeated exactly what Dan had told him to say. Dan could hear the Governor's chair push back from his massive desk at which time a boisterous uproar of laughter began. Dan began to smile. The huge doors opened, and the Governor walked out and reached for an embrace from his most famous nephew. The Governor laid his head on Dan's huge chest as he began to describe the feelings his mother Margarita had for him. The Governor said, "Dan, my sister has told me many times she and General O'Shea didn't know of life until your life became their lives. I just received a message from General Washington, who addressed you as Lieutenant General of the Continental Army and Commanding General of the Army of the Southern Revolutionary Forces." Dan was embarrassed as he thought of his little private war to get Spain out of Florida and now, he was on the same side of Spain against Great Britain. The Governor was filled with joy as he told Dan some of the stories Margarita had revealed to him about Dan's youthful exploits. The Governor said, "Dan, I have kept close to you by hearing of some of the tactics you have used. I know General O'Shea would have loved to have been with you on some of them."

Dan began bringing the Governor up to date on the birth of his great nephew Cathal Brendon O'Flaherty O'Shea and his beautiful mother, Mary O'Malley O'Flaherty O'Shea. The Governor asked where they were located. Dan told him in Eastern Tennessee. The Governor demanded of Dan to send for them immediately to get them out of harm's way, because of some information he had received that harm could come to them if they remained in that location. Dan's thoughts began running wild. He asked the Governor if he could be excused. The Governor replied, "Dan, if you are sending a troop to get your family, I want to, in fact, I insist upon General O'Reilly's men be involved in the transporting of them back here for safety." The Governor then told one of the guards to ask General O'Reilly to come to his office. Within minutes, General Alexander O'Reilly (Don Alejandro) was in Governor Galvez's office. The Governor introduced Don Alejandro to Dan O'Flaherty O'Shea as his nephew, the adoptive son of General Phillip O'Shea and his wife, Margarita O'Shea. He also pointed out Dan is now serving as a Lieutenant General in the Continental Army. General O'Reilly stood and saluted Dan, with an explanation of having admired his parents for years. General O'Reilly told Dan of Margarita's stories, as she had told them to him. Dan had begun to feel relaxed as he said, "I often told my mother not to complain about my misbehavior because she knew I was Irish before she adopted me." They laughed. Dan got serious when he began telling the two Governors of his mission. Dan explained he had some of his men with his wife and family in Eastern Tennessee under the protection of a Cherokee Tribe whose Chief is named Attakullakulla. He explained some of his men are serving as security for the Washington family at Mount Vernon in Virginia and some are serving as General Washington's personal security. He told them General Washington had advised him of the two Governor's support of the Continental Army. He also revealed his unit was stretched from New York to Tennessee. He informed them there was a need for a company of regular Army trained soldiers to serve as a core group. The two governors looked at one another with a smile on their faces. General Washington was requesting them to become personally involved in the Revolution; they were more excited than they could allow anyone to know. They had an Army, a battlefield and their training was going to be displayed for the world to know their involvement. General O'Reilly asked to be dismissed to make the necessary preparations. The Governor asked him, "How many troops he was thinking of sending to retrieve your family?" The General replied, "I was thinking of 500. What do you think?" Governor Galvez agreed.

When General O'Reily had gone, Dan asked if he could have some time with the Governor in private. The Governor could tell it was a matter of great importance. The Governor asked the Chief of Security to come in his office. When he arrived, he told the Security Chief to see he was not disturbed.

Dan began by telling the Governor of his concern for the quality of information General Washington was receiving from the spies to properly advise him of the British troop movements. He revealed to him of having two sisters, Maureen and Shibeal who has the talent and capability of infiltrating the enemy's command. He said, "My youngest sister Maureen was raised as an indentured slave while in prison in Georgia with my birth parents. Shibeal was raised by a deceased cousin and has survived the brutality of the British Army in Ireland. Both of my sisters need training to become effective spies. I have an attorney in Spain whose name is Matthew Collier who is willing to supervise their training as well as placing them in New York in a strategic position to obtain information." The Governor inquired, "Dan how can I help facilitate the plan?" Dan replied, "They need transportation to Spain." The Governor quickly told Dan, "Consider it done." Dan was extremely happy to know the Governor would place Maureen and Shibeal in good hands for the journey.

Very soon thereafter, as they opened the Governor's office doors, a Blue Celt informed Dan his sisters had arrived. Dan thanked and excused himself to the Governor to meet with his sisters.

Dan was fond of the backyard of the Governor's Mansion. He and his sisters found a swing and Dan began telling them of the plan to train them for service to the Continental Army. Their eyes lit up by thinking about, *being allowed to serve their country*. Dan told them of his relationship with Mr. Collier and how important it would be for them to allow him to manage their lives until they became competent to understand their duty. To emphasize what he was saying, he told them they would be in a position to not only save lives but also to have an impact on winning the war.

Dan said, "Ladies, I want you to understand, I love you the way you are but when this adventure is over, you are not going to be the innocent baby sister I once knew. You are going to be full grown, with more experience in living life than most people ever know. I have been trained by the best combat soldiers in the world. You are going to be trained by the most qualified secret service personnel in the world. My question to you is this, are you agreeable to entering a training program for this purpose?" Maureen said, "Big Brother, I know how much you love all of us. I know you would not be asking us for help if you thought we weren't capable. The answer is yes, as far as I am concerned, I am ready to help win the war."

Dan knew that Shibeal was endowed with a mind to grasp numbers better than anyone in the family. She had been the bookkeeper for Eamonn and the O'Malleys after Bridget died. All the

O'Flaherty's regarded her as the one who knew how to handle money. Dan had discussed with Weston and Mr. Collier the necessity of having a well-known investment house in New York as a conduit for European supporters to contribute to the revolutionary cause. Shibeal would be the perfect choice to assist Weston in the management of those funds. Shibeal said, "Big Brother, the day I first met you when Eamonn was dying, I knew we would be involved in something of value together, I am ready."

Dan said, "Ladies, I am going to leave you in the care of the Governor of Louisiana who is my adoptive uncle, whom you will refer to as Governor Galvez. He is arranging for you to sail to Spain where you will be put under the care of Matthew Collier who has been a family attorney for us for many years." Maureen said, "Big Brother, I guess that's it. We'll see you after we win the war. One more thing, when we win where will we find you?" Dan said, "When you hear we have won, give me ten days to find you and then we will go home together."

Dan was considering the moment, thinking, *of how simple his life began in Ireland, and had evolved into a life of wars between nations.* Dan stayed with the Governor as General O'Reilly dismissed himself. Dan told his uncle how grateful he was to have such a wonderful response to the needs of America at this desperate hour. Governor Galvez told Dan he was considering coming to America after he retired from his duty to Spain. Dan said, "If you do, I hope we can be neighbors."

Dan decided to delay rejoining his men because he had to see his family before going into a battle that had to be won, which meant taking whatever the risk became to defeat a powerful enemy. The one thing he wanted to do was talk to his mother before he sent Shibeal and Maureen to Spain for covert operative training. When his family arrived, it became a very meaningful time for all of them to express their love for one another. At the first opportunity, Dan told his mother and father, "We need to talk." When Dan had finished telling his parents about the importance of having the girls trained as spies, they wanted to know if he thought they would be in a safe place. Dan said, "No Mam" to his mother. He said, "Mama, you know how the British have been toward all of us every day of our lives. They have done everything in their power to destroy our family. God has kept them from killing us. The only way I know to express our loyalty and gratitude to God for all he has done for us is to do whatever it takes to defeat these people. We will never know peace until we defeat them."

Delia said, "Coleman, are we ready to give up three of our children to try to find freedom from the cruel hands these people have lifted toward us?" Coleman said, "Delia, we have lived for this day. We have been willing to give back to God our all, no matter what it takes to have peace on this earth. It looks like to me the time has come for us to do all it takes to win even if we must die. I trust God will do whatever it takes to protect our children as well as us." Delia said, "Dan, do whatever you have to do, we will be praying for each of you to return safe." Delia and Coleman hugged Dan one more time and went to find Shibeal and Maureen.

After Dan had thanked the Governor again and rejoined his men, he informed the men of the plan to allow General O'Reilly to protect his family while in New Orleans. Dan began sending scouts to locate the other militia to advise them to rendezvous at Gilbert Town.

As the militias began to gather, all the men of each troop began making their way to meet Dan who had found a log to relax on from the days of travel from New Orleans. When they had gathered, he told them General Washington wanted them to know their efforts were not in vain, because he was working as fast as he could to guide the British Army into a trap. He told them the British had become concerned they might lose the north to General Washington and might change their plans to settle with the Southern Colonies in a negotiated surrender. Dan told them, "That is the reason we are seeing the influx of British troops in all the Southern Colonies. The King knows the land in the south is better for farming than the north.

General Washington wants everyone in the south to become aware that an attack is being planned on the Southern Colonies." Dan said, "That is the purpose of this meeting. The plan is for all the Militia to be under one flag, for the leader to better organize the communication between the various Armies. I know for a fact there is an attack being planned, very close to where we are now. Lord Cornwallis has sent another of his henchmen named, Major Ferguson, who is of the same character as Banastre Tarleton. British officers below the rank of General are all alike trying to show their Generals which one has the greatest skill to spill innocent blood. From what I understand, his favorite, Tarleton, is ill at the time, but make no mistake, Ferguson is a battle-hardened warrior. (14) The difference will be the execution of the plan we have prepared for their defeat. I am sending some of our troops to East Tennessee to get my family away from a British plan to attack the Colonies from the west. The remainder of the Continental soldiers will remain here with us. Out of those troops, we are going to divide our detachments into separate units. Our attack will be a complete surprise, all yelling as loud as we can. Each detachment will be fighting separate from one another. I am asking you to remember they have bayonets, and we have none. After you have fired your first volley, get prepared to run for your life, then hide behind a tree and wait until they get back to the top of the hill, and attack again repeating the same maneuver." Dan asked, "Do any of you have any questions? If not, I am going to get the men prepared for the journey." Dan went to talk to the men who were going to Tennessee. He began telling the men about the Cherokee tribe who had taken care of his family, he told them the Chief was known as "First Beloved Man." Dan said, "Do not be misled by his name, he is a brilliant man who has been Chief of a large group of Indians, who have come to trust his decisions. I am probably the first white man to ask him to care for his family. He is a good man. He is not a foolish man. The Chief has trusted me with members of his tribe who are the Indians you see in camp. My hope is, they come back to continue the good work they have done."

Dan was up early the next morning as one of the scouts came into camp. The scout reported a large troop traveling toward Gilbert Town. Dan told the Sergeant to wake the men up to get ready for a battle. Battle ready excitement began to hum in the camp as each man began to ready himself to, *walk through the valley of the shadow of death.* Dan met with the Commander of each group and discussed the attack plan with each officer. Dan told them to remember the battle called the Waxhaws incident, when Banastre Tarleton slaughtered soldiers who had surrendered. Dan said, "It is time to even the score."

When they attacked the Loyalists on October 7, 1780, at Kings Mountain, South Carolina their attack was made by surprise. Every group of Americans fought as an independent unit. The Americans knew how to fight a war under the cover of the forest. The Americans attacked and fired. When the Loyalists finally recognized what was taking place, they made a bayonet charge down the hill chasing the Americans. When the Loyalists walked back to the top of the hill, the Americans attacked again. The Loyalists made another bayonet charge and again, they failed, because the Patriots knew how to conceal themselves with the tree foliage. [14]

After an hour of combat, the Loyalists were heavily damaged. Three of the other groups attacked the Loyalists from the rear. They were driven back and began to surrender. One of the Americans came out of hiding and asked Major Ferguson to surrender. Major Ferguson shot and killed the officer. The American riflemen then shot and killed Ferguson. [14]

In the aftermath, the Loyalist's had lost 290 killed and 190 wounded, with 668 taken prisoner. The American's had lost 29 killed and 58 wounded. The battle plan was executed to perfection. The victory was complete to the extent Lord Cornwallis changed his plan to invade North Carolina and instead evacuated Charlotte and retreated to Wilmington, North Carolina. The American victory was the turning point of the American Revolution. [14]

As Dan began to unwind, the joy of seeing his Mary and his family came to his mind and heart. When the time was right, he talked to Captain Milledge and told him he was elevating his rank to Lieutenant Colonel, to reward him for the excellent service he had been in every task to which he had been assigned. Dan told him to get the men ready for another battle. Dan was thinking some of the same thoughts he had in Florida against the Spanish. His desire was to kill the spirit of the Loyalist Militia first and save the big battles with the regulars for the climax. He felt Cornwallis was trying to hide the regular British soldiers behind the dead bodies of the Loyalist's, while he drifted further into obscurity in Wilmington, North Carolina.

Dan had to see his loved ones who were in New Orleans waiting for him to return. He brought Lieutenant Colonel Milledge up to date on all the dispatches he had received from General Washington. One of the dispatches in particular had caught his attention which was the arrival of Brigadier General Daniel Morgan, who had been released from British captivity in an exchange of prisoner releases arranged by General Washington.

Dan told Colonel John Milledge to place the Continental troops and the Militia under General Morgan's command, upon his arrival. Dan told Colonel Milledge to listen and learn from General Morgan because, "He fights war like we fight war and he will be bringing 500 handpicked riflemen with him." General Morgan was the key figure for the Revolutionary forces no matter where he was placed to command.

General Washington chose Nathanael Green to command the Southern Department of the Continental forces after he had decided Dan was better suited to command the Guerilla and Special Force's units, which generally were the troops from the south and were adjusted to the night fighting and hit and run tactics. (15)

Dan told Colonel Milledge, "We need one more decisive victory to change the attitude of the British Generals and the Loyalists. Dan said, "Once they see our unflinching courage, they will change their strategy and head north. Their concern is to end up in New York and in the final settlement that will be the Colony they try to preserve."

Dan rode off with two spare horses trailing him. He was in a hurry to again be in the world of love and peace, to enjoy the fruits from heaven's orchard. He rode night and day to reach New Orleans ahead of the troop that escorted them to New Orleans. When he arrived at the Governor's Mansion, it was after midnight and he was tired. He then rode to the stable and unsaddled his horse as a caretaker approached to help him with the horses. Dan asked the soldier whether the men had arrived from Tennessee. The soldier said, "That is why I am here, they should be arriving in a short time." Dan felt most relieved. In about two hours, Dan heard the sound of many hoofs coming toward the stable. He stepped out of the stable to see how many of the troops would be returning from the western battle.

The first sign of life he saw was his father. The sun was wanting to rise as members of the family began to gather in the kitchen. There was a child that Dan did not recognize. He thought his son, Cathal, would have remained a baby, but there was a young man with arms out spread reaching for his daddy. Dan was overcome with joy. It was beyond belief how his world had changed in seemingly a short while. Dan took Mary's hands as she stepped into the kitchen. At last, they were together again. Tears filled their eyes as they attempted to drink in the blessing's God had so richly granted to them. The whole O'Flaherty family was together again. It seemed too much to comprehend had been laid before them to enjoy. Mary held Dan's arm and looked into his eyes. Dan felt from the way her hand was clutching his arm, there was something of importance for him to close out everything else he was considering. Mary took him to a bed where there were two children sleeping he had never seen. He looked at them very closely and saw the resemblance in each of their faces. He then looked at Mary and asked, "Is there something I am supposed to know and don't?" Mary said, "Dan, do you remember the lake in the Appalachian Mountains where we fished and camped before you went to war?" Dan said, "I have thought of that memory every day since I left." Mary asked, "Would you like to know how I will remember our time together forever?" Dan asked, "Mary, are you trying to tell me something?" As Mary was smiling, the little boy awoke as she whispered to him, "What is your name?" The child said, "Dan O'Flaherty." Then she faced the little girl and asked, "What is your name?" She said, "Bridget O'Flaherty." Dan looked at Mary with a look of complete bewilderment and asked Mary, "Are these our children?" Mary asked, "And whose children would they be, if I am their mother?" Dan bowed his head as tears began falling like rain. Again, the true blessings of God had come to their lives. He fell to his knees in front of the twins and placed his arms around them as they held their daddy for the first time. Dan asked Mary, "What has the war cost me?" Mary said, "Nothing, but your time and effort to cause freedom for our children to be real. You have given them the greatest gift any father could bring home to his family." Cathal had joined with his brother and sister ready to get to know their daddy.

Dan asked Mary, "How did you decide the names you gave the children?" Mary answered, "Before we left the Indian village to come to New Orleans I remembered when Cathal was born, you said he needed to be his own man. After several days of thinking, Chief Attakullakulla wanted to see the twins. Several of us went to his teepee where he had gathered the other leaders of the tribe for a meeting with us. It turned out to be an Indian ritual ceremony for the newborns. They sang, danced and lifted smoke upward as if the children were members of the Cherokee tribe. Apparently, they had adopted the children as Cherokees. He cut his hand and their hands and tied them together to become one blood.

The Chief then asked me the name of the girl child. Your mother whispered to me the name Bridget, which was the name of the angel that came to the slave ship and saved the lives of Siobhann and Shibeal. When I said Bridget, he held the baby up and prayed in Cherokee and said, her name Bridget and the tribe said, Bridget. The ceremony continued after he gave Bridget back to me. He then took the male child and the tribes began a similar ceremony, which continued with all the leaders saying words in Cherokee. After about an hour, the Chief held the baby over his head and looked toward the sky and said, "Two Dan." He did not ask me our choice of names. The tribe began regarding our family as Cherokee tribe members. After we were adopted Cherokee, the Chief began to indicate his health was failing." Dan told Mary his life felt complete again. He told her she had made him so happy.

The Governor had made arrangements for the family to stay in some guest houses behind the Governor's mansion. Mary asked, "Dan, do you suppose you could arrange for us to clean up for a while. It will take a long time to scrape the trail dust off all of us." Dan said, "My guess is, you will have all the good clean warm water available. You will need to get as clean as you want us to be."

Dan couldn't keep his eyes off his two sons and daughter who were walking around looking at a new world they had never seen before. Joy filled the air, as they gathered together to have a family prayer.

Coleman began by saying, "Lord, here we are again to continue our praise, honor and glorify Your divine presence in our lives. Lord, You have pulled us through again, and we are thankful to You again. Lord, we know it is another gift from You, and we are thanking You for it. Amen."

Dan held his blessed mother, as tears fell from their eyes. Each of them knew none of what they had been given could have come from any other source, but the Lord Himself. Dan whispered in his mama's ear, *thank you for loving me so much.* Delia said, "You have been so good to me." Dan said, "Mama, I love you."

The Governor had food, clothes and anything else they needed to be transformed from the hidden life of the wilderness back to a civilized surrounding. The three children were running everywhere enjoying the good life. When they had raked the dust off and were ready to find out where they were, food in abundance began to be served by several servants. They had a menu from watermelon to pork ribs to select from. Their meal was the first Irish meal they had tasted in a long time. As soon as they had filled themselves, a need for sleep filled the dining room. The tension and fear the family had lived through had been with them night and day. They were ready to be at ease if only for a brief moment.

Dan and Mary, went hand in hand, walking through the Governor's beautiful garden; it was like the gardens Dan had to care for in Spain for his Margarita. Memories of those days filled his mind as they strolled along smelling the beautiful flowers that grew everywhere.

Dan and Mary's joy whispered as they pretended the end of the war and divisive turbulence of life had come to an end. They knew their joy was temporary, but they had the moment, and they intended to hold on to every breath of it. Dan knew from the grasp of Mary's hand, she was thinking of, *the future separation again.* Dan interrupted her solemnness with this statement, "Mary, the war will be over soon, and we will have won a beautiful nation from those who told us we are animals. We will live to behold the greatest nation ever known anywhere on this earth. And, remember this, it would not have been possible without the blood, sweat and suffering of the Scottish and Irish Americans. My hope is our children and our children's children will remember the Irish and Scottish blood that was paid to purchase their days of freedom. I hope they will remember us." Mary said, "Dan, there will always be those who remember to remind the others the cost was the lives of millions of us who held to the faith that a day would come when no one was more important than anyone else, because in God's eyes, we are all the same. Jesus paid the same amount for each and every one of us."

CHAPTER FIFTEEN

FREEDOM ACHIEVED

As Dan began to leave the Governor's mansion, he learned Governor Galvez and General O'Reilly were in Florida involved in fighting the British to keep them from building a staging ground to invade the Southern Colonies. The family stood on the front porch as Dan waved farewell to them once more. He had told his father General Cornwallis was occupying their land in South Carolina, and he was headed there to persuade the British to go back to Europe. Coleman was glad to hear Dan had his mind on protecting their land for farming.

Dan was ready to get this war brought to a close. He and every Scots-Irishman wanted the British out of America. Spain, France and many other countries in the world wanted the same. Some of those countries were shipping money, men and weapons to America to aid in the victory. As Dan rode into camp at Charlotte, North Carolina many things had changed. Large numbers of troops from the Northern Department of the Continental Army had arrived.

Dan went to the Blue Celt headquarters to meet with Lieutenant Colonel Milledge to be briefed. After the Colonel had brought Dan up to date, Dan went to the headquarters of General Nathanael Greene, who had been sent by General Washington to command the Continental Forces of the South.

After conversing with General Greene, it was decided to attach the Blue Celts to General Daniel Morgan, who had the experience and knowledge to use their clandestine talents effectively. The decision had been made to avoid direct confrontation with the British Forces. The two southern Armies were divided into two branches. The first order of business was to make their presence known among the locals to restore the morale of the Americans that had begun to fade away. Dan took command of a Militia Rifle and Sniper Brigade taking a position in the river bottoms of the Broad and Pacolet Rivers.

Information had come to the Americans that Cornwallis had planned to reoccupy North Carolina to renew his desire to launch an invasion toward the north. Cornwallis had also received invalid information the Americans intended to attack the fort at 96 South Carolina. Cornwallis ordered Lieutenant Colonel Banastre Tarleton to save the fort and defeat Morgan's Army. Tarleton was the most despised British soldier of the war. He was the brash, loud mouth poster child of the arrogance, which was the norm demonstrated by every British soldier under the Cornwallis command. Tarleton's reputation was based upon having killed Americans who had surrendered at the Battle of Waxhaw's. (16) (17)

When Tarleton arrived at the fort, he learned General Daniel Morgan's Army was not there. Enraged by having lost an opportunity to again demonstrate his murderous attributes, Tarleton decided to pursue Morgan and ask for reinforcements of British regulars. Cornwallis granted the request for extra troops, as Tarleton took off in hot pursuit of Morgan's Army. After learning of Morgan's location, he drove his command with hard marching, without rest, crossing rivers that had flooded from winter rains. Morgan's scouts reported Tarleton was in hot pursuit so Morgan decided to retreat north to avoid being trapped between the Tarleton and Cornwallis' Armies. (16)(17)

When Morgan approached the Broad River, it was flooded due to heavy rains, which made it difficult to cross. By night fall, he had reached an area known as Cowpens, which was a well-known grazing area for local cattle. Morgan decided to stand and fight. Tarleton learned of Morgan's location and decided to attack after marching the men at 3:00 a.m., instead of resting for the night. (16) (17)

Tarleton did everything he could to display his obsessive arrogance, and frowardness of an untamable mind set, beginning with marching his exhausted dragoons to attack the first line of Americans who opened fire and killed fifteen of his men. The Tarleton dragoons retreated when Tarleton ordered an infantry charge without knowing the alignment of the Morgan troops. The main body of British troops had not made it out of the woods. Every move Tarleton made was proof of his ineptness as a qualified Commander. Dan's Blue Celts used the Tarleton led troops as targets and ultimately destroyed the battle effectiveness of the unit. By 8:00 a.m., Morgan's Command had the battle under control. The mass of bewildered men began to turn and run as volley after volley of shots dropped mislead soldiers to their death. Morgan's men then mounted a bayonet charge as the British soldiers began to collapse. Nearly half of the British and Loyalists infantrymen fell to the ground whether they were wounded or not. Their fight was gone as many began to surrender. Tarleton had one last hope for personal glory, when he found the Legion Cavalry still in one piece. He ordered them to charge, but they refused and fled the field. One last act of desperation caused Tarleton to at least try to salvage the two cannons. He pulled together about 40 Cavalry men and with them tried to save the cannons. When they arrived at what he thought was the location of the cannons, they had been removed. Tarleton escaped and fled to find Cornwallis. (16) (17)

When the final numbers were tallied, 110 British soldiers were killed in action; 712 prisoners were taken which included 200 wounded. The reputation of Banastre Tarleton was destroyed and he became known as the British officer who led the Americans to victory over Great Britain. (16) (17)

Dan could finally sense ultimate victory. Cowpens was a surprising event and a turning point that changed the attitudes of the participants and the spectators of the war. The observers on the side of the Revolutionaries were elevated with hope, they had not experienced since the beginning of the fight. Those of the Southern Colonies came to know victory was possible over the world's mightiest Army. Americans were sure they could go on to victory. The British Army was adjusting to slow, but sure defeat as the certainty of defeat began to plague their false pride. The final result of the Cowpens Battle was the British lost a strategic portion of their forces it could not afford to lose. The actual effect of the battle had on the outcome of the war could not be calculated, until Cornwallis later surrendered in Yorktown, Virginia. When he later evaluated his lack of ability to respond to the snare in which he trapped himself and his Army, *he admitted to himself that it was the Battle of Cowpens, where the designed disaster took the certainty of victory from his grasp.*

The American victory at Kings Mountain and now Cowpens was the decisive jolt to General Cornwallis, who abandoned his efforts to return to South Carolina to persuade more loyalists to join in the Crown's efforts to defeat the Revolutionaries.

Cornwallis was enraged that a novice group of pretend soldiers could defeat the best soldiers Great Britain had to offer. He set about to make General Greene pay for his embarrassment by pursuing his small Army across North Carolina.

During the pursuit, Dan and General Greene felt if they could cross the Dan River, they would have a buffer between the two Armies with an American advantage. Because of the successive victories the American ranks began swelling with American volunteers. Dan had scouts and spies well placed to keep them aware of Cornwallis' movements. Cornwallis also had a group of Loyalists spies. The Loyalist reported to Cornwallis the American General Butler was moving to attack the British troops. The information proved to be incorrect, in that, General Butler was moving his troops to join General Greene's Army. (18) Dan told General Greene he intended to organize, along with the Blue Celts, a detachment to harass the British, while avoiding direct confrontation. Dan's group operated at night, and kept the British demoralized with dead soldiers, who had been killed in their tents while sleeping.

General Cornwallis received a report the Americans were camped near Guilford Courthouse. When Cornwallis verified the dispatch, he began marching toward the Guilford Courthouse, despite having only 1,900 men on hand. Green had re-crossed the Dan River and established a defense of 4,400 men. The battle plan laid out by the American's General Greene was flawed by having his men placed too far apart to support one another. (18) Dan had kept Cornwallis busy trying to avoid the snipers Dan had placed on the way to the battle field.

When the Cornwallis troops began to enter the battlefield, the fighting began over 4 miles from the Courthouse where Tarleton's Light Dragoons had encountered Lieutenant Colonel Henry "Light Horse Harry" Lee's men near Quaker New Garden Meeting House. After a sharp fight the British 23rd Regiment of Foot advanced to aid Tarleton, as Lee withdrew back to the main American lines. (18)

As Cornwallis advanced, his troops began to encounter heavy fire from the Militia. They were supported by Lee's men, who had taken a position on their left flank. When the British entered the woods, they were met by another Militia. As the action continued, Cornwallis ordered the artillery to fire grapeshot into the middle of both troops of men. The desperate move cost as many lives of the British as Americans, but it did halt Greene's counter attack. (18)

At the close of the battle, America had lost 79 killed and 185 wounded. The British had 93 dead and 413 wounded. The British losses continued to whittle away at the numbers of key combat units that could not be replaced. Low on supplies and irreplaceable men, Cornwallis took the remainder of his troops to Wilmington, North Carolina to rest and rebuild. (18) After a while, he then embarked on an invasion of Virginia, while General Greene and General O'Flaherty were scattering the Loyalists and scant military personnel from South Carolina and Georgia. Cornwallis went from North Carolina to Virginia on the grounds that Virginia needed to be chastised in order to hold the Southern Colonies under British rule.

Cornwallis was venturing into territory that had just been invaded by turncoat, Benedict Arnold. He and his raiders began moving through the countryside, destroying supply depots, mills, and other targets of interest. General Washington countered Arnold's destruction by sending General Lafayette a dispatch to stop Arnold. Arnold received reinforcements from New York and his Army was joined by Cornwallis in May. The Americans continued the strategy of avoiding large scale battles, while waiting for the approval of the people to bring reinforcements to the ranks.[19] The good part of Cornwallis's invasion of Virginia was, his Superior officer General Clinton despised Virginia. He did not want any concentrated effort to be wasted in such a large disease-ridden area with such a wide spread, deeply hostile environment, when the area could be pacified with a limited force. General Clinton wanted Cornwallis to conduct operations further north in Maryland, Delaware and Southern Pennsylvania where he believed a large Loyalist support was available. Clinton specifically ordered General Cornwallis to build a naval base with fortification and to send several thousand troops to New York to respond to an attack by the American and French forces. [19] General Cornwallis fortified Yorktown and avoided Lafayette, while awaiting the arrival of the Royal Navy. The American Northern and Southern Armies, along with the naval war ships met at Yorktown, Virginia, in 1781 in an effort to trap the British forces. The French held the strategic position over the British by being able to move against Yorktown or New York. General Washington favored attacking New York, but the French decided to send the fleet to their preferred target at Yorktown. When General Washington learned of the French fleet moving to Yorktown in August, he began to move his Army South to cooperate. The British did not know the French had moved their entire fleet to America. The British did not have the naval resources to match their opponents every move. [19] In early September, French naval forces defeated the British fleet at the Battle of Chesapeake, cutting off Cornwallis's route of escape to New York. Cornwallis hesitated to move his troops because he was waiting to receive support from New York. The time had gone for him to breakout. As Washington's Army entered Yorktown, Cornwallis moved his defensive positions, thus allowing the Americans ever closer, which hastened Great Britain's eventual defeat. [19] On October 19, 1781, the terms of the British surrender were signed by the opposing parties. British arrogance kept Cornwallis from surrendering his sword to Washington as well as his successor. The thought of a group of rabble troops having defeated the King's Army was unspeakable, much less possible. King George III took the news calmly and delivered a defiant address pledging to continue the war with the House of Commons' endorsement. When France and Spain began taking several West Indies Islands, the Parliament in 1782 voted to cease all offensive operation in America and seek peace. Lord North resigned his position as Prime Minister, and the Whigs readily replaced him. The Whigs accepted American Independence as a basis for peace. [19] Dan received a dispatch from General Washington to meet with him before he left to return home. Dan sent him a note saying he was available at any time. Dan went to his own personal tent and closed the flap to be alone for at least a few moments, to drink in the Grace of God that had come to a nation of people that had been freed from the tyranny they had lived under, for all the days of their lives.

Dan stepped outside his tent and beckoned to Colonel Milledge. When the Colonel walked up to Dan, he began asking about the troops and whether any of them had suffered any wounds. The

Colonel reported the troops were too excited to know if there were any injuries. Dan told Colonel John Milledge, Jr. what a fine soldier he had become, since his days with the Rangers.

Dan said, "John, you have made this nation proud for the service you have rendered. I have been blessed by having the opportunity to serve with you." John said, "General, what are we going to do next?" Dan smiled and said, "Whoa! War has a purpose and the purpose is, you go somewhere else to kill the bad folks, so you can go back home and not have to worry with them anymore. John now is the time we can prepare to go home and think about other things for a while. I will tell you this though; we are going home to Georgia and South Carolina, after we go to New Orleans and get our family. It is hard for me to believe we can make that trip and not be watching for a redcoat behind every tree."

General Washington was most anxious to see Dan as the celebration began to create a need for rest. When Dan walked in the General's tent, the General stood and embraced what he termed as, *the most loyal of my friends*, as they sat and stared at one another tears ran from their eyes. After a long period of time of allowing their tears to bathe their souls, the General finally spoke. He said, "What we have done we will never know, because as the years pass others will come to enjoy this gracious gift from God who have other motives than the one you and I share. Those who have not known the grasp of tyranny around the throats of justice and freedom will never know the blessing we share at this moment of repose." Dan said, "General, I have been under the heavy hand of a King every day of my life on this earth, and now to know that no man who walks this earth will ever be over me again to do his bidding, is a blessing beyond compare. The question is, how do we operate a country with everyone being in control, and at the same time, no one person being in control?" General Washington said, "After God has granted us the freedom, we sought, I am sure he will send us a plan to cause it to function if all we do is done to His glory. Dan, the reason I wanted to visit with you is, to personally thank you for the financial, military, and personal support you supplied at the most critical times of the campaign. You told me in the beginning to call upon you when I needed money to keep our army together. You never hesitated or failed in your commitment to support the cause. I have done as you asked me to do, I have not shared the knowledge of your generosity with any other living soul. I know there is a huge debt owed to you. I will disclose what you have contributed and as time develops a method of repayment will be established. You will be repaid. I personally think each family of our new nation needs to be involved in paying those who made it possible. Right now, all I have for you is a medal, which is the highest honor this fledgling nation has to give to those who made this victory possible. Dan there is something else you and I need to discuss before our time together begins to come to a close. As you and I have considered this entire matter, I know some of the conclusions we have reached are the same. The one conclusion I know we share is, if God had not had His Holy Spirit involved in this conflict; there would have been a different outcome. I have had time to reflect upon these matters from the standpoint of observing seasons of depressed trade, great sickness, terrible wars and public disasters, but I have also observed that no matter what conflict comes to mankind, Jesus remains the same. I have seen the times when sin abounds without ceasing, the light of the Word burns low, the prince of darkness destroys mankind with his mighty deceptiveness, but nevertheless, and this truth stands sure; Jesus is the I Am. Dan, at certain periods, diabolical influence seems paramount, the reins of nations appear to be taken out of the hand of the Great Ruler, and yet it is not so. Look through the darkness, and you shall see the Lord God of all mankind amid the hurricane, walking the water of politics ruling national convulsions, governing, overruling, arranging all, making even the wrath of man to praise Him and restraining the arrogance of man according to His wisdom. If you listen closely during these times of doubt, you can hear His voice saying again, "It is I, be not afraid, I am ruling all things. I am coming to rescue My people that they may reach My desired haven for them."(20)

Dan if there was ever a conflict between nations that clearly shows Gods involvement in the affairs of all men, it is our present war. The outcome of this war started in 1695 when the first anti-Catholic Penal laws were introduced in the British Parliament. Those laws had their roots in the hearts of vile men who sought to profit by stealing property that was owned by innocent land owners. At that time, the Catholic land owners owned but seven percent of the total land of Ireland. The Crown of England, with cowardly disdain for the Irish culture, decided to take the land and award it to wrong doer's who supported the King. The Parliament enacted laws to exterminate the entire culture of Irish Catholics. The laws were framed for the commission of genocide. During the period of Oliver Cromwell's, protestant control of the British Empire, the Irish population was reduced by two thirds by being killed in battle, starvation or being sent to work as slaves on plantations in the Islands of the Caribbean. (21)

From 1641 to 1652 over 300,000 Irish people were sold as slaves. The Irish slave trade expanded to Virginia and New England, and then to other Colonies. The usual periods of slavery for the Irish lasted for seven to twenty-one years. The cost for one-way passage to America was seven years of slavery. The first Irish immigration to America therefore started with the forced migration of the Irish race as involuntary indentured servants. The protestant slaves were known as the Scots-Irish, distinguishing themselves from the Catholics. The reason I wanted you to think along with me about this great victory we, by God's Grace, have been given is, every Irish and Scottish family in America are the true sufferers that brought America into becoming the nation it will prayerfully become. Dan, remember this, over half of the American forces were Irish and Scottish soldiers. Many of my Generals, like you, are of Irish decent. And, don't ever forget the number of Irishmen who signed the Declaration of Independence pledging their blood, their lives and their treasure. Somehow, I feel the Irish have carried the torch for all humanity, to show it is within mankind's ability to govern themselves. Dan, to sum it up, I have never been as proud as I am now to have been allowed to serve with such a gallant band of warriors. Without the Irish and the Scottish there would not have been a victory.

The problem we will face when we become self-governed is that plague which has destroyed all nations beginning in bondage growing in faith, increasing in courage, then to strength, and finally to Liberty where we are today. But, then comes leisure, selfishness, complacency, apathy, dependence, weakness back to bondage. I thank God we are at the beginning of a nation that can grow into the greatest nation on earth. I pray for those who will forget the sacrifices we have made to allow them to know freedom. May God bless America's leaders of the future who have to face the issue of being a nation of the people, by the people and for the people instead of their own personal self-interest. America will rise or fall by the character of the leaders they select. What I have enjoyed is being allowed to observe the coming together of same minded men willing to sacrifice their all to become responsible, through their government, for the safety and defense of every other individual American. This same mind set is what will become necessary in years to come as the lamp of vigilance has grown dim; at that time great Americans will again be called upon by the same voice that called each of us forward in this present battle. That same voice will again call out for the warriors of those future days to respond to the call to arms to share the responsibility for their neighbor's defense. That same spirit of America will again rise up to shoulder the responsibility of defending this great land. So long as there are those who care for their neighbors as they care for themselves, there will always be an America."

Dan said, "General, I want you to know, and only you, the funds I have advanced to this cause are funds willed to me by my adoptive parents, Phillip O'Shea and Margarita O'Shea. While visiting with me, when I served General Oglethorpe, they told me they wanted to move from Spain to become a part of this new nation. The funds I have advanced to you would have been with their blessing, if they were here today. General, we thank you for all you have done to cause this victory to have become attainable. No other man could have accomplished this freedom, but you. Our family knows what it is to be despised and rejected by those who are filled with hate for our beliefs and our culture. We now know the burden of a living death has been lifted from our lives. We thank you for allowing our people and our culture to participate in the elimination of the demonic power of evil over our lives."

General Washington said, "Dan, I do not have any idea what form our government will take, but I favor a plan that if we do make wrong choices in our selection of leaders, we have a way to replace them." Dan said, "General, I am going to leave the politics to you. If I had my way, I would want you to become the King of America." The General bowed his head and said, "Dan, I want to be a farmer. Something tells me I can cause Mount Vernon to become a good farm, all it needs is some good workers."

Dan said, "General, I have got to ride to New Orleans and get my family back together. I left them under the care of my uncle, Governor Galvez. We will then be going back to South Carolina, Georgia and maybe Florida to begin again. This time we will not be fighting the Spanish and British Armies." General Washington said, "I have got to bid the troops farewell, and then go home, I would like to rest a few days."

The General extended his arms again and embraced his most admired Irishman, as the two great leaders went their separate ways. When Dan was leaving, General Washington said, "Dan, be sure to tell Governor Galvez I send him my highest regards, and most humble gratitude for the blessings of his efforts along the coast. Also, tell him this enemy is still very angry, and most untrustworthy. Tell him my thoughts are, they will be back. Give your precious family my fondest affection and hope for a blessed future."

Dan stepped out of the General's headquarters and asked Colonel Milledge the location of the men. The Colonel reported they were guarding the prisoners. Dan said, "Do you need me for anything?" The Colonel said, "If something comes up, I know where to find you." Dan said, "Increase the security around General Washington. If we lose him, the war will not be over. Also send more troops to Mount Vernon to protect Mrs. Washington. I may go by there on my way to New Orleans to check on her. Where do you have the spare horses corralled?"

Colonel Milledge said, "Down there behind the two redoubts, which Cornwallis had constructed." Dan made his way to find three good mounts for a journey toward New York to find his sisters. As he rode off toward New Jersey, his chest was completely filled with the breath freedom had supplied. While riding through the forest, his mind began to shed the strategies and military tactics that had been with him night and day, since the first day of the war. His thoughts were focused on Maureen, Shibeal and Weston.

It wasn't long before he found a beautiful stream to wash the stench of war from his body and soul. As he swam in the luxury of just being alone, without fear, he concentrated on the magnificence of the beauty of America. He thought to himself, *just think, we own this place.* He slept for the first time with nothing but the sounds of the night prowlers, trying to find a meal. It was good to hear the silence of the canons.

CHAPTER SIXTEEN

ESPIONAGE REMNANTS

The next morning Dan's mind shifted from the stress of combat to locating Maureen and Shibeal to keep the commitment he had made to find them when the war had been won. He made his way to Richmond where he bought a change of clothes. He was ready for a new image which was being, just another American who had been blessed with all the treasure heaven and earth could offer. As he rode along, he began to see evidence of a new spirit easing out of the shadows. Men, women and children were walking as if a burden had been lifted from their shoulders. In one town, he heard children laughing and playing in front of a school building. In another town he saw patriots walking through the streets of the town, with men tipping their hats to the ladies. A great change was awakening the hidden spirits of a humanity that had known oppression, fear and death from organized murderers and thieves. It made tears run from Dan's eyes to behold the faces of those for whom he had willingly given his all that all men could know freedom as a daily blessing from God.

After several days riding he rode into an area which appeared to be under the control of the British even though he saw some American soldiers standing guard as the British stacked their weapons in designated locations. But, it was not until he rode through the heavily occupied areas of New Jersey did he see the impact of defeat on the men who had lost the battle. He did not see any emotion. The soldiers seemed to be in a trance of doom, as opposed to the arrogance and brutality that had dwelled in their spirits. Some appeared as if their souls had been jarred from them as they wrestled with the shame and humiliation of defeat.

Dan's mind recalled, *how these very men had stripped the dignity and hope for a breath of life from millions of those who were starved and beaten to death.* The Americans suffered because of a desire and choice to worship their God in a manner which brought balm and connection to God within their spirits. As a warrior, Dan reminded himself of his teaching *those who live by the sword shall die by the sword.* Dan uttered a silent prayer, *Lord as they learn Your mercy, may You show them peace and mercy.* Dan was becoming more anxious by the minute to locate Maureen, Shibeal and Weston. He had received information from Mr. Collier as to the approximate location of Weston's office.

When he arrived in New York he found a livery stable to care for the extra horses and then proceeded on his search for Shibeal, Maureen and Weston. He soon came to the area that appeared to be the hub of commercial activity that did not appear as active as Dan had anticipated. The loyalists seemed rather busily involved in moving office furniture from the buildings under the supervision of American troops. Then he saw a building with a sign that read, "Weston Collier, Foreign Investments Counselor." Dan soon found the correct door and knocked. He heard a voice say, "Please come in." As he entered several clerks were busy working. Dan asked one of the clerks if Mr. Collier was available. The clerk told him Mr. Collier was at the jail talking to a client. Dan asked, "How do I find the jail?" When the clerk described the facility, it became clear to him the client was in a

British prison. Dan asked for the location of the prison, the clerk told him it is near the port.

As Dan was mounting his horse, it occurred to him the possibility of both girls being loaded on a prison ship bound for England. Dan knew the stockade would be well guarded. He decided to find the Continental Army Headquarters first, to inform them of the peril of his relatives, and his concern for them being transported to England. Dan introduced himself to the Commanding Officer as General Dan O'Flaherty. The name was very familiar to Colonel Grady Jackson. Dan quickly asked if he had relatives in east Tennessee. He told Dan he had a cousin named Andrew he corresponded with quite often who was being trained to become a lawyer. Andrew had written his cousin three years before telling him of a man named O'Flaherty who had paid his way to college. He then asked, "Would that perhaps be you?" Dan said, "Andrew is a young man I met when he was a young teenager. I admired him then and admire him now." A huge Irish smile came on the Colonels face when he said, "It is beyond belief that this coincidence could be unfolding before my eyes." Dan was thinking about, *God's tender mercy that is new each morning*, as he said, "Colonel, I need your assistance which involves a personal matter."

Colonel Jackson said, "General, you need but say the words and I am at your command." Dan said, "I have just learned my two sisters are possibly being wrongfully forced onto a prison ship probably bound for England. I need help to determine whether my information is correct." The Colonel didn't hesitate. He yelled, "Captain." Captain Benjamin O'Rourke came through the door. Colonel Jackson said, "Captain, this is General Dan O'Flaherty and he has information his sisters are being wrongfully held by the British in a stockade by the port, and he needs our help to rescue them." The Colonel advised the Lieutenant he was in command of headquarters security until he returned. A company of Continental Army soldiers mounted their horses and headed for the port at full gallop. The Continental Army as yet had not penetrated very deep into the British stronghold in New York. All the soldiers under Colonel Jackson's command were on the alert for combat.

When the troops arrived at the stockade, they saw hundreds of Americans being held as prisoners which was baffling to the Colonel. When they dismounted the Colonel went to the stockade entrance and asked to see the Commanding Officer. The guard led the two Continental Army officers to the British Commanding officer.

The Colonel out ranked the Major in charge of the stockade. The Colonel asked the Major to explain why the Americans were being held as prisoners. The Major answered, "I just follow orders, I do not ask questions." The Colonel asked, "Have you heard the war is over and the Americans have won?" The Major replied, "Yes Sir." The Colonel then asked, "Whose orders are you obeying now." The Major replied, "The Americans." The Colonel said, "Major, I need your help. I want you to go with me to the stockade and order all those prisoners freed." The Major said, "As you desire, Colonel."

They walked to the stockade gate. He told one of the guards to inform all the other guards to assemble at the gate. Within a short time, thirty-five British soldiers had assembled. The Major told the soldiers, "The Americans are here to free the prisoners, lay your rifles down, now." The British soldiers were stunned. The surrender of England to America was in the process of being understood in the very heart of the British Army. The British Major ordered the gates to be opened. When the prisoners heard the command, they were stunned but, they soon realized they were being rescued by the Continental Army. All of them had been imprisoned to the extent they were dehumanized and did not fully comprehend being told they were free.

Dan began to mingle among the prisoners searching for Maureen and Shibeal. As he walked closer to the dock area he saw a young lady with black hair sitting on the ground. She had been beaten and wounded. Dan walked over to her and stooped down and asked if she knew Maureen. The young lady's mouth and eyes were bleeding but as she looked at Dan, he saw her blue eyes which told him it was Maureen. He touched her hair and learned she had on a black wig. He removed the wig as her beautiful red hair unfolded and touched her shoulders. Dan's heart was broken because he realized he was responsible for persuading her to become involved in the horror of warfare. Within several minutes, Maureen became more conscious of what was happening. She looked at Dan and even though it caused great pain, she managed a smile. Dan and Maureen bowed their heads as the tears of freedom flowed from their eyes and hearts. Dan lifted her in his massive arms and carried her to his horse and put her on the saddle. Dan saluted Colonel Jackson and told him of his gratitude.

As Dan began to think of, *Shibeal,* Weston Collier walked up and said, "The clerk guessed you were here at the docks." Dan said, "Weston, God bless you for being here." Weston had been to the British Headquarters seeking a Writ of Habeas Corpus attempting to talk to someone in General Clinton's office, but everyone refused to discuss the release of Maureen and Shibeal with him. Weston told them he had a writ to present for them to be freed on the basis of mistaken identity, but he soon learned the British high command knew them as Olivia Peel and Katherine Thorpe. They were being held responsible for Cornwallis's surrender. They told him he would have to find a judge to hear his complaint. Weston knew they were playing for time to get them shipped out of the country to try them for treason in an English court because they knew there were no judges in America to hear the Habeas Corpus petitions because the Continental Congress had not established a court system. Weston said, "Thank God, you went to the stockade with the soldiers. I think the British soldiers yielded because you are an American General." Dan said, "Weston, whatever the reason, they are free, and I am deeply grateful for the blessing. Maureen needs medical care, and I have not found Shibeal. Could you take her to your office and get her medical treatment as soon as possible?" Weston began leading the horse to his office as Dan began to look for Colonel Jackson.

Dan located Colonel Jackson to tell him Maureen was too injured to tell him where Shibeal was located. He said, "Colonel, when I stood on the dock and looked in the harbor, I saw a prison ship being maneuvered to the south side of the harbor. If we could use one of the skiffs tied to the dock, we could overtake the ship before it sails for England." The Colonel ordered ten of his men to row the skiff toward the ship. Colonel Jackson ordered the British Major to go with them to stop the ship.

When the skiff caught up with the prison ship, the Major ordered the first mate to turn the ship back toward the dock. While the ship was slowing to make the turn to return to the docks, the Major ordered the seaman to drop the ropes for them to board the ship. Dan was the first to grab a rope to climb up the side of the ship. As soon as Dan's feet stood on the ships deck, he asked, "Where is the Captain located?" The seaman answered, "In the Captain's quarters." Dan said, "Show me." By that time, six of the soldiers, the Major and Colonel had boarded. The smell of rotten flesh and human waste filled the air as they walked to the Captain's quarters. When they arrived, Dan moved to the front of the line and kicked the Captain's door open. When the door opened, Shibeal cried, "Dan, thank God." Dan looked at the Captain and asked him what he had in mind for the lady. The Captain said, "I was making sure this beautiful lady was comfortable." Dan asked Shibeal if she was comfortable. Shibeal stood up and ran to Dan and pulled him to her as she began to tremble and sob. The Captain asked Dan, "What is she to you?" Dan said, "This lady is part of everything I hold sacred and precious in this life." The Captain's face began to show the fear he was experiencing from his toes to his hair. Dan asked the Captain how quick he could get this filthy boat turned around. The Captain said, "Not long." Dan told the Captain to go upon deck and order his men to remove the chains from all the prisoners and help each one of them to come up on deck.

Dan asked Shibeal if she could walk the stairway to the deck. Shibeal said, "I will try." Dan helped her up the stairs where the Colonel was waiting to lift her up over the last step that was broken. The Captain began following Dan's orders. By the time the ship docked over two hundred prisoners were standing on deck. When the boat docked, Dan carried Shibeal to the dock. The Colonel told the Captain to free all the prisoners as soon as possible and have the people treated by the Continental Army Doctors.

Dan asked Weston if he had a place where they could rest for a few days before they returned home. Weston said, "General, I am glad you asked me that question, because I want you to see the home my father and I bought with your money."

They continued to provide water and care to Shibeal and Maureen; it was obvious they were dehydrated. After approximately two hours, Dan asked her, "Do you feel like riding a horse?" Weston interrupted by saying, "General, these ladies should be riding in the best carriage in New York for all they have done for America." Weston asked one of his clerks to get his carriage. Within a short time, the carriage arrived, and Dan carried Maureen and Shibeal to the carriage. As they rode along, Maureen laid her head on Dan's shoulder and said, "Well, we did it, Big Brother, didn't we?"

Tears began flowing in Dan's eyes as he came face to face with the full responsibility of what he had done to the lives of three precious, very special individuals who trusted him with their lives by becoming involved in the war for freedom. The impact of that thought *caused him to sob, but in his heart, he knew the combination of their tears had made freedom possible.*

Weston said, "General, I want to thank you from the depth of my heart for including me in the greatest adventure that could have ever occurred in my life." As the carriage entered the iron gates of one of the most beautiful homes in New York, Dan was reminded of the palace of which he was raised in Spain. Dan said, "Weston, this place is magnificent." Weston said, "Now, you know how I felt the first time I saw it." As the carriage pulled up to the front door, the butler came to open the side door of the carriage. Dan stepped out and carried Maureen in his arms as he walked inside. Weston took Shibeal to the master bedroom. The girls decided to share the same room since it would be more convenient to provide care for them. Dan told

Weston to get medical help as soon as possible and, he also asked some of the ladies to help them take a good bath with lye soap. Weston told the butler to give Dan the bedroom next to the master bedroom. While they were waiting for the doctor to arrive, Dan took the opportunity to bathe himself because he knew some of the prisoners were suffering from typhus fever.

When the doctor arrived, Dan told him the two ladies would be treated in the home. The doctor agreed. When the doctor examined them, he became concerned how much damage had been done to them from blows they had received to their abdomen. After several days of care, they began to drink chicken broth; within two weeks they wanted to sit outside to get some sunshine if the weather permitted.

The one thing Dan had longed for was getting to know his family and here was the opportunity of a life time for them to truly get to know one another. Dan was very patient waiting for them to indicate to him how deep in their spirits they had been injured. The doctor continued to check their abdomen for any indication of an intestinal puncture. Their appetites began to improve, but it was clear their spirits had been severely harmed. Weston and Dan were very attentive. Sharing the same living quarters gave them the opportunity to share their feelings. Shibeal was the perfect big sister to Maureen. The four of them had formed an inseparable bond. They had walked hand in hand in a dark world few people had visited and survived. Dan could tell it mattered a great deal to Weston for Maureen to return to the good health she had always enjoyed.

Dan was so proud of them, but they would come to know their experience would remain a private joy that probably would never be revealed. As time passed joyfully by being constant company for one another, their being together became a requirement for their daily happiness. On one occasion, Dan was strolling through the home and discovered a guitar. Dan told Weston he would like to play them some Irish songs after he had knocked the rust off of his talents. Weston told Dan he enjoyed playing the guitar. It wasn't long before they were singing together to entertain themselves. They began to truly heal being surrounded by the love and care they had received for several weeks.

After many weeks had passed, Maureen and Shibeal were doing much better. One morning they had the opportunity to share some of their infiltration of the enemy experiences with Dan. The servants had the day off and the doctor was treating Shibeal and Maureen once per week.

Weston began by telling them the Retreat Center they had built near the bank of the Hudson River had become the center of General Clinton's interest for rest and relaxation. The British officers also frequented the facility as planned. He told Dan it had been designed in such a manner so as to provide for the British officers to ride Thoroughbred and Arabian horses. He told him the facility had twenty-five separate luxurious rooms for the British officers to rest and be entertained. Weston further explained he had designed a meeting place in the center of the facility where the military officers could and did have discussions pertaining to the detailed plans of the war.

Weston had designed, in four different areas in the room, a fake wall that allowed the sound of the room to be heard in a basement below the room. In addition to that, he had designed a ballroom for the Commanding General to entertain the British officers and the

King's Ambassadors along with their ladies. Weston then began telling Dan of the magnificent work they had done to manage the Retreat Center and the horse farm. Shibeal also monitored the number of British ships in the harbor to match the number of troops Maureen had heard the officers discuss from the confidential relationships she had established with the British officers. Weston further disclosed the horse farm was a perfect cover for their covert activities because the horses had to be ridden two to three times a week which gave the couriers of the information a normal appearance to suspicious observers. Weston and Shibeal also received money from Matthew Collier, Weston's father, who had shipped the money in barrels filled with wine from Spain. When the barrels were delivered to a wholesale liquor store, the wine was then drained from the barrels. There remained tightly sealed metal cylinders that appeared to be bottles filled with money, which was then taken to the Retreat Center. The cylinders were then wrapped in potato sacks and taken to the courier to be delivered to General Washington for him to use at his discretion.

The Continental Congress did not have the money to pay the soldiers. The General was able to keep the Army together with money he received from individual contributors and financial support from allies in Europe.

Weston revealed General Washington did not know the source of any information that had been provided to him. The delivery of the information was done on three occasions each week by giving the information to a rider who delivered it to another agent who was waiting in a small boat on the Hudson River. He then took the information to the other side of the river to be delivered to General Washington, personally. Weston disclosed it took some time before

General Washington had faith in the validity of the information. When he became convinced the information was valid, he sent a bottle of vanishing ink for Maureen to use. As the war began to come to an end, General Clinton and all his officers became more and more suspicious of everything and everyone. Weston said, "During the Battle of Yorktown, one of Clinton's officers discovered the secret door to the basement under the assembly room. By the grace of God, no one was in the basement when the discovery was made. The British command connected us as being responsible for the outcome of the war. A warrant was issued for our arrest, but I was able to hide until the war ended. They took Shibeal and Maureen to British headquarters and tortured them for hours. As the ill-fated reports of the status of the war began to be delivered to General Clinton, indicating the possible defeat of the Cornwallis Army, their torturers began becoming self-concerned. If they killed them after the war was over they would be charged with murder. After thinking about it, they decided to put the girls on a prison ship to be shipped to England for trial."

Dan said, "Weston, I am going to request that none of this information ever be disclosed to any living person beside us. I want them to know the fruits of their labor in helping freedom to become a reality, but no one else. They are not the kind of ladies that need the adulation of people to be who they are."

Weston said, "General, there is one thing you need to know. In British circles, Maureen is known as Olivia Peel, and Shibeal is known as, Katherine Thorpe. No one has ever heard their names mentioned. One more thing, the nation owes General Fredricko de Longoria the very highest tribute the new nation can give to a patriot.

If it was not for his commitment and his superb training, the British would have discovered the operation which would have resulted in our death."

Dans response to their report was well received. He told them he had prayed for their safety each day and now he knew his prayers had been answered. He expressed his gratitude from the depths of his heart. He said, "Everyone who makes a great sacrifice as you have done causes those who know what you have done to reward you. There will come a day when your efforts in behalf of America can be revealed. Until that time, it is imperative our secrets remain our secrets." Everyone agreed.

As their health began to improve, one morning Dan was visiting with them about their mother teaching him to do the Irish jig. When Dan said, "Irish jig," Maureen's eyes lit up and she said, "Mama taught me to do the jig too." Dan suggested they ask Weston to play them a good tune while they did the real Irish jig. Maureen liked the idea and Dan quickly invited Weston to the party. Weston began playing as Dan and Maureen began the ancient joy of jig dancing, which was passed to them through hundreds of years of their culture. While they were dancing, Dan asked Shibeal if Bridget had taught her the "jig?" Shibeal said, "Somehow I missed out, but I would like to learn it now." Dan said, "Get yourself up here and we are going to learn the "jig." Shibeal had begun to laugh like she had never laughed in her life. As the three of them arm in arm with one another danced the "jig." Their stamina was returning. Dan was ready to hear them laughing again as the winds of healing took all the memories of harm away from their souls.

CHAPTER SEVENTEEN

RECLUSION

As time passed the question of what to do next became the subject of the family discussion. Dan said, "I would like for the three of you to consider us leaving this area of America and travel to where I know some children and their beautiful mother are waiting for us to return." Weston asked, "Are you talking about me going with you?" Dan said, "Well of course, did you have something else planned?" Weston said, "No, in fact, I was wondering what the other part of America was like." Dan said, "Good! Let's plan on getting prepared for a journey back to where we call home. There are some folks I want you to meet you might find very interesting."

Dan continued, "I promised General Washington I would go by his home to check on his family. That shouldn't take too long." Weston asked, "Are you serious? You mean to tell me we are going to General George Washington's home?" Dan said, "And, I must stop by an Indian Chief's village that cared for my family, to whom I am deeply indebted."

Weston asked, "Well, who is going to take care of all of this property?" Dan said, "Tell the butler to manage the house and hire someone to take care of the farm. We can have your law firm's correspondence sent to Georgia." Everything Dan had said to Weston was like living in a world of dreams that suddenly was becoming reality. Weston was ready for the next scene.

It took them the better part of two weeks to get prepared for the journey. When Weston told them he was getting a carriage for the trip, Maureen and Shibeal looked at one another and grinned and told Weston how much they appreciated the thought, but they preferred to ride a horse. They told Weston they had traveled some of the roads they were going to travel, and they knew a carriage would not make it through the country. Weston took their word because they knew what they were talking about and he was guessing.

Dan had taken his time selecting the horses for the journey. He had ridden several of them to make certain they did not become a problem. Dan had a great interest in horses and had, in the back of his mind, bringing the horses from New York to Georgia. As they began their journey Weston and Dan were of the same mind, which was, to travel at a pace that would not cause Maureen and Shibeal further discomfort.

Dan began pondering the trip in his mind the day they began and noticed he didn't have to consider military maneuvers because he didn't have any enemies. That was the first time he had realized the British were actually defeated and the survivors were on their way to Europe. He thought, *thanks be to God.* In Dan's mind his intention was, *to cause their journey to be a very memorable occasion for Weston, Maureen and Shibeal to learn about the landscape of America.* Each of them had on their minds, *going to the home of General Washington.* The three of them had never imagined themselves standing in the presence of the General who defeated the most powerful Army in the world.

Weston had lived his childhood in Spain, the son of the most prominent lawyer in Europe and had never experienced the difficulties of life as Dan's family because all the O'Flaherty's had been thrust into adverse circumstances of life beyond their control. Dan felt it was time for the different views of life be joined by mutual experiences. Maureen's life experiences were limited to being born in a prison, rescued by a brother, being a fugitive from justice, and ultimately becoming a spy in the American Revolutionary War. Shibeal, because of her mother and father becoming indentured slaves and transported to a foreign nation, was left with a cousin who very fortunately turned out to be a blessing from God. Upon Bridget's death, she and her sister, Siobhann were again orphaned and became cared for by an uncle whose name was Eamonn O'Flaherty. None of their life had been to experience the time and opportunity to just stop and look around at the magnificent creation God had given to them as a birth place for the soul to prepare for its journey to forever. Dan enjoyed watching them grow each day in the knowledge and understanding of how great it is just to be given a beautiful day in a land where everyone is free from the horror imposed upon them by the Crown.

Dan loved fresh pork and soon found some half-grown pigs eating acorns. It didn't take him long to have some pork ribs and pork ham smoking over an open fire. This was a meal they could remember. Weston was settling into being an American with great enthusiasm. About half way to Mount Vernon, the concern Weston had for Maureen's health became a concern for Maureen generally, which was unexpected for them because, after all, their views of their relationship were to be covert partners in an attempt to set a nation free from tyranny. But, they found their new identification with one another a pleasant set of thoughts to consider.

Dan and Shibeal were aware of the attention Weston and Maureen had begun to share with one another. They stayed amused at Weston and Maureen as they attempted to conceal their feelings. It reminded Dan of the days when he first met Mary. The imagination of love is more powerful than the will of human beings. Dan learned the best path was to surrender to the desire of what God was in the process of joining together.

Every time they stopped to make camp, Weston and Maureen enjoyed walking together in the woods to find firewood. Just before they reached Mount Vernon, they noticed Weston and Maureen had begun to hold hands as they went in search of firewood. Dan was aware the negative remnants of their joint efforts in espionage was in the process of working itself out of their systems allowing the matters of joy, happiness and love to fill the wounds that war had caused. Dan chuckled when he thought of, *Weston having to tell his father he had become an American.* After many days on the trail they were getting closer to Mount Vernon. As they rode up the path to the Washington home, he could see the security Colonel Milledge had designed to protect the Washington family.

Apparently, Mrs. Washington had been looking through her front window as Dan approached the home, because she met him at the front porch. She said, "Dan, you have been on my mind for a while, because I wanted to tell you personally how great your men have been to my family during this period of time. I cannot thank you enough for the protection and peace of mind you have provided for our family and all you have done to cause this dream to become real.

We all are so blessed. It is a time when all of us are so filled with the joy of our victory; words cannot express the depth of gratitude we are experiencing. I know this, the entire countries of Scotland and Ireland are rejoicing with us. My prayer is for those who are still under the tyranny will be blessed by God to come to America. America was given to those who have suffered abuse to have a place to heal their wounds and live good lives.

I want to fix you and your family the best breakfast you have ever eaten, so tell me how some smoked ham, biscuits and gravy fit with your appetite." Dan said, "Sounds perfect to me." Mrs. Washington asked, "Who is this you have brought to see us?"
Dan said, "We are on our way home and I promised the General to stop by and inspect the security. I wanted you to meet my sisters, Maureen, Shibeal and my attorney's son, Weston Collier." Mrs. Washington was overly joyful to meet Maureen, Shibeal and Weston. She told Maureen and Shibeal, "I can see the family resemblance." Dan said, "We all are so blessed."

Mrs. Washington said, "There is someone who has been wanting to see you who is by the river in the back yard. Dan peeked through the door and much to his surprise; General Washington was under the big oak tree looking toward the east. Dan said, "I don't want to interrupt him." Mrs. Washington said, "Dan you are the one person he knows that could never be an interruption." She suggested they visit with the General, while she prepared their meal. When General Washington saw Dan, he looked very surprised and then a teeth shining smile broke out from ear to ear. He reached out to welcome Dan and meet three strangers. The first words he said to Dan was, "I thought I had lost you." Dan said, "General, I had a commitment I needed to keep locating my sisters and when I arrived to get them things became complicated. But, as soon as we got everything worked out, we headed your way." Dan very proudly introduced Weston Collier, Maureen O'Flaherty and Shibeal O'Flaherty to General Washington who was grateful to meet Dan's family members.

The General told them the wind was too chilly to sit outside and invited them in for breakfast. Mrs. Washington prepared a breakfast they would never forget. Maureen was most appreciative because the meal reminded her of her mother's cooking. The occasion was truly a gathering of the eagles who knew in their hearts, the price that had been paid to be allowed to eat in peace. After the meal was served, General Washington was anxious to talk of victory and planning the design of a new nation and how anxious he was to plant his spring crops. The great General told them he was glad it was over because he was ready to be a full-time farmer.

The General asked them to please sit in the living room to continue their visit. When everyone was comfortably seated, the General began bringing Dan up to date on some of the unknown events that took place at the close of the war. He began by telling them of Dan's great work in establishing a spy network before he left to command the Continental Army of the Southern Colonies. He told Dan if they had not had that network of patriots, America would have lost the war. The General said, "Dan, before you left I remember you bringing the members of the spy group to meet me, so I could know them personally." Dan said, "That was the plan, General." The General said, "That was what I thought too, but about two years ago, I began receiving information from an unknown source. At first, I thought it was a trap that General Clinton's people were setting for me. However, as time passed I began receiving information that not only was vital to our survival, but was also timely, in fact, most of the information I received was three days before the event. After a while I began to completely trust whoever the patriots were to the extent I sent them a bottle of ink by the courier. Near the end of the war the information I received from those wonderful people kept me from attacking General Clinton's Army in New York. I received information that Cornwallis had trapped himself in Yorktown which ultimately led to his surrender."

When Weston, Maureen and Shibeal heard the words of the Commanding General of the Continental Army, George Washington, stating the effect their concealed efforts had upon the eventual defeat of the British Army, they were amazed what they had done could have been of such importance. The humility of their sprits prevented them from knowing the true value of their efforts. Dan was on the brink of tears, because of the knowledge of the impact their work and risk had been for America's victory. The General asked Dan if he knew anything about that particular group of spies. Dan said, "General, I was busy with the southern campaign. When I left your tent that day, I introduced you to everyone I knew at that time who was active in covert activity. It could be some New York patriots took it upon themselves to support the Revolutionaries for example, Spain and France." The General's insight told him Dan was obligated to protect the identity of those people. He understood Dan's attempt at secrecy was to protect their lives in the future. He smiled at Dan in such a manner Dan understood he knew the truth.

General Washington said, "It could be they did not want to become known, so they could go home and live in peace when the war was over." Dan said, "That is probably the truth." Dan said, "General, we have taken up too much of your time away from your family; we need to get on the road to New Orleans and get our family back together."

As he rode down the path to the front gate, he turned his horse quickly toward Mount Vernon raised his hand and saluted the General. The General raised his hand in fond farewell, saluting his most faithful friend. Then his thoughts shifted to*, the road toward his family*. He began thinking of, *the Appalachian Trail to east Tennessee and the "First Beloved Man," Attakullakulla, the Cherokee leader, who had cared for and watched over his family while he was separated from them by the war.* He was considering the great debt he owed such a good man, as he thought of, *something to give him as a gift to memorialize their friendship.* The Chief had been like a brother to Dan and he was considering a special gift for him. It was when they reached the southwest region of Pennsylvania before Weston began to settle in some kind of comfort mounting a saddle before dawn each morning. Maureen had begun to become very attentive to the needs of Dan and Weston which was an answer to the many prayers they had prayed for her recovery. After the adjustments were made the remarkable beauty and grandeur of America began to take over their thoughts as they entered the mountain ranges in the mid-west.

Dan re-discovered the trail he had traveled years before. Dan began to recognize the region where he and the Blue Celts had hunted to keep the Celts and the Indian tribe supplied with fresh meat.

One afternoon the area became very familiar, as they found the trail and headed for East Tennessee. As they traveled, Dan could see signs of where the tribe had hunted. The closer they got to the camp ground, the more Dan became excited to be with his friend once again. Dan finally located one of the young men who was hunting at the time and made him understand he had come to visit the Chief. When they arrived at the Chief's teepee, and as they were dismounting, an Indian stepped out, whom Dan did not know. He asked to see Attakullakulla. The Chief made a hand sign from his heart to indicate the Chief had gone away. Dan finally understood that his good friend had died. He left a son whose name was, Dragging Canoe. Dan asked the Chief if he could see him. The Chief sent one of his sons to find him. Dan decided he would give his son his personal hunting knife to show his friendship for his wonderful father. The young man was very grateful, and Dan told the Chief how grateful he was for the tribe caring for his family. Communication was difficult, but Dan was able to make him understand.

They traveled on through Mississippi and finally reached New Orleans. When they rode up to the Governor's Mansion, there was a battalion of soldiers guarding the area. Dan dismounted, introduced himself as the Governors nephew, and was escorted to the quarters behind the mansion. Dan led his horse slowly up to the door, while noticing a young man climbing a rope hanging from a tree. When he had climbed to the top, he let go, and fell to the ground, and started climbing the rope again. Dan walked over to tell his young son he was back from the war. Dan was looking at his son and hardly recognized him, because he had grown so much, which saddened his heart. Dan wasn't sure Cathal knew who he was. He asked, "Where is your daddy? The young man replied, "Fighting a war for freedom." Dan said, "Oh, no he isn't." The young man asked, "Well, where is he?" Dan said, "I am your daddy." Cathal ran to his father and grabbed his leg. Dan kneeled, placed his arms around his son and held him close. Cathal said, "We have been waiting for you." Dan said, "I am here to stay." Mary glanced out the window and saw Dan talking to his son. She ran through the house yelling "They are here." The whole family followed Mary outside, and each one of them had to touch them to see if they were real. Dan finally said, "It is really us. Where are my twins?" Mary said, "They are coming, they have been taking a nap."

The Governor was in the upstairs bedroom as he looked into the yard, and there was his nephew, his nieces Maureen, Shibeal, and a stranger. He hurriedly dressed and ran downstairs into the backyard to welcome them home. There were chairs under the big oak tree. The family gathered to thank God; the circle had not become broken. Dan told the Governor some of the comments he had heard General Washington say concerning the Governor's support of America.

The Governor had to tell Dan of God's intervention in the war. He told Dan Great Britain secretly declared war on Louisiana and New Orleans. He told of the King and Lord George Germaine sending orders to General John Campbell at Pensacola, Florida instructing him to take all the troops necessary to take New Orleans and Louisiana from Galvez. The Governor said, "But unfortunately for Great Britain, the secret orders fell into my hands, which gave me time to prepare for the attack. We defeated the British in every location they tried to attack." He also said, "A year later, we attacked Pensacola and Mobile by land and sea, and recaptured the land the British had taken earlier. The victories left the British with no bases along the Gulf Coasts." Dan told him the General had given him credit for keeping the British from encircling the Americans, and kept open the vital conduit for supplies, which was provided by Oliver

Pollock. General Washington so respected Bernardo de Galvez, he had him stand to his right during the July 4th parade. (12)

The family visited for hours as they watched Cathal perform his skills of climbing the rope and the other two children watching Cathal as they played with a puppy. Dan was thinking to himself, *this family of ours is closer now than it would have been if we had been together every day of our lives.* As he thought of the reasons, one of them was because, *Patrick and Barbara had given their lives to the welfare of their parents.* Dan was compelled to tell them how he felt about the sacrificial life they had given to their family. He beckoned to them to come to him to share some private thoughts. Dan began with his head bowed and then he turned to them and said, "Patrick, I want you to know there has not been a battle of which I was involved that I was not aware of your efforts to keep me from being killed. Of all the soldiers I know who have stood by my side, you are my hero." Dan then looked at Barbara as her eyes began to tear up and he said, "Barbara, when I see that Irish smile on mama's face, I know it is you who kept her smiling all these years. Just know how much I love and respect both of you and I am completely aware the largest portion of our happiness as a family today is dedicated to the both of you." As he walked away he glanced toward the edge of the barn area and there was Shibeal and Siobhann holding hands with a look of complete and total peace for the first day of their entire life.

The Governor insisted they have a meal together as one family. The meal was fit for the attendance of royalty. Dan told his uncle of his appreciation for caring for his family during his absence. The Governor said, "I have never enjoyed anything as much in my life." The Governor asked Dan of his plans. Dan told him his father wanted to raise cotton in Georgia and South Carolina. He also told him of his desire to bring as many Irish and Scottish immigrants to America as he could. Dan's comment was, "I would pray everyone who has been under British rule would have at least one opportunity for freedom." He said, "I am thinking sincerely about buying some ships to transport farm products to Europe and providing passage for the Irish and Scottish back to America. This nation needs hearts and minds that yearn to be free to provide for themselves without government involvement." The Governor said, "Dan that is a wonderful thought, we really are relatives in the spirit. For something as wonderful as America to have been accomplished when all General Washington had to work with was the unknown, the ignored, and the meekest people on earth, who are known as the Scottish and the Irish; it had to be another one of God's miracles. Let us praise God for the gift of America."

CHAPTER EIGHTEEN

HOMEWARD BOUND

Dan met with his family prior to leaving New Orleans to make sure living in South Carolina, Georgia or Florida was what they wanted to do. The family was set on becoming farmers. Dan had learned something during the war he wanted to share with his father which was: the land in South Carolina was more suited for farming rice and indigo than cotton. Georgia was the place to grow cotton. Dan had begun to marvel how easy it was to adjust to a life that didn't involve being harmed or thinking of some way to harm another person. By the time Dan had finished organizing the necessities and the family passengers for the trip home, he had to buy twelve wagons to make the journey. He thought to himself, *traveling didn't use to be this complicated."*

With most all the participants involved in the journey being Irish and Scottish a plan was made to make this trip the most fun filled trip of their lives. Dan made up his mind because every person in the O'Flaherty family had missed major parts of their lives under the rule of a ruthless, tyrannical King who had caused suffering to be the only life they knew, it was time for them to know the joy God intended.

Dan and Mary knew the trip could be remembered as everyone having time to get re-acquainted and truly getting to know the qualities of one another and perhaps, even learning secrets some of them had, that had never been shared with one another. As they prepared to load the final items, Dan was nowhere to be found. In about an hour he returned with a case that appeared to be a case for a musical instrument. They were all shocked, but no one asked any questions. Coleman told Delia, "I guess he gets that from your side, but he will tell us about it when he wants us to know." Dan put the case in the wagon he would be driving.

The Governor had insisted Dan take thirty Spanish bred horses for breeding stock. The Governor had also accumulated a large herd of jersey cows as well as three bulls for breeding; even though the jersey was not well known, the breed was becoming known as the best milk cows in America. The Governor brought the breed from Spain to help feed his troops. When the Governor mentioned milk, Dan's mind went back to, *the time of living on the Bryan O'Flaherty's farm in Ireland, where he remembered his mother warming his milk in the morning for his breakfast.*

Dan had never been as completely happy as he was at this special moment. The only missing element to truly have heaven on earth would be for Phillip, Margarita O'Shea and Eamonn O'Flaherty to be making the journey with them. Dan had made arrangements for half of the men to be riding ahead of the wagon train and half behind with some of the men driving the horses and cattle. Mary wanted Maureen and Weston to ride in their wagon.

Managing the problem of crossing the vast Mississippi River was a difficult undertaking. The ferry was not built to transport the number of cows and horses they had brought. It took a full week to get everyone and everything across the river safely. When they had successfully crossed, Dan looked at Mary and said, "We are supposed to be resting. I think we really need to rest for a while." The Blue

Celts wanted to catch some catfish and Coleman was the man who could show them how to fish. "Two Dan" and Cathal caught a frog for bait, some of the men had found some earthworms, Coleman had the hooks and a yearning to fish that dated back to years before Dan was born when he fished off the coast of Ireland. Within an hour, they were fishing for catfish in the mighty Mississippi River, and for once in a long time, they were enjoying their lives. Everyone was at peace for a change, the troop was not under attack or preparing to kill or be killed or being attacked by an Army which outnumbered them four to one. There they were drying off from a nice swim in some good clean water preparing to eat fish until they were filled to the brim. As one of the Celts put it, "This feels just like being an Irish American."

Dan had given his hunting knife to the Cherokee, Chief Attakullakulla's son, Dragging Canoe. But, he had bought a new knife at a hardware store in New Orleans. It had not been sharpened, but Cathal and Two Dan wanted to look at it. Dan said, "It is time for you boys to learn how to sharpen a knife." Dan had a whet rock in the wagon he retrieved to sharpen his new knife. Dan was sitting on a stump when he pulled out his knife and began pulling the fine metal across the stone. The boys were intrigued and as they stood by their dad, he asked them, "Do you want to learn to do this?" Both said, "Yes Sir!" Dan put Cathal between his legs and took his left hand to hold the whet stone as he carefully pulled the knife across it. After they had pulled the knife across the rock on both sides about 20 times, Dan used his finger to test the sharpness of the blade. Then he took the knife and shaved some hair from the top of his forearm. Dan then said, "What do you think?" Cathal said, "It sure seems sharp to me." "Two Dan" wanted to learn also. Dan showed him how to put the edge on the point of the knife. About that time, one of the Celt soldiers brought five hump back blue catfish to the fire. Dan said, "Now we are going to find out if the knife is sharp." When they had skinned four of the five fish another soldier brought seven more catfish. When they decided to start cooking the fish, they had caught thirty-two averaging eight pounds per fish. Dan said, "All of the sudden, I am not in a hurry to go anywhere." With that statement, they decided to stay where they were for four more days to catch fish, rest and swim in the mighty river.

After Mary and Delia, and some good help from the troops had cooked the fish the occasion turned out to be a real Celtic get-together. When they reached their fill of the meal, Dan brought the mysterious leather case to the circle and pulled out a guitar. Very few had ever heard Dan play a musical instrument or sing a song. Mary had heard him humming a little tune now and again, but not any tune with words. Dan had already put the strings on the guitar. He began to tune the strings and then he began a ballad he had written after the last battle. He said, "Here is a song I wrote a few days ago. I named it, Spirit of Freedom."

SPIRIT OF FREEDOM

Let me tell the story how our freedom all began
This nation born of spirit with its people in command
A land with snow top mountains, freedom to do my all
I wondered who those hearts were who answered that first call

Once upon a time in a faraway land
Kings had all the rights and made slaves of man
But something began to happen as the time went by
A prayer rose up for liberty, freedom was their cry

Brave hearts began to gather from far across the sea

They'd ride the waves to freedom for a taste of liberty
Many weeks on ships at sea were we, no place to lay our heads
We touched the shores of freedom where our dreams had led

CHORUS:
We told ourselves America is where we belong
We'll cast our nets and farm our fields to make our nation strong
We called ourselves Americans; with grace we would stand tall
With solemn vow we'll live our lives with liberty for all

With England's chains to bind us, no longer were we free
A call rose up for freedom and their cry for liberty
This new nation would be born amidst the cannon's roar
With Washington to lead them and our country ever more

We can't forget those heroes who fought and gave their lives
They won the fight, bought your rights, for you those heroes died
And all of you must carry on; take your place in freedom's song
Live your lives keep their dreams alive and keep our nation strong.

CHORUS:
We told ourselves America is where we belong
We'll cast our nets and farm our fields to make our nation strong
We called ourselves Americans; with grace we would stand tall
With solemn vow we'll live our lives with liberty for all
God Bless America, My Home Sweet Home.

When Dan had completed the song, there was complete silence. Tears began flowing from the eyes of all those present. Delia stood up and walked to Dan, who stood up when he saw her coming. His mother said, "Dan, that song pretty well says it all. I am proud to be an American, and even more proud to have a son who helped make it possible." Mary's tear-filled eyes turned to Dan who had reached out to embrace her to share those memories on top of memories that had brought them to America's shores. The song touched Weston's heart, even though his parents were from Wales. Weston walked up to Dan and embraced him saying, "I want to be an American if you think I am qualified." Dan said, "Weston, if you aren't, none of us are."

Dan turned to the crowd and said, "There will come a day very soon when our struggle will vanish as a dream. When the day comes, we forget this awesome blessing we are now enjoying, remember this, that will be the day we begin to lose the dream. Regardless of what circumstances we wake up tomorrow having to face, we must always begin our day with gratitude in our hearts for God allowing us to become Americans. Remember, we are not here by accident; we are here because of God's Grace. We will always have the opportunity for being known as a family of overcomers. We have overcome every reason that has ever been placed in our path. Every hardship that was placed there was to cause us to become ready for the battle. The reason we have overcome all that has come our way is, it is in our blood to endure. We have voluntarily given this nation our every breath, every heartbeat and every tear it took to prevail over the greatest military Army on earth. We gave all and now we have won all, because God has heard our prayers. We must now seek refuge in our thoughts and plan ways to supply our own needs as we wait for another call from General George Washington to defend our shores. Until we receive that call, we must busy ourselves with good purposes, one is to love the Lord our God with all our hearts, our souls and our minds and our neighbors as ourselves while we do the best we can to provide for our families. Now let's get some good rest."

Weston said, "Dan, there is a matter that Maureen and I would like for everyone to know. We have discussed whether it would be wise for us to consider the marriage to one another at this time. We have reached the decision the time is now, therefore we would like for everyone to know at the first opportunity we shall become man and wife."

Delia and Coleman had observed the interest that Weston and Maureen had shown to one another. They were very grateful to have Weston as a son-in-law, and began thinking of, *the wedding arrangements, because they did not know of a Christian church located within the Cherokee territory.*

Dan woke up on the fifth morning and said, "This place has got a way of growing on you. If we are going home, we had better get started." For once, everyone was rested for the first time in years. The children were having the time of their lives. Bridget was one for Delia to appreciate because she had missed being with her two daughters when they were young. The children felt very comfortable being in the outdoors after living with a Cherokee Indian tribe. The jersey cows were doing their part by keeping the troops filled with the best milk in America. Shibeal and Maureen were recovering from the abuse. They were enjoying being with their mother and father.

In years past, Dan had learned of a trail used by Indians who were known as mound builders for their construction engineering ability. (22) The bottom land of the Mississippi was extremely difficult to travel if there had been any rain. Once they found the trail, keeping the wagons out of the mud bogs was a big improvement. It seemed every Irishman loved the venison stew Mary and Delia prepared. They had loaded several sacks of cornmeal which Delia developed into a cornbread that was a favorite for everyone. The trail they were traveling was ridden with a history of violence between Indian tribes and later the French and English attempting to lay claim to the exclusive use of the trail which was preferred for travel and commerce between at least three Territories, later to become known as States of the United States. Originally, the trail was a dense forest where buffalo, deer and other animal made paths, which eventually became paths that could be widened for wagon trails. The path at that time could be traced back to 800 AD and was inhabited by several tribes of Indians, (later known as the Natchez Trace.) Dan took his time to teach the children the great value of knowing all you can learn about everything in order to cultivate a deep appreciation for all of God's creation.

Dan had to keep reminding himself he and his family were not being ruled by anyone. Every time he would say freedom to himself, he was reminded of, *the answered prayers his family had prayed to be allowed to know freedom in their life time.* No joy had ever been better than being with his family traveling toward a destination they could call home. Dan was very aware they were traveling through territory claimed by native Indians who had begun to oppose the other cultures for invading their territory and laying claims to large portions of the land.

Dan began to notice evidence of unshod hoof prints which he knew to be Indian horses. Because of the family's connection with Attakullakulla he felt he had arrived in friendly territory. As they traveled the paths toward a common destination, it became obvious all paths lead toward the same location.

On three occasions Dan had seen three Indians hiding but as the troop came closer the onlookers vanished. Dan began to become concerned something had changed causing unrest among the Indians. Dan decided to send out the four remaining scouts that had fought with him in the war. Dan told them to find a village to gather information as to what was taking place that had caused the war paint to be on the faces of the Indians he had seen. Dan decided rather than expose the family to an unexpected battle without cause; they needed to stop and rest awhile. The family settled in and began enjoying their surroundings. Within four days, two of the scouts returned. They told Dan they had located a tribe in an area near a river. The Indians referred to the location as Tuscaloosa which was an Indian name for "Black Warrior." The scouts reported the village to be inhabited by a Choctaw tribe that was not opposed to the family entering their territory.

Dan and his naturally suspicious nature decided to go with the scouts to the village to determine whether or not it was a trap. Dan took Lupe and four Blue Celts dressed as pioneers. When they entered the village, it was obvious to Dan trouble had come to the tribe. He could not tell if the source was Indians or Whites. As Dan dismounted and led his horse to the teepee of the chief, members of the tribe began to come close as they saw how big Dan and the Celts were.

Dan was beginning to decide the trouble had come to the tribe because of another Indian tribe, which put his mind at ease. Dan continued to wait on the chief to appear when much to his surprise an Indian woman stepped out of the door of the teepee. She had a warrior by her side who spoke English. Dan walked toward her with his eyes fixed on her eyes. Dan knew in his spirit he would be talking with a very smart woman. The lady had dark skin and dark black hair. Her facial features were not the same as the other tribe members.

As they sat and visited, Dan learned her name in English was "Dark Lady." She was the great granddaughter of the former Chief "Black Warrior" who was known for his superior intellect. The members of the tribe had selected her as their leader. Dan explained to "Dark Lady" of their travels toward Georgia which brought them to traveling across the Indian land. Dan apologized for the intrusion but asked her if there was a peaceful way they could cross the land without interrupting the village. The Chieftess told him of the low water crossing of the river which would allow their wagons to cross without having to unload them.

Dan was becoming more at ease as they visited. He told her of his friend, Attakullakulla. When Dan said his name, "Dark Lady's" eyes lit up when she said, "Beloved Man." Dan could tell he had finally touched on a name she knew. Dan told her of the chief's friendship and care for his family during the war. He told her his twins had been named by the chief and had been made members of their tribe.

"Dark Lady" told Dan she knew Attakullakulla and had high respect for him because of his love for all people. Dan then began telling her of his sister Maureen and Weston and their desire to become married. Dan asked her if she would perform the ceremony with the blessings of the one true and living spirit. "Dark Lady" became noticeably excited she would be asked by a white man to perform the ceremony. She told Dan she would, and it would bring her joy to do so. Dan noticed tears falling from her eyes as she told the interpreter of her approval. Dan sent the scouts to the family telling them to come to the village. When they arrived, Dan brought Mary and the children to meet "Dark Lady." Maureen and Weston came later.

"Dark Lady" visited with Maureen and Weston. She sensed their purity and devotion to one another. She told them there was an area that was used for the marriage ritual which would be purified and cleansed for several days as a special wood was gathered to build the fire of purification. She explained how the bride and groom approached the sacred fire they would be blessed by the Chieftess who was known as the Priestess for the ceremony. Each of those in attendance would also be blessed. The bride and groom would be covered in blue blankets. The Priestess would then remove the blue blankets and cover them with a white blanket as they began their new lives together. The groom will then give the bride a piece of meat as a commitment to always have meat in the home. The bride would deliver corn to the groom indicating her willingness to make a home for the family. When Maureen and Weston heard the ancient rituals, it brought to mind how similar the rituals were for each culture. The final act was for both of them to drink from one pitcher with two openings. At that point the ceremony was completed.

Within two weeks Maureen and Weston had become man and wife as the troop departed for Georgia. Dan approached "Dark Lady" and knelt before her and bowed his head as he held her hand in deep respect. Dan told her interpreter to tell "Dark Lady" he would not be far away if she needed his help.

CHAPTER NINETEEN

AMERICA

Many weeks had passed since leaving New Orleans. Some of the scouts reported the Challahoochee River was about one more day to travel. Dan decided to let everyone rest before entering Georgia. The closer they got to home the more anxious they became to get to work. Dan told the scouts to head for Savannah. As they traveled through Georgia, they began to remember about the days with General Oglethorpe.

Dan had noticed when the family had crossed the Great River later named the Mississippi River, Colonel John Milledge Jr., had been showing subtle interest in a member of the O'Flaherty family named, Shibeal. The Colonel had always been truly dedicated to duty and was the most reliable man Dan had ever met. When Dan had assigned the Colonel to the security of General Washington and his family, he knew Colonel John Milledge Jr., was the best man in America to oversee such an important duty.

While they were traveling toward Georgia, a courier rode up with a message from General Washington. The message stated that Colonel John Milledge had been promoted to the rank of Brigadier General by the Continental Congress as recommended by the Commander and Chief General, George Washington. General Washington included a personal note of gratitude for not only protecting him, but also his family. General Washington included a medal which represented the highest honor he could award a soldier under his command. When he saw the General's handwriting verifying all the qualities John had in him as a soldier, as a man and as a close friend, he was proud beyond words. Within a short time, Dan told the scouts to find a camping place to rest for a while. After they had unharnessed the mules and horses and had come together to eat, Dan told them he wanted to take a minute to read a message from General Washington. Dan asked Colonel Milledge to stand up. Dan read the message for everyone to hear. He then asked the Colonel to step forward. When he was standing in front of the General, Dan asked him who he would like to place the medal on his uniform as well as the Star signifying his rank. John looked at Shibeal with his eyes asking her to place the star on his coat. Shibeal was most honored to decorate a man who had become her hero.

Delia and Coleman had known John Milledge for many years and they were extremely fond of him. After the ceremony was completed and John had been embraced at least once by everyone in the troop, he and Shibeal walked away from the camp site to visit with one another.

Two scouts reported being close to a fort outside Savannah; after learning their location, they decided to stay at the fort until they had time to find out the status of their property which they had bought from General Oglethorpe. Dan rode with the scouts the next morning to Savannah. It seemed strange to all of them not to have to be aware of the British presence. Dan rode on to General Oglethorpe's home which was occupied by one of the Trustees of the plan General Oglethorpe had designed to create a system of "Agrarian Equality." When Dan started thinking about what the General had put together, he recognized it was the same plan all the Irish and Scottish soldiers had just completed by defeating the British and getting them and their government out of America to become a government of the people. Dan thought to himself, *even though the English Parliament passed a law, which to some extent was freedom for the chosen few; the King could change whatever he wanted to change and destroy the hopes of those who were led to believe they were free to govern themselves.*

Dan rode to the property his mother and father had owned. The cottage had been burned and it was obvious, the land had fallen into disuse. Dan was comparing the Georgia land with some of the land he had seen in Mississippi and he determined the Georgia land was a waste of time when compared with the Mississippi land for farming cotton and sugar cane.

When Dan returned to the fort, he told his mother and father what he had found. Dan reassured them the last thing they would need to be concerned about was land. He said, "We have land in Florida we have never seen. I intend to go look at the Florida land in a week or so." Dan recalled some of the beautiful land he had seen in Florida when he was at war with Spain.

In 1781, Spain attacked Pensacola, the capital of West Florida, and defeated the British which left the British with no bases along the Gulf Coast. With his uncle being in control, Dan felt comfortable to settle his land in Florida. Some of the first Europeans to land near St. Augustine had brought different species of citrus fruits. There was something God given in the soil of Florida that was very conducive to some citrus species. When Dan was fighting the Spanish, he found a range of citrus fruit growing wild in the forests of Florida. His troops found the wild fruit most tasteful. Dan had pondered the prospect of farming citrus fruit in Florida. He had previously found a tree growing in the wild and took some of the fruit to his family. Delia, in particular, liked the taste very much.

As they continued to plan their places to locate, another courier from General Washington's office delivered a message to Dan. The letter contained the General's most cordial blessing to Dan and his family and he wanted Dan to know the Colonies were making progress on the peace negotiations even though England was making a most difficult adjustment by having to treat former British subjects of the King as equals. General Washington also wrote Dan the following: "The Colonies are bankrupt from the cost of the war, but it appears there is a proposed agreement for the new government of the United States to take the individual debt of the Colonies into a united obligation." He informed Dan there would not be any immediate money coming from the Federal government to repay him, but he wondered if Dan would consider a federal grant of land of his choice in exchange for a portion of the debt.

After Dan had thought about what General Washington had proposed, he decided to again tell the General as far as he was concerned; the Federal government did not owe him a debt. He wrote the General, "The Colonies have given my family a gift that no other nation on earth has ever given to any of their citizens, and we considered the gift of freedom as more precious than gold." Dan then wrote, "However, if the government insists on paying me something, I would consider some land located somewhere along the Great River, (later known as the Mississippi River bottom,) should any of that land ever be under the control of the Federal Government." Dan then gave his response to the courier and began getting serious about a house for his family.

Dan asked his mother and father where they would truly enjoy living. Coleman told Dan he knew how to raise cotton and didn't know anything about raising indigo and rice. Dan asked his mother and father how much land they wanted to work. Coleman said, "Dan, I don't know what to say, all I know is, we have to make a living." Dan said, "Mama and daddy, I want you to listen to me, you do not have to make a living, we have all the money we will ever need. Let me ask you this, what would you really like to do?" Delia said, "Dan, all I have ever wanted to do was be with my children and your father." Dan asked, "Would you like to live in town, or do you like living out in the country?" They both replied, "We do not like towns." Dan said, "I have heard of a place not far from Savannah that has about 500 acres. What do you think about looking to see if it would take care of our needs, temporarily?" Coleman said, "Dan I need to get a little rest first before I do any more traveling." Dan said, "Daddy, there is no hurry. You and mama rest for a few days. I need to check on the troops to see if they need anything."

Dan rode up to the Blue Celt headquarters at about 2:00 p.m., and he could tell the rest and relaxation they needed had grown into a habit for an afternoon sleep. But, as always, Brigadier General John Milledge Jr., was awake and taking care of the details. Dan was glad to see his most trusted fellow soldier. The General told Dan he had learned his father, John Milledge, Sr., had recently died and he was glad to be where he could take care of his mother and a brother of his who was an invalid. Dan told the General to be sure and let him know if there was anything he and his mother needed. The General asked Dan if he thought they would be fighting the British again. Dan told John they had to remember the ruling family of Great Britain was of German ancestry, not English. Dan told him from what he knew about the German culture, nothing about a dispute with the German ancestry is ever over until the German's prevail. He told John, "I am encouraged the British are still negotiating a peaceful settlement." He also told him, "But, even if England signs a peace treaty, they will be back for more war. The only time we will ever be friendly with Great Britain will be when they need our help."

Dan decided to stay at the fort until he learned from his mother and father as to what they would be interested in doing. Their health was good, they were enjoying every day of their lives. From where they had come from in their lives of abuse and slavery, every moment lived with their loved ones in complete peace was more than they ever thought would be possible. Delia told Dan, " "Two Dan" had the same heart as his father." Dan was devoted to causing his family to be allowed to realize hope which had not been known to Irish Catholics in many decades. Dan wanted his sons to have military training along with the training of a profession such as engineering or a degree in law. Dan knew the worst mistake that could be made would be for the Irish to submit to a rule of law established by some of the left-over Loyalists residue from the north. Dan had learned the right to have a voice in all decisions regarding the basic God given rights placed in the hands of a body of governors needed very close scrutiny.

Dan recalled having met a young lad whose name was Andrew Jackson while on his way to avoid being captured by the British for killing three of their soldiers. The lad had truly impressed Dan, in that; he seemed to know what to do with life at an early age. Dan decided to take a trip in his direction for renewing his relationship with Andrew Jackson to determine whether he needed more money to complete his education and Dan was ready for a hunting and fishing trip with his sons.

Dan and the two boys saddled up to try and find where Andrew Jackson had gone. One of the real reasons Dan wanted to go in that direction was to take his time teaching his sons how to survive in the woods. They set out in the direction of the Asheville settlement. It took them almost two weeks to get to Asheville. Dan went to the blacksmith shop where he had left Andrew years earlier.

When he walked in the door, he saw Andrew fitting horse shoes to a Bay mare. Andrew immediately came to attention to salute his favorite General. Dan said, "Hold it Andrew, the war is over, I hope." Andrew looked behind the General and there was two of the best-looking Irish cowboys he had ever seen. They both tried to hide behind their Dad, but he told them Andrew was their friend. Andrew stuck out his hand and said, "Hi, partner." Cathal said, "Hi, Mr. Andrew." "Two Dan" asked Andrew, "What are you doing?" Andrew said, "I am putting shoes on this good horse, so she won't hurt her feet. "Two Dan" asked, "Can I help you?" Andrew said, "Come here boy, let me show you how to make a living." Andrew picked the mare's front foot up and put some tacks in his mouth, ready to nail the shoe to the hoof. "Two Dan" asked, "Can I do it?" Andrew, said, "Yes Sir, little General, give it a good lick." "Two Dan" picked up the hammer with both hands and Andrew held the tack. "Two Dan" hit the tack dead center three times and Andrew said, "You are hired." Dan asked Andrew if there was anywhere to eat a meal. Andrew said,

"I normally eat at Benny McGee's place. He can cook meat better than anybody around here."

They had a good meal consisting of fried steak, potatoes and cornbread. Dan asked Andrew if he had made any plans since the war was over. Andrew said, "General, I have a hankering to do two things. One is, I want to be in the Army of America." He told the General he had entered the study of law about a year before. He also told him he had returned to help the blacksmith to earn some money to continue his studies. Andrew said, "General, if it had not been for you, I would never have made it this far." Dan smiled, because he had found a young man who had the same spirit in him he had all his life. When they had visited more, Dan told Andrew he wished him well in all his pursuits and if he could ever be of help to him, he could be found somewhere around Savannah, Georgia. As Dan was leaving, he handed Andrew a sack of money. This time it was 1,000 pounds. Dan said, "Andrew, you remind me of myself at your age and I know you need some help. I know you are going to do very well in life and I will help you when you need me." Andrew said, "General, you couldn't have come at a better time. I am headed toward Northeastern Tennessee to learn how to practice law. Let me have an address to write you a letter when I get settled." Dan felt it was the appropriate time to tell Andrew of meeting with his relative in New York named Colonel Grady Jackson, who actually saved his sister's life as well as hundreds of other prisoners who were being imprisoned in ships in the New York harbor. Andrew told Dan he did not know his cousin well, but he could tell he was filled with the spirit of a warrior by the letter he had written him after he had met him and his family.

Dan said, "Andrew, there is one more thing I want to mention to you." Andrew said, "General, I am ready." Dan said, "These two boys will be right behind you by ten or twelve years. Should you have two O'Flaherty's asking to speak with you, I hope you will allow them the privilege of visiting with you." Andrew leaned over and said, "Cathal and "Two Dan", if you ever need me for anything, start looking in Northeast Tennessee, I'll be around there somewhere."

As they rode away, Dan knew somewhere along the road of life, they would meet again. On the way back to Georgia, Dan took full advantage teaching the boys about the difference in trees, what kind of wood to use to build a fire, the right kind of wood for cooking and building a house. Dan built both of them a bow and made them some arrows. Dan said, "You need to know other kinds of weapons, in case your powder gets wet." They wrestled and played, swam, fished, shot guns, threw knives, built tomahawks and much more Dan loved teaching his sons.

Dan had learned all kinds of tricks Indians had taught him while wrestling. Dan said, "The two most important things to learn about Indian fighting is how to run and when." Dan taught them the joy of being in the forest and respect for the wild game.

One evening, after a full day of play and fun, Dan built a fire out of red oak which was a good wood to cook meat. As they were turning the meat while it roasted Dan said, *"Shhh."* They fixed their eyes on their dad. He then took their hands and moved away from the fire to hide in a grove of myrtle bushes. In about ten minutes three men walked up and went to looking around. One saw Dan's rifle and walked over and picked it up. Dan whispered to the boys, *"Stay here and be quiet."* Dan eased out the back side of the myrtle grove and walked around the fire to where the three men had entered the camp area. The three men had begun to rummage around in Dan's belongings, obviously to take whatever they wanted. Out of the darkness, Dan asked, 'Who are you?" The men seemingly froze in their tracks and answered, "Just traveling through and got hungry." Dan said, "Put everything down you have picked up and leave." One of the men said, "We know you are by yourself and there are three of us. Why don't you settle down and be neighborly?" Dan said, "I will tell you again to put down what you have picked up and move on." The one that had the Pennsylvania Rifle in his hands pulled the hammer back. Dan asked, "Before we begin deciding one another's rights, are you sure this is what you want to try to do?" The one with the rifle pointed the barrel in the direction he thought Dan was hiding and pulled the trigger. Within three seconds, Dan's knife was stuck in the man's heart area up to the hilt as he dropped to his knees. Dan again asked the remaining two, "Is there anything more I need to say?" The two men began walking away, then Dan said, "Take my knife out of your friend's chest, and lay it on the stump, then take your friend with you and get out of here." The two men hurriedly picked their friend up and left without any more discussion. After about thirty minutes, Dan walked back around to the myrtle bush and the boys were still in their hiding place. Dan said, "Are ya'll about ready to eat some supper?" The boys answered, "Yes sir." Both of them snuggled close to their daddy as they lay there looking at the stars and thanking God for a good day.

On the way back to Savannah, Dan asked them, "How would you like to go hunt some alligators?" "Two Dan" asked, "When?" Dan said, "Well, we need to go by and check on everyone and eat some home cooked food first and then we will head for Florida and get us some gator meat." When they arrived at the fort, Mary was so glad to see her men again. The two boys were about to burst to tell their mama everything that had happened. Mary listened to each word as she recalled, *some of the life experiences she and Dan had survived through the years.*

Dan asked Weston whether he had any plans for the day. Weston told Dan he wanted to see more of the nation he was adopting as his own. Dan told Weston he had heard of a piece of land for sale near Savannah, Georgia he wanted to see. Weston told Dan he would like to look at the property with him. Dan said, "I have heard there is a lawyer in town that seemingly knows most of the business of Savannah." Weston said, "Let's go check him out." Upon arrival in town, they learned the lawyers name was Ned Sharkey. Dan thought to himself that sounds like a Celtic name.

When he went inside the door, a lady asked them who they wanted to see. Dan replied, "Mr. Sharkey." She told them to have a seat. The lady's voice could be heard as she said, "Two men are here to see you." The lawyer said, "Show them in." Dan and Weston stood up and walked toward the door as the lady stepped out and said, "He will see you now." They thanked her as they went into Mr. Sharkey's office. Mr. Sharkey was overwhelmed by Dan's size as he stood up to shake Dan's hand. Dan said, "My name is Dan O'Flaherty O'Shea, and this is Weston Collier. We are here to ask about a piece of land I heard was for sale southwest of town." The lawyer asked, "Mr. O'Flaherty, were you in the military service?" Dan answered, "Yes Sir." Mr. Sharkey said, "There was a General O'Flaherty that was from somewhere in this area, would that be who you are?" Dan said, "I am from this area, and at one time, I served under General Oglethorpe in

Georgia, but when the war began, I fought for the Colonies." Mr. Sharkey asked, "What rank do you hold?" Dan answered, "Major General." Mr. Sharkey said, "Now, I know who you are. When General Oglethorpe was in Georgia, he visited me several times about some land transactions, and he never failed to mention Dan O'Flaherty and to tell me what a truly remarkable individual you are. Let me say, I am very grateful to make your acquaintance." Dan said, "I am certainly glad to meet you also. The General had mentioned your name to me and said very good things about your ability and character." Mr. Sharkey said, "Lawyers do not get compliments very often, but with the source of today's compliments being from General Oglethorpe and you, I feel most complimented, thank you. How can I help you?"

Dan said, "Someone made me aware of a place consisting of a home and about 500 acres of land, reasonably close to town and I was wondering if that information is correct?" Mr. Sharkey said, "Well, it might be." There is a fine place west of town that is owned by a family named Priestly who has moved back to England, due to the outcome of the war. I don't know what you have in mind, but this home is magnificent. The soil has produced some of the finest cotton and a portion of it is good for tobacco. Mr. Priestley is aware he will never get the price he wants but is willing to consider any offer." Dan asked Mr. Sharkey, "What would be the lowest amount he thought would be acceptable to the seller." Mr. Sharkey said, "Mr. Priestley knows the Savannah area, after the war, is inhabited mainly by people who at one time were indentured slaves. He also knows absolutely no one has any money and those who do have it are back in London, England." Mr. Sharkey continued by saying, "I think 7,500 pounds would be acceptable."

Dan asked, "How do I make arrangements to see the place?" Mr. Sharkey asked, "What are you doing now? Dan said, "Hoping to go see the place." Mr. Sharkey said, "Let me get my carriage, and we will go look."

When they arrived, they were very impressed with the entrance which had been manicured by the gardeners. The house had the appearance of a small castle and was immaculately done with good taste. There were barns and sleeping quarters away from the main house, like the house in Spain, where he grew up. Dan asked about the farm machinery, and the furniture in the house. Mr. Sharkey took them to the barn where there was enough farm machinery to do some serious farming. Mr. Sharkey took him to the horse stalls, where he found thoroughbred race horses and farm stock as well as some jersey milk cows.

He then led him inside the house and Dan could not believe his eyes. The home was furnished with the finest furniture from Europe. Most of the wood was hand crafted by the finest carpenters. The rugs and drapes were of the highest quality. Dan was completely astonished that the owners had abandoned a fortune.

After Dan and Weston saw the home and everything that went with it, they were surprised the price was so low. After they took everything into consideration, it was apparent very few people had access to any kind of money of that magnitude. Weston said, "Dan, this is too good to be true, but the truth is, it is true. My advice to you is pay the money and thank God for the blessing but, I do find it rather strange that a gift like this would come to you from an English family."

Dan told Mr. Sharkey to draw up a contract for 7,500 pounds. Mr. Sharkey said, "Mr. Priestly has appointed me Power of Attorney and I am prepared to issue you a deed upon full payment." Dan said, "I have that much available now. If you need some time to prepare the deed, tell me." Mr. Sharkey said, "The deed is prepared, all I need is the name of the purchaser." Dan said, "My mother and father's names are Coleman and Delia O'Flaherty." They went back to Mr. Sharkey's office, and within an hour the transaction was completed.

Dan and Weston rode back to the fort to get their family and arrived late. The next morning, Dan got up very early and went to where his mother and daddy were sleeping. He eased the door open with just enough light to see his mother. He walked quietly to the side of her bed and kneeled by her side, and laid his head on her arm, as she loved holding him again to begin another day. He then gently whispered, *"Mama, let's go home."*

CHAPTER TWENTY

RE-ACQUAINTING

Very few siblings ever have the opportunity or means to express their personal gratitude to parents who have given their lives as a sacrifice for their children's lives to be made better. Delia and Coleman O'Flaherty were two parents whose very breath was devoted to the welfare of their children. Every motive, every thought, every desire and every prayer they prayed was for the protection and guidance of the children God had placed in their care. But, their family existed as victims of a brutal empire motivated by greed and godlessness.

Regardless of every drop of the King's venom attempting to destroy their very existence, the O'Flaherty's endured. God in His infinite mercy had rejoined the family in America where they could seek to break the chains of tyranny. They endured, and they survived having played a huge role in the defeat of a British despotic ruler. When their family was again as one, heaven's mercy had provided those last years of the torment of separation to become a togetherness only the love of heaven could have provided.

When Dan brought his parents to the mansion that would be theirs for the remaining days of their lives, Delia and Coleman had no words they felt were adequate to express the joy in which their hearts were filled. For once in their lives there were no boundaries. They could do whatever had become their desire for that particular day.

Delia's joy came from being surrounded by the next generation of Irish blooded children who would be known as Americans. Coleman's joy was from being involved in locating good dirt to grow beautiful crops of his choice. The siblings joy was being with their parents to erase the days of separation as if there had never been sorrow in their lives of any kind. Their combined assets of Irish laughter, playfulness and mischief eventually eroded the memories confusion and slavery had caused in their lives.

Dan, Mary and three children had plans every day for a new adventure. They had cultivated special fishing holes, places to trap wild animals and birds and perfect wilderness to enjoy the pleasures of being together alone as a family. Joy filled their hearts because of the efforts they had put forth to cause freedom to become a reality.

The years passed too quickly. Coleman had begun to slow his pace of breaking new ground each spring. Dan could tell the time was near for them to begin to adjust to not having the presence of one another. Coleman's funeral service was held near the family home and those who had partaken of his life's efforts joined to hear the life of a fisherman from Ireland who became an American.

Delia never adjusted to the loss of her soulmate she had known for most of her days. Within a few months, she joined him in death. The memories she took with her were filled with God's mercy even though her family's life had been gripped by an unmerciful empire.

When Dan had placed the last stone on his mother's grave, he had finally come face to face with a burden he could not bear. He asked his family to allow him time to be with her alone. He thought, *if he could only lay his head on her clutching arms one more time to thank her for loving him with each breath of her life, he could defend against the pain and sorrow.*

King George II and King George III used their supreme authority to strip the O'Flaherty family of most of their days of basking in the sunlight of one another's presence, but little did the King know he had taken nothing of their love for one another that had endured his bitterest assault to destroy their very being. Once the family was reunited in America and freedom had become the reality of each day's blessing, they saw the meaning to their early life as the preparation to help create one nation, under God, with liberty and justice for all. They knew in their hearts the O'Flaherty family had given their all without regret. They shared the same commitment with hundreds of thousands of Irish and Scottish former slaves that eventually became a victory over tyranny for all mankind. Dan could not leave his mother alone. He laid his body by her grave to embrace her memory. Through the night he wept the tears his heart had gathered from the years of his life being under the care of others; he truly loved his mother and father with his whole heart.

As the morning began to dawn, he kneeled by her side and the side of his father, Coleman O'Flaherty, to bid them farewell to continue to complete his walk to the same destiny. Dan had massive responsibilities to manage. He had arranged for all the military personnel, those who had served with him in the Blue Celts, to be awarded tracts of land for their individual families. Dan had been awarded huge tracts of land in South Carolina, Florida and Georgia, by the King of Spain and the King of England for arranging a basis for a Treaty between the two nations to end the Seven-Year War. Dan gave each of the Blue Celts and their family's time to select the tract of land that suited each family's needs. He also provided enough money to provide for their provisions for at least one year as a reward for their faithful service.

Dan gathered the troop together to attempt to get a general area in which each man would settle. He insisted each man lay out their land in six hundred forty-acre sections. He told them once they made their choice of tracts to get back with him to have the land surveyed and the deed recorded. Dan gave them a farewell blessing which was for them to know the Blue Celts would never be disbanded. He told them he would contact them if the British returned. When Dan had the beginning of his concerns of the Blue Celts off to a good start, he began wanting to meet with other members of his family to help them find a satisfactory beginning for their lives in the new territory.

Dan began the discussion by asking them to consider where they wanted to live in a town or in the country. Each of them was considering issues they had never faced before, because all they had known was their lives being at the will of others who profited from their existence through the labor they performed. He told them there was no hurry to decide anything, because adequate temporary lodging was available until they decided. He told them he had found three matters to be of the utmost importance. One, the education of their children in the future; two, the decision to provide a living for their family was the center piece of their lives, because that was the decision that provided them the value they would place on themselves. If they decided to work for someone other than themselves, they would be limited to the value someone else placed on their labor. However, if they worked for themselves, they had the opportunity to allow God to direct their steps. The third decision was to select a method of the worship of God each day. Dan told them he would be available to help them in any way he could to help them get started.

After he had met with his extended family members and had given each of them some things to consider, he turned his attention to his own family. Mary was waiting for him to visit with her to decide the direction their lives would take with their new-found freedom. Dan decided he could think better when he was in the open country. He asks Mary if she would like to get everyone together and spend some time by the river making plans for their family. Mary smiled at Dan's suggestion asking him if having to make these decisions is what freedom was all about. Dan smiled back at her and said, "That is what freedom is all about, when you make a wrong decision, there is no one to blame but yourself." Mary asks, "How does it feel to wake up and not be responsible for the lives of others who are being abused by a foreign country?"

Dan said, "Mary, you know what I think, you have given me the answer to what I must have wrong with me. I have been under the dark cloud of war and despair for so long; I don't know what to feel like without the burden. Why don't we gather up our family and go to the river and allow God to help us figure out which direction we need to go?"

After two weeks of basking in the bliss of American freedom, Dan and Mary decided to discuss the options of life that lay before them. Dan began with reminding Mary of the knowledge of the other cultures of the world they had accumulated through their years of suffering. He also reminded her of the property they purchased in New York, as well as the property they owned in Spain.

Dan expressed his desire for their children to be exposed to the different cultures of the world as part of their education. He told Mary how important it was for them to reveal the people that had become mentors in their lives such as General Phillip and Margarita O'Shea. He told her he wanted Maureen and Weston to become a part of their children's education by meeting Weston's father, Mr. Collier, who was recognized as the most famous lawyer in all of Europe. Mary told Dan she wanted the same things for their children as him, but he had to understand her family were Irish seaman that for the most part were uneducated. Dan reminded her of the O'Flaherty and O'Malley blood lines in Ireland, as being clan leaders and survivors of the blood bath brought to Ireland by the British rulers. He told Mary the single most important lesson for the next generation to learn is no matter how difficult the hardships are, their culture must survive. Dan told Mary it was their obligation to teach the children what happens when good people remain silent.

Dan woke up one morning wanting a challenge that would be something the boys would remember. He had noticed the river had changed courses through time and left what was referred to as 'Oxbow' lakes, which usually was the perfect place for alligators to hide. When the boys were full of their mama's cooking, he told them to get a sack to take some meat and bread with them. The boys looked at one another wondering, *what kind of adventure their daddy was under taking.* "Two Dan" asked his father, "What kind of clothes should we wear?" Dan grinned and said, "The kind that can get wet." Mary told Dan she and Bridget were involved in practicing their sewing of buckskin leather for some winter clothes.

As the adventure began, Dan told them to step in the tracks he made to keep from making racket and whatever they did not to step on a dry stick and break it because it can be heard all over the forest. Dan explained to them if they didn't learn how to be very quiet, they would never be good hunters or good soldiers. He told them to remember the wilderness and wooded areas is the home of all kinds of animals, some of which are good for food, but if they didn't learn to be very quiet, they may not be able to see a squirrel or hog because they would run and hide.

The adventure began for Mary's three hunters. After they had gone about two hundred yards, "Two Dan" turned and waved goodbye to his darling mother. She had a smile on her face as a tear appeared in the corner of her eye, because of seeing her men get grown which meant danger, she could not control. When they had gone nearly a mile, Dan looked back and "Two Dan" was jumping from one of Dan's foot prints to the next one as quick as he could.

He remembered he had told them to step where he had stepped so he shortened his steps for "Two Dan." They began to come upon the edge of one of the 'Oxbow' lakes, as he slowed his pace. He squatted down to listen to hear for some ducks that might be on the pond. Dan whispered, *some duck meat would be good for supper.* They waited for a while and began their approach to the pond again. When they were within fifty yards of the water, Dan stopped dead in his tracks. He turned and whispered, *there is a baby deer getting a drink of water.*

The boys looked in the direction of the water in time to see an alligator's head rise out of the water and catch the fawn with his teeth and pull it into the water to kill it. Dan told them it was time to get serious about gator meat. Dan knew after the alligator had eaten the meal, the gator would want to lay in the warm sun and sleep. He told the boys they had to get closer to get a good shot. Dan found a cluster of bay trees, one of which was crooked which made a perfect bench for them to sit on.

After an hour of waiting for the alligator to reappear, the boys had fallen asleep on each side of their father as he waited for the alligator to rest in the sun. The sun was warm, which was the perfect place for a gator to want to rest to digest his meal. Dan whispered to the boys telling them, *the gator is ready to come up*. They woke up as the gator drug himself through some soupy mud to find a dry place for a snooze. Dan had made many shots at alligators before he found out how difficult it was to kill one, but he had learned of a soft spot just behind the top part of the skull where the head joins the back bone, was the best place to shoot. Dan was hoping the gator would crawl out and then turn its body back toward the water to expose the soft spot. He whispered to them, *maybe he will turn around toward the water.* Just as he hoped, the gator turned and came to rest. Dan whispered to the boys to, *put their fingers is their ears, because the shot would be loud.* Dan fired, and it was obvious the way the gator spread his feet out, he was dead. Dan said, "Let's go look at him."

The gator was about nine feet long and weighed about 200 pounds. Dan put a piece of rope around his tail and they pulled him to a tree to cut some gator meat for their supper. When Dan cut the gator open, the stomach fell out with the dead fawn inside. Dan told the boys, "Killing and eating is what nature is all about." When they had cleaned their hands, they cut the gators tail in three pieces and put it in a cloth sack and went back to the campsite. Mary made her men a good supper with alligator meat. The next day, Dan and Mary had time to discuss a plan for their family's future. Dan suggested they first travel to New York to help Weston and Maureen re-establish themselves in New York. There were several matters Dan had been considering he needed to talk to Weston about. Mary thought that was the perfect plan.

When they returned from the river hunt, Dan contacted Mary's father, Gregory O'Malley, who was also Dan's partner in the shipping business, to determine the best time to make the trip to New York. Gregory told Dan a ship was due in on Thursday, which would be available to go to New York. Gregory reminded Dan of the storm season by telling him, "Now is the best time to go."

Dan was very mindful of the storm season, as he recalled his adoptive parents General Phillip O'Shea and his wife, Margarita being lost at sea years before. Dan went back to their home and told Mary he had talked with her father and it appeared possible to leave for New York within the week. Mary told Dan she would be ready to go when he was. Mary told the children they would be going on a voyage to New York within five days and she needed their help to get ready.

Everyone began getting excited about being on a ship. Gregory O'Malley sent word to Dan advising him of Saturday being the best tide and wind for the voyage. Dan sent a message back to him, "We will be ready." Weston, Maureen and Shibeal were the only members of the family who had become familiar with New York.

Dan and Mary prepared for the voyage while Weston and Maureen made plans for their future. Weston said, "If possible, I want to return to New York to continue the law practice of foreign investments. He reminded Maureen how important it was for his father to have assurance from Weston of his personal knowledge of the quality of the investments. Maureen told Weston she hoped there was a way for them to continue their lives together in New York. They agreed there needed to be consideration given to the war years and the danger they had encountered. being involved with the highest-ranking officers in the British Army. As they recalled the experience, they began to wonder if, *it would be safe for them to return to that area.* They decided to discuss their feeling with Dan. When they disclosed to him their concerns, Dan told them he certainly understood how they felt, but they would have to understand the changes in everything that had taken place since October 19, 1781, the date of the surrender of the British Army. Dan said, "In fact, I am looking forward to seeing this country since it has been placed in the hands of the people as opposed to some monarchs in Europe." When Dan reminded them the British were gone, their spirits improved.

Saturday morning began very early because the Captain wanted to take full advantage of the high tide and the early morning breeze. As they were preparing to sail for New York, Dan began thinking of his earliest memories of the sea were, *when he sailed with his Uncle Eamonn O'Flaherty, who had rescued him before the British had arrested the members of Dan's family to be placed on a slave ship bound for America as indentured slaves. The reason stated for the arrest was, the man they worked for in Ireland, Bryan O'Flaherty, was accused of failing to pay his farm mortgage debt. Under the British Penal Laws at that time, the creditor was entitled to all the property, including their employees, who were Irish Catholics. During this period, King George II, a protestant with approval of the parliament had passed the necessary laws to slowly exterminate all Irish Catholics in Ireland. At the time of the arrest, Eamonn O'Flaherty, a relative of Coleman O'Flaherty, Dan*

O'Flaherty's father, was at the farm purchasing supplies for his ship. When Delia, Dan's mother, saw what was taking place, she placed Dan in the care of his distant cousin, Eamonn O'Flaherty. During his early years, Dan rode the waves of the sea with his "Uncle Eamonn" who cared for him as his own son.

As the ship gently cleared the docks and the sails unfurled, they caught a breeze out of the southeast and the O'Flaherty family was on their way toward another part of America. They were excited. Mary was excited as she recalled, *their first voyage together by remembering the message God had whispered to her of the birth of their first son, Cathal in approximately nine months.* Dan watched Bridget's excitement. She was her father's child and he delighted in all her ways. She was the image of her mother in her ways of caring for everyone to make certain everything in their lives was as perfect as she could help make it. He stood by her as the ship cleared the harbor and held her hand to assure her she was in a safe place. It took time for everyone to adjust to riding the waves of the sea. Mary was certain enough of her genes were in her children to keep them from being seasick. No O'Malley had ever been known to suffer with sea sickness and Mary didn't want it to start in her family.

Dan took the boys to the upper deck where the Captain was steering the ship. The boys were fascinated by everything that was happening. At any uneasy moment, the children would look at their daddy's eyes for reassurance and Dan was always ready to cause those he loved to feel secure. Bridget moved over by her mother to hold her hand until the waves began to smooth out. Once they cleared the shallow water, they reached the even waves of the ocean where each wave was exactly the same distance apart. The Captain gave the crew the order to open all the sails as the ship began to increase its speed.

Dan was happy to see Maureen and Weston enjoying themselves. It had been a long time since Weston had seen his father. He was anxious for Dan to consider a trip to Spain; he had so much to tell his father, Mr. Collier. They had communicated but it was not the same as being able to visit with a man of his father's integrity.

The journey was into its sixth day when land appeared on the horizon. Two other ships appeared with full sails apparently bound for Europe. As the O'Flaherty family began to grasp the moment of sailing into a nation they had help create, a double breath of pure, clean exhilarating air filled their bosoms as they silently gave God full credit and gratitude for allowing them to participate in such a wonderful blessing.

As the ship entered New York harbor, the area reminded Dan of, *the last visit he made to the docks of New York to rescue his sister Shibeal, who had been loaded on a prison ship bound for England to stand trial for treason.* Maureen moved over by Dan to hold his hand as the ship was being tied to the dock. Maureen and Dan held one another as they recalled. *that moment in time. when he found her on the wharf having been beaten by her captors after British General Cornwallis had surrendered to the Continental Army of America.* Weston, Maureen and Shibeal had supplied General Washington's Army with information of General Cornwallis's Army's intentions to invade New York. When the information was received by General Washington, the Continental Army had the advantage to trap Cornwallis at Yorktown, Virginia. They looked at one another as Maureen said, "It was worth the trouble." She also reached for Weston's hand as they savored the moment together.

When they arrived, Weston took charge of all the arrangements. He had a carriage brought to the docks to take the family to the most beautiful home in New York. Other arrangements were made to transport their luggage to the house. When they arrived at the mansion, Weston talked to the butler who had never been introduced to the owners of the property. Dan took Mary by the hand to show her the house. The three children had never seen a home that large in their lives. The grounds were beautiful, and all the facilities were in superb condition. Dan recalled, *at the end of the conflict and the rescue of his family was achieved, Dan had wondered what would happen to the home when the owner's involvement in the war was revealed. It was certain if the British learned of their involvement; they would have retaliated by burning the house to the ground.* None of that occurred, everything was in order.

After they had rested from their voyage, Dan told Weston he would like to see the horse farm. Weston took Dan to the facility, which Dan had never seen. Dan asks Weston if there were any fond memories he had of his participation in a war in behalf of a country he was not connected with in anyway except through the relationship with the O'Flaherty family. Weston told Dan once he understood the malice a nation had toward those who were helpless and had no defense, but their faith in God, he understood how justice was at the basis of the Irish cause and began to enjoy participating in dismantling the arrogance, abuse and injustice of Great Britain.

They walked to the stables to see some of the Arabian horses; Dan enjoyed the pure blood animals. He had a deep appreciation for their ability in combat. Weston suggested they ride the area to better comprehend the procedures they had established to transmit the British secrets to General Washington. Once Dan saw the intricate details of the method in which the information was sent, the more he realized the risk and stress Maureen, Shibeal and Weston suffered every day and night the war endured; his appreciation for their contribution became more deeply embedded in his heart.

They had also developed an entertainment center for the high-ranking British officers. Weston took Dan to see the room under the floor that contained air ways to the twenty-five areas that had been set up for British military officers. Weston pointed out the hidden door that was uncovered by the British that led to the arrest of Maureen and Shibeal. Dan took time to sit and think of how close his family came to a family tragedy. He thought to himself, *except for the Grace of God, the three of them, would have been hung.*

As they made their way back to the main house, thoughts of the risks they took for America was going through their minds. They were telling themselves, *if I had to do it again, I would without hesitation.* Dan said, "The greatness of America is based upon people like us who had no other place on earth to go."

When they arrived at the main house all the beautiful women of the family were even more beautiful. As they roamed through the palatial home they were selecting parts of the home they liked the best. Shibeal loved the gardens and the marvelous landscape. Maureen enjoyed the huge dining area. Mary loved the balcony which was reminiscent of General Oglethorpe's home in Georgia where she and Dan stayed when they had arrived in America from Spain. She and Dan sat on the porch at every opportunity and enjoyed the company of one another.

When the family gathered to sit down to eat, it was a meal they would never forget. The cooks were talking in the kitchen about, *who the big man was.* They learned listening to all the family talk; the *big man was the real owner of the facilities* and when they did learn who Dan was, they wanted him to enjoy his food. He met with the cooks after the meal and told them how wonderful the food tasted.

The next day, Weston and Dan decided they would go to Weston's office where he advised clients concerning their foreign investments. When they arrived, Weston met a young man Weston's father had sent from Spain to oversee the investment business until Weston decided to do whatever he wanted to do. During their visit, they learned foreign investment in America was the best business in New York. The most frequent reason given by foreign investors' confidence to invest in America was, what they referred to as, American ingenuity. In other words, the investors understood the populous of America had a basic set of good work ethics and good intelligence, along with the teaching of Christian values, one of which was for servants to be loyal to their masters. Europeans knew, there was a basis for good work ethics and good intelligence in American character.

Jokingly, Dan said, "Weston, I know that isn't completely true, because most of what is going on in America is being done by the Scots-Irish and no person from England has ever accused us of having good work ethics or having good brains because they accused us of being somewhere between a monkey and a baboon. Some of them accused me of having gorilla blood because I was so big."

After they had completed the tour of the investment office, Dan told Weston he would like to go by the Continental Military Headquarters Building, which was walking distance from Weston's office. When they arrived, several military horses were tied, causing them to assume someone was in the building.

Dan went to the sergeant's desk and asked to see Colonel Grady Jackson. The sergeant said, "Sir, we have a General Grady Jackson, maybe he is the man you want to see." The sergeant said, "May I ask, who wants to see him?" Dan said, "Tell him General Dan O'Flaherty would like to see him."

The Sergeant snapped to attention and saluted Dan. Dan returned the salute and said, "The war is over for me, sergeant." The sergeant told General Jackson, General O'Flaherty was here to see him. General Jackson ran to the door and when he opened it two comrades saluted one another and then embraced. Dan told him he was in the area and couldn't leave without thanking him for all he had done for his family as the war began to come to a close.

Dan said, "General, I wanted you to know without your taking charge of an Army that had not quite surrendered, I would have lost two precious members of our family." The General thanked Dan for remembering his efforts. He also told him he had heard from his relative Andrew Jackson, who told him of the financial help he had given him to help him complete his study of the law.

After visiting with General Jackson for nearly one hour, Dan told him, if there is ever anything he could do to serve him, or anyone connected with him to contact someone at my brother-in-law's office in New York. They saluted one another with the highest esteem. As they walked away, something kept telling Dan he and General Jackson would cross paths again.

CHAPTER TWENTY-ONE

TRAVELING EAST

They continued to stroll around the inner city of New York being aware of the changes that had been made since the defeated had gone to Canada or England. Dan would be hard to convince all his enemies and the enemies of the new nation had gone.

He was walking around hoping none of his military enemies recognized him and wanted to get even. Dan's training and experience caused him to keep an awareness of all those around him, especially in areas where the smoke from the cannons of battle had barely cleared the air. However, he was encouraged to see there were some new others in the business district with newly painted signs with Irish names that had hidden the fact they were of the Catholic faith. But now, there was a different atmosphere surrounding the old thoughts of prejudice, which were now known as freedom. Within a brief span of time, American thoughts were suffocating the thoughts of the remaining British imperialist. The thoughts of those who waded ashore to the new nation named, the United States of America was evidenced by being governed by the richest man and the poorest man allowing equality to all citizens. The adjustment to freedom was a gradual process because no person on earth had ever experienced complete freedom to exercise the right to life, liberty and the pursuit of their individual happiness. Before America, no nation on earth had ever been governed by themselves with none having more political power than the other because of equality of all Americans becoming the law of the land.

As the sun slowly vanished in the west, the O'Flaherty family began to select which side of the house and which level they preferred to rest in the most beautiful home in New York. There was no doubt they were the happiest family in America. The next morning, Dan went to the kitchen early to do some planning. He was very concerned about the welfare of their children. He knew from experience the best schools in the world were in Europe. As a young man, because of the concern General Phillip O'Shea and his wife Margarita had shown to him, Dan received the best education available in the world, because of the General's influence with the King of Spain. In addition, the General and Margarita hired private tutors for advanced training in the use of weapons both military and domestic. Dan became the most skilled swordsman in the Spanish Empire and was taught horsemanship and military strategy by the best military minds in Spain.

In many years past, General O'Shea became the most decorated soldier in Spain. When Dan's mind became focused on the gift's others had given him, he bowed his head in gratitude to God for giving him the opportunities to be of benefit to others. At sunlight, he took his sons into the garden area for a talk. He told them of the gifts others had given to him, allowing him to be elevated to do many good things for others. The boys had never heard the story of their father's past. When he had completed telling them a small portion of his adventurous life, he asks them if they would enjoy learning all there is to know about everything he knows. Big smiles came on their faces as "Two Dan" asked, "What do I have to do?" Dan said, "All you have to do is tell me what you would like to know that you do not know now." Cathal said, "I want to know everything." Dan said, "OK, let's talk to mama and we will be getting ready for the adventure of a lifetime." When Mary came to the kitchen, all she saw was smiling faces wanting to love their mama good morning. Mary suspicioned the two boys had been talking with their daddy and she thought to herself, *I wonder what they are up to now?*

Dan was the first to speak; he began telling Mary, "We have been discussing all the different things I learned when I grew up in Spain with my adoptive parents, General and Margarita O'Shea. We have been thinking about how advanced the education knowledge is in Europe. I know there is an opportunity in America, but not of the quality there is in Europe. What do you think about moving to Spain for their education and military training?" Mary told Dan she had become concerned about the same thing, but she didn't know what to do about it. Dan assured her there is a better education for the children in Spain than in America. The family agreed to go to Spain as soon as arrangements could be made.

Mary and Dan met with Maureen and Weston after they awoke and told them they were moving to Spain for an undetermined amount of time. Weston told Dan he needed to visit his family in Spain after which he and Maureen would be returning to New York to continue the Foreign Investment Firm he and his father had started. Dan was most agreeable to their decision and suggested they continue to reside in the New York home. Weston and Maureen were very pleased with the arrangements.

Mid-morning, Dan went to the docks to talk to Gregory O'Malley to inform him of the decision they had made. Gregory told Dan he could be prepared to sail two days from now. Dan told

Gregory they would be ready. Sailing east was the farthest thing from Dan's mind. He thought Ireland and Spain were places he would never see again.

It was not until he began thinking of his three children's education that he began to understand the most he could ever teach his children was all he knew, but he wanted them to know more than he knew. So many changes had occurred in the world of finance, law and economics, as well as the sciences, he knew the future would be dim for his children if he failed to expose them to the best teachers in the world. All these were matters of great importance to him because he was the son of former Irish slaves who was torn from his family at a young age and fell into the arms of some of the most lovingly, kind people on earth by the grace of God. Had those events not occurred, he would have remained a slave until the British were defeated.

As Dan continued to ponder the truth of his family's circumstances, he knew the wealth he had inherited from his adoptive parents would eventually become a crutch for the children to use to fail in life, because he knew great wealth causes families to become weaklings. Dan had an awesome task ahead of him he was willing to confront with Mary's help. Dan told Mary the worst mistake they could ever make was for their children to learn they didn't have to try to do their best at everything. Dan said, "Mary, life does not allow time to rest and play. A good life is a series of very deadly serious decisions we have to make to provide for our children. The opportunity for an abundant life begins with the fundamental unwavering belief that Jesus is the Son of the living God. Once our children understand we are in God's care, we can understand our responsibility to obey Him.

Our duty is to see that His will be done in all things. What we are to do is make sure God is using the best of ourselves to do His will." Mary and Dan talked until they had a complete understanding and agreement to the plan they were implementing for the future of their children. Dan explained, "The blood that flows in our veins, and the ancestors from both of our families demands we train the next generation to meet their responsibility head on to be ready to participate on the biggest stage the future of the world has to offer."

When they completed talking to one another, they turned to God to get His guidance and directive for the future decisions they were to make. When they had dried one another's tears of supplication and determination, Dan told Mary he had to visit with General Grady Jackson regarding a message to General Washington and General John Milledge before they sailed. He told her he would eat when he returned. Dan found Weston and Maureen to tell them the responsibility he had before they sailed to inform General Washington and General Milledge of their plans. Weston arranged for a carriage to take Dan to General Jackson's headquarters.

The General was again delighted to visit with his friend. He told General Jackson of his plan to sail for Spain and needed to inform General Washington of his whereabouts and how he could be contacted should the need arise. He also told him General Milledge was in charge of the Blue Celts and needed to know because he had the responsibility of providing security for General Washington and Mrs. Washington. General Jackson told Dan he had dispatch capability and would take care of taking the message to them. Dan wrote the messages and gave them to the General. Dan thanked him for his prompt attention to his need. Dan again bade farewell to his trusted comrade and went back to the mansion for the evening with his family.

He told Mary as soon as everything leveled out he would like to spend some time with their family because he wanted to discuss with them some of the options they had to be thinking about as a course of study. When they had gathered, Dan could sense the anxious anticipation beginning to build in each of them. Dan told them the first lesson General O'Shea taught him was, "To know where you are going, you must know where you are." Dan told them the voyage on a sailing ship to Europe would be a fascinating experience as he taught them the constellations and stars of the northern hemisphere." He told them in the darkest night, God has arranged for you to never be lost if you learn astrology which is the study of the stars. He told them the stars keep ships on course in rough seas. He told them of learning to sail a ship when he was their age. His teacher was his Uncle Eamonn O'Flaherty. The children were more excited than ever getting to stay up late on the voyage and keep the ship on course.

The family was ready to go to the dock Thursday morning early. The O'Flahertys especially had not become accustomed to an abundance of clothes; they lived a very frugal life style. It didn't take them long to pack their clothes. They had lived with the Indians during the war and learned the value of being very grateful for each morsel of God's blessings.

The weather was beautiful as the captain began to guide the ship through the harbor into the open Atlantic Ocean. The wind had shifted to the southwest which was the perfect wind for their voyage. The children began to familiarize themselves with everything about a sailing vessel. They went to the bow of the ship to feel the cool salt water spray them as the ship split the waves. Each child had their own adventurous spirit, but Bridget had a certain quality she inherited from her father that was different from the two boys. There was a very confident air about her that indicated in advance she could conquer whatever challenge that lay ahead of her. Bridget was developing into a size much taller than her mother. She had a desire to learn all the ways of her father. She had learned the Irish Jig at a very early age from her father and was always ready to do the jig with her father when he had time.

When the ship was well at sea, Dan had developed a habit of meeting the children at their grandfather O'Malley's quarters where the maps and location devises were stored. Any sea Captain treasured the quadrant, which was a device to keep the direction of the ship on the right path. The children enjoyed their grandfather speaking the Gaelic language as he explained each detail of the devices and each purpose. There were no better teasers than one's own family members. With each new word, the children could tell what was of importance and what was not by the voice inflections of their kin. The greatest blessing to each of the O'Flaherty children was, their blood lines were not only clan member blood lines but were clan leader blood lines. From the 1500's, the Chieftain of the O'Malley family was Grace O'Malley. She became famous for fighting against England to keep Ireland separated from being ruled by Great Britain. That information was of the greatest interest to Bridget. She had wondered whether any of her ancestor women were involved in the leaderships of the clans. For some reason, Bridget did not see her future as being a caretaker of a family and not becoming involved as her father had done in the Revolutionary War. She had never voiced her desires, but when the opportunity came, she would reveal her choice to her father. She knew she had the basic knowledge of many different subjects to learn, but she wanted her efforts at learning to be for a purpose to achieve goals unknown to her now. She had a desire to learn military skills with weapons and basic strategy of military maneuvers to counter act the strategy of an enemy. To Cathal and "Two Dan" knowledge of military tactics and strategy was in their blood. They had heard the Blue Celts telling of the different victories won by their father against the English at a time when it appeared all was lost.

After the children had accomplished a basic knowledge of sailing the ship, their grandfather took them to the main deck to teach them the purpose of their knowledge. When "Two Dan" was given command of the wheel that guided the full ship, his eyes were opened wider than ever before. Once he knew the responsibility for everyone was in his hands, he grew in stature, in his own mind, to be someone who could perform when called upon. Each day every member of the family grew more confident of their ability and knowledge to be passed on to the next generation.

The voyage was at the close of the second month and no land had been seen. Gregory had hoped the southwest wind would have cut the time somewhat, but so far all they had left was hope and prayer. Yet, the family was high spirited the same as if the trip had only taken one week. The O'Flaherty's were very happy people, because they put gratitude ahead of any discomfort that came to them. All the Irish culture were known for making the best of the worst, always searching for the most hidden parts of life to become a source of thunderous laughter. Even the Irish soldiers armed with nothing more than a stick or club could find reason to laugh. It has been said, *there are no down hearted Irishman.*

After another ten days had passed, Gregory was gazing due east, when he thought he saw an image of something. He did not want false hope, so he said nothing but as his eyes began to bead up, he squinted harder and saw another gift from God. He remained quiet in hopes one of his grandchildren would see land before anyone else. "Two Dan" had decided to ride the bow for a while and walked toward his grandfather to take his place. Gregory kept hoping he would see what he had seen and in about five minutes, he heard "Two Dan's" voice yelling, "Land-Ho, Land-Ho!" When it caught everyone's attention, they hurried to the bow to take in the gift of a successful voyage. Dan and Mary stood close to one another and held hands remembering, *the first voyage they took together to America.*

Within two hours they had docked as their good friend Sam O'Keefe Jr., was the harbor master when they landed. Dan was so glad to see Sam Jr. and asked him how his father was doing. He told Dan even though his eyesight had worsened, he could still see the cards well enough to play with his friends daily. Weston made the arrangements for a coach to take them to their palace. The children had heard their father talk of his life in La Coruna, Spain. When they arrived at the front door of the palace, that had been part of the estate willed to him by General and Margarita O'Shea, they could never have imagined a home as magnificent as the one they were beholding. Dan had given instructions to Mr. Collier, his attorney, who was also Weston's father, to maintain the place to the exact perfection his mother Margarita O'Shea would have required.

Mr. Monroe, the butler met the family at the door along with the other servants. Three of them remembered Dan as a young man in his formative years as he was being trained and mentored by the O'Sheas. They knew Dan would become a major force in whatever or wherever he was called upon to see that justice was done. The Irish culture is the culture that brought the characteristic of 'fair play' to all the other cultures of the world as the necessary ingredient to establish a civil society and for peace to prevail. For example, if a person was accused by another of a wrong doing, the accused had the right to be confronted by his accuser and the right to defend himself.

Successive English monarchs were blinded by the grace given humility of the Irish people who at first blush appeared to be a culture that would surrender their faith and belief if ordered to do so by the Crown, but they learned the Irish culture would never surrender the spiritual gifts that God Himself had granted to them in double portions.

After hundreds of years of bad judgment legalized theft of property, torture, abuse slavery, and murder the English learned two things, one of which was the Irish cannot and will not ever be defeated. Two, they will never submit to the government by a foreign nation by having to surrender their faith.

The amazed O'Flaherty family wanted to see the home after they had rested in the garden behind the main house. While they were enjoying themselves, Dan went to the library Margarita had built behind, but connected to the main house. When Dan opened the door, the spirit of General O'Shea swept over his soul. Dan went to his knees and bowed his head in gratitude for the memory of being allowed by God to have lived his early years in the presence of such great souls. Dan could feel the warmth of their presence and the memory of their gentle voice's as he mentally unfolded page after page of life lessons the General and Margarita had so lovingly given to him. Nothing on this earth could ever be of more value than for Dan to have been invited into the hearts of those two precious souls who loved him with their whole hearts. His adoptive mother Margarita was in the line of succession to become Queen of Spain but abdicated that position to become the wife of General Phillip O'Shea.

Dan recalled, *the memory of General O'Shea being injured by the back blast of a canon that was being demonstrated by a manufacturer to the Army of Spain. General O'Shea lost an arm and a portion of his lower leg. His face was disfigured because the blast had blown most of the flesh off the bones of his face. He lingered on the brink of death for months and became a shell of the man he had been. Margarita persuaded him to live and within a year, he had recovered to a limited extent, but God in his mercy had allowed him to keep all his superb mental faculty intact.*

The O'Sheas closet friend was Eamonn O'Flaherty who had become the care taker of Dan whose parents had been forcefully taken to America by the English government and forced into slavery. At the time of the arrest of his family, Dan was placed in care of Eamonn O'Flaherty who was persuaded by the O'Sheas to allow Dan to live with them. Their purpose was to allow General O'Shea to train and teach Dan to become a Special Force soldier. Eamonn and Dan agreed. Dan received the best education available from the most distinguished scholars of the day. He received military training of the highest order from General O'Shea and the skills of the use of weapons by the most accomplished trainers in Europe. As Dan walked through the library, he recalled, *the screen Margarita had built to allow Phillip privacy for his wounds to heal.* He recalled; *the special day General O'Shea wanted him to perform the Irish Jig.*

Dan had become familiar with the privacy of General O'Shea to the extent he told his mother he would do the jig if his father would come from behind the screen. General O'Shea agreed. Dan did the jig and the family celebrated the spirit of being cured and well from all the injuries. It was one of Dan's most memorable days.

A thought began to come to Dan's mind, *of using the library to teach his own children in the same manner as his adoptive father had taught him.* The library contained more reading material than most other librarys, even those designed for public use. Dan began recalling, *the different subjects General O'Shea had taught him.*

After they had inspected their new home, the family prepared for a good night's rest without being tossed by the waves of the Atlantic Ocean. Dan's head was spinning from one thought to another. He had never perceived himself as a teacher of geography, astronomy, mathematics, chemistry and world science. He decided he had best begin with some refresher courses himself by hiring a tutor. The war had dimmed the focus the knowledge his children needed.

The next morning, he prepared the family to go with him to visit his friend and attorney, Matthew Collier, who was also Weston's father, and a person who believed in having a plan for living life with balance. Weston had enlightened his father on most all his adventures, except for those he could not run the risk of putting in writing. For some reason, Maureen was not feeling well and was hesitant to run the risk of causing others to become ill but about mid-morning, the queasy feeling in her stomach became better and she decided to visit her father-in-law, Mr. Collier. Weston was so hopeful Maureen would be up to the visit and it began to appear she would be able to go with them.

When they arrived at Mr. Collier's office, Dan recalled his first visit with him, *when it became timely for the O'Shea's estate to be probated in which Dan was named as the heir to their fortune.* Except for the expertise of Mr. Collier, the entire estate would have escheated to the Crown, but because of Mr. Collier representing Margarita she had abdicated her rights of succession to become the Queen of Spain. Mr. Collier had an agreement with the successors she would retain her share of the property she would have received had she become the Queen of Spain. Had that agreement not been recognized by the court, the property would have reverted to the Crown.

When the wills were combined and probated, Dan became one of the wealthiest men in the world. When Dan returned to America as a prisoner of War under the supervision of British General James Oglethorpe (known for his establishment of the Colony of Georgia) he was later pardoned by the Crown of England for his gallant military service against Spain. His involvement ultimately ended the Seven Year War. The English Crown awarded Dan and the O'Shea's millions of acres of land in Georgia and Carolina. Spain had awarded General O'Shea land in Florida for his efforts in bringing the Treaty to finality. Dan gave all the responsibility of managing the gigantic estate to Mr. Collier who had caused the estate to grow in large amounts by his participation as one of the largest land investors in America. Dan had used a huge portion of the estate to supplement the cost of the Revolutionary War. He gave the money to General George Washington to pay the Army and by doing so could keep the military actively engaged against Great Britain for years of warfare.

Mr. Collier was delighted to see his best client who had with Weston's marriage to Dan's sister Maureen almost become a relative. Mr. Collier was overjoyed with the combining of the two families. Mr. Collier and Dan were ready for Weston to get back to work, investing money in America. Mr. Collier told Dan he would have never guessed Weston, Shibeal and Maureen would have become the most effective group of spies in the war. Everyone sat staring at one another in complete amazement because so much had been accomplished by so few. Mr. Collier was having a difficult time controlling his tears as he looked at his son with such beaming admiration. He said, "Weston, let me make the most understated statement I have ever made in my life." Weston said, "Let us hear it." Mr. Collier said, "Weston, I am so proud of you." The room fell silent as the most prominent lawyer in Europe and perhaps the world beheld a son of his own flesh that impacted the future of the world by the contribution he made to the cause of freedom. They embraced and allowed the tears that freedom had produced to flow freely from their grateful hearts. Only Maureen, Weston and Shibeal knew the hour by hour escapes from the enemy as they probed the depths of the enemy strongholds of war secrets to save the lives of American soldiers. Mr. Collier began to see the qualities of Maureen and why Weston would have been attracted to a person who was born in a slave camp in America and had not one day of formal education in her life. Mr. Collier could not have been prouder of Weston's choice for a life partner. Dan knew he was among the most unique group of people anyone could have imagined.

Dan told Mr. Collier of his plans to educate his family in Europe as opposed to America. Dan was convinced he could become qualified to train his family to gain the knowledge he had gained from

General O'Shea and Margarita with the assistance of exceptional tutors. Mr. Collier agreed to locate a qualified instructor for the O'Flaherty family.

CHAPTER TWENTY-TWO

FAMILY PLANNING

It wasn't long before Maureen and Weston began to move around the office to recall some of the memories Weston had being a law clerk for his prestigious father as he was deciding his field of endeavor to earn a living for his family.

Dan needed some time to visit with Mr. Collier. Mr. Collier also needed to discuss some of the questions relating to business decisions regarding the management of his estate.

Dan knew Maureen would enjoy visiting some of the dress shops in the inner-city shopping area, so he suggested meeting them there after he had completed his visit with Mr. Collier. That pleased Weston and the other family members.

Dan was very grateful to Mr. Collier for taking the time to discuss the personal matters that had begun to weigh heavy on his mind. Dan's life was filled with life changing events of great joy and great sadness. but there seemed to be a wealth of blessings that always came at the right time which enhanced his life to be better prepared for the next set of circumstances. Even though there were times circumstances became life threatening, but in the final analysis the experiences made his life better. As he considered the future of his children, his highest hope was to prepare them, as best he could, for the turbulence of each day of the future.

He discussed with Mr. Collier the prospect of enlarging the O'Shea estate acreage to approximately four thousand acres. The purpose for the expansion was to have a training facility constructed like the one in New York. He disclosed to him he intended to hire the best trainers in Europe to train his family and others, that had the potential to learn what the academy had to offer. As Dan was telling Mr. Collier some of the details, Mr. Collier was thinking of, *discussing the plan with some of Spain's military leaders whom he knew would have an interest their officer's being trained by General Dan O'Flaherty O'Shea.* Mr. Collier was also considering asking, *the military leaders to share the cost of such an elaborate training ground.* After Dan had given Mr. Collier his plan, he thanked him again for his time and they agreed to meet again in approximately one week.

When Dan found his family, the ladies were having the time of their lives. Dan could see they were enjoying every moment, considering themselves to be ladies of distinction. Dan was quick to tell them of his experiences of visiting the clothing shops with his adoptive mother, Margarita O'Shea. He told them he had been trained by a lady who knew the difference in good clothes and clothes suited for royalty. Dan was especially interested in Bridget having an opportunity to become acquainted with the finer clothes women seemed to enjoy. Her mother told her the background she had on Clare Island in Ireland when she was young. She also told her how her father brought her to the same stores and bought her beautiful clothes at the time they were preparing for marriage.

Bridget decided she would make her parents happy by trying on some of the finer dresses. Dan and Mary remembered Mary's first blue dress they bought and went about trying to find one similar. The clerk brought out a beautiful blue silk dress that was almost the duplicate of her mother's first dress. When Bridget came out to show them the dress, Dan could tell Bridget finally realized how much God had blessed her. She was stunningly beautiful, which was something she had never realized. Maureen and Weston were enjoying every moment of the shopping trip, but Maureen had begun to suspect her upset stomach was more than she had expected. She had been around enough morning sickness to know she should expect more later. She whispered to Weston she didn't feel like trying on clothes today, maybe later. Weston had never been around morning sickness before, but he did wonder what had made Maureen ill.

When the family returned to their home, Dan told his family he needed to take a ride and would welcome anyone who wanted to go with him. Bridget was the first to volunteer and then her brothers told their father they wanted to explore the wooded area. As they rode together Dan began telling them of the field maps he and some of the Blue Celts had drawn before the American Revolutionary War. Dan said, "The biggest advantage we had over the British soldiers was we knew where we were at all times and knew where to hide if the battle got out of hand. I am thinking of enlarging the five hundred acres we own into four thousand acres or more, if the land is available. My purpose is to set up a training facility to train the most qualified military soldiers in the world. What I am wanting to know now is, whether the land around us is suitable for such a plan. After the three heard the purpose, they became more attentive to the terrain. They were mounted on four Arabian horses that needed to be ridden to gentle out their better qualifications as war horses.

When Dan was young, he would venture into the surrounding forest to hunt for wild animals. He wanted his family to know the art of survival. The first lesson he taught them was paying attention to the slopes of the earth to learn where there may be a channel that would hopefully lead to water. He asked them to remember their days of living with the Cherokee Indian tribe. Dan had become a fugitive from the British courts because he and Maureen killed four British soldiers before the war began. He took his family to east Tennessee in the Appalachian Mountains to hide. He developed a friendship with a brilliant Cherokee chief named Attakullakulla, otherwise known as "First Beloved Man." Dan left his family under the care of the Chief while he fought the British during the Revolutionary War. At wars end, he learned the chief had died. While he was alive, he cared for Dan's family as if they were Cherokee. The memories Dan's children had of that experience began to come alive as they ventured further and further into the wilderness.

At evening, Dan asks them if they had brought anything to eat. As he began to build a fire, Cathal looked at Bridget and "Two Dan" looked at his father and said, "We didn't bring anything to eat." Dan smiled and said, "I did." And everyone felt relieved. They had no idea their training had begun. The three O'Flaherty military recruits didn't mind what their father had planned for them, they were with him with no outside interference and they were enjoying every minute of being with him in the forest. Dan was so proud of his family. It appeared to him Bridget was enjoying herself more than her brothers.

Dan had his family with him and it was hard for him to give up the evening with them, but he knew Mary would be looking for them by the time she was ready for rest. On the way back to their home, Dan stopped his horse as he gazed into a star lit sky. He said, "It is time for a test." "Two Dan" asked, "Is it a race?" His father said, "No, it is for each of you to tell me all you know about the stars and of course, ladies are first. It was too dark for them to see one another but, if the boys could have seen their sister they would have been embarrassed because Bridget knew more about the stars than her brothers. Dan said, "This part of your education is so important because most of the field training you will learn will be done at night because most of the combat you will be involved with will be at night. General O'Shea taught me everything he knew about military combat at night and that is the reason the British lost the war. As you practice your night vision, your brain makes an adjustment to the greater use of night vision and you can see more clearly at a further distance. Also, remember this, your learning ability is more sensitive at night than in daylight hours. I have reached the point I can hear a snake crawling if I can't see it.

Each of Dan's children had learned more about their father in one day than they thought possible. Each of them went to bed excited and ready for their next adventure which they hoped would be very soon.

Just before daylight the next morning, Dan went to the bedside of each of his children and whispered, "Let's go hunting." Each one of them woke up ready to continue their adventure. Dan didn't have to tell them to bring food and water because they had no idea where their daring father would lead them. Just as the sun cast its first hint of another dawn, they were saddled and ready to go. Dan entered the wooded area from the opposite side he had gone the day before because the east of the five hundred original acres appeared to be denser which indicated the possibility of fresh water.

Dan told them to be aware of any indication of signs of human intrusion on the property. He had been told some of the woods could possibly be hiding places for gangs of thieves. As they entered the wooded area, the birds had begun their morning welcome with a melody only God Himself could create. As they quietly moved along Dan silently signaled for them to see the squirrels and other animals as they began their uninterrupted foraging for the family meal of nuts and berries. Dan was so blest, in that, his entire family loved to be in the forest. They especially enjoyed the bottom areas where the nut producing trees grew in large clusters and provided food for all the nut gathering animals of the forest.

After they had traveled to mid-morning, Dan decided to let the horses have a breather. They all released the girth to allow the horses to get a full breath of air. As they gathered around an old hollow log, Dan asks, "Has anyone got an indication where there may be a source of water?" "Two Dan" said, "For the last hour, I've had the feeling we are going downhill, and I noticed the ground has become softer because the horses are leaving prints." Bridget said, "I've seen some birds flying east, it could be toward a water supply source." When they had rested for a while and chewed on some dried meat, Dan turned due south. As the afternoon began to approach, he abruptly halted because he saw some wagon tracks which put him on alert; he whispered, *we may have visitors.* As they began to follow the wagon tracks, he noticed the tracks were joined by another set of wagon tracks coming from another direction. After they saw evidence of several wagons gathering on to one trail, it was evident there was probably a campsite further on down the trail. After Dan had pondered the evidence he decided to move away from the trail and wait until it was dark to find an answer to the gathering of the caravan. They waited for the cover of night to give whoever it was time to gather for the night. Just as the darkness of night had set in, they began to hear music. Dan recognized some old Spanish folk songs with all kinds of musical instruments, some of which he was hearing for the first time.

Dan had heard talk on the docks, when he was young, about a cult of people referred to as Roma or Gypsys. The seaman couldn't explain their origin other than a group of reclusive travelers that had no homeland. It was reported they had their own language, customs and had been exiled by most every country under the threat of extermination.

Since Dan's family had been in America for years, he had no knowledge of the invasion of the Roma or Gypsy population in Europe. In the beginning, they were a natural specimen for the churches to exercise brotherly love and compassion. The purpose was to persuade them to abandon their unchristian heritage of the practices of witchcraft, weird medical practices as well as the art of palm reading. The Roma presented themselves as the needy which enthused the church members to meet the needs of a group of harmless vagabonds.

As observing free hearted practitioners of the church acted upon their beliefs of giving and sharing, the flood gates of more and more Gypsies poured into the European countries until the knowledge of the Gypsy culture became known as a threat to the entire culture of Europe. Germany was the first to pass laws to prevent the massive immigration of beggars and thieves. As their populations exploded and began to affect all the nations, laws of expulsion began to be passed by all the nations. The gypsys were a culture without home or master and with few exceptions could not be assimilated into any known culture known to man. When they eventually became known as having no willingness to become responsible to any form of cultural or social order, they began to be stigmatized as a threat to all other cultures. The mass annihilation of them began in Germany in the fifteen hundred, sixteenth and seventeenth centuries with the passage of the anti-gypsy laws. It took France almost 150 years longer to learn of the destructive force a Godless, lethargic, hopelessly lazy culture could cause to any nation. (23)

Dan did not want to risk involving his family in something none of them knew anything about. He had decided to involve the military to do what was necessary to remove them from the land. Until that had occurred, he did not want to take his family back into that area. But, because of the closeness to his property, he would place night sentry's around his home.

Within a week, he had received notice from Mr. Collier of the necessity for a meeting. The next morning, he went to see if Mr. Collier had decided whether the expansion of his property was possible. When Mr. Collier heard his voice, he came to welcome Dan at the door. While they were being seated, Mr. Collier began an inquiry as to whether he had inspected any of the property he intended to purchase. He told Mr. Collier of taking his family on an excursion until they discovered wagon tracks which led to the sounds of a Gypsy campsite. He told him it apparently was a hideaway where several different groups were meeting. Mr. Collier told Dan he was wise not to involve himself with them because there are several fugitive gangs of gypsys who have begun to rob and pillage families which are now being sought by the Army of Spain. Dan told Mr. Collier that was good news to him because he had posted sentries around their home. He also told him they needed to make a visit to Army Headquarters to discuss sending troops to arrest them as fugitives from justice. Mr. Collier asks Dan if he had the time to go with him to discuss the matter of the training facility and the removal of the intruders. He added, "I know everyone would be very excited to see you again." Dan agreed. The General was well pleased to see Dan and Mr. Collier. They had become well acquainted when Dan was living in Spain as a youngster.

Mr. Collier began the discussion by inquiring of the status of the fugitive Roma groups that were suspected to be hiding in the deep forest areas. The General replied by telling them the King was most intent in ridding the nation of the remaining gangs to the extent of having agreed to pay a bounty to those who report their whereabouts. Mr. Collier told him he needed to let Dan tell him where there may be several groups within proximity of his home. Dan told the General he would like to make his services available to him to trap the ones he had located. Dan said, "General, it would probably be wise to attack at night, because there appeared to be several wagon loads of them. The General told Dan if he would agree to lead the Special Force Troops on a night attack, it would almost guarantee the capture of most of them. Dan replied, "General, I am ready when you give the order."

Within a week, three companies of Special Force soldiers came to Dan's home at dusk dark. Dan had a plan of attack and knew the exact location of the fugitives. Dan did not think it wise to involve his family in a full-scale battle before he had completed their training. Everyone understood it was not the time to run the risk of injury.

Dan's plan was to encircle the camp after dark. The Roma later called Gypsy usually concluded the day with dance, gaiety and musical performances as well as singing mixed with alcohol and boisterous laughter. The plan called for an approach to the camp site from four directions with an order to disable the sentries, should there be any. Stealth was the secret to success of the attack. Dan planned to walk into the camp alone and request there be no resistance to the arrest. The timing had to be perfect. Dan would give each group twenty minutes to get into place after the music began. Approximately thirty minutes after the music started, Dan walked into the Gypsy camp that consisted of one hundred men, women and children.

As Dan approached the fire in the center of the camp, the music stopped, and all eyes were fixed on Dan. The first words out of his mouth was to inform them they were surrounded by the Army of Spain and they were under arrest. Dan was waiting for the first wrong move which came in a second's time as one of the leaders threw a knife aimed for Dan's heart. Dan saw him as he threw it and turned his side as a shot was fired by one of the soldiers who saw the man throw the knife. The bullet hit the Gypsy's head at the top of his nose. When the others saw his body lying on the ground, the remaining group believed they were surrounded. Dan asked one of the leaders, "Do you surrender?" The man said, "Yes!" The Special Force soldiers moved into the light of the fire and began driving stakes to tie ropes to surround the prisoners. Some of the others began to rebuild the fire for the night. The prisoners were told to disarm themselves by throwing their weapons across the rope line.

At daylight, the prisoners were taken from the enclosure in groups of ten and placed in their wagons to be taken to the fort. Dan could tell the group was a dangerous group of people. They arrived at the fort at dusk and the prisoners were placed in the military's stockade.

Dan reported to the General the mission was a complete success with no injuries. Dan told the General he was thinking of building a training facility to train military and civilian troops to become Special Force combat soldiers. The General was encouraged to know how Dan would be in charge of training the troops. He asked Dan what he needed to do to be of assistance. Dan told him he was in the process of purchasing the land to expand the acreage to become the best facility in Europe. Dan told the General as soon as he had the land purchased, he would have a plan drawn for his approval.

When Dan got back to his home, the whole family couldn't wait to hear the details of the adventure. Dan told them the story in its entirety. When he finished, Mary asked him, "And what would have happened if you had not seen the man throw the knife?" Dan said, "Mary, God will never allow harm to keep me from coming back to you." Mary asked Dan, "Does that include our three gifts from heaven?" Dan said, "Mary, look back at all we have had come to our lives and you will see we could not have made it through except for God's constant protection, guidance and mercy. Mary, I have recognized for many years, we have received special care beyond our ability to care for ourselves. I have concluded we are involved in a special mission God has designed for our lives. It is our duty to accept the responsibility to do everything in our power to cause righteousness to prevail. I want both of us to be involved in training our children to know and recognize not only the blessings they are given every day but to also be willing to accept full responsibility to cause right to be done in all things." Mary said, "Dan. I suppose you know how deeply I feel for you and our family but, having been with you these years, I have learned there is more responsibility to life than just to ourselves and our family. I have learned we have a responsibility to be aware of the needs of our neighbors. I pray with your guidance you will train me to walk the path we should walk together." Dan said, "The good part is, we love one another more today than we did yesterday. With that to look forward to every morning we will not take the wrong path. But Mary, besides all that, I love to make you happy." Mary said, "Dan you have made me happier than I could have ever hoped. Thank you for loving me and our children."

Cathal, his brother and sister had been sitting in the swing on the back porch talking about the plans for tomorrow. He asked his father whether they would be proceeding with their plans to develop an academy. Dan asks, "What made you ask that question?" Cathal told him there could be other bands of Gypsys on other parts of the property. Dan said, "Cathal that is a good thing. Cathal asked, "Why?" Dan responded, "Because that will give us purpose for getting up in the morning." Cathal smiled at his father saying, "Does that mean we are going back and look for some more intruders?" Dan said, "Cathal, that is what the O'Flaherty family does every day. Now get some good rest and we will explore what is known as Mino River Basin. We may find more than we could expect in that area."

The next morning when Dan went to the kitchen where he discovered Bridget waiting to have a private talk with her father. Dan was so pleased with Bridget. Deep in Dan's heart he felt Bridget had more of his spirit than Cathal and "Two Dan". She had a sureness about her that caused others to trust in her ways. Dan amused himself by thinking of a description of her ways. He thought to himself, *she is a solution looking for a problem to solve.* She began by telling her father how anxious she was to begin the adventure of life. She knew to achieve the heights of being of benefit to others she must prepare herself in every known field of education. She told him she wanted to become skilled as a warrior but with finesse and cunning to accomplish the mission with a subtle delicacy.

After hearing Bridget reveal her deepest yearnings, Dan revealed to her, even though their family had become Americans, there are those who are still suffering more than ever before as the King of England tightens the choke hold around the necks of the Irish, Catholics. He told her the hundreds of thousands who remained under British rule. The inhumanity of the protestant rule of Irish Catholics had reached a severe level of cruelty. For example: The Anglo Parliament had rejected a bill that allowed Catholics to lease a cabin with a potato garden. The brave soul who had presented the bill was voted out of his seat in parliament for attempting to provide an element of humanity to the dying Irish culture.

Another such atrocity was learned of a soldier shooting a Catholic for refusing to sell his beautiful horse to a Protestant for five pounds. Anything educational being exposed to the younger Catholic children which pertained to the historical greatness of the clans was forbidden. The ancient greatness of the clans was forbidden being imparted to the lower order. All the teachings that had been held as the reverent Irish teachings became nonexistent because it was forbidden by English law.

But, regardless of the laws some of the Protestant hearts continued to break the morsels of knowledge to the poor scholars on the sly because of the love and honor that prevailed in the hearts of some of the protestants who knew by God's spiritual messengers the English cruelty was wrong before God. The persistent grains of knowledge kept being systematically distributed to some few who would not be denied because of their eagerness to learn. The sharp edge of hatred and bitterness began to dull. The word Catholic began being used by some in open conversation by the Throne. A degree of tolerance began to fill the air in the mid 1790's which gave hope of a restoration to at least some who were suffering the extinction of their culture.

Bridget had never known the depth of the inhumanity of England until her father revealed the truth to her. She asks her father whether there was time to do something to correct the prevailing immorality of the Crown. Dan responded by telling her, "There is always hope when the will of God is being done, but first you must prepare yourself to enter the den of evil by being trained by those who have survived other murdering regimes."

CHAPTER TWENTY-THREE

INAUGURATION

Dan knew it was time to reveal to Bridget the truth behind the family becoming Americans. He began by telling her the rich history of the Irish culture. He told her of the scores of years of warfare, starvation and cruelty that had not resulted in the Irish Catholics relinquishing their belief in God in the manner set forth by the teachings of the Catholic church. He revealed the conflict Britain always had with Ireland was the Protestant British coveting the Irish Catholic land. He told her no amount of imagination can bring to the human mind the persecution imposed upon the Catholics against the Irish by the British. Every wicked imagination that could be contrived was told as truth to the English people from every Protestant pulpit in the British empire. For example, an event was told of a massacre of 610,000 Irish Protestants by the Irish Catholics. The news was magnified by the pulpit ministers calling for the blood of all Catholics. When the truth was finally revealed 4,028 British soldiers were killed within a two-year period of warfare. The total amount was reduced to 2,109 over a ten-year period of warfare. (24)

The truth was, there were 1,466,000 Irish Catholic land owners in the year 1641. That number had been reduced to 616,000 by the year 1652 which was nearly one-half of the population of the whole country that had been sent to other nations as slaves or exterminated.

Centuries of bitterness had existed between both nations. As the British bitterness increased the population of Irish Catholics decreased. The resistance by the Catholic church to the governance of Ireland by England produced a never-ending war that was fought by the Irish heart that never knew defeat. Any defeat suffered by the Irish simply meant another conflict would begin on another part of Ireland. When England had taken the land by the extermination and enslavement of almost five sixths of the population, a humane decision was made to exterminate the remaining few by enacting laws that would further suppress the hopes of the Irish.

In the 18th century the most prominent British legal scholars designed a plan of extermination based primarily upon denial of any form of civil liberties. Those that have analyzed the "Penal Laws" agree the object of the specific laws enacted by the British Parliament had four goals:

(1) To deprive the Catholics of all civil life.
(2) To reduce them to a condition of most extreme and brutal ignorance.
(3) To dissociate them from the soil.
(4) To exterminate the Irish culture.

As Protestants developed the "Laws of Extinction" a legal finesse developed in achieving oppression, impoverishment and degradation of the Irish people was achieved by artful words of legalese to disguise the inherent cruelty not for the sake of mercy but as a bath for the guilt of conscience. (24)

After listening to her father reveal the British inhumanity toward the Irish each word she heard caused her heart to make a deeper commitment of purpose for her life effort. She inquired as to when the training would begin. Her father revealed he had in mind a special training for her in addition to being trained as a military combat soldier. He told her of a very dear friend named Colonel Frederico de Longoria, who had served as Chief of Security for the Army of Spain. He also revealed Colonel Longoria had trained her Aunt Maureen and Aunt Shibeal for covert service. He asks her if she had thought about becoming involved as a trained spy. Bridget told her father she had envisioned herself as being most useful by covertly gathering information from the enemy.

Dan advised Bridget of his desire to enroll her for training with Colonel Longoria. The next day, Dan sent a message to Colonel Longoria requesting an appointment for him and Bridget. Within a short time, a message arrived setting the time for 11:00 a.m., the following morning. Bridget could hardly sleep. She was ready to begin the adventures life had for her.

They arrived at Colonel Longoria's academy the next morning. As soon as the Colonel learned of Dan's presence, he hurriedly went to the waiting area to see his beloved friend. When Dan saw the Colonel, his mind flashed back to the days of being tutored and guided by General Phillip O'Shea while being trained to become a Special Forces soldier. Colonel Longoria had served as Chief of Security under General O'Shea when he was in the active service of the military.

Dan had a heart full of gratitude because the Colonel had trained his two sisters for service in the American Revolutionary War.

Colonel Longoria revealed to Dan the training of Maureen and Shibeal was a most pleasant undertaking, in that, both students were most capable of performing their tasks at the highest levels because of their natural skills.

Dan was most proud to introduce Bridget to the Colonel. The Colonel was astonished at the beauty Bridget possessed. He revealed to them she may very well be the most beautiful student we have ever enrolled in the academy. Dan told the Colonel the mission she would be sent to perform would require the highest level of skills.

Colonel Longoria could not believe Dan would be sending someone so precious to him to the world of espionage. He told the Colonel she has special talents to overcome the risks. Colonel Longoria told Dan his son had just retired from the Spanish military and was an instructor at the academy. He said, "We will see to it she receives the best training available in Europe." He also told Dan we are ready to begin when she is ready. Bridget told them she was prepared to start at any time. Colonel Longoria escorted them to the registrar's office. When Bridget had completed the registration, she was told to report the following Monday. Monday morning Bridget reported for duty to learn the art of infiltrating the enemy at the highest level to learn the secrets of how to defend against their plans.

Captain Esteban Longoria met Bridget at the assembly room and escorted her to the captain's office. The first words spoken to Bridget by Captain Longoria was, "I am going to teach you how to stay alive in enemy territory." Bridget said, "Captain, I will say Amen to that." The Captain was very impressed with her intelligence and her beauty. Each of her trainers knew she would become an effective operative wherever she was assigned.

The academy was primarily based upon training the students to become qualified to be placed as a workman at any level of knowledge within any setting. Bridget excelled at every level. She had come from a family that knew the value of hard work and commitment. She knew farming and was also very qualified as a scribe for important documents. Her hand writing was regarded as some of the most elegant writing her instructors had ever seen.

When the instructors learned of her skills as a scribe, they stressed the importance of learning the art of secretly memorizing documents. Dan had insisted his family know the English language and the Spanish language with variations of dialect. Dan's military training had become very useful for his children's training as they prepared to be of service to others.

With Bridget being well settled in the academy, Dan became involved in completing the purchase of the additional acreage to construct a world class military training facility. He had the experience of being involved in the American Revolution with men who had no military training. Dan knew the war between America and Great Britain was far from over and he wanted to train career soldiers for the next encounter.

By the time Dan had put together the available acreage, the training ground was over ten thousand acres. The facility contained areas for most every type terrain from dense forest to open arid territory. He had designed a portion to train the special troops to operate all known military heavy artillery.

The central theme for training the Special Force units was based on warfare from ambush at night. All major armed militaries at that time in history were conventional armies meeting in open fields and firing muskets at short distances. General Phillip O'Shea was the creator of snipers hiding by the cover of nature and darkness armed with rifles that are accurate at one hundred yards or more.

The general staff of the Spanish military selected the most qualified personnel to enter the Special Force. With Dan having been promoted to General during the American Revolutionary War by General George Washington caused his prestige to soar among the Spanish military general staff. Many of them were trying to volunteer to be trained by General Dan O'Flaherty O'Shea.

Bridget was developing a reputation for her use of the sword. She was being presented as perhaps the best female swordswoman in Spain. Dan could not be prouder of his three children when the reports of their physical and mental accomplishments began to come to him from those who were charged with educating them for competition on the world stage.

Once Dan had set up the basic structure of the military school and had placed each of his children in the hands of his most trusted military educators, he had a yearning to go home to America. Weston and Maureen had reestablished the New York Investment office as well as the home and the horse stable. Dan asks Mary to accompany him to America. Dan and Mary agreed to sail to Savannah, Georgia first to see the other members of O'Flaherty and O'Malley family.

The ships owned by the O'Malley and O'Flaherty's were enjoying a good year in the shipping business. Trade between America and most of the European nations was well established even though the Continental Congress had not completed the final details of the American Constitution.

When they were ready to leave Spain, the whole family had gathered to bid them a safe journey. The family knelt in prayer as they tearfully told one another farewell. Dan was glad to know the ship they were on was the sturdiest vessel of their fleet. Trade between Spain, France and America was very good. Tobacco was a huge export for America which was in abundance after the colonies had settled into hard work and cultivation of their land.

Dan and Mary were anxious to visit with all their family members who had for the most part settled in Carolina, Georgia and Florida. When they arrived at the dock in Savannah, Georgia it was filled with the O'Malley's and O'Flaherty's to greet Dan and Mary. Many of the Blue Celts who had served with Dan were there to welcome their leader home. As they approached the palatial home Dan had purchased for his mother and father, southwest of Savannah, deep precious memories came upon him that, *brought gratitude to his God for allowing the O'Flaherty family to be with one another during the war and have time together when the war was over.*

Evidence of just how much his father loved farming was everywhere to see, as he saw field after field his father had plowed. Before Coleman O'Flaherty died, he had become known as one of the major farmers in the area even though he had begun his life as a fisherman in Ireland. Dan was so glad his father and mother had several years of peace and comfort before they were called to heaven.

Dan and Mary enjoyed every moment of time with their loved ones. After they had settled in to the extent Dan was feeling lazy, a courier arrived with a message from General Washington requesting his attendance at the inauguration ceremony of him becoming the first President of the United States of America. When Dan read the letter, he handed the letter to Mary as tears began rolling down his cheek. When Mary read the letter, she embraced Dan as they recalled the war-torn years of being slaves, fugitives from justice, battle field warriors, adopted members of a Cherokee tribe and eventually victors over the greatest army in the world. They were speechless as they held one another. After they had time to collect their thoughts, Dan said, "Mary, we need to be a part of the ceremony. I know General Washington would like to see us."

As both prepared to travel to Washington for the Inauguration, independent thoughts raced through their minds. Mary recalled, *the first time she saw Dan and her father and General O'Shea when they negotiated a partnership in the shipping business such a manner as to avoid the Penal Laws of England that forbid Irish Catholics from having investments that made a profit.* The second occasion, *they had seen one another was the funeral at a Ballynakill of Dan's mentor and relative Eammon O'Flaherty who had been wounded on the field of battle in the second Jacobite uprising. At that meeting they had vowed to one another to be soul mates for life.*

She also recalled, *Dan being captured in the Jacobite War and just before being shot he was rescued by General Oglethorpe who had begun a colony in Georgia. General Oglethorpe and Dan became friends even though Dan was a prisoner of war. Dan was instrumental in saving the colony of Georgia because of his intervention with Spain which prevented Spain from expanding land holdings known as Florida. Dan and his adoptive father, General Phillip O'Shea promoted the signing of a Treaty which brought about the end of the Seven Year War. The fortunes of Dan's efforts to assist England against his native land of Spain brought about great wealth for the O'Shea family. However, just as the Treaty was approved by both nations, General Phillip O'Shea and his wife Margarita were lost at sea because of a hurricane as they were traveling to America to become*

American citizens. Dan was their only heir and became one of the wealthiest men in the world. Dan used his fortune to help subsidize the cost of the war against England.

As they privately considered memorable events of their lives, a smile appeared on their faces generated by the memories they had been pondering. They had recalled their backgrounds and recognized that but for God's mercy they would have not been alive to experience the honor of being involved in founding a nation.

As their ship entered the New York harbor, it became evident the celebration had begun. As the ship was being moored, Dan saw a carriage surrounded by a company of what appeared to him to be soldiers, dressed in blue, which was not the color of uniform of the Continental soldiers. When he and Mary walked the gang plank to the dock, he glanced up and standing at the end of the walkway was General John Milledge to greet him. Every light in Dan's memory bank flashed on as he saluted the man that had been with him from the first day of his coming to America.

As Mary approached General Milledge, he kneeled and kissed her hand. Dan said, "John, this is becoming embarrassing to two immigrants from Ireland." As tears of welcome flowed from the faces of all the Blue Celts, General Milledge said, "General Washington is waiting for you, sir." Dan and Mary walked toward the company as the emotion rose beyond their capacity to withhold their joy. Mary threw open her arms as did Dan, and the entire Company surrounded them with a familiar joy not known in the military. When the circle surrounding Dan and Mary began to loosen, General Milledge said, "We don't want to keep General Washington waiting, he has a schedule to keep." Dan and Mary could not have received a more royal welcome if they were in fact of royal blood. The O'Flaherty family had included the Blue Celts as family from the date of its origin.

Weston and Maureen had made their way through the crowd to welcome them to New York where the first President of the United States was inaugurated on April 30, 1789 on the balcony of Federal Hall. The Executive Branch of the United States government officially began operations under the new frame of government established by the 1787 Constitution. The Senate and the House met in joint session and counted the electoral votes on April 6, 1789 and Washington and Adams were certified as having been elected President and Vice President. (26)

Dan and Mary were so glad to see Maureen and Weston again. They were also glad they had come several days early to enjoy the festivities before the actual inauguration ceremony began. The Generals aides met Dan and Mary and gave them a message from the General to meet him at 3 Cherry Street, which would become Washington's official residence.

Weston and Maureen knew the locations and after he had maneuvered them through the crowd, they took the carriage to the residence of General Washington. When they arrived, Dan was met again by another group of the Blue Celts that was the official security force for the President of the United States. General John Milledge had made certain General Washington was the most secure American in America since the end of the war. Dan and Mary were led to the door that swung open as they stepped on to the first step to the door. Through the front door came General Washington and his wife, Martha. Dan gave the General the sincerest salute that had ever been given to a Commanding Officer. The General affectionally returned the salute and then reached to embrace the man who he regarded as his true friend. Dan and Mary embraced Martha Washington together. They were so glad to see one another and could not wait to exchange the news of the two families.

The first question Mrs. Washington asked them was whether they were hungry. She told them the kitchen was filled with political food of all kinds. She invited them to the kitchen to get whatever they desired. After they had selected their food, General Washington asks Mary if it would be rude for him to visit with Dan alone. Mary told the General she would be busy visiting with Mrs. Washington.

When the General had closed the door, he asked Dan to sit down. The General's face became somber. The General asked Dan what he had become involved with since they were together. Dan brought the General up to date on the Special Force Academy in Spain, and the education of his three children. When Dan told the General the children were being trained as Special Force soldiers, he became extremely interested because of some information he had received from England. When Dan had brought the General up to date on his activities, the General said, "Dan the war is not over." Dan was stunned because he had assumed King George III had given up on his plan to regain the colonies as property of England.

General Washington explained the colonies are exposed to infiltrators more than ever before. He told Dan a huge number of Loyalists that had remained under cover are involved in a plan to burn all the government facilities and infiltrate every level of government to cause the government to fail. He told Dan what he needed most was a group of trained people that could help determine who these British agents are to give him time to organize a military group to counter act their plans. Dan told the General he felt compelled to reveal to him who the spies were that had provided him with the information to capture British Cornwallis and his army.

Dan began by telling the General he had purchased property in New York in 1778 through his attorney in Spain and had developed a retreat center to entertain 25 of the British Generals. Part of the amenities was a 200-acre farm for breeding thoroughbred horses. He further told the General his two sisters and the son of his attorney in Spain, Weston Collier had developed the most effective spy network of the war.

As Dan was talking, the General began peering out the window of his headquarters grasping for recollection of the messages he had received from several sources. He finally turned to Dan and told Dan he had suspected the three relatives he had brought by his home on his way back to New Orleans when the war was over. He said, "Dan, those are the people this nation needs to undermine this latest threat by Great Britain." Dan told the General his sister Maureen had married Weston Collier and were living in the home and had recently become parents to another prospective Irish American soldier. He told him they had reopened the training facility for the horses. General Washington told Dan he was to give his oath of office on April 30, 1790 and his first official act will be to organize the military.

He told Dan he was to be promoted to a Four-Star rank as General charged with the responsibility of the Security of the President, the Vice President and all the Cabinet Officers. He further told Dan he would have a budget to pay all the personnel under his command including those not officially employed by the government.

General Washington's attitude had completely changed from wonderment to an attitude with full faith and confidence the mission would be accomplished.

The General said, "Dan, you have taught me there are men available in this nation who are trustworthy and capable of doing a great service for this nation. I think I may have found one more beside yourself that I regard as a man of your stature. Dan was most interested to learn more about the General's new protégé. Dan asked the General his name. General Washington advised Dan to keep his eye on a young man from Tennessee named, Andrew Jackson. A smile slowly spread across Dan's face which caused General Washington to ask, "Do you know him?" Dan responded, "Since he was thirteen years old working as a blacksmith in the Carolinas." General Washington told Dan he would be wise to draw himself close to Mr. Jackson who will be of help to this nation someday. Dan told General Washington his two sons will be graduating soon and would be looking for an army to join. General Washington with a big smile told Dan to bring the two to see him. Dan gave the General his word he would begin immediately to set up the communications he could rely upon to make wise decisions for America.

After they had visited into the night, Dan and Mary dismissed themselves and was escorted to their home with Maureen and Weston. The next morning a courier arrived to advise Dan and Mary of the General's desire for them to be involved in the inaugural ceremony. Dan sent a reply of his gratitude for his mentor and close personal friend to allow him to participate in the ceremony giving birth to a nation governed by themselves.

Most women Dan was familiar with would have been placed in a complete dither, not Mrs. Mary O'Flaherty. From the suppression by Great Britain, while living in Ireland to the front steps of Federal Hall in New York City, she had seen a journey that would have intimidated most any woman, but not an Irish O'Malley bred survivor with a will of steel and a heart of purified gold. To her, it was the successful outcome of a plan that began the day the first English thief stepped on Irish soil to steal the land of her ancestors. Her heart was filled with joy for the Irish and Scotts to have found a battleground to settle the dispute with the reward being that of freedom to be who they were and to worship God in their chosen manner.

She was so proud of Dan and all his accomplishments on the field of battle, but most of all his defeat of his human desire to be placed in positions of wealth and power to lord over his fellowman. She had learned by experience most men are humble because they have no other choice. Not so with Dan. He had the choice to be ruler of anything his heart desired, but he chose to love and honor God, care and guide his family and serve his fellowman with his whole heart. Mary was well prepared to be proud of her family and friends as God endowed them with the ability to lead and serve others.

Those involved in the ceremony were to meet on the balcony of the Federal Hall in New York City known as the Constitutional Capital of the United States of America. As the participants gathered, the President elected beckoned Dan, General Milledge and two Blue Celt Colonels to serve as security for the ceremony. When the ceremony began, Dan walked ahead of the President to be, while General Milledge took the rear guard. The two Colonels walked at the right and left of the President.

As the band began playing, Dan walked ahead of the President toward the awaiting crowd which was immense. The Chancellor Grand Master of Masons in the City of New York, Robert Livingston stood in wait with the Congress of the United States for the leader of a new nation to begin a history never matched by any other nation on earth.

As the ceremony was ready to begin, it was discovered a Holy Bible had not been provided on which the President Elect could swear his allegiance to the Constitution of the United States of America. John Morton, Marshal of the parade was serving as Master of St. John's Lodge volunteered to retrieve the Altar Bible of the St. John Lodge a short distance away. (28) The Bible was brought, and George Washington took the oath with his right hand resting on the bible. His head was bowed in reverence as he said, "I swear, so help me, God." He then bowed over the Bible and prayed the following prayer:

"Almighty God; We make our earnest prayer that Thou wilt keep the United States in Thy Holy protection: that Thou will incline the hearts of the citizens to cultivate a spirit of subordination and obedience to government; and to entertain a brotherly affection and love for one another and for their fellow citizens of the United States at large.

And finally, that thou wilt most graciously be pleased to dispose us all to do justice, to love mercy, and to demean ourselves with that charity, humility, and pacific temper of mind which were the characteristics of the divine Author of our blessed supplication, we beseech Thee, through Jesus Christ our Lord, Amen." (27)

At the close of the prayer Chancellor Livingston exclaimed in a loud voice;

"Long live George Washington, President of the United States."

CHAPTER TWENTY-FOUR

MILITARY ORGANIZATION

Two weeks after the inaugural ceremony, Dan received a message from President Washington to meet him at Mt. Vernon on June 4, 1789. Dan and Mary made arrangements to again become accustomed to the discipline of military life. When they arrived at the familiar setting of life at Mr. Vernon, the President was near the smoke house talking to one of the foremen. When he saw Dan and Mary, he completed his conversation and hurriedly walked to assist Mary's stepping from the carriage. Martha had seen the arrival of the two people she adored above all others. She also came to the carriage to greet them.

After an hours' time of the four visiting, President Washington told the ladies he needed to talk with Dan privately. Dan and the President walked to the same old oak tree they had used for shade to plan the tactics to defeat the British Army. The President began his conversation by saying, "All the sudden, I don't know who anyone is any more. The one thing I have always enjoyed is truth spoken between honest men. In the few weeks, I have been in office, I have learned people are now saying what they think I want to hear. Everything is political in government. The one thing I have learned is, I know for sure, when someone wants to meet with me, the reason is to benefit themselves. My plan was to be a farmer not a politician. The reason I wanted to talk to you is, you are the one man I have met that has never asked for anything. Your only concern has been how you could do more for our nation. After a pause, he continued in the most solemn manner, Dan, I am extremely concerned about the infiltration of spies hired by foreign nations stealing our secrets. And, even more than that, I am concerned about well-meaning patriots not knowing who to talk to as well as what not to reveal. You and I learned during the war there were some good soldiers, good fighters, who didn't know how to keep their mouths closed. I am learning in politics knowing what the most top secret is, should be kept secret. Some I have noticed are using our secrets to gain power and prestige. That is why I need your advice in organizing the military. I want you to be a vital part of the military high command, but I also want you to oversee a group of highly qualified operatives who can gather information in Continental United States as well as Great Britain or any other foreign nation. I am aware you are personally involved in the shipping business which will be vital as we gather information from the countries of Europe. I appreciate you making me aware of your family's involvement with gathering the most valuable information of the war that allowed us to trap Cornwallis at Yorktown. This nation needs your help in re-establishing that same type network of spies without anyone but you and me knowing its existence or the information obtained."

Dan responded by saying, "Mr. President, God has entrusted me with four lives consisting of three children and their precious mother. I have lived my life ready to give my life for this nation and my family. Before I can expose our children to such a task, I must talk to their mother. I have not talked with them in some time. I know our daughter Bridget is becoming very qualified for clandestine work because she has told me she was drawn to that type covert military activity. Before we have completed our visit, I will talk to Mary about this matter."

The President said, "Dan, the decision to involve your children at the risk of their lives is a grave matter. I do not want you thinking I am thinking that your family must become involved in this plan. I have experienced the work your family has achieved, and no other group of people could have achieved the performance level your family did. Remember, this entire operation will be under your command and I know you know how to keep your loved ones from too much risk. I don't know about you, but I would like to have a bite to eat before we continue." Dan said, "I agree, but I would also like for you to consider General John Milledge to continue with his duty as Chief of Security for your family." The President replied, "No one else is as qualified as he is to perform this vital task."

Martha had prepared a meal to be remembered. When they were finished eating, Dan and Mary walked along the Potomac as Dan saluted each of the Blue Celts standing guard around Mt. Vernon. Dan asked Mary whether she thought the children would enjoy working with their father in military matters. Mary responded by saying, "Dan, I think that would be what they were expecting to do when they had completed their training." Dan asked Mary to find out as soon as she could how far along they were with their training.

When the President and Dan had resumed their conversation, Dan began by saying, "Mr. President, after you revealed to me the Loyalists still being actively involved in New York, I began thinking how to best infiltrate the meeting places of those who are suspected of being activists for Great Britain. I have assumed most of their members would be some of the wealthiest people in New York. My suspicion is based upon there being vast real estate investments financed by English citizens. The President agreed with Dan because he knew the reason for the King's continued threats of war was based upon his friends wanting to regain financial control for themselves which would ultimately give them control of our government.

The concepts of freedom and self-government had begun to be embraced by the nations of Europe. The best monitor for Europe's financial interest in America was Weston Collier, who gave Dan the investment reports of all Great Britain investors. Dan made the President aware of his connections to the financial world which was vital in making a determination of who the infiltrators and spies would be.

The President was anxious to get back to the plan for setting up the military. He told Dan how appreciative he was for the many times, when his command was under attack, he appeared out of nowhere. Dan most of the time would arrive from the opposite direction with sniper fire at long range and win the battle. The President reminded Dan of the conversation about the Pennsylvania Rifle that was accurate at 100 yards. The President reminded Dan about the two problems with the weapons being difficult to operate and the cost being too much. The President told Dan how grateful he was for not taking his advice because those rifles saved the lives of his soldiers many times because of their accuracy at 100 yards or more. Because of those experiences, he wanted Dan to train an elite group of soldiers like the Blue Celts, but different, in that, they could operate in separate groups unattached from the main body of troops. He told Dan he wanted to include cavalry training as part of their curriculum.

Dan began to smile, which told the President he was in the process of learning something he did not know. Dan began by reminding him he had enrolled his children in an academy in Spain. The President told Dan he vaguely recalled the information. Dan said, "Let me start over. I have established an academy in Spain which consists of approximately 10,000 acres with most every kind of terrain a soldier in our world would encounter. The facility also includes training in heavy artillery and espionage. It is located on land attached to land, on which I was raised by General Phillip O'Shea and my adoptive mother, Margarita. This entire facility is underwritten by the nation of Spain because my step-father was the developer of the Special Force Units of Spain. The reason I have revealed this to you is to save our government money by having our troops trained at an existing facility by some of the best soldiers in the world. Another asset is, the troops are taught the language of most every European nation as part of their espionage courses. With your permission, I would like to begin a selection process from those we now have enrolled in the academy, as well as, from those who will become soldiers in our military.

The President stood up and began staring in open space across the Potomac River. When he began speaking he said, "Dan, this just may solve more problems than either of us realize. For example, we will not have to reveal to anyone the whereabouts of the soldiers we have enlisted for this kind of training, which was nonexistent until you arrived here in the 1740's. I like this idea, because I am sure we can find qualified inductees if we look hard enough." Dan responded by saying, "Mr. President, with your permission, I will begin a search among our present trainees and inductees." The President said, "You have my qualified permission. The qualification is, this secret will be the first secret we share in our new organizational efforts of the military.

The President said, "Dan I consider you my closest confidant. I promise you I will be relying upon you to advise me in the future involving matters that are not of a military nature. I have been two things, a farmer and an army officer. I will be asking you for help in most everything else." Dan said, "Mr. President, I have followed the same path you have traveled, but I have learned, when I don't know the answer to a problem, someone else does, so all I have to do is find that someone who is usually Mr. Collier, my attorney."

As the sun began to fade in the West, the President insisted Dan and Mary stay the night, which they accepted with gratitude. The President said, "Dan, some of the best nights rest I have received through the years has come after I have had a visit with you. I am grateful beyond measure for your wise counsel." Dan said, "And the same is for me, Mr. President."

As the sun rose the next morning, the carriage was ready for Dan and Mary to return to New York to begin the task of preparing a defense against those who were planning to cause harm to the well-being of a new nation. Dan was 67 years of age as all these events began unfolding in his life. However, Dan was much of a man and was capable of taking on new challenges, if it was for the good of his nation. He viewed the main purpose for the remaining days of his life was to participate in the formation of a nation's military that will protect its borders to protect the primary culture of the nation to allow it to be given time for its identity to develop and grow. By far the dominant culture in America was, the Scots-Irish. When the vote was taken in Congress to determine the national language, English was selected over German, by one vote. The great number of immigrants who came to America were slaves, of the British Empire having been harvested from Ireland and Scotland.

Dan was ready to hear some good news from Spain about his children. When Dan asked Mary the plan to be with their children, she replied, "All we need is a boat." Dan visited with the harbor master and learned one of the ships owned by O'Malley and O'Flaherty would be docking in about 10 days. Dan suggested Mary prepare for a trip to Spain to possibly gather the children together for a trip back with them to America. The ship arrived on time. Dan advised Weston and Maureen when they returned, he would like for them to have done what was necessary to formulate a plan to infiltrate the group of loyalists that were making plans to destroy the new government of America. Weston and Maureen were excited to receive the news of being involved in defeating England again.

Dan and Mary were such good friends of one another. Anytime they could have time to be with one another for prolonged periods was considered a pinch of heaven's grace. The voyage was so peaceful. The crew was so helpful to them. The food was wonderful. They delighted being in the presence of one another. Their memorable days were without end. They were truly at the peak of their happiness when they were together out of reach of interference by the interruptions and chaos of the world.

Sam O'Keefe, Jr., was on duty as harbor master when they arrived in Spain. Years prior, Dan sailed the oceans with a cousin who rescued him at the age of seven. His mother and father were sold into slavery as part of the foreclosure of land which was owned by another distant O'Flaherty cousin where his father was working. At that time, the harbor master was Sam O'Keefe, Sr., who became instrumental in directing Dan to the law office of Matthew Collier which resulted in Dan becoming one of the wealthiest men on earth as the result of his adoptive mother, and father the O'Sheas, being lost at sea because of a hurricane that sunk their ship on a voyage to America. Because of Mr. O'Keefe's partial loss of his eyesight, he was forced to retire. Dan put him in his palatial estate as a caretaker to assist Mr. Collier in managing the estate.

As the ship was being moored, Sam Jr., yelled his welcome to the O'Flahertys. Dan recalled how heavy the rope was he would try to throw to Sam O'Keefe, Sr., when Eamonn O'Flaherty docked his ships. Memories, precious memories, raced through his thoughts, *recalling the names of precious souls that had been placed in his life by the Almighty God to lead him to the position he now held as a leader of men and a help for those whose burdens had caused them to become weary. He looked at Sam Jr, who was smiling to know this favorite person, other than his father, had returned to Spain.*

When Dan and Mary had walked on to the dock, Sam Jr., was there to shake hands with Dan and kiss the hand of Mary. Dan asked Sam Jr., how his business was going. Sam Jr. told him of the military ships bringing supplies to a new training academy close to the land where the O'Flaherty home is located. That was encouraging to Dan because it told him the military leaders were serious about training Special Force soldiers. Sam Jr. told Dan he had seen some of the biggest cannons he had ever seen as well as hundreds of horses. Dan was getting excited to see the improvement the military had set up.

There was a carriage for him to take them to their home. When Dan and Mary arrived, it developed into a real home coming.

The butler met them at the door very surprised and excited to know the family would be together again. As they walked past the children's rooms, Mary could see an improvement in the care they were taking with their clothes.

Dan was ready to relax and prepare to be with his children. At approximately 6:00 p.m., Bridget walked in the door looking like a queen in search of a nation to rule. When she saw her mother and father, she was overjoyed. She looked at her father and said, "We have some things to talk about." Dan smiled, indicating he was ready to be with his daughter to hear of her progress in the academy. The cooks prepared a meal for them that could be eaten out of doors. Mary was ready to hear of the adventures of her daughter. Bridget began by telling them of her skills with the sword. She had won all the matches involving female opposition. She told them she was ready to graduate to become involved with the real world. Dan asked her how her brothers were progressing. Bridget told them both boys were now men and had won the respect of their fellow students. While they continued to visit, the two brothers came running through the back door into the garden area. Mary and Dan could not believe their eyes. Cathal stood eye to eye with his father, at more than six feet tall, as did "Two Dan". All three of them were dressed in their academy uniforms, and their parents were very pleased with the way they had developed into adulthood. Dan asked them, "Are you glad we did this?" Bridget said, "Daddy, I cannot think of anything that could have been more correct than for us to be prepared for the future." Dan asked them if they were prepared to enter the dark world of warfare. "Two Dan" told his parents he felt like he needed to be with his daddy to get experience before he would feel capable of that much responsibility. Dan said, "General Washington has asked me to be responsible for developing a Special Force Unit for the American military." Bridget asked him if that meant they would get to work together. Dan told her, "Within a close proximity of one another." Dan told them when the war was over, the Continental Army did the best they could to move the British sympathizers out of America, specifically out of New York City. However, President Washington has now learned about a group of very wealthy Loyalists who are involved in a plot to take down the government of the United States. He also revealed the necessity to begin in some manner, to infiltrate the loyalist camp to prevent their plans from becoming a reality.

Dan revealed the statement made by General Washington of Weston, Maureen and Shibeal being the most effective spies of the war. Dan said, "The question is, do you think we are capable of avoiding being caught?" Bridget said, "Daddy, we have been with the best espionage trainers in the world. I do believe we have the training and skills to be of value to our country, when do we get started?" Dan told them there is no big hurry. I would like to visit with Colonel Longoria to get his advice as to how to penetrate the Loyalist's traitors. Dan asks, "What do you have planned for tomorrow? I was thinking we could ride over to the training facility for an inspection." "Two Dan"' said, "That is a good way to start this operation." The next morning, Dan was alone in the kitchen waiting for his family to get ready for the day. He heard noises which meant they were getting prepared to be with the real General of Special Forces.

When they arrived at a facility with "Headquarters" over the door, Dan was very surprised. The Army of Spain had built a training facility second to none in Europe. He thought to himself, *I wish the*

President could see this place. They had built barracks that could house as many as four hundred soldiers. The horse stables were immaculate. The King of Spain was so impressed with the idea of the training facility, he authorized an additional 100,000 acres being added to the existing facility. The facility was of an ideal design to train the Special Force Units Dan had in mind for the American military. After Dan had observed the development, he went to the headquarters building to tell those in charge what a good job they had done.

When he walked in the building with his three cadets, they were escorted to the Commanding Officers office whose name is Colonel Alexander de Hernandez. When Dan and his family walked in, the Colonel stood to salute the son of perhaps the greatest warrior that had ever served in the Army of Spain. The Colonel began with a congratulation to General O'Flaherty and America's victory over Great Britain. Dan responded by saying, "God blessed a group of outcasts who had nowhere else to go. We had to fight, and we did." The Colonel told Dan he had heard others say the knowledge of Special Force tactics he had learned from his father was the difference that won the war. Dan told the Colonel, "There is no doubt the knowledge of my father's tactics made the difference in several major conflicts." Colonel Hernandez was anxious to give Dan a report on the status of his children's training status. Colonel Hernandez said, "To summarize their status is rather brief, we are amazed each day. In my twenty-two years of service, I have never known of any other trainee who started with their level of knowledge and ability." Dan got quiet as the Colonel verified Dan's thoughts of their ability. He told Dan, Bridget is the most outstanding female recruit we have ever had in our covert training program. He summarized his report by saying,

"They will be a compliment to any nation they serve." After they had visited for more than an hour, the Colonel insisted they have lunch together, and they did.

Dan was most anxious to visit with Colonel Longoria regarding his opinion of their readiness for covert activities in America. Dan told the Colonel how appreciative he was for his kind remarks regarding his children. He told the him they needed to visit again regarding training American combat soldiers for duty in Special Force Warfare. The Colonel was surprised by Dan's statement until he recalled the entire facility was on Dan's property. He then told Dan it would be an honor to help prepare Americans for another battle.

The afternoon was becoming evening when they arrived at Colonel Longoria's office. It delighted him to see Dan again and to be able to give Dan his report of his children's preparedness for covert activity. He began with Bridget. He told Dan, her only weakness was, her astonishing beauty. The Colonel humorously told Dan it will be very difficult for you to disguise her beauty. But, then he said, "Once she opens her mouth, she will be perceived as whatever roll she is to play, from a Duchess to a Nanny. She is a brilliant girl who will be able to infiltrate the enemy's secrets at whatever level she works. She has a humility like yours, which allows her to penetrate secret conversations of the enemy.

Colonel Longoria advised Dan to consider placing Cathal and "Two Dan" in positions of actual combat. He said, "Both of them are fierce warriors and potentially great leaders, very frankly, they are both blessed with such superb military skills, it would be a shame to waist their talent on spying. Cathal was the first to speak saying, "I think we have too much Irish blood in us to do work as spies." Dan agreed.

After they had discussed the future of Dan's children for three hours, Dan apologized for taking too much of the Colonel's time. The Colonel told them what a blessing it had been to him to be allowed to train members of the O'Shea family. He told them General O'Shea was a blessing to his life in so many ways, and he enjoyed every minute of being allowed to be a part of their lives.

CHAPTER TWENTY- FIVE

SEPARATION

After spending the day at the academy, they returned to their home. The three graduate cadets walked to the front door ahead of their father as he beheld in front of him was the living, breathing answer to prayers his heart had prayed years before they were ever born. Mary was the love Dan had prayed for from a young age to be allowed to have the opportunity to be a good husband to a good wife. When God had so completely answered his prayer by allowing him to become the husband of a lady beyond any hope he could have ever dreamed, he then prayed for children, and again his prayers were answered beyond any prayer he knew how to pray.

Dan could not, in any way, be made prouder than he was at that moment. He could hardly wait to share the joy with Mary the achievements of their children. All he could think about was, *God bless Mary, because he knew during the time they had been separated by the war years she was the one who was responsible and the only one who deserved to get the credit for keeping the family together and headed in the right direction.*

The truth is, it was very difficult for her to be living with a Cherokee tribe during the war, but there was no choice. They were fugitives on the run because the British courts had charged Dan and Maureen for killing four British soldiers. Mary had to be very cautious, because had it not been for the Cherokee Chief Attakullakulla, they would have been in the wilderness of the Appalachian Mountains in the heart of Indian Territory, alone. The chiefs name meant "First Beloved Man," and he lived up to his reputation. Mary was constantly concerned about her children being raised in the Cherokee culture, because with Dan being called to war by General George Washington, she was left to depend upon the leadership of the Cherokee Chief who loved her children.

The Chief was a very wise man, and he made certain Mary's culture prevailed in all things. The twins, "Two Dan" and Bridget were born while Dan was away fighting the war. The Chief named Dan Jr., "Two Dan" in a Cherokee ceremony given in honor of a male son. Mary chose to name Bridget after the wife of Eamonn O'Flaherty's son's wife named, Bridget who rescued Dan's infant sisters, Siobhan and Shibeal from being placed in a British orphanage. Bridget rescued the two infants as the slave ship was being filled with Irish slaves bound for America. Dan's father and mother along with Dan's sister, Barbara and brother Patrick had wrongfully been enslaved by British courts for debt. Many years later Dan found his sisters, when, even though he was a prisoner of the Jacobite War, he was allowed to attend the funeral of Dan's cousin, Eamonn O'Flaherty. On that occasion, he met with Mary, at which time they committed their lives to one another.

As they entered the home, Mary met them and wanted to know every detail of their day at the academy. Dan asked Mary if they could talk while they ate a bite of whatever, because he was hungry. Dan made up his mind to listen to them tell their mother all about their day. He was anxious to learn whether they heard the same things he heard. At the close of a two-hour glowing report to their mother, Dan said, "I have got to get some rest."

The next morning as Dan was thanking God for his bushel of blessings being pressed down and running over, Bridget came and sat by her daddy and held his hand. Dan ask, "Do I need to say how proud you have made your mother and me?" Bridget said, "If you were not the proudest man on the planet earth for being the parent of the three of us, I would say, you needed to go see a doctor." Dan smiled and said, "Bridget, that is the problem, I may be too proud." Bridget ask, "What do you mean by that?" Dan said, "The spy game is the most dangerous game in the world. It is so dangerous, you cannot make even one mistake. If you do, it is instant death. Bridget said, "Daddy, I told you one day, I wanted to be involved in doing all I could for my country. Colonel Longoria and his son have given me the best training the world has to offer. The next stop is up to me. At this stage of my life, I do not think I would enjoy anything else." Dan said, "Bridget, I hope I have not given you the beginning of a cursed life. You have inherited a bountiful amount of my traits and characteristics. The only reason I am alive today is because I relied upon my God, and the training I received from the most knowledgeable people in the world. So far, it has worked for me. I am praying it will work for you. You are going to be exposed to a different enemy than I had to fight, because my enemies wore red coats. Your enemy will be wearing the same kind of clothes as everyone else. But, remember this, they are going to be just as deadly. It is going to be difficult at first for you to be authentically different from any person you have ever been before. Have you thought of the method of infiltration you are going to use?" Bridget responded by saying, "I have selected the role of a "Nanny", which hopefully, puts me in the center of family activity, performing a vital service, while being personally unnoticed most of the time."

Colonel Longoria and I discussed this issue, and he advised against me being a high-profile debutant, which is expensive and very tiring. On my days off, I can go home and practice my weapon skills. Dan asked her if she had considered how alone she was going to be. Bridget said, "Daddy, that is my greatest weakness. I am going to miss my family. The other concern I have is all the suspects I will be surveilling have money and methods to know my whereabouts at all times. But, I do know you and I have the cunning to know how to arrange a meeting without getting me caught, don't we?" Dan smiled at her as if he was staring himself in the face. They talked through the afternoon until bedtime.

By the time the family was awake the next morning, it was time for a big breakfast. When they had finished eating, Dan asked if any of them wanted to go with him to visit with Sam O'Keefe. Dan and Sam were very close friends dating back when he was nine years of age. He was also the person that advised him to hire Matthew Collier when he needed to have the O'Shea wills probated.

When Mr. Collier had completed the legal work of having the Court of Spain award him two fortunes, Dan insisted that Sam Sr., become a permanent resident in the estate while Dan was in America. Sam agreed to care for the estate with the agreement he could stay in his own home from time to time. When Dan and Mary arrived, Sam went to his own home. Now it was time to make arrangements to return to America and Dan needed an expert to find him a good ship to make the voyage.

Dan always enjoyed his visits with Sam, because Sam and Dan's Uncle Eamonn were close friends. Dan enjoyed being reminded of his day as a ten-year-old sailor, on the open seas. It didn't take Eamonn long to learn Dan had more talent than being a seaman. As Dan began to grow, Eamonn became concerned about Dan not getting an opportunity for an education.

At that same time, Margarita O'Shea was doing everything she could to keep General O'Shea alive. He had been injured by a shell explosion in the Army. It was reported after the accident General O'Shea had died from the accident. After several years, it became apparent he was going to live, she asked the Generals permission to inform Eamonn that he had survived the explosion. The General gave her permission. because Eamonn was General O'Shea's best friend and he felt it was wrong to keep his friend in grief when it was apparent he was going to survive.

At the meeting when Margarita informed Eamonn the General was alive, she also asked Eamonn if Dan could live with them to give the General some company and provide Dan an education. The four agreed to the plan, which involved Dan residing with the O'Shea's. As time passed, the O'Sheas learned to love Dan and he loved them. They agreed to adopt Dan with Eamonn's blessing, because they did not know the whereabouts of Dan's family, whether dead or alive.

As time passed, the O'Shea's saw to it Dan received the best of education in Spain and the General's health improved to the extent he and Eamonn became business partners with the O'Malley's who were the parents of Mary O'Malley, Dan's wife.

As Dan and Sam recalled the time gone by, they both confessed no matter how much it hurt Dan to be separated from his parents in America, the life God planned for him was far better than he could ever have dreamed. Sam said, "Eamonn, was your Savior from Ireland?" Dan told Sam he was not sure he would have endured the Penal Laws, because most of them are against God and the nature of man. But, I am grateful I found my family in America, in fact, I am glad I found America and the O'Sheas. I pray God's blessing on all those who have come to our families' rescue.

Dan ask Sam if there was anything he needed before they left for America. Sam told Dan he was getting accustomed to living in luxury in that big house. Sam said, "Dan, did you know those maids change my bed sheets every day?" Dan said, "They do that because you don't give them enough work to do. You need to invite some of your friends over for supper." Sam said, "Dan, I don't have any friends that would feel comfortable in that palace." Dan said, "Maybe you need to upgrade your friends?" Sam laughed and said, "The few friends I have I can't trade off, because I have had them too long." I like things the way they are." Dan then asked Sam to help him find a good ship to take his family back to America. Sam told him he would check with his son and would have him a good ride located in a few days.

When Dan got up the next morning, Sam was standing in the kitchen ready for some coffee. Sam asks Dan if he would mind sailing on an O'Malley ship. Dan said, "I would prefer it above all others." Sam said, "Get ready by tomorrow, there is one due in tonight at midnight. Sam told Dan he would talk to the captain for him and make the arrangements. Dan enjoyed his morning coffee with Sam before everyone else awoke.

Mary was ready to get her family back to America. Her family was ready to get back to an environment of work and predictability for their lives. She knew they needed to go to New York and establish themselves because of Dan again being involved with the military. After they had packed their clothes, they wanted one more wonderful meal prepared by the best cook in Spain.

The next morning, they arrived at the dock at the break of dawn. The seaman had spent the early morning hours scrubbing and cleaning the ship for its prized cargo, the O'Flaherty family. They would be delayed for a short while to load some cargo bound for New York. Bridget and her brothers had become attached to Spain, but they looked forward to putting all their knowledge into action to help build America.

Dan and Mary found two deck chairs and went to the back of the ship to enjoy one another's company while the ship was being loaded. The seaman had never seen such a gorgeous creature in their lives as Bridget. She became self-conscious and found her way to where her parents were sitting. The sea gulls flying around the ship were making a terrible noise and didn't mind using the ship as a toilet. Everyone was anxious to set sails for America. Mary was quietly, thanking God, *for allowing them to be together again.* When Dan heard the gang plank being hoisted to the deck, he stood up to wave to Sam Jr., and his father. The day was beautiful, and the wind was brisk, which would allow them to get some miles behind them by the next day.

Unfortunately, a rain had set in, which would keep them in their quarters for three days. Finally, the sun reappeared, and they were back on deck enjoying their trip. Mary kept her eyes on them as if they were small children, probably because of habits she had formed from the day they were born.

On the eleventh week at sea, the scouts in the crow's nest spotted a ship going east which told them they were on the right path for New York harbor. The journey was about to be concluded. Dan told them to dress for the landing in ordinary clothes as opposed to the academy uniforms. After they landed, they went directly to Weston's office.

The timing could not have been better. Maureen was visiting with Weston as their children sat and listened to their parents talk. Maureen knew the necessity of teaching children how to act outside their home in the business environment of a professional office. The one ingredient that prevailed in the Scots-Irish culture was the discipline of respect for others. Maureen and Weston were taught discipline, and they knew the importance of that being one of the main ingredients in the American culture.

Weston and Maureen were astonished at the growth of their niece and nephews. Weston asked about his father's health and they assured him he was in perfect health. After a two hour visit of bringing them up to date on the development of the academy, and Spain's development of its military for Special Force training, a quietness began to prevail because each of them knew it was time to get down to business.

Dan began by making the statement, "The enemy is still with us. The problem is, they are not wearing red coats. and as far as we know, none of them have infiltrated political positions of power in our government. We have been assigned the duty of locating and identifying the Loyalist who remained after the war and swore a false oath to our flag. We will find some whom we relocated in Canada or Nova Scotia who have come back to America secretly. Nevertheless, the President has chosen our same group that served him so well during the war to be involved with infiltrating the Loyalist camps to prevent the beginning of another major conflict. I recall during the war, when General Washington summoned me to his headquarters to attempt to uncover a plot to have him assassinated. The Loyalists at that time had infiltrated our ranks to the extent Thomas Hickey, one of the General's most trusted bodyguards, was discovered to be a spy. He was tried for treason and hung. When the truth finally prevailed, over 600 other Loyalists were exposed. The present thinking is that same mind set prevails, right here in New York City.

As a beginning, Bridget has volunteered to become a Nanny known as Emily Emerson. The thing she needs the most help with is locating a suspect, probably with extreme wealth that has a family and needs child care." Weston told them he had a long list of suspects all of which fits the requirements mentioned, but I don't know who needs a Nanny. He suggested reading the want ads in the newspaper first to see if someone is advertising their need and if one of the names appears on the suspect list. I would recommend this office to be very discreet about becoming openly involved in the matter at this time. However, the butler we now have on staff could begin a whisper campaign with some names from a list of suspects, I will furnish to him. The servants generally is aware of who needs help.

He shared a thought for everyone to consider, which was for Bridget to have just arrived from Europe, where she had worked with the royal family of Spain as a care taker of a prominent family's children. He said that will eliminate the suspicion of who, what and where in America Bridget was derived and for sure, they will not feel at ease to be researching whom she served in Spain. Bridget thought that was a great idea.

Dan told Bridget they would not be seeing her for some time, but she knew how and when to get out of harm's way. He told her to be very patient in developing the relationships with the suspect. He told her, "It could take years, but in the meantime, you need a place of your own to stay until you get appointed. I will leave all the funds you will need to live on with Weston. I would recommend you not come back to Weston's office until you have earned enough money to hire Weston's services as your investment counselor. When information becomes available, you can use Weston as your contact. He will know how to get in touch with me. Bridget felt very comfortable with the training she had received in Spain. Dan suggested she have some Spanish money to exchange for American money at the bank. After they each had embraced her, Bridget began her adventure into the dark world of espionage, deceit and fear.

She found a temporary dwelling near Weston's office, and began searching the newspapers for employment. One of the first opportunities had a refined address, but the job was house keeper, and she did not want that as a reference. After three weeks of seclusion and becoming familiar with her surroundings, she received a note from Weston to go to a certain address in the most refined home district in New York, which she learned was within a few blocks of the O'Flaherty home where Weston and Maureen resided.

She hired a carriage to take her to the address that had been provided by Weston. She asks the coachman to wait for her. She went to the door and saw a name plate with the name, Robert Milton Montgomery on the name plate. Within a short while, a butler answered the door. She told him she had been advised the Montgomery family was seeking permanent child care. The butler smiled and said, "We have been waiting for you." He asks her name and she replied, "Emily Emerson."

The butler took her upstairs to the bedside of Mrs. Anne Montgomery who extended her hand in welcome. Seated on the opposite side of the bed was her husband who stood and introduced himself as, Robert Milton Montgomery. When Bridget's eyes met with Mr. Montgomery's eyes, a sensation covered her body she had never felt before. She quickly returned to the bedside of Mrs. Montgomery who began the story of the need to have child care in their home. She told Emily she had been highly recommended by a family who knows your ability. She asks Emily to tell them her background and training. The reality of her training surfaced as she began to speak words that told a story of fabricated lies. When she was finished, the Montgomery's were more than pleased to have her as their Nanny. Mrs. Montgomery told Bridget none of the doctors had told her what had caused her to develop very suddenly, a shortness of breath. She told her she had been bed ridden for three weeks. She explained to her the ages of the four children was from 5 years to twelve consisting of two boys and two girls. She disclosed to Emily there was a study on the third floor they had used as a classroom. Mrs. Montgomery had been the teacher and care taker of the children until she became ill. It was very apparent the parents were good parents and wanted the best training available for their children.

Emily told the Montgomery's she hoped she would be allowed some flexibility with the children's curriculum, in that, she was prepared to share her knowledge of the out of doors and exercise, which she believed would give them a more well-rounded education. When Emily said that, she glanced at Mr. Montgomery who was smiling from ear to ear. He remarked, "I think you are the person we have been waiting on to care for our children.

When the interview was completed, and the financial arrangements had been agreed upon, Mr. Montgomery said to his wife, "If it is with your approval my love, I would like to introduce Emily to the children." Mrs. Montgomery said, "By all means and tell them to come by to see me after their first lesson." Mr. Montgomery looked as if a heavy weight had been lifted from his shoulders. When they walked through the back door of the home, the four children were sitting in lawn chairs waiting to meet someone they knew they were not going to like. Mr. Montgomery introduced Emily to them as their "Nanny." He explained to them that Emily was not going to be a person who was like some of their friends had described, as their "Nanny." He told them he and their mother had given her full authority to teach them about America, and how to improve their knowledge. With that bit of introduction, Mr. Montgomery returned to his wife's bedroom.

The first words out of Emily's mouth was, "Who likes to fish?" The oldest one Robert said, "I like to eat fish." Emily asked, "What kind of fish do you like to eat," Robert replied, "Cod, mostly." Emily asks, "Have you ever eaten a fish that you caught?" The children looked at one another, and Robert asked, "Caught, what do you mean?" Emily smiled and said, "Let's go fishing." The four children's eyes opened wide and they said, "OK."

Emily told the Montgomery's she needed some get acquainted time with the children, and with their permission, she was taking them on a picnic and fishing trip. Mr. Montgomery asked, "What do we need to do?" Emily said, "Say OK, and give me some money for fishing line, bait and hooks, and we need to get the carriage driver to take us to the river. Mrs. Montgomery gave Emily money, and the cook made them a picnic lunch. They were off on their first adventure ever.

As they were leaving, Emily said, "Mr. Montgomery, don't worry about a thing, I know what I am doing." Mr. Montgomery said, "I can tell, have fun." Within an hour, the carriage driver had taken them to his favorite fishing hole, which was a small creek that flowed into the Hudson River. Emily had cut some poles from the brush cane that was growing on the creek bank. Sarah was the five-year-old daughter, Emily's personal assistant. It wasn't long before Emily and the children were having all the fun they could stand for their first day of being together.

When lunch time came, they opened the basket and found some sandwiches made in their home kitchen. Each child was having an especially good time telling how many fish they had caught for the first time in their lives. The two girls needed to rest after lunch. The carriage driver took the two boys back to the creek side to catch some more fish. After the girls had rested they were ready to do some more fishing. The carriage driver had made a stringer to hold the fish and keep them alive until they were ready to be cleaned.

At about four in the afternoon, Emily asked them if they were ready to have a fish supper. They told her they were ready. Emily told them she didn't think there was enough fish for them and their parents too. They looked disappointed, because they wanted their mother to eat some of the fish they had caught. Emily said, "Let's say a prayer, are you ready?" Emily said, "Lord, we need your help to catch enough fish to feed all of us, Amen." Emily said, "Now, everybody go get ready to hang on, because someone is going to catch a whopper." After another thirty minutes, their faith began to wilt, and Emily could tell what was happening. While Robert Jr., was looking at Emily shaking her head in despair, his line tightened up, and he pulled in a twelve-pound catfish. All the children gathered around looking at the monster, wondering what it was. Emily said, "Well, we prayed and here's the answer." The carriage driver was amazed, because the biggest fish he had ever caught out of that hole was a two-pound bass.

When they returned home, Mr. Montgomery was standing at the upstairs bedroom window anticipating their return. When the carriage driver took the stringer of fish out of the bucket, Mr. Montgomery turned to his wife and said, "My Lord, Anne, they have caught a bucket of fish." The children ran through the door way toward their mother's room. When they arrived, she was anxious to hear the fish story from everyone's personal point of view. Robert Jr., waited until last to tell them how he was looking at Emily, shaking his head to indicate he had given up. Then the line tightened, and he pulled the big fish out of the water. He said, "Mother, we didn't catch the big one until we prayed, and I said a prayer, asking to catch a big one for you."

The carriage driver helped the cook clean the fish for the family to have dinner in their mother's bedroom with the carriage driver and Emily invited. So, they ate their meal together. Emily could tell the mother's illness had stripped them of their family joy.

She was so happy she could share those moments of happiness with them. During the meal, Emily told them how much she was going to enjoy being a part of their lives and thanked them for the opportunity to become a part of their family.

As she began to close her eyes to sleep, she said to herself, *if he is who he is suspected of being, this is going to become a very complicated situation.*

CHAPTER TWENTY-SIX

THE NANNY

When the children came to the class room at 8:00 a.m., Emily was impressed but as she thought about it, *the Montgomery's impressed her as very serious parents.* Emily was wondering, *how Mrs. Montgomery had arranged a curriculum with a wide range of differences in their ages*. Emily ask Robert Jr., to help her begin where their mother had last taught the class. Robert Jr. took her to the school library and helped her collect the correct book for each grade level. Emily was very impressed with their intelligence. Robert Jr. though only twelve, had a grasp of mathematics above his age. Emily told them she did not want to repeat the lessons their mother had already completed. Robert Jr. helped Emily locate the lesson plan their mother had prepared for each of them. At mid-morning, the day had begun to level off, so Emily suggested they take a nature walk around the neighborhood.

A beautiful trail with small pebbles had been used to carve out a path through the densely wooded area. The youngest child named Sarah, the second child was named Charlotte who was ten years old, and the third child was named William who was seven years old.

As they walked along Sarah held Emily's hand. It was obvious the children were missing their mother's care. They returned to the home at almost noon. Emily suggested eating a snack in their mother's room, if she agreed. Emily and the children went to Mrs. Montgomery's bedside to ask her if she wanted to visit with them during the lunch break. Emily did not realize two doctors had come in while they were walking. When she recognized their presence and purpose, she took the children back to the kitchen. Sarah asked Emily what was the matter with her mother. Emily told her, "She is ill." Sarah asks, "What kind of sick?" Emily said, "That is why the doctor is here, we should know very soon."

After lunch, they returned to the class room to complete the days study. Mr. Montgomery had never left her bedside since Emily had arrived. Emily was faced with a huge problem, because the children sensed their mother was very ill, and they wanted to be with her. Emily decided to tell Mr. Montgomery of her concern. Mr. Montgomery told her the doctors had not determined the cause of her high fever, but they did agree she had some kind of infection. She would possibly need to be hospitalized.

Five more days passed with no improvement. Mr. Montgomery knocked on Emily's door at 4 a.m., on the sixth day to tell her she would be placed in charge of the children because he was taking his wife to the hospital. They decided not to disturb the children.

At 7:00 a.m., the children were awakened for breakfast. Before breakfast began, Emily told them their mother was in the hospital and they needed to pray for her. Robert Jr. said the prayer as they all held hands asking for God's deliverance of their mother's illness. At 9:00 a.m., they were all in their places ready to begin another day. Emily had planned some music. She had found a guitar in the music room. Her father had taught her to play and she had become proficient at playing the guitar. She began with children's songs that told the love of Jesus. Some of the songs she sang were some the children had been taught in Sunday school. After she had sung church songs, she began singing songs of love for one another, most of the songs she had learned from her father from the time she could pronounce the words.

As they were strolling along the nature trail one morning, Emily saw some cane growing near a creek. She stopped and broke four pieces of cane, one for each of them. When they returned home, Emily went to the kitchen and found a knife. She used the knife to cut the piece of cane into four joints when she did that, she then used the knife to cut a slot in the cane and then she put four holes in below the slots. She put the cane up to her lips and blew air into the slot and the cane made a musical sound.

Robert Jr. said, "Let me see that." He blew, and another musical sound came out of the cane. Sarah said, "I want to do it." William said, "Me first." Emily said, "Let's make four whistles." They replied, "OK." Emily's plan had worked, which was to get them to thinking about something besides worrying about their mother.

Emily would sometimes hear Mr. Montgomery come in at night, apparently to get a change of clothes, and he would return to the bedside of his beloved wife at the hospital. As the time wore on, the children became closer to Emily. Each of them had their own distinct difference of personality, which caused them to have different needs to handle this traumatic life experience, that had invaded their lives. Emily had never considered she would have an emotional involvement with the children of a suspect who could possibly be found guilty of treason and could be put to death. As each day passed, she became closer and closer to the children and they had become extremely close to her. The length of time Mrs. Montgomery had remained in the hospital told her there may be a new and entirely unexpected involvement with this family. She felt it was time to somehow communicate the information to Weston. The length of time she had worked and the amount of money she was being paid, caused her to have accumulated a tidy sum of money she needed to deposit. She made arrangements on a Tuesday to take the children on a field trip to the business center of New York. She told the butler her plans, which the butler agreed was vital to relieve some of the tension the children were having to endure.

When the carriage was ready, the children were eager for a change of pace. The coachman took a route which involved passing in front of the O'Flaherty farm. The coachman turned to the children and said, "This is the largest home in New York." Emily could not help but smile to herself as she thought about, *how twisted the path of life can become.* The coachman was aware of the location of the Collier Investment offices. When they arrived, she asks the children to remain in the carriage with the coachman. None of the children had ever been to the center of New York commerce before. They were interested in how people made money with money.

When Emily saw Weston, she whispered to him, *"The children are in the carriage with the coachman. I must hurry to get back to them quickly. My employer's wife is apparently deathly ill, and could possibly die, soon. I need instruction from you and daddy about what to do if she dies, and I am asked to remain."* Weston said, "Bridget, I understand the impact the mother's death will have on the family, but from our perspective, that will put you in a better position to learn whether this man is involved in treason. Bridget said, "Weston, I just needed reassurance I was thinking correctly." Weston said, "You are in a better position now to learn the truth than anyone has ever been." Bridget said, "But Weston, the children love me, and I love them." I thought I was the most cold-blooded woman in the world, but I am not sure I could break their hearts." Weston said, "Bridget at the right time, you will do the right thing, believe me, your name is O'Flaherty, and don't forget that. We will be praying for you, and this family." Emily said, "Thank you, Mr. Collier for your sound advice."

The children were excited when Emily returned. As they were coming into the city, she had noticed what was called, a "Sweet Shop." She asks them if they had ever gone to a "Sweet Shop." They told her, "No", but they had always wondered what it was like. The coachman heard the conversation and took them straight to the front door as if he had been there before. When they walked in, Robert Jr., was the first to speak by saying, "I have never seen anything this good in my life." Sarah and William saw some candy with different colors. Charlotte found candy with peanuts covered in the sweet part, but the one they wanted was the candy on a stick that they could lick with their tongue. They went from one candy ben to another, some of which, was in a glass jar. They finally decided there were too many choices to make a decision, so they settled on what was named a "sucker."

Emily asks the coachman to go by the hospital, but she did not want the children to know what it was. She wanted to know the location in case she had to take the children there when no one else was available. She asked the coachman to return home by the same route he had taken to town, because she had seen some horses she wanted the children to see. The coachman took them to the stable where the horses were located. Emily told them to follow her to look at the beautiful animals. They saw what appeared to be a worker at the end of the stable, working in one of the stalls. The closer they got to her, Emily could see it was Maureen, who would be careful not to expose her identity. When they reached the stall, Maureen was in the stall shoveling horse manure. Emily held out her hand and said, "I am Emily Emerson. We are neighbors. I am the Nanny for this family known as the Montgomery's. Maureen was aware of what Emily was doing when she asks, "I would guess you are on a field trip. Because of this beautiful weather, it is way to pleasant to be inside if you can be outside. Emily said, "We have been inside for quite some time, because Mrs. Montgomery has become very ill, and hopefully, she will get better soon, but in the meantime, the family wanted to see some of these beautiful horses. Maureen looked at Robert Jr, and introduced herself and then she met Charlotte, William and Sarah. Maureen had to hug Sarah. Then she said, "Come with me, and let's look at something that might be of interest to you."

She took them to a pen that contained several very tame, very friendly ponies. She asks them if they would like to ride one of them. Robert Jr., and Charlotte responded by saying, "Yes, I would love to." Maureen asked them which one was their choice. Robert Jr. chose a brownish, black Welsh pony and Charlotte chose a Shetland. When they were saddled, Maureen told them the rules, as she led the horses around with them mounted. Robert Jr. was anxious to be allowed to ride on his own. Charlotte was not yet that brave. Sarah and William had not worked up their courage to ride yet. After a while, Maureen allowed Robert Jr., and Charlotte to ride slowly around the pen. They enjoyed every moment of the excitement. After about an hour, Emily told them it was time to return home. Maureen looked at Emily saying, "I hope Mrs. Montgomery gets better soon. If I can help in anyway, let me know. The children were very courteous, thanking Maureen for allowing them to ride the horses. Everyone was tired when they returned to their home.

After a good meal, they all wanted to go to bed early. Emily was exhausted because of the tension she was under, anticipating the untimely death of the children's mother. They were all in bed before the 9:00 p.m., bed time. During the early morning hour, she heard a soft knock at her door. She lit the lamp and opened the door. Mr. Montgomery was standing there, not uttering a sound. He finally whispered, *"We lost her."* Emily reached for his hand, and said, "I am so sorry." Is there anything I can do to help you?" He said, "I need someone to hold me." Emily said, "Sir, come sit on the sofa." Mr. Montgomery sat down, and Emily put her arms around him and cradled him as if he was her child. He began to sob uncontrollably. She handed him a towel. He cried until dawn. Finally, he stood up and said, "I want to apologize for my behavior, but I had no one to turn to." Emily said, Mr. Montgomery, "I am very blessed to be here to help you and your family at this tragic time." He said, "Emily, I must go get cleaned up and dressed to meet with the children at breakfast. Emily said, "I will be there to help you."

When the children came down for breakfast, their father was there to greet them. They could tell their mother was not yet well. Robert Jr. was the first to speak asking, "When will mother be back home?" Mr. Montgomery's eyes filled with tears, as he considered the fact for the first time, *their mother would not be returning*. The children gathered around their father and everyone including Emily, shared the pain of the loss of a dear, precious mother at such a young age. When the children had comforted their father, they turned to Emily. who held each one of them as they poured out the tears of separation.

When everyone had found a respite from the pain of loss, Emily asked when the arrangement would be made for the funeral service. Mr. Montgomery told her he would be expected to meet with the funeral directors before noon. Emily asks him whether she should have the children ready. He told her he would appreciate it if she went with them to make the arrangements. When breakfast was completed, she took the children outside to discuss with them the details of what to expect for the remainder of the day. She explained to them death is part of life, and everyone eventually must return to the Creator. She told them, "God is not mad at any of us. Your mother became very ill and was called by God to be with Him. You will see your mother again someday. Until that time, you will have her in your heart every day." Charlotte asks Emily, "Are you leaving?" Emily answered, "Only if you don't want me to stay." Robert Jr., said, "I want you to stay." He fell to his knees, put his head on Emily's lap and began sobbing again. Then all the children grabbed Emily and held her as they sobbed. Mr. Montgomery walked in while Emily was nurturing each child in a special way to help them bare the most difficult day of their tender lives. He joined with them by kneeling in front of Emily and caressing each child with her.

At 10:45 a.m., the carriage was ready to leave. The children entered the carriage holding to Emily. While Mr. Montgomery was talking with the funeral director, the children were in complete silence. When they entered the room to select the casket, the children held to Emily. When Mr. Montgomery had selected three choices, he asks them to decide which one of the three they chose. They all agreed on the same one as did Mr. Montgomery. When the family had agreed, Mr. Montgomery ask Emily if it met with her approval. Emily told him, "I know Mrs. Montgomery would have chosen the same one."

As time passed very slowly before the ceremony, the children more and more ask Emily questions about where their mother would be while they were waiting to meet again. Emily told them., "She waits in your heart. Your heart is where your mother will continue to live until we meet again."

When the ceremony was completed, and they had returned home, Emily asked to be excused. She needed to be alone. She had begun to wonder if she was doing what was right by remaining with them to complete her mission. As she sat alone in the garden, she prayed for God's mercy to be upon the children and her. She asks in her heart for God, *to lead her in the path He would take, and His will be done.*

As days passed after the funeral, Emily forced herself into becoming a teacher. She wanted to impart to the children every piece of knowledge she had to assist them throughout their lives, because she did not know where this tragic event would lead with Mr. Montgomery. The one piece of evidence she wanted was the names of all the Montgomery friends who signed the attendance record at the funeral. That list would perhaps give them the names of most of the Montgomery co-horts, if he was in fact, a part of a conspiracy to topple the new government of America. She knew eventually the funeral home would deliver the names to him. She didn't know if he had a business office or whether his business was in his home. She was hoping he would not do anything drastic, which would affect her relationship with the children. For the time being, he remained in his bedroom alone. He from time to time would have breakfast with

Emily and the children. On one occasion, he did eat an evening meal with them. Each day that passed, the children drew closer and closer to Emily. When she prayed with the children at breakfast, and at bedtime, she would pray a prayer for their father.

The business office in the home was located on the first floor. All his mail when delivered was taken by the butler to Mr. Montgomery's room. One mid-morning, Sarah came up missing during the morning recess. Emily found her in Mr. Montgomery's office. She noticed his mail had begun to stack up. She noticed there were several personal notes regarding the loss of his wife that needed to be answered. She waited until one morning at breakfast to tell him when she had gone to retrieve Sarah she noticed the unopened mail. She asked him if there was anything she could do to help him acknowledge their friends concerns about the loss of Mrs. Montgomery. He told Emily he did need some help and was thinking of hiring someone to keep up with the correspondence. Emily asked him if she could assist him until he had made a decision. He said, "Today would be a good day for us to go through the mail." Emily had the cook prepare a picnic lunch for the children to play outside on such a beautiful day. Mr. Montgomery was in his office when Emily came through the door. Mr. Montgomery was looking at the sky as tears ran down his cheeks. Emily sat down and didn't say a word. She knew he had allowed his sorrow to build to the point where he had lost hope or interest in anything including his children. Emily began opening some of the mail that appeared to be personal and regarding the loss of his wife. As she opened each letter, she would glance at the contents which was a message of sympathy for the loss of such a beautiful spirit and life partner.

She saw some thank you notes with their names engraved on the stationary, which was the perfect answer to each of the sympathy cards. When she had written ten of the responses, she laid it in front of him for his signature. Emily said, "Mr. Montgomery, these good friends deserve your acknowledgement. He picked up the pin and signed his name to everyone she would put in front of him. Within two hours, they had answered the majority of the cards. Emily broke the silence by saying, "Mr. Montgomery, this is what life is made of, and when one part of our world gets broken, it doesn't mean everything in our life is broken. Listen to me, we have four precious souls who are depending on us to lead them through the valley of the shadow of death. They are completely dependent upon us to teach them how to respond to the reality of death. If we quit, they will quit, and grow up helpless. If we reassure them they have a way through this tragedy, their lives can be made better by this experience.

Mr. Montgomery said, "Emily, I need your help. I feel it is wrong to impose our problems on you. My children love you and are dependent on you to teach them life. I am willing to pay you whatever you ask to stay with us. I have felt for a long time there is probably going to become more to this relationship than you, being our Nanny. I am not ready to discuss what I just revealed to you, but I do think this family needs you, and I also need you. I don't like details. I am going to set up an account at the bank for you to take care of all these details. I am not capable of doing that right now. Will you help me handle my affairs?" Emily said, "Mr. Montgomery, I offered to do that for you, and I will be glad to help you through this crisis."

They decided to go to the bank on Monday, to open an account for Emily to take care of the family affairs. She told him if at any time he needed to hire someone to replace her to just simply tell her, because she did have plenty of other things to do. She said, "I am going to ask you a personal favor. Would it be possible for you to have breakfast and prayer with us each morning?" Mr. Montgomery said, "We will begin in the morning, after which we will attend church, if that meets with your and the children's approval."

Emily said, "Mr. Montgomery, I agree to attend worship services with you however, I will not agree to sit with you and the children. I do not want to be responsible for even the slightest blemish on the memory of your blessed wife." He said, "The children will not understand why you are not sitting with them." Emily said, "It will take time for me to explain the reason to them, which I will do in due time. I will not allow this precious home to become the seed for busy body, gossiping, religious tongues." Mr. Montgomery would have desired otherwise, but he knew it was way too soon for another woman to be sitting with him and the family especially because of Emily's striking beauty.

Emily sat in the back of the service. When it was over the entire congregation gathered around Mr. Montgomery. Emily had walked on to the carriage. Mr. Montgomery did not tarry long. He told all those gathered how much their prayers in the family's behalf was answered. He told them they had come a long way from where they were three months ago.

The cook had prepared a delicious Sunday meal. The children asked Emily to come be with them in the garden. Mr. Montgomery told them he was feeling much better and was going to try really hard to be a father to them. When they had changed their clothes, and had gathered by the back-door Emily said, "Why don't we take your father fishing?" Mr. Montgomery looked at Emily with a surprised look. Emily asked, "You do know how to fish don't you, and then winked at him." Mr. Montgomery caught on to her playing and responded, "I will probably catch the biggest fish." Robert Jr., said, "We will see about that!" They gathered their fishing equipment and the coachman. Emily brought some roast beef sandwiches and they were off to an afternoon fishing trip.

The coachman took them to the same creek but decided to take them a little closer to the river where the creek and the river connected. Emily made note of the children cutting their own cane poles and tying their hooks to their lines. Sarah tried and finally said, "Daddy, will you help me fix my line?" Mr. Montgomery had never experienced being with his children in an outdoor environment such as they were experiencing. It appeared to Emily, Mr. Montgomery had not, at any time, been exposed to knowing how to fish in a creek. Emily went to Sarah at the same time as Mr. Montgomery. Emily said, "Sarah, show us all you know about tying your hook". Sarah picked up the hook with one hand and the fishing line with the other. Emily said, "Sarah, you are doing good. Now what is next?" Sarah looked at Emily and said, "I'll have to guess." Emily said, "Don't be afraid, go ahead and guess." Sarah saw the hole at the top of the hook and pushed the fishing line through the hole. Sarah yelled. "I did it." Her father's face broke into a smile as he said, "You are doing so good."

Sarah looked at Emily and said, "What's next?" Emily said, "Ok, here comes the tricky, fun part." Emily got behind Sarah, reached around her and took both of Sarah's hands. She then guided the line into a knot that could hold the hook. Mr. Montgomery then asked Sarah, "What's next?" Emily looked at Sarah and asked what is going to make the fish want to bite the hook?" Sarah said, "Worms." Emily said, "Who is going to put the worm on the hook?" Sarah said, "Daddy." Emily asks Sarah, "Is that really why you wanted your daddy to help you, just so you wouldn't have to touch the worms?" Sarah looked at Emily and said, "That's what friends are for."

When Mr. Montgomery heard Sarah's answer, his laughter could be heard a block away. He picked Sarah up in his arms and said, "You little sneaker. I am going to have to watch you very close." Sarah's line was the last one to be put into the water. As they sat watching their lines, William's line began to slowly ease away. The coachman said, "Jerk!" When William jerked, the line got very tight. William began walking backwards and pulled a huge turtle out on dry land. Charlotte asked?" "What is that thing?" Emily said, "It is a snapping turtle, don't touch him." Emily said, "William, it looks like we are going to lose your hook, because once a snapping turtle closes his mouth, it won't reopen until it thunders." Emily looked all around and said, "I don't see any clouds so we will have to cut the line." The coachman got as much of the line as he could, cut the line and back into the water the turtle crawled.

Robert Jr. was being very still and quiet. He wanted to catch the biggest fish. Mr. Montgomery was sitting on a log, as he dropped his hook by an old dead tree. The worm had no more than touched the water, when all at once, the pole began to bend, as the line tightened. Mr. Montgomery had stepped upon the log to try and keep his line from getting hung. As the fish pulled, the farther out on the log Mr. Montgomery walked. He was not aware the green slime growing on the log was slick. When his feet reached the damp, green colored area of the log, his feet slipped, and Mr. Montgomery found himself in the creek with the fish still hooked to the line. As he walked toward the shoreline, he felt a huge tug on the line. He walked up on shore and started pulling the line in with his hands. When the fish reached shallow water, he could see the fish was huge. Mr. Montgomery kept pulling the line, backing up at the same time. He pulled the fish out on dry land as the family gazed in amazement at the size of the catfish. The coachman ran a stringer through his bottom lip and tied him to a root close to the water. The children looked at their father and began laughing out loud. The children could tell their father was in a position where he had never been before. He had no other choice than to laugh with them as he and Emily embraced the children and one another. When they arrived home the coachman weighed the fish. The fish weighted twenty-two pounds. The coachman said he had never heard of a catfish being caught out of that creek any bigger than that fish. The cook asks them if they wanted fish for supper. Everyone wanted fish. They ate all they could hold, even after they asked the butler and the other staff members to eat with them.

As Emily closed her eyes for sleep, she began to wonder where she was being led with this family. She resolved the question by saying, *Holy Father, may Thy will be done.*

CHAPTER TWENTY-SEVEN

THE ENTRAPMENT

As each of the children came to the breakfast table the next morning, they found Emily and their father waiting. Mr. Montgomery was unusually joyful. As each one of them entered the room, he embraced them asking if they had rested. They responded by saying, "We feel like we have been on a vacation." Mr. Montgomery said, "That is precisely the topic I wanted to discuss this morning. I am considering a destination we all can decide to reach within a few days, perhaps to the west of the city. Robert Jr., said, "I have heard people talk of the Catskill Mountains. Have you ever been there?" His father said, "Come to think of it Robert Jr., I haven't been any farther than New Jersey." Charlotte said, "I would love to see a mountain." Mr. Montgomery said, "Emily, where would you like to go?" Emily said, "I love the mountains, let's get ready and go."

The next morning, they were ready for a real vacation. They took two carriages, one for clothes and camping and one for transportation. They also brought the cook. The roadway was not what they thought it would be. At times, they had to walk because they couldn't sit in the coach while the horses were pulling through the mud. But, there was not one hardship they weren't prepared to meet. For some reason, Mr. Montgomery felt like there was no problem Emily couldn't solve. He had begun to have full faith and confidence in her abilities and her as a person. He knew she had been exposed to hardships in her life. She had too much knowledge that could not have been taught in a classroom. It took them four days to reach the mountains. The wilderness was a kind of serene peace their souls needed to bathe some of the sorrow from their hearts.

When they arrived at a location that appeared to have been a habitat at a previous time, they camped near a running creek. Emily asked the children if they had ever captured a wild rabbit. Since there was no answer, Emily asked them if they would like to build a trap to capture some quail or rabbits. She went about searching the area to find the type tree limbs to build a bird and rabbit trap. They worked on the trap all day and set the trap near the creek, where she had shown them some rabbit tracks. They used some corn the cook had brought to grind for cornbread. As they were sitting by the fire in the late evening, Emily began telling them the different animals that lived in the wilderness. She told them the one that worried her the most was the black bear because he was always hungry, especially for something sweet.

As the sun began setting the timber wolves began howling. Each time a new sound was heard, the children got closer to Emily. Emily was glad they had brought Mr. Montgomery's musket for protection. As they snuggled closer to Emily, she began naming the stars and constellations she had learned from her father while at sea. Her goal was to teach them all they could remember on this one trip, because she was not sure there would be another. Mr. Montgomery was as interested as the children and he too became a part of the snuggling close to Emily. She taught them whether on land or sea, the heavens remained the same and would always be their guide if they were ever lost, but they had to learn what the stars were whispering to them.

The coachman had gathered sufficient wood to burn all night. The higher up the mountains they had climbed, the cooler it became. At the end of the first night, they awoke safe, sound and hungry. The cook had brought some salt bacon and flour for pancakes. The coffee had never tasted as good to Mr. Montgomery. The first thing the children wanted to do was check their trap. When they were still a good distance from the trap, Emily could see the trap was sprung. When they were all close to the trap, they could see they had a rabbit. The good part was, it was not much more than a baby. Emily asked Sarah if she wanted a rabbit to pet. Sarah was excited to have a friend to play with her. They decided to leave the baby rabbit in the trap until they had built a cage. Robert Jr. gathered the small limbs from the tree Emily had shown him, and they began building the rabbit cage. By late afternoon, the cage was ready for the newest member of the family. Emily reminded Sarah the rabbit needed food and water. She helped Sarah find a container for the water and put some corn in the pen.

While they were building the rabbit cage, Mr. Montgomery decided to walk in the woods, just to be alone. When the sun was setting, he came back to the camp site with a very rested appearance. The cook made them a delicious meal and then they were ready to sit by the fire. William told them tomorrow he was going to swim in the creek, no matter how cold it was. Emily asked, "Even if you turn blue?" William asked, "Will I turn blue?" Emily said, "If you get cold enough, you will turn blue." William asked, "How cold is that?" Emily said, "Too cold." They laughed, they played and really enjoyed being with one another. The next morning Charlotte asked Emily, "What will be in the trap today? Emily said, "Anything that is hungry and small enough to fit." When they arrived at the trap, it was full of a family of quail. Emily asked them if they had ever eaten quail. They said, "No." Emily said, "It is very good. You will like it." Mr. Montgomery told them he had eaten quail and he really liked it. The cook prepared it with brown gravy and everyone loved the taste of quail.

The next morning, Mr. Montgomery asked them if they would like to go for a walk in the woods. Everyone thought that would be wonderful. Mr. Montgomery led the way along a path that eventually became a bluff bank on the side of a huge mountain. When they walked out on the bluff, they could see in every direction. It was higher than any of them had ever knowingly been before. Emily held Sarah and William's hands, as they walked playfully across the bluff. There was a group of stones knee high in the center. Mr. Montgomery sat down to give the children a rest. As they half laying and half sitting on the stones, their eye lids closed and without expectation, they were napping in the Catskills, out of reach from all humanity. They had not had such a relaxed moment in months. When they awoke, the sun was beginning to slip away for the night, as they made their way back to the camp.

The impact of the loss that had shattered their lives had begun to fade to some extent. While they were sitting by the fire, Emily was sitting across from Mr. Montgomery. She said, "Mr. Montgomery, I want to thank you for this time you have arranged for us to be together, this will be a memory I will cherish forever." After a long silence, Mr. Montgomery said, "Emily, I need to ask you a favor, if you don't mind." Emily's response was, "Ask and your wish shall become as my command." Mr. Montgomery said, "Emily, in the future would you consider referring to me as, "Robert." Emily said, "That will not make me uncomfortable at all. Is that the name you preferred from your wife?" He said, "Yes, it was, and I would like to hear you say it, also." Emily said, "I also have a request." Robert asked, "And what would it be?" Emily said, "For the benefit of the children, I would never want them to ever think I am here to fill their mother's shoes. Therefore, I would like to continue to use the name Mr. Montgomery in their presence and I will refer to you as Robert in our private moments." Robert said, "Emily, you are a very wise lady and you need to know how much we treasure your presence in our lives."

The next morning, a fog had covered the mountains which blinded the beauty of their surroundings. Mr. Montgomery told them it was time for them to go home. They loaded everything including the rabbit and down the mountain they began the joyful journey home. Everyone was more rested than they had been in months. They were sure their mother had been with them on the mountain. Charlotte told them she could feel her mother in her heart. All the others said, the same. Mr. Montgomery told himself, *this is not the last time we will do this.* When they arrived home after the long journey, they crawled into their beds, and their eye lids closed immediately. They had matured beyond their years by having the opportunity to be with Emily during the past months. The substance of the truth of reality had begun to anchor their souls.

At breakfast, their father announced he and Emily had business in the city and he wanted them to go with him, if possible. They all agreed to go. When they arrived at the bank, they entered the bank by the back door which was locked, but Mr. Montgomery had a key to the lock. They walked along a corridor to another door that was also locked. Mr. Montgomery had a key for that lock also. Once in the main building, they walked a flight of stairs to a room that had the word, "Private" engraved on a gold-plated name plate on the door. When they entered the room, he asked them to remain seated at a large table until he returned. Within a brief time, two men entered the room with him. The first man was the approximate age as Mr. Montgomery and the other appeared about ten years younger. Mr. Montgomery introduced the first man as the bank president, Mr. Stewart and the second man as the cashier, Mr. Taylor.

Mr. Montgomery did not begin the conservation in a manner indicating he was asking the two men for anything. He told them to arrange for Emily Emerson to henceforth have check writing authority on his personal account. Mr. Taylor left the room and returned with signature cards for Emily to sign. Mr. Stewart asked him if there was an amount authorized. Mr. Montgomery said, "Whatever the amount she writes, honor the check. I trust her explicitly. She will be in charge of my affairs. The two men were without any doubt employees of Mr. Montgomery. Emily had entered the very heart of New York financial power and influence, unknowingly. The answer she needed, was whether these people were loyal to the United States of America or were they the treasonous traitors that had come with the blessings of King George III to retake America and continue the Penal Laws that prevailed at that time. For a time, she had allowed her thoughts of, *caring for the family to dim her purpose by being involved with their lives.* The dilemma of attempting to serve two masters had clouded her purpose. When she saw the massive financial power in the heart of New York and Robert Montgomery being one of the primary suspects, she settled back into her original purpose. She reminded herself of, *the possible conspiracy against the American government.* As her training began slowly evolving, she became more determined than ever before to expose the truth regardless of whose lives it might hurt. She began to complete the plan to invade the trader's secrets. The children had no idea what their father did to provide them with a home in the most prestigious section of New York.

Her plan was to take the names of everyone who attended Mrs. Montgomery's funeral to Weston. She began by delivering him the names of those who signed the record of their attendance at the funeral. She told Mr. Montgomery she did not want to upset him again by bringing up an obligation she felt he had to fulfill, which was acknowledging the presence of everyone who had attended the funeral. He told her to do whatever she needed to do to meet and complete the obligation. She labored to write the acknowledgements while developing another list of names with the addresses to deliver to Weston.

Along with her other duties, she was able to produce the names and addresses of every person on the funeral record. She delivered the names and addresses to Weston who along with some expert help would select the list of suspects needed. After receiving the names, the decision was made to focus on each individual in the same or similar manner as Emily was focusing on Mr. Montgomery.

During one of their informal meetings while the children were studying an assignment Emily had given them, she asked Robert if he felt like inviting a select group of his best friends and their wives over for a meal soon. Robert told her she was able to read his mind, because he was being bothered by the same thing. He told Emily his life was completely content with her and the children. Emily said, "That is exactly how I feel also, but sooner or later, we have got to get back to reality and become a part of the human race again."

Robert said, "I will have you a list prepared before the week is over." Emily asks, "In preparation of the occasion is there anything I could do to assist you?" Robert replied, "I would like to have a place away from the wives where I could meet with the men for a short while. You could arrange that for me if you would. During that time, you could perhaps think of some entertainment for the ladies, what do you think?" Emily said, "That would be a nice gesture on your part and you would not have to hurry your meetings with the men. I will take care of that as soon as I can. Do you have a date in mind?" Robert said, "The twelfth is a good day for me, how about you?" Emily said, "Remember, Charlotte's birthday, the fifteenth." Robert said, "See there, Emily, what would I do without you?" Emily said, "Probably be saying, I am sorry, I forgot all of the time." Robert laughed at her quick remark and said to himself, *how blessed I am to have Emily to care for us.*

It was now Emily's duty to arrange a place where she could hear every word that was said by Mr. Montgomery and his guest who could possibly be the most destructive force of traitors in America. She thought of the connections of the fireplaces on the first floor and the second floor. The perfect answer would be the room she could hear from while in her room. As a test, she took the children to the first-floor room below her room one morning during recess. She told them she had a surprise for them, but she needed to finish its preparation. She told them to remain in the room while she went to her room to get it ready. She went to her room and closed the door to listen. She sat by the fireplace as the children played and visited. The sound was such as she could plainly hear the words spoken and she could distinguish who was speaking. She went to the room and told them she was ready to get back to the classroom for their surprise. She had the cook prepare them cupcakes as a treat and she had put chocolate icing on top of each of them. They were delighted and so was she.

Emily knew if those invited to Mr. Montgomery's were the core members of the conspiracy, they would want to bring him up to date. The financial status of the United States was very fragile at the time even worse than it had been before the Revolution. The British had not allowed a mint to be built in America and would not allow the British to ship large amounts of silver and gold to the colonies. The Crown demanded all debt owed the British be paid in sterling silver or gold. This prevented an excess of hard money from building up in the colonies. The Americans relied on the Spanish milled dollar, a silver coin about the size of a modern silver dollar. French money and Portuguese gold coins as well as German and coins from the Netherlands were circulated. Because of the shortage, the colonies began printing paper money even prior to the Revolution. The Revolution began by financing the war with paper money. The reason was, paper money was all that was available, but as the war continued, the colonies continued to print too much paper money.

When the war had reached a conclusion, it took 600 Continental dollars to equal one Spanish silver dollar. If they were the men suspected of destroying America, Emily had come to believe the plot probably included forcing the United States into bankruptcy, which would render them helpless to pay its debts and which would cost the nation its financial credibility. If any of this had one grain of truth connected to it, she knew her father needed to know this as soon as she was sure.

Prior to the twelfth, Emily took Robert into the meeting room which pleased him very much. She also suggested a renowned poet to read poetry to the ladies. She did not want loud singing or a musical instrument interfering with her ability to hear every word spoken. She had note pads in her room available to record the words spoken by each speaker at the meeting.

After she had seen to it, all the guests were received and were in their places, she dismissed herself to care for the children. After she said a prayer with Sarah, she went to her bedroom for the evening. She dressed in her night clothes and had a book available to read should Robert knock on her door. She remained very quiet as she waited for the meeting to begin. She heard Robert's voice tell the guest they would be meeting in this room. She could hear the chairs being moved and glasses clinking. Finally, Robert said, "I want to thank you for responding to my invitation to meet with me this evening. I am sure you know how I must feel with the loss of Anne. For a time, I had wondered if I would ever become interested in anything again. But after a while with the help of our Nanny, I was able to struggle back to realizing how important it is to Great Britain that we do all we can to prevent the new government of the colonies from becoming financially self-supportive. We agree with the King that the group of rabble rousers who seized power will never be capable of causing America to become anything but a nation of slaves without knowledge or capable leadership. I have examined their President Washington. He has no background in financial matters and does not have the capability of keeping the colonies together. For the most part, I view this experiment as nothing but a waste of time. Do any of you see it different than I do? One of the participants said, "Well, they did win the war." Robert again spoke, "The war we have planned is not with guns and bullets, it is a war of financial knowledge. It is a war of economics and there is not one of the leaders in America that has a clue about economics.

The colonies voted to put all the debt of the war on the central government that is already bankrupt. Should that occur the central government will turn to our bank to fund the payment to the colonies. Once we loan them the money and they default, as sure they will, all we have to do is demand payment and the game will be over. We represent the most powerful group of investors in Europe. If we call our debt the government will fall, and we can convince King George III to divide this nation into equal shares among us." Emily did not hear a response to Robert's words. They began talking about other investments in other nations. Finally, as the meeting was about to conclude, Robert asked them, "Are we ready to drop the axe?" All the voices said, "Yes!"

Emily didn't sleep at all after she had heard Robert's plan to destroy America. The next morning, she was in the kitchen when Robert arrived. He could tell she did not feel well at all. She told Robert she needed medical attention and needed his permission to use the carriage. She went upstairs to dress and when she returned the children met her and began to cry. When she told them, she would be back in a short while, they felt much better.

Emily (Bridget) was waiting in Weston's office when he arrived. He could tell her visit was urgent. He took her to his office.

She began by saying we were right, there is a plot to destroy America not by invasion of the Army, but with money. She explained the whole plan to Weston. After Weston had all the facts in his mind he told her he was on his way to Washington D.C. to talk with her father. He encouraged her to get hold of herself and do not let Robert have any suspicions about her behavior. He said, "I want you to go to our doctor's office before you go back, we will be in contact with you."

When Emily had finished with Weston, she went to the doctor's office for her upset stomach. He gave her some medicine and she returned to the Montgomery home. The children were overjoyed to see her. They led her upstairs and made her lie down. The cook brought her some broth and drinking water. The children were all standing around her bed when their father walked in the room. He came and kneeled by her bedside asking her what seemed to be the matter. She said, "Oh, Mr. Montgomery, I have been so worried about you and the guests becoming ill also. Have you been feeling sick at your stomach?" Robert said, "No, not so far." She said, "Children, we must pray I am the only one who has this upset stomach, because it hurts so much." When she said that, the children kneeled beside their father while he prayed for Emily to get well. She said, "Maybe I need a little rest, if you don't mind." They said, "You rest all you want to, and we will be really quiet." They walked softly out of the room. Their father remained kneeling as he asked her, "Emily, have I put too much on you? If there is anything I have done to cause you to become ill, please forgive me."

Emily looked at him and said, "Robert, all I need is rest for a day or so and I will be feeling better." Robert got up from his knees and kissed her lips, as tears rolled from his cheeks. She put her arms around his neck and kissed him. She then said, "Let me rest." He said, "I will be by the door, if you need me." She tried to smile and turned over to close her eyes.

Her mind was where she knew she would eventually be. She had arrived at that line between the purest form of hate and the purest form of love. There had to be a location where God's will could be done, but she did not know if she was capable of finding that place.

She truly loved Robert and his family, as much as she loved life itself. What would she do when the day came to take the witness stand and condemn him to death for betraying their country. She was the only hope he had to stay alive. Then her mind raced to the welfare of the children and how they would hate her for having their father put to death.

She prostrated her soul before God and prayed with her whole heart to deliver her from this burden that had crushed her soul to dust. She had not slept in two nights and was beginning to feel exhausted. She told herself, *since America's worst enemy was at her door, the time had come for her to become the warrior she was trained to be, because this man was tampering with the security of America.* With that thought as a valid excuse to close her eyes, she fell asleep.

When she awoke, it took her a few minutes to realize she was in the same world, she had left when she closed her eyes. She decided to continue the sick stomach routine to keep Robert occupied. She said to herself, *anyone with the potential for harm that Robert has, needs to be kept busy thinking of good things.* She very softly said to him, "Robert", and no faster than it took her to say his name, he was through the door and standing by her bedside. He asked her if she would like to sit up for a while. She said, "That might be nice." Robert gently removed the pillow from under her head and leaned it against the headboard, as he placed the other pillow at an angle for her to scoot up to a 45-degree angle. He then placed his arms around her back, just below her shoulder and lifted her up to place her head on the pillow. She asked him if he had rested. He said, "Enough". She asks, "Where did you sleep?" He told her he had dozed in a chair. He asked her if there was anything he could get for her. She replied, "I wonder if the cook has any of the broth left." Robert said, "I will be back in a moment."

When he left, it gave her a moment to freshen up and comb her hair. When he returned with a tray, on which there was broth and choices of other things she might enjoy. She began to think to herself, *about being loved by one of the most dangerous men on earth. A man who would think nothing about betraying millions of people, who had won their freedom from a tyrant that knew no boundaries to his greed and insane tyranny.*

King George III had been judged by his fellow rulers as the cruelest despot in the world. She was thinking of all the British had done to her family and then she began thinking of the millions he had killed while some in his group viewed the harm as acts of mercy. Ireland and Scotland were the birthplaces of the application of fair play and freedom between neighbors. That belief was contradictory to a despotic ruler's mind.

When she had finished the delicious morsels, Robert had brought to her, he removed the tray and pulled a chair to her bedside. He said, "The children are missing you." She said, "And I, them. Robert, they are so wonderful. Each day, I am allowed to be with them, I learn more and more of their ways. When they grow up, they will become admired by all their friends. My prayer is for one of them to become a lawyer, perhaps even a Senator." She asks, "What is your prediction for Charlotte?" Robert said, "She will become the one with ways of her mother. She will love everyone, and everyone will love her." Emily asked, "What of Sarah?" Robert said, "She gives me concern of perhaps, having some of my obvious bad traits." Emily asks, "Such as what? You cannot name one bad trait you possess." As quick as lightening had struck, Robert stood up and in a loud tearful voice, he said, "You don't know me. You think you know me. I am an evil man."

Emily spoke very softly, "I have not seen any traits you describe as evil in the Robert I know. Is there another Robert I don't know?" Robert was sobbing when he said, "Yes, there is a terrible Robert, you have not met." Emily said, "From the way you describe him, I don't think I want to meet him. The Robert I know is a fine man of dignity and integrity who loves God, his country and his family above all things he loves his neighbors as he loves himself." Robert lifted his face from his hands and said, "You could never know how much I pray that could be the truth." Emily said, "Whatever we want to be the truth about ourselves, we can cause it to become the truth." Robert ask her, "Have you ever gone too far to turn back?" Emily said, "Not yet, but life is a long time and I am sure there will be times when I will feel I have gone too far." Emily said, "Robert, I can't imagine you being an evil man." Robert said, "Emily, I am an evil man." Emily said, "Maybe you need some help getting back on the right path."

CHAPTER TWENTY-EIGHT

SHOWDOWN

On the third day of Emily's illness, she asked Robert to sit in the garden with her and the three children. As they gathered around her, she told them she was feeling much better. She assured the children she had missed them. They sat next to her, as Sarah held one of her hands and Charlotte held the other. Emily said, "We need to do some catch up on our lessons." Robert said, "We decided while you were sick, the most we could do for you was keep up with our lessons." Emily said, while she was smiling, "We will see tomorrow when I give you a test." As they gathered around her each one of them tried to be the closest to her. Emily ended up with a double arm load of love and everyone was enjoying every minute of that moment of wellness and togetherness.

Robert did not come to breakfast that next morning which caused Emily to wonder, *if there were some serious things on his mind.* He had indicated his mind was filled with trouble. She knew his guilt was what was bothering him. She knew it was his conscience which gave her hope to keep him from following up on the plans he and others had made to harm America and its people. Emily told the children she would be ready to resume their lessons in the morning. As the day slowly closed, Emily could tell Robert became more depressed and withdrawn. She prayed he was having second thoughts about his plan.

She held to the possibility of him changing his mind. She could feel he was already feeling his regret.

The next morning, the family including Robert, was at the breakfast table ready for another day. Emily said, "I want to say the prayer this morning." Everyone was thankful because Emily always knew what to pray for because she knew what they needed most. She began by expressing gratitude for one another and the great gifts of divine grace that surrounded them at all times, especially in time of secret needs. She asked for a special blessing for Mr. Montgomery, who had provided his work and labor to allow God to provide His blessing to them each day. Finally, she prayed for guidance in every decision they would make today, that it be the decision that pleased God the most. She thanked God for allowing her to get well and be with such a wonderful family. As they were completing their breakfast, they heard a knock at the front door. She heard the butler talking to the visitor and then it became quiet. The butler came in the breakfast room to tell Mr. Montgomery a General Dan O'Flaherty and an attorney, whose name is Weston Collier, has asked to speak with you. As Bridget heard her father's voice, she knew she had reached the end of her pretending to be someone she wasn't. Robert asked the General to come in the office. Just as they were seated, Bridget walked in the office and closed the door. Robert was very surprised. She began by walking to Robert's chair to introduce herself as Bridget O'Flaherty, the daughter of General Dan O'Flaherty, who was in Command of Special Forces for the United States of America. She told him the man seated next to the General is an attorney. She said, "Robert, I am an investigator for the government in matters relating to treason and espionage." Robert asks her, "What does that have to do with me?"

Bridget said, "You have been the focus of an investigation for more than a year. I was sent here to determine whether or not there is any truth to the reports our department has been receiving regarding a plan by you to cause harm to America. When I verified your involvement and more important your leadership in causing the government of the United States to fail financially, I notified my father of your involvement." When Robert heard the words Bridget said, he began sobbing and saying, "I have no excuse for what I have been planning to do to America. I am that evil man that I told you I am, and yes, I think I have gone too far, and I need to be hung by my neck, until I am dead."

After the General heard Mr. Montgomery admit his guilt, he wondered if he might be remorseful enough to help capture the traitors before the plan was executed. Dan asked Mr. Montgomery if he had set a date for the plan to begin. Mr. Montgomery replied, "No Sir." The General inquired, "Are you advising me there is time for this mission to be aborted?" Mr. Montgomery answered, "Yes Sir." The General ask, "Who has the final authority to abort the mission?" Mr. Montgomery answered, "I do." The General said, "Good because if the mission is aborted, we will have more mercy available than there is at this moment, because I have come prepared to kill you myself, if need be." Mr. Montgomery said, "That will not be necessary. I am sorry you will have to forgive me, but there is something I need to say so we will all be on equal footing in our attempt to understand one another. Please do not misunderstand, I am not asking for mercy, because I don't deserve any mercy.

My background is that of extreme wealth, political influence and power as granted by the King of England. I have had very little to do with amassing any of the wealth of my family. My parents were Loyalists before the war began. At the conclusion of the war, they were sent to Nova Scotia. I remained in America planning to do as much damage to the new government as I could. With the full approval and support of the King, I set about to prevent the new nation from functioning financially. I organized a large group of the most financially capable Loyalists who had been deported to create a large amount of money to be used to bankrupt the nation by purchasing the balances of payment the United States owed other nations. Most of the larger trade creditors have been paid by our syndicate, and we are now the creditors of most of the American outstanding debt. We had the countries remain as the credit holders to avoid suspicion. At this particular time, we are prepared to call the obligations owed several foreign governments which in fact, is a syndicate for Great Britain.

Dan listened to Mr. Montgomery pour out his soul. He had apparently lost his will to cause harm after the loss of his wife, because her death had taken the joy his family had known. He had lost heart to desire harm to his fellow man. He perhaps was one of the British who had learned how it felt to have harm and suffering come to the innocent. Dan asked Mr. Montgomery if there was anything else planned to bring harm to America. Mr. Montgomery said, "Cornwallis and some of the other Generals who lost the war are wanting to launch a major offensive probably in the south around New Orleans. Another group is promoting the idea of burning the new government buildings. At this time, the groups have not gained the full support of the King and parliament, but they will eventually prevail because the King remains very angry about losing the war."

Dan said, "And now, we must decide what to do with you and your fellow elite relatives and friends. For the first time in the history of humanity, a group of people fight and win their freedom. My question to you is, why would a man like you be opposed to all other men having the opportunity to do better for their family, become landowners and stand on equal footing with all men?" Mr. Montgomery said, "Conceptually, that all sounds good except for one thing, we want it all. We do not want the hordes of humanity sharing in the wealth, we want all the wealth because we deserve it, because we are of an elitist class. That is what I was taught to believe. However, I have come to know that is wrong and I want to change my way of living and thinking." Dan asked, "How did you come to more understanding than you had two years ago?" Mr. Montgomery said, "Because, I came to know your daughter, Bridget, whom we know as Emily Emerson. She came into our lives when we were in a most desperate situation. Bridget came out of nowhere which now, I know was a plot by the government to prevent harm to America. She did her duty and at the same time, she loved us. She nursed us back from the grave of my dear wife and has shared her strength with us to be whole again. We have learned to love her and depend upon every word that comes from her lips. She taught me if I hurt America, I would hurt her, and I would give my life before I would hurt her or anyone that is close to her. General, this may seem strange to you, I am in a position of having to fight for my life because of the wrong I have planned, but I have never been this happy in my life. I feel free because I do not have to bear the burden of evil any longer. Regardless of what you decide to do with me, I know my Emily will take care of my family for the rest of her life, because we love her, and she loves us, and no one can take the blessing of her pure heart away from our family. I am before you now, because of your daughter's pure heart and faithfulness to the United States of America and even though that is true, she loved me enough to prevent me from being evil the remainder of my life. I thank her from the bottom of my heart for the time she has given to us regardless of her original motive. Well, General where do we go from here?"

The General said, "I have been sitting here wondering if you can be as good as you have been bad. For us to try and completely undo the mess you have plotted and planned will take too many reasons for too long a time. I am trying to think of a way to get you to help us end this plot you have put together. I am assuming all of the participants are good, clean upstanding citizens who attend some protestant church of high religious regard." Mr. Montgomery said, "General, you have pretty well described us." The General said, "What do you think about helping us round up your gang just because it is the right thing to do." Mr. Montgomery said, "I would consider it an honor and a privilege to serve America with attempting to undo my evil." The General said, "I need to visit with my daughter while you and the company lawyer write down the names and addresses of all you know who are participants.

The General and Bridget went out the back door into the garden area to visit about her future. When they were seated, the butler brought a tray of fruit, crackers, coffee and tea. Dan said, "Bridget, I don't know why, but I get the impression Mr. Montgomery is ready to approach you to become his wife." Bridget said, "That was something he mentioned to me in the very beginning, because he had lost his wife. I have been very nurturing to this family because they needed me.

They mean a great deal to me and I do to them. Now, that he will probably be in prison, I don't know what that would do about us. I do know this, except for him planning to destroy America, he is a good person." Dan looked at her while asking himself, *now, how does she expect me to understand that?* "She smiled and said, "Daddy, I said that for humor, let's lighten up a little bit, come on. We have him captured. He is not going anywhere, besides all that, he is a sweetheart." With that statement, Dan cracked a small smile. He said, "Daughter, I take matters that involve America very serious." Bridget said, "And so do I. All I'm asking is, what is the plan for this gang? I think the whole bunch is a group of spoiled brats that can and will be willing to give America the financial improvement it needs to become solvent. The thing I love about our position is, we can use the King's money and his little co-hort's money to make America solvent or hang the lot of them." Dan had to laugh at that one. He told her she may be having fun, but she was coming up with the best plan to hurt the enemy where they hurt the most he had heard of in a long time.

Bridget said, "Daddy, Colonel Hernandez and Colonel Longoria taught me many ways a cat can be skinned. Take for example, in this case, there will be enough money come out of this one group of criminals to probably pay off the national debt." Dan knew he had been blessed with something special with her being born in a Cherokee tribes' village, but he never thought she would be this smart. After she had her Daddy ready to laugh a little, it was time to revisit the criminal to decide on the disposition of the rest of his life.

When Dan and Bridget walked in, Mr. Montgomery out of respect for them, stood up. Weston told Dan he had been very cooperative and had an abundance of information remaining he was willing to reveal. Dan told Weston to take his time, they were not in any hurry because they were less than a mile from their home. Mr. Montgomery asked the General if he owned property in New York. Dan said he did and it was the property where the horse farm is located. Mr. Montgomery told them he had always admired that piece of property and had intended to buy it. Dan said, "It has served us well."

Dan could see the circumstance had begun to wear Mr. Montgomery down. He asks him if he would like to adjourn the meeting until tomorrow when everyone was rested. Mr. Montgomery was stunned by Dan's suggestion because he had envisioned himself being taken to a prison to prepare for a trial. Weston had begun to yawn and therefore agreed more could be accomplished when everyone was rested. Mr. Montgomery agreed that he needed the rest and had begun to need some food. He said, "You will have to forgive me, but I do not know the protocol for being arrested for espionage, but I was wondering if it was permissible for us to have an evening meal together with the children." Dan said, "I don't think anyone in the government would object to such an offer." Dan was observing the children when they were around Bridget. He could tell they worshipped her. When it was time for the meal to begin, Dan said, "Would you object to an Irish Catholic prayer for the meal?" Robert said, "That will probably enhance the taste." Dan was enthralled with the children. Each one had a distinctive charm all their own. When one of them would address Bridget, it was with the utmost adoration and respect. Dan had begun to understand what Bridget's spirit had meant to the family when their mother died.

When Dan began the prayer, he asked God for His blessing upon the household and the food. He asked for God's blessing to be upon their wisdom to find a way to benefit others. He asks that their hearts be opened to the opportunity to give of themselves to their great nation and then he asked for forgiveness for their sins. Dan glanced at Robert, as a tear rolled down his cheek. It appeared the meal was a perfect end to a good day. Dan asked Robert when a good time in the morning would be to meet again. Robert said, "We have breakfast and prayer at 8:00 a.m., and you are invited."

The next morning, all the parties had slept soundly and were ready for another day. Bridget announced at breakfast she had to get back with the children. Dan and Weston had no objection. When they had closed the door to the meeting room, Dan began by giving Robert a brief statement about the fact of him being born in Ireland and his family becoming slaves and shipped to America. He told him about him and his two sisters being rescued before the ship sailed, the outcome of which placed him in Spain under the care of General Phillip and Margarita O'Shea. He revealed to him of being captured by the British in the Jacobite War and shipped to America as a prisoner of war under the command of General James Oglethorpe. He told him also about working with his father, General Phillip O'Shea to bring an end to the Seven Year War between England and Spain. He disclosed the fact of his adoptive parents being lost at sea during a hurricane and him becoming an heir to one of the largest estates in the world. He mentioned also to him of General George Washington telling him his Army had not been paid because of the length of time the war had endured. Then he disclosed he had paid the troops with his own funds which ultimately saved America. Dan allowed what he had just disclosed to Robert to sink into his thoughts. He then said to Robert, "I had the money to demand and get anything I wanted out of America. The only thing I have ever asked for in return is that all our people be safe and be given equal opportunity to be free. My question for you to consider is since you have decided you do not want to become the owner of America, what are you willing to give to keep America free?" Without hesitation, Robert said, "All my treasure, my blood and my life, if necessary.

Dan then said, "Robert, I am thinking of offering you an opportunity to become an active part of this government to help set up a department of skilled people to do as my daughter is doing to keep America secure." Robert said, "After I get out of prison, I would probably be looking for employment and I would sure consider your offer." Dan said, "At this time, I do not see that you have, in fact committed an act of treason. I do know you have planned to commit an act of treason. Let's consider my original thought. There is a world out there that is full of people like you and your friends who are living and praying for the day America will fall. Would you consider working with Bridget, Weston and me to prevent that from happening?" Robert said, "I would consider that opportunity the greatest blessing of my life." Dan said, "You do know, you will probably end up broke and living on a government salary, don't you?" Robert said, "That sounds good to me, when considering the alternative." Dan said, "And of course, you do know you will be under house arrest and the supervision of Bridget until we complete the mission." Her supervision of you after that will be up to you and her. Dan suggested they take a break to walk around in the garden. While they were drinking tea, Dan asked Robert when he would like to get started on the plan to persuade his co-conspirators to cooperate with them, as opposed to going to prison for the remainder of their lives or be deported.

Robert said he would like to have a few days to organize his thoughts as to the most effective approach to each individual, since he knew all the parties intimately. Dan asks Weston in Roberts presence, "What would be the best method to use to get the amount of money they would be receiving from each of the contributors into the Treasury of the United States of America." Weston responded by saying, "It is not unlawful to give the nation a gift of any amount of money." Dan said, "The first thing I want to consider a portion of the money contributed to build a mint to press hard money. Since the King would not allow a mint to be built in America, I would like to find a way, whereby the King contributes to the building of the mint."

It had become time for Bridget to end school for the day. The cook had prepared some cookies for the children and the guest. When the children came down from the classroom, everyone went outside to enjoy the fresh air. Sarah was attracted to the General, especially the gold buttons on his coat. She came to Dan and courtsied, saying, "My name is Sarah." Dan kneeled in front of her saying, "I know your name, Sarah. You are so pretty." Dan said, "Did you know I had a daughter your age one time, but now, she is a big lady." Sarah asks, "Where is she now?" Dan said, "That is her standing by the bed of flowers, she is your Nanny." Sarah said, "My Nanny has a Daddy?" Dan said, "I am him." Sarah said, "I love my Nanny." Dan said, "She told me, she loves you too." Sarah laughed saying, "I know that."

After they had visited for about thirty minutes, Dan said, "Sarah, we have to go home. We will see you tomorrow." Sarah said,

"See you tomorrow." Dan took time to bring Bridget up to date on the discussion with Robert. She was most encouraged they would not have to get into a long drawn out process of infiltrating each home. Weston and Dan went on to the mansion to check out the new horse Weston had bought for breeding. Dan wanted to ride one of the Arabians. Weston wanted to ride with him to the river to show him the contact point they used to send the messages to General Washington. Dan was very impressed with all the details they had put together to get the information to the General faster than any other spy group during the war.

The next morning, they met again with Robert who was becoming more convinced each day he was doing the right thing, regardless of his parents being deported after the war. The family problem was, they had chosen the wrong side to support and lost. Robert had no animosity toward the British, because he did not know the brutality the King and parliament had passed to exterminate the Irish. After he learned why the Irish and Scottish were hostile toward Great Britain, he understood their reasons for wanting freedom.

Robert revealed his plan to dismantle the traitors he had organized. He began by asking Dan and Weston the question concerning their method of working on his case. Weston asks, "What do you mean?" Robert said, "If you set up a massive arrest of everyone, they will all eventually flee the country and the threat to financially topple the government will remain. That is why I am asking; why don't you achieve everything you want to achieve, by approaching them the same way you have done me?" The objective is to gain possession of their weapon, which is their financial power, i.e., all their money in exchange for their freedom and silence about the transaction.

To try and force them, the money will end up in Great Britain to pay legal fees. If it was me, I would offer them their homes and enough to exist on for at least two years after the matter is resolved. They will be able to explain to their parents, they made a bad investment and had to pay all their money to keep from becoming bankrupt. With being prison or death, the alternative is obvious none of them would select that method to resolve this matter. There are two in the group that will be rather stubborn, but I can assist you with those two.

Weston told Dan, "I am not completely certain, but I don't think we need to talk to anyone about this proposition." He then asked Robert who had possession of the cancelled debt agreements that was executed when your group paid the trade balances owed to foreign governments?" Robert responded, "I do." Weston asks, "While we are on that subject, what do you do to generate income for your family?" Robert said, "I own the second largest bank in America." Weston then asks, "What degrees do you have?" Robert said, "I have a law degree and an accounting degree; however, I have never practiced either profession." Weston asks, "Do you see any problem with assigning the bank's annual profits to the United States Treasury?" "Not in the least," Robert responded. Weston then asked, "Would you object to having three new directors on your board?" Robert said, "Of course not, consider it done." Robert said, "Each one of us have vast amounts of real estate in America. It will take some time for us to divest ourselves of the property." Weston said, "My firm represents a large number of investors who want a piece of America. Give me the information on the property and I will see if there is any interest." Robert suggested they go to the bank as soon as possible to get the documents he needed.

Dan asked, "Who would be the next person we could talk with to see if they would be as interested in a peaceful settlement of this matter as you have been?" Robert suggested Theodore Walpole. He has been a very dear friend for years and is a man of reason. He has a family of which he is very proud and would do nothing to tarnish the Walpole reputation. He is a rather passive soul and at the same time is a brilliant man who has made money in large sums for years. He did inherit his family's wealth which he has invested wisely. I would not reveal to him you know of the others who are involved. The more you can do for him as you have done for me, without consequence for our immature insanity, the better response you will receive."

Weston asked, "Are you saying, the General and I should knock at his door as we did your door?" Robert said, "I would suggest any other method would expose his privacy and that is what you want him to have when the transaction is completed." Weston assured Robert they would follow his recommendations without deviation.

Three days had passed before the General and Weston Collier knocked at the door of Mr. Walpole. His butler answered the door and asked, "Who may I say is calling?" Weston replied, General Dan O'Flaherty, Commander of the Special Forces of the United States of America and his attorney, Weston Collier. Within five minutes, the butler asked them to come in. He took them to an office that appeared well used. They could tell he was a man that liked to be busy. They could tell by the opulence of his home, he had accumulated a great deal of wealth. He met them at the door way of his office. They were both surprised by the man's size. It was obvious he had eaten his share of food and more during his life time. He displayed a jolly type personality and was most delighted by visitors. His first words were,

"How can I help you?" The General began by saying his department had received information naming him as a person who was involved in doing certain acts, so as to bring about the bankruptcy of the United States of America. The General's demeanor and presence said more to Theodore Walpole than what he had said. Sweat began popping out all over his face. He removed his jacket while trying to calculate how anyone could know of his involvement. However, his response was, "Well, this sounds most interesting. Just how was I supposed to bankrupt America?"

Dan said, "We have copies of obligations owed by the United States to other nations that have been paid by you and we think you intend to call those notes which could cause the government to fail." Mr. Walpole did not bother with asking to see the documents. He began by saying he bought the debt as an investment because he believed in America's economy. Weston asked him, "How did you plan to make money when there is no interest to be paid on the notes?" Mr. Walpole by that time had wet his shirt with sweat. His attempt to appear innocent had betrayed him. He knew they knew the truth. He began revealing every secret Robert had already revealed. They were glad to hear it repeated to check out Robert's story. Mr. Walpole talked and talked some more about his love for America. When he had run down, Dan asked him if he knew the penalty for betraying America. He said, "Death by hanging." Dan asked, "Does life in the penitentiary sound better?"

Dan and Weston allowed him time to consider his options, when he asked them, "Is there an option?" Dan said, "Theodore, "What if I told you, yes, how would that make you feel?" Mr. Walpole said, "Much better." Dan asked Weston to explain the plan to him which he accepted immediately. Dan said, "There is one other requirement for you to thoroughly and completely understand and that is you cannot reveal this to any other person because if you do, you will be tried for treason. If that is agreeable with you, Mr. Collier will make arrangements to meet you at the United States Treasury office. Tell him when you are ready, and I assume that will be soon. Mr. Walpole asks, "Is tomorrow too soon?" Weston said, "Next week is better.

CHAPTER TWENTY-NINE

RECOLLECTIONS

During the first two years of Washington's Presidency, the dark cloud that the need for more money brings seemed to be the main topic everyone had on their mind, when they came to talk to the President. It was not until April 2, 1792 a bill was passed to operate a federal mint in Philadelphia.

Alexander Hamilton established the standard for coinage which was based on a gold standard eagle ($10.00), half eagle and quarter eagle, silver coins of one dollar, half eagles, and quarter eagle, silver coins of one dollar, half dollar, quarter dollar, dime (disme at the time) and half dime (5 cents). The pure copper coins of one cent and half-cent were the final two denominations in the coinage series.

President George Washington appointed David Rittenhouse, a Philadelphia scientist, to be the first director of the new mint building at Seventh Street and Arch, a few blocks from Independence Hall. (29) Martha Washington donated some personal silverware for the manufacture of the first coin. General O'Flaherty and Weston continued the collections from the traitors until each of them had paid all they possessed to pay the United States of America for their acts of treason.

Robert Montgomery was never as proud of himself in his life as he was for what he had done to expose the plot to destroy America. There was never any mention as to the reason for his withdrawal from the plot to the other. They continued to visit as friends. Their children attended one another's birthday parties. As was agreed, no one ever betrayed the oath they gave to General O'Flaherty and Weston to keep the whole matter secret.

Robert continued operating the bank under the scrutiny of Weston and two of his employees. Bridget continued to be Nanny to the Montgomery family. Everyone in the family continued to call her Emily which was their private way of holding to the memory of their mother. From time to time, Emily would, of government necessity, have to be absent from teaching which was carried on by another lady none of the children liked because she was not their Emily.

Robert had become an extremely valuable man for Weston to rely upon in matters associated with any kind of banking. Once they became better acquainted, Robert began to refer business to Weston and the Collier empire began to grow with Dan's estate being one of the largest investors.

During the years when the colonies had printed its own paper money, each colony had its own artistic flare to the money that was printed. When money became the responsibility of the United States government, the counterfeit money business began to flourish.

Since New York City became the money capital of America it soon became a haven for counterfeit money operations. Dan and Weston agreed Robert would be the man to put in charge of solving the counterfeit problem for all the banks. It wasn't long before he learned the best defense was to use a paper that was not for sale to the public. Once the government began using the paper, the difference was obvious.

When Dan returned to their New York home, he told Mary he was tired. He asked her if she was up to a visit with the President and his wife. She told him she was ready for a visit with Cathal and "Two Dan." The next morning, they told Maureen and Weston they needed to visit the boys. They had wondered how Mary had been able to be without their company for such a long time. When they arrived in Washington, D.C., it was difficult to decide which of the Blue Celts were their sons. Dan told Mary he was feeling so old, everyone else looked like teenagers. The closer they got to the President's house, the more Blue Celts they saw. It wasn't until they arrived at the President's door, they were able to find their sons. The President had insisted they be the last line for his defense between him and any villain.

When the President saw Dan and Mary, he told them he was ready to visit awhile. He said he needed the refreshment of their presence each time he was able to be with them. It wasn't long before Martha came by to check on him and when she saw Dan and Mary, she was so overjoyed to see them. She told them, "There are no other two people in America she and the President held closer to their hearts than them." Martha asked, "Do you see where the President has both of your sons? They are the only two that makes him feel completely at ease when General John Milledge is not here." Mary thanked her for the kind words. Martha asked Mary to go with her upstairs while those two men visit. She said, "The President has been asking when Dan was coming to town." Martha told the President to visit with Dan and they would be upstairs.

When the President sat down, he told Dan he had some most unexpected good news to tell him that should restore his faith and trust in his government. He said, "General, I hope you don't think I have forgotten about the money this country owes for your contributions during the war. Dan, I would not have been able to keep the troops together if they had not been paid. Dan, that is the topic I am so glad to report to you. The Secretary of the Treasury has reported to me a group of patriots from New York has made this nation a gift of an unbelievable amount of money. In addition, they have also paid for the construction of a mint to print the money. I know to the dollar how much we owe you and I am sending for the Secretary of the Treasury, Alexander Hamilton to bring you a check. Don't even try to come up with a reason to not let this nation pay you what it owes. This has been our secret and will remain our secret, so please no more on that subject.

Dan this nation is growing every day. People are coming to our shores from most everywhere but Great Britain. The bitterness of defeat has never left the King's mind. He continues to blast out cursing and hatred toward us. I know there will be a day when he sends an army to our shores again. I don't know if you and I will be here to fight the battle, but he will return some day. In the meanwhile, we must keep our rifles ready for battle. Have you thought any about the numbers of Special Force troops we need to have ready at all times?"

Dan said, "Sir, I believe we need twenty-five-hundred men to serve as Special Force combat soldiers, snipers, spies, and we need to think of having its own separate medical unit." The President asked, "Dan, how many trained fighters do we have now?" Dan responded, "Sir, we have sent six-hundred men to Spain for training at the academy." When we add those to the troops, we have now, we are approaching 1,600 men." The President said, "As soon as you can, find more qualified trainees and send them to Spain. We need 600 more troops." Dan told the President the academy in Spain was ready to accommodate approximately seven hundred more trainees that qualified for the training. Dan also reminded the President the academy was involved with training soldiers from other countries that would volunteer their assistance, should Great Britain attack unexpectedly. The President complemented Dan for having the forethought to have troops from other countries trained and ready to join with America if there was an attack.

Dan inquired into the world of American politics. The President responded by telling Dan how peculiar it felt not to have someone else to blame when something went wrong. He said "Dan, every person involved in America's great experiment of obtaining freedom has been under the rule of some monarch. Now, there is no one to hold responsible for anything but ourselves. That has taken quiet an adjustment. Dan, perhaps the greatest gift to come from all the freedoms people are now enjoying, is the right to be heard by a jury of your neighbors when you are accused of a crime. To be out of arms reach of the accusations of any one human being from being able to decide guilt or innocence, is a blessing from God Almighty." Dan said, "Mr. President, before the war, I personally experienced that right before the war began. The British Army stationed in Georgia decided to hang me without a trial and I was not guilty. I thank God every day for the protection the Constitution of the United States protects me and my personal rights against the government." The President said, "Dan you and Mary should attend some of the meetings of the Senate and the House of Representatives to better understand the gift of freedom our Constitution now guarantees for all men. Dan told him they had discussed doing that while they were in the area.

Later in the afternoon when Cathal and "Two Dan" had finished their duty, Dan and Mary had the opportunity to visit with them. The two boys told their parents they would like to go somewhere to get away from guard duty for a while. They talked to General John Milledge who told them to go fishing with their parents and he would take care of their duty. It didn't take them long to locate some line, hooks and bait to catch some fish. All they could talk about was the trip from New Orleans to Savannah after the war. Dan had taken full advantage to teach them about everything they would need to survive in the woods. That journey made a lasting impression on them. When they had established the camp, they began fishing for catfish. For some reason, the ones they caught were small, but perfect for one person. Mary enjoyed the precious time together, as did they all. The longer they stayed, the more they recalled the life lessons their parents had taught them. "Two Dan" said, "Well, what else would you expect when your father is the General of the Army?"

When they were ready to rest, Dan began reminding them of the hunting trip they took after they arrived in Savannah. Cathal told them, "The thing I remember most is meeting Andrew Jackson when he was a blacksmith in North Carolina." Dan told them the blacksmith is now a lawyer and a member of the House of Representatives. "Two Dan" said, "I would like to see him again. Dan suggested they try to do that tomorrow.

The next morning Mary had bacon and coffee cooking when they awoke. The boys felt so good to be away from guard duty for a change. They were not the guard duty type soldier. They were trained for combat and that is what they wanted to do. They arrived at the Congressional buildings in time to hear some of the members debating a new bill that had been introduced. Cathal was enthralled by the words being used by Representatives which would eventually become the law of the land for everyone without a ruler or King being involved. Mary whispered to Dan asking him, *"Is this what the war was all about?"* Dan looked at her bewildered and didn't know what to say. He thought to himself, *there has to be more to it than this.*

When he began looking around the room, he saw Andrew Jackson. It didn't take him long to get his attention and when he did, Andrew came to the family with arms outstretched to embrace the General. "Two Dan" and Cathal recalled being with him when he was a blacksmith. Dan looked at Andrew saying, "You have come a long way since North Carolina." Andrew said, "With much gratitude to you for providing the money and prayers for the journey." Dan said, "It appears you have given a good account of yourself with the Tennesseans sending you to Congress." Andrew said, "General, I am here, but I am not here because I asked to be here. This is not the place for me. This place reminds me of trying to pour honey out of a jar when it's cold. If you remember, the honey comes out real slow. I've had just about all I can take of this part of the new government. I think I need to think about something more active. I'm thinking about being involved in the militia of Tennessee and if I do, I want to be talking with your sons about coming to Tennessee to help me."

Dan asked Andrew, "Are you aware they were born in Tennessee?" Andrew said, "That is hard to believe. What were you doing in Tennessee?" Dan said, "Getting ready to fight the British and send what was left back to England." Andrew said, "I'm thanking you for what you did for all of us. I do not have a very high regard for the British. I am the only survivor in our family. They had a hand in killing all my family, but me." Dan said, "You had better be getting prepared to fight them again. From what I understand, the King is still mad about what he has lost. They will return."

Cathal and "Two Dan" asked Andrew if he was serious about setting up a militia. Andrew said, "I probably will, if both of you will come help me, if I am successful." Cathal said, "You can count on me." "Two Dan" said, "And me too." Cathal began telling him about their Special Force training in Spain. "Two Dan" said, "I don't think our training would be a good fit with conventional combat soldiers." Andrew was quick to respond by saying, "I don't know how to operate a conventional army. I'm from Tennessee. We like to slip up on them, do all the damage we can and run to hide behind a tree." "Two Dan" said, "That's what we know how to do." Andrew asks them what they were doing in the blue uniforms. Cathal said, "We are in the Irish group known as the "Blue Celts," who has the duty of security for President Washington. Andrew said, "You have got your hands full because the Loyalists are still trying to assassinate him." "Two Dan" told him the Blue Celts were aware of the gravity of the responsibility and the risk the President was taking to be around Washington D.C.

Andrew told them he would not seek public office again, because he had been asked to serve as Judge of the Supreme Court. He said, "If I am appointed to that position, I intend to take the job. I will be keeping both of you aware of my whereabouts when I return to Tennessee. Your father told me when I was younger, we may serve together some day." Dan recalled the statement he had made to Andrew when he was a teenager. Cathal and "Two Dan" later told their father they would like to be assigned to Andrew's army, if the need ever arose. Dan told them he knew they would enjoy serving with Andrew.

Andrew did not seek re-election but was again appointed to serve as the Senator from Tennessee, which he agreed to do. As before at the end of one years' service as Senator, he resigned and returned to Tennessee to be appointed Supreme Court Judge. He served in that post until 1804. During his term of office, he was also elected Major General of the Tennessee Militia, a position he held at the beginning of the War of 1812.

As soon as he was promoted to Major General, he contacted Cathal and "Two Dan" to join with him with the rank of Colonel to train and make ready a Brigade of Special Force soldiers for the State of Tennessee. At that time, they made General Jackson aware of the training academy in Spain his father had established. They suggested to General Jackson the cost of training two-hundred-night fighting combat soldiers to be a very expensive adventure. Their suggestions were to keep the troops under the command of their father in the United States military until the need for their service was necessary. General Jackson agreed with his Colonels to keep the militia well trained and affordable for the tax payers. General O'Flaherty assured General Jackson if the need for additional troops arose in Tennessee he would send the force needed from the Special Force Unit under his command.

At that same time, Andrew Jackson became aware of the political power being under the control of a group of self-interest wealthy industrialists who were out of touch with the needs of common ordinary Americans. He began an effort to form a party that focused on the democracy of America. It wasn't long before the term Jacksonion democracy became the name of the new party, later known as the Democrat Party, which included all those who had been ignored by the Republican party.

Dan continued to serve President Washington in every capacity that involved a risk of his assassination. Dan had received a message from personal acquaintances in Ireland, setting forth the intensification of the application of the Penal Laws. The message disclosed Dan's old advisary, British General, Charles Cornwallis had been appointed in June 1798 to serve as both Lord and Commander in Chief of Ireland. As the Parliament and the King continued to annihilate the Irish Catholics, other nations with populations of Catholic believers became aware of the protestant plan to dehumanize the Irish race. A French Revolutionary force landed in Killala Bay in August 1798. When the uprising was quashed, the political climate with regard to Ireland became dominated by the idea of forming a Union of the two Kingdoms, both Irish and Britain under the sovereignty of King George III. The premise for the Union was to improve conditions in Ireland. Cornwallis favored Union but believed for the Union to correct the centuries old problem between the two nations would also require Catholic emancipation which granted basic civil rights to the predominately Roman Catholic populations to create a lasting peace.

When Dan was informed of the political position of General Cornwallis, he felt the possibility of change had finally come to Ireland. Dan sent messages to old acquaintances to do all within their power to assist General Cornwallis in getting the legislation be passed to unify the two nations, if the amendment of emancipation was included.

General Cornwallis was instrumental in the passage of the Act of Union in 1800 by the Irish Parliament, but he and Prime Minister William Pitt were not able to persuade the King to set aside his hatred of the Irish Catholic people. The difference of opinion led to the fall of Pitts government. Cornwallis was also reassigned. However, the atrocities and sectarian violence witnessed by Cornwallis left a mark on him. He learned even when he attempted to provide amnesty to the rebels, court martials continued to be held in the field by soldiers under his command. Cornwallis began the requirement of his personal review of all sentences issued by the courts to ensure that justice was consistently applied to the captured rebels. The hatred for Catholics was prevalent among the British command. Executions continued without disclosing the sentences to General Cornwallis for review. He later wrote in his memoirs, "My service in Ireland comes up to me of a perfect misery."

When Dan heard of the failure of emancipation to be included in the Act of Union, he knew there would come another day soon, when the Irish could again avenge the suffering of his people. He looked forward to the day to settle the score between the two nations. Toward the end of President Washington's second term, Dan was called to meet with the President at Mt. Vernon. The President inquired of Dan the status of his family members and Dan gave him an update on each one. When the President had completed the second term of office, he told Dan, he for the first time had control of the remaining days of his life. Dan reminded the President their enemies view your life as the only reason the colonies, now known as States, remain bound by the Constitution agreement. He told him King George III intends to take over where you leave off at your death. Dan told him, "Mr. President, I intend to remain in your personal service until we are separated by death." The President said, "Dan, there is no wonder we defeated the British with the kind of loyalty and dedication the Irish and Scottish displayed while serving this nation." From the day President Washington exited Washington D.C., the Blue Celts remained as his personal guard.

When the winds shifted to the northwest in the first few days of December, the retired President, in the typical style of farmers throughout the region, began to make ready for the change of weather conditions to fall, with the probability of being exposed to the cold weather. He summoned Dan to ride with him to evaluate the preparations that were being made for winter. They began their ride toward the fields to make certain most of the late harvesting had been completed. That particular year, he had planted an abundance of corn in early spring and mid-summer. The weather had allowed for the planting of a fall crop. The riders began the supervisory tour after the fog had cleared in mid-morning. The President thought there may be a few hours to allow them to escape the wet rain. At mid-afternoon, as they were completing their ride, the weather shifted from a light snow to hail. They found a grove of half-grown oaks to shelter the horses and themselves. Within a short while, the hail became a bone chilling rain. When they arrived at Mr. Vernon, their clothes were soaked to the skin. Because of his stern belief in punctuality, Washington decided to remain in his wet clothes. The heat in the dining room was such the upper part of his body was warm, but the lower part of his body remained cold, because of no air circulation.

The next morning, he developed a sore throat. With lighthearted disregard, he and Dan went to a wooded area to select trees for removal. Throughout the day, his voice became hoarser. He habitually read the news to his secretary, Tobias Lear and wife, Martha, but that evening he could not complete the reading because of a severe sore throat.

During the night, he awoke in extreme discomfort. Martha was alarmed and wanted to send for help. Washington would not allow her to leave his bedside because she was recovering from a cold herself. As the cook arose to light the fire at daybreak, she was told to contact Tobias Lear who rushed to his room immediately after being notified. Lear sent for George Rawlins an overseer at Mr. Vernon who bled him at the request of George Washington. Lear also sent for Dr. James Craik, the family doctor who was Washington's trusted friend and family doctor for forty years. Dan had soon been contacted and went to the bedside of his President and friend.

While they were waiting, Doctor Rawlins extracted a half-pint of blood at the President's request. Martha objected to the treatment however, he favored the treatment because it had improved his condition many times during his life time for numerous other ailments. While waiting, Washington was given a mixture of molasses butter and vinegar to sooth his throat. The mixture was hard to swallow which caused him to convulse and nearly suffocate.

When Dr. Craik had not arrived timely, he requested Tobias Lear to send for the second doctor, Dr. Gustavus Brown of Port Tobacco. Dr. Brown was a physician that Dr. Craik felt had an excellent reputation for diagnosis and moderate medicating.

Dr. Craik finally arrived and by examining and produced a blister on Washington's throat, in an attempt to balance the fluids in his body. Dr. Craik bled Washington a second time and ordered a portion of vinegar and sage tea. Dr. Brown had not yet arrived causing Dr. Craik to send for the third physician which indicated the seriousness of the ailment. At noon, an enema was administered, but the President's health continued to fail. Again, for the fourth time, he was bled for a total of 32 ounces of blood was extracted during the bleeding procedure.

Following that procedure, Dr. Craik administered an emetic to induce vomiting, resulting in nothing beneficial. As the friends, servants and family gathered at his bedside, his conditioned worsened. Washington called Martha to his bedside and asked her to bring his two wills from his study. After reading the wills, he discarded one which Martha burned.

George Washington then called for Tobias Lear. He told Lear, "I find I am going, my breath cannot last long. I believed from the first the disorder would prove fatal. I want you to arrange and record all my late military letters and papers. Arrange my accounts and settle my books, as you know more about them than anyone else, and let Mr. Rawlins finish recording my other letters, which he has begun"

At five in the afternoon, George Washington got up from bed, dressed, and walked to his chair. Within thirty minutes, he returned to his bed. He told Dr. Craik, "Doctor, I die hard, but I am not afraid to go. I believed from my first attack I would not survive it; my breath cannot last long." Soon afterward, he thanked all three doctors for their service. He then asked to hold the hand of his most trusted soldier, General Dan O'Flaherty. When he looked up at Dan, his eyes were as bright as they were on the days of their hardest fought battles. He said, "Dan, whatever flows from my passing, whether gratitude for heroes' deeds performed or any and all forms of honor, you and I know there was one reason I continued to stand when I should have fallen. That reason was because you were by my side. I will carry the treasure of your heart with me to the throne of God as I await your arrival. I ask you to continue to protect my family as you have done for me. May God Bless your soul and the souls of all the Scots-Irish whose sacrifice has allowed freedom to weep no more."

George Washington asked that he be, "Decently buried, and not let my body be put into the vault in less than three days after I am dead." Between ten and eleven at night on December 14, 1799, George Washington passed away. He was surrounded by the people who were close to him, including his wife who sat at the foot of the bed, his friends, Dr. Craik and Tobias Lear, house maids, Caroline, Molly and Charlotte and his valet, Christopher Sheels who stood in the room throughout the day and his most trusted and admired soldier, General Dan O'Flaherty. On December 18, 1799, a solemn funeral was held at Mt. Vernon. (31) After the funeral, Dan told Mary, he had a mind to be alone.

CHAPTER THIRTY

LIFE'S CELEBRATION

As Dan reflected back on the days of being a prisoner of war as the result of his capture during the Jacobite War, he thought of how his life had been directed by an unseen and hidden sprit that seemingly appeared to provide the best path for him to take, even though the path that led him to become a prisoner of war would not have been his choice. The path led him to the oversight of British General James Oglethorpe, who was the originator of the Colony of Georgia. The relationship with General Oglethorpe led him to become the Commanding officer of the Rangers which eventually became the core group for the Blue Celts. General Oglethorpe had organized the Rangers to protect the settlers of the Georgia Colony from the invasion of Spain from the Spanish held peninsula of Florida. That decision allowed him to request his adoptive father, General Phillip O'Shea, who had great influence and standing to persuade the King of Spain to enter a peace treaty with England to end the Seven Year War. General Oglethorpe was very close friends with George Washington who became the military leader of the Continental Army. He introduced George Washington to Dan O'Flaherty. When the Revolutionary War began Dan was promoted to General of the Special Forces because he had the knowledge necessary to train a combat unit that could affect the plans of the British Army. Because of his close and respected relationship with General Washington, General O'Flaherty used his great wealth to provide money to pay the Continental Army troops.

Dan also reflected upon having established a spy network in New York City that provided information to General Washington regarding British General Cornwallis troop movements at Yorktown, Virginia. That critical information allowed General Washington to cause the British to surrender.

Dan pondered the series of great relationships that grew out of seeming despair and developed into his relocating his parents and siblings in America where they had been enslaved by the British Empire for sale to the highest bidder. As he considered each monumental step of what appeared to be circumstance, he saw how nothing, but the spirit of the living God could have provided the light, when darkness covered his world. It was a time of gratitude to God for him being so blessed and selected to be of service in the different capacities he had served. But, the one gift above all other that kept him blessed at all times was, Mary. She was the answer to prayer he did not have the wisdom to pray, and for her he was eternally grateful. She had given him a taste of heaven while still on earth. She had given birth to three of the most outstanding children any father could have ever hoped.

After he had recounted some of his greatest blessings, he knew he would miss his good friend, President George Washington. He was prepared to confront life without his friend and leader, but he knew he had to continue his fight for freedom. He did not think the new President would deem his service as vital as President Washington. Nevertheless, he had determined his troops would provide the security for Mrs. Washington as long as she felt it was necessary. Mrs. Washington had told him privately she did not think she would be able to do without his security. He had assured her he would always be available. Dan had discussed the continued security for the Washington family with General John Milledge, who agreed to provide the services so long as Mrs. Washington requested the protection.

Dan was aware the new President was unaware of the Special Force troops that had been set up with General Washington's approval. Dan felt his service to the new nation as an active General had come to a close because of his age. He met with the President who agreed it would be a good time for him to retire. Prior to his official retirement, Dan transferred approximately 200 Special Force troops to the Tennessee militia as a training group for General Andrew Jackson. His hope was the personnel he transferred would be a core group to form an army should the British attack somewhere from the south or the northwest. He also sent his two sons to Tennessee as United States Army Training officers with the rank of Colonel. When the group arrived, Andrew Jackson was never more satisfied than he was when his militia in Tennessee was recognized by the United States Army as a nucleus for the future to begin a defensive buildup should the British begin again. Mary was on hand when her two sons began leading the soldiers to Tennessee. To her, it was a reminder of when General Dan O'Flaherty led the Blue Celts out of the Appalachian Mountains to join with the Continental Army led by General Washington at the beginning of the Revolutionary War. The Blue Celts were in East Tennessee because the O'Flaherty family had become fugitives from justice after General O'Flaherty and his sister,

Maureen had killed four British soldiers who wrongfully attacked his family prior to the beginning of the war. When Dan had made all the decisions that affected his family members, he decided to retire and become a farmer in Savannah, Georgia.

Before he and Mary decided to leave for Savannah, he wanted to make certain the spy operation in New York was continuing to observe and locate the Loyalists who were at war to undermine the new government. He was certain he had a military man in the army in Washington named, General John Milledge who would become the recipient of the government secrets, as well as being the commander of the participants of the spy operation. Dan had set aside a week, or as long as it took, to put everyone in place to know all each of them knew and to set up a reporting procedure.

When Dan and John Milledge met in Washington, Dan told him he didn't like to talk in rooms, he preferred to be in the outdoors to discuss matters of grave importance. As they walked along together, Dan told John of the entire spy operation. John was completely surprised that Dan would risk his family members to become involved in the welfare of the nation. Dan told John, "This nation has provided us more than we can ever give in return. We are dedicated to the good this nation has provided for the whole world. We learned early in life, freedom is a gift from God and is not to be placed in the hands of other men to design it to suit their desires." John responded by saying, "Since my father died, I have dedicated my life to the services of this nation because of my love, admiration and respect for you. There is no other man I have known whom I have a deep affection for more than you. I will continue to serve you even though you are no longer physically commanding the army. I will assure you Bridget, Maureen and Weston will be protected to the full extent of my ability." Dan said, "John, keep in mind, politicians use secrets as the throne of their power. Be extremely discreet with whom you share names and information. I am beginning to see a group of employees of the government become self-important and it is giving me great concern. Let us be mindful the idea of government we have fought to create is the government of the people. I did not risk my life and treasure for a group of self-indulgent bureaucrats who will do everything they can to form this new government into their own image and for their own welfare. United statism can become worse than a monarchy, especially aristocratic statism. John, do you know what I mean by that term?" John replied, "Not exactly." Dan said, "It in its simplest form is a government of the people, but the will of the people has no effect on the law of the land. The government is actually run by those we have hired to serve the will of the people." Dan had provided John the insight he needed to understand the nature of men. Dan told him the heart of governments is power and money. Only those seeking those two things are involved in the affairs of government. Dan told John to be very sparing with his trust for anyone in government.

After Dan completed his meeting with General John Milledge, he suggested they meet in New York at the mansion occupied by Weston and Maureen. When they arrived, Bridget was so glad to see her father and General Milledge. All of them had been lifetime friends. When the meeting began, Dan told the group he was retiring soon and wanted to select his successor personally. All the family agreed John was the man of choice to maintain the quality and excellence of all the military oversights Dan had put in place. Bridget reported to the group her involvement with Robert Montgomery had become more serious than she had expected, because he had asked her to become his wife. Dan expected that news would be forthcoming. He asked when the wedding was planned. Bridget told them the wedding would be a private matter which meant it could be at any time. Dan told them he would be leaving office in about a month. Bridget said, "We can arrange to meet your time schedule." Since they were all together, Dan wanted Weston to give John an update on the bank and its profit sharing with the government. John was surprised there was a bank that cared enough for the government to share its profits. Dan told John, "It is a long story, I will tell you on our way back to Washington."

After a delicious meal prepared with Maureen's Irish oversight, Dan and John returned to Washington. As they were traveling, Dan told John his intention to return to the O'Flaherty home in Savannah, Georgia. General John Milledge, Jr., was the son of John Milledge who was the most successful Scotsman in the Colony of Georgia. John Jr. had shown an interest in the military when General James Oglethorpe had organized the original Ranger force to protect the settlers from the invading Spanish Army. When Dan was put in charge of the Rangers, John Jr., became the leader of the company. After the treaty with Spain and Great Britain was signed, Dan organized the Blue Celts from the remnants of the Rangers. The Blue Celts consisted of a group of former Scottish and Irish slaves that became the best soldiers in the colony militias and Continental Army. They were known as a Special Force Unit that primarily fought at night and in the daylight hours as snipers. They served as the security force to protect the lives and property of the Washington family and other military officers assigned by General George Washington himself. Dan told General Milledge he was in the process of setting up a plot of ground on the Savannah property as a cemetery for all the Blue Celts and their families. John thanked Dan for being that caring toward all those who served under his command.

The ceremony commemorating Dan's retirement was very discreet as ordered by Dan. It involved those who had served with him. It was a very meaningful ceremony because none of them ever expected anyone of their group would survive the war. Cathal and "Two "Dan" were in attendance. as well as General Andrew Jackson. When the ceremony was completed, General Jackson sat down beside Dan to tell him what an honor it was to serve with his two sons. The General told Dan he could be most proud of his sons and, "They are without flaws." Dan smiled and told General Jackson, "They will serve you well when the next battle begins." General Jackson said, "The battle has begun."

Dan returned to New York to sail to Savannah with his beloved Mary. As they left the harbor, they were waving at their family with hopes to see one another again. The trip was again memories for Dan and Mary to cherish forever. One of the first things Dan did upon arrival in Savannah was to contact Mr. Sharkey their Georgia attorney. He told Mr. Sharkey he wanted to have a survey crew lay out a ten-acre plot around the area where his mother and father were buried for the Blue Celt cemetery, walking distance from their home site.

After all the papers were signed and recorded, Dan and Mary stood by the gate as Dan said, "Mary, my prayer is, we will be the first to occupy this land and not have to bear the sorrow of the loss of our loved ones." Mary replied, "I also pray that same prayer. We have carried our share of sorrow." Dan decided he had been away from work too long and the way to make up for it was to plow a field. He chose a place where his father and mother had planted a garden. Dan enjoyed this time with Mary as they shared memories of their lives together. Their lives had consisted of every joy two people could have ever known. Both had been born under the tyranny of King George II, who had set about to exterminate the Irish race. Their lives had been lived doing everything in their power to free mankind from the rule of a brutal empire. Dan had done everything in his power to erase the scars of humiliation, shame and brutality that had been inflicted on his family.

At the close of each day, he would visit the grave sites of his mother and father to express his gratitude to them for all they had done to try and give the family a good life. He was grateful to them for never losing hope. Dan was so grateful his crop had produced more than he expected. They shared with all their neighbors.

Dan woke up one morning wanting to visit General Oglethorpe's home. He hitched up the wagon and off they rode to a field of memories. When they arrived, they learned the house was occupied by a family that was a distant relative of General Oglethorpe. Dan and Mary introduced themselves and they were welcomed in for a visit. Dan told them his connection with General Oglethorpe and had lived there when the Oglethorpe's occupied the home. As they walked through the home, Mary remembered the birth of their first son, Cathal. When they visited the upstairs, Dan and Mary looked at one another as they saw the second-floor porch where they sat the night of their wedding. They thanked the people for allowing them to visit their memories. Then they visited the original home General Oglethorpe had provided for his family when they were released from the slave prison. Because of Dan's outstanding service preventing the Spanish Army from invading the Georgia Colony, General Oglethorpe had the O'Flaherty family released from prison. The General also allowed the O'Flaherty family to own fifty acres of land, even though they were of the Catholic faith which was prohibited by the Charter issued by King George II.

When they returned to their home, Dan told Mary he was tired, and had developed a pain in his left arm. He decided to take a bath and get some rest, while Mary had the cook prepare a good meal to make him feel better. The two years they had been home had passed so quickly, but they had enjoyed every minute of being with one another. The cook prepared a meal of all Dan's favorite foods. Mary had bathed herself and was ready to eat. She kept waiting for Dan to return to the kitchen. She allowed another twenty minutes to pass before she went to check on him. As she opened the door to the bathroom, a cold chill was in the air. She looked in the tub and it was as if Dan was asleep. She didn't want to wake him, but she could tell there was more involved than sleep. She whispered, "*Dan.*" He didn't answer. She touched his face and then she knew, her Dan had crossed the River Jordan and was waiting for her on the other side. The loss she felt could never be removed. The love of her very existence was not with her any longer. Tears that she expected would flow from her eyes one day began to move toward her heart. She had never known what being alone was until Dan's life had gone out like a candle. She had expected someone to come to her door someday to report his death on the battlefield. She had not thought death would come to separate them during the only peace they had ever known.

She turned and went back to the kitchen to report his death. He had asked her to bury him after three days had passed. She sent messages to her sons in Tennessee and the family in New York and Washington D.C. Mary knew it would take four weeks for all the family and friends to gather. She set April 30th as the date for the ceremony. Savannah had never witnessed a burial ceremony with that many in attendance. A priest directed the service, but when he had completed the Catholic ritual, those who had served with Dan had to say something. Everyone who spoke had something to report concerning how Dan touched their lives. After four hours, no one had left his grave site. Mary and the family joined the others with joyful tales of being with one another. No one wanted to turn him loose and let him rest. Finally, as Mary began to tire, she asks Cathal and "Two Dan" to take her to the house. At sundown, there remained a huge crowd. Mary thought to herself, h*is parents would have been so proud of him.*

Cathal and "Two Dan" got permission from General Jackson to remain with their mother for a while. The General told them to stay as long as they were needed. After the crowd had gone, the next morning they went back to the grave to personally share their father's memory with their gratitude. Bridget said, to herself, f*inding another one like him to respect will never happen again.* Her work in the secret service had taught her how evil men could become. She felt so fortunate the man she married got to know her father because she had the same expectations from Robert Montgomery she was taught to expect from her father. She and Robert had brought the children with them because she wanted them to know everything about her.

Dan kept several horses for riding. The next morning, Bridget suggested they go for a ride. They all agreed. The two boys wanted to ride horses. Bridget told them she and their father could ride with them. They rode, they played they had more fun than they had experienced since their mother died. Sarah asked Bridget if she could ride with her. Bridget asks, "Will you hold on tight?" She said, "Yes mam." They found a grove of oak trees and decided to have a picnic. While they were eating Bridget told them, "This is how I was raised, in the out of doors." Robert told Bridget, "I have missed a lot by growing up in the environment of a city." Bridget said, "Robert it is not too late for us to live in the country. We can move down here and take care of my mother and Weston can run the bank." Bridget was thinking, *how her life had changed from being an undercover spy for the government to an adoptive mother of four children.* Robert was enjoying the spy game. Bridget had grown to love the children and wanted more. Bridget asked her mother if she would like to return to New York with them. Mary told her she didn't want to be far away from Dan. Bridget was able to watch her parents caring for one another most of her life. She knew Mary would never leave his graveside to go anywhere.

Cathal and "Two Dan" had to get back to Tennessee, as word of a British invasion of America became the topic of conversation. Bridget and Robert had begun to become aware of strange faces coming into their New York neighborhood. Robert and Weston were keeping a team of people busy checking out the new people in town. The real secret was, there was talk about spies burning the White House. General John Milledge had increased the number of troops by 400 men because evidence of the Kings ill will toward America continued to fester.

General Andrew Jackson's troops were positioned perfectly in the center of where they should begin which was just outside Memphis, Tennessee. It had become evident the British would not attack from the eastern shores of America. General Jackson sent "Two Dan" to the New Orleans area and Cathal to an area to the northwest in areas which would later become known as Ohio, Indiana, Illinois, Michigan and Wisconsin. Unfortunately, the war had not settled the dispute of which nation the northwest territory would be governed by. As the issue became heated, the British became involved with the many different Indian Tribes that had occupied the frontier by equipping them to fight against the European American settlers. The settlers assumed the land contiguous with the land they had defeated Great Britain to gain was America soil. The British had laid claim to all land known as Canada. Three separate interests came together to assert claims to territory that would eventually become a part of the reason to begin another war. Great Britain wanted to preserve the land north of America known as Canada. The native Indians wanted the northwest territory which comprised the land now known as the states of Ohio, Indiana, Illinois, Michigan and Wisconsin. The land had been ceded by Great Britain to the United States government by Treaty in 1783. Neither party to the agreement recognized the land was occupied by many different tribes of native born Indians. The Indians desire was to create their own nation in the northwest. Two Indian Chief's named Teniskwataws and Tecumseh formed a confederation of numerous tribes to block American expansion. The British supported the Indians because they saw the Indian occupation of the land as a buffer for its Canadian colonies. The British provided all the weapons of war for the Indians to begin attacks on the American settlers. The raids by the Indians slowed the American settlement of the farmland. Julius W. Pratt wrote:

There is ample proof that the British authorities did all in their power to hold or win the allegiance of the Indians of the Northwest with the expectation of using them as allies in the event of war. Indian allegiance could be held only by gifts, and to an Indian no gift was as acceptable as a lethal weapon. Guns and ammunition, tomahawks and scalping knives were dealt out with some liberality by British agents.

The British plan back fired because after every Indian raid, the settlers found evidence of muskets and equipment furnished by the British that caused the death of the settlers. The settlers began an outcry to remove the British from Canada to eliminate the problem with the Indians. Neither Britain or the United States was prepared for another war. The Indians, with weapons supplied by the British, were the only participants that knew exactly what they needed to accomplish. The British did not deem it wise to over supply the Indians with the tools of war because they feared after the defeat of the Americans, the Indians would try to take Canada. But with westward expansion becoming the goal of the settlers, the political pressure became intense for the United States government to fund the money and supplies for protection to settle the land.

Even though it took years of debate, the War of 1812 began with Cathal leading the charge. General Andrew Jackson was sure both regions of potential war were well commanded by the two most outstanding military leaders in America. "Two Dan" had been assigned to a friendlier environment because of his father being adopted by General Phillip and Margarita O'Shea. His adoptive mother was the sister of Governor Bernardo Galvez who was the

Governor of Louisiana and Cuba. Governor Galvez was a very close ally of the colonies during the Revolutionary War. General George Washington held him in the highest regard by asking him to stand to his right at the formal surrender of the British Army. Another patriot, who was held in high regard as a patriot was an Irishman named, Oliver Pollock who was extremely wealthy and had supplied money to the colonies to continue the war against the British. His relatives were prominent citizens in the New Orleans area. General Don O'Riley was another Irishman who was the commander of the Spanish Army of Cuba and New Orleans when Governor Galvez was in command.

"Two Dan" was very aware of being recognized by those who had relationships with his father because he did not want his position revealed which would have caused him to become ineffective as a spy. He knew the British would attack in New Orleans in an effort to control the Big River shipping. All his time was being taken by learning the terrain and advantageous positions for a land battle.

His strategic problem was the massive number of British troops that could and would be shipped to that area being defended with 1 schooner, and 1 sloop-of-war. He knew there would be over 50 ships to transport as many as 10,000 troops. His training and planning would be put to the test. The good news was, he had time to organize because he was aware the politics in Washington did not favor another expensive military campaign.

CHAPTER THIRTY-ONE

MARY BELLE

When "Two Dan" got back to the New Orleans area after his father's funeral he wanted time alone to consider the blessing of being the son of a man named O'Flaherty and a woman named O'Malley. His hope and prayer was to find a lady of his mother's likeness who knew the meaning of enduring. His thoughts drifted to how it must have been for them to suffer the hatred of the British Empire. His father and mother did not dwell on the abuse they had suffered. They did whatever it took to survive and care for their family.

"Two Dan" enjoyed the river. All his experiences with the Big River involved his family moving to Savannah, Georgia to settle after the war. He recalled the catfish and camp fires with all the Blue Celts. He for sure remembered the crossing of the river by ferry boat. He could remember the look of concern his father had while that river crossing was taking place. But now, most of his new time was taken up by looking for anyone who appeared to be out of place. He knew some of the Loyalists were involved in extending their help to spies being shipped into New Orleans from other areas. "Two Dan's" training in Spain by Colonel Longoria was vital for him knowing all there was to know as the nations prepared for conflict.

One of the headquarters for the Tennessee Militia was in Memphis, Tennessee. "Two Dan" received notice from headquarters one of the officers had received an inquiry regarding strangers coming to the Natchez area. The request was for one of the Special Force officers to consider the matter. When Dan received the inquiry, he decided it was time to expand his knowledge of the Big River to the north. The trip would give him time to ponder all those precious memories of being with his father and mother. He missed being with his family which made him wonder if it was time for him to begin considering a family. That thought had never entered his mind before. He thought to himself, *I must be thinking about things like this because I know I will never be with my entire family again.* He laughed at himself thinking, a*nd besides all that, no good woman would put up with someone like me anyhow.*

The next morning, Dan left at daylight for Natchez to get serious about finding British spies or whatever he could find that needed his attention. Scavengering off the landscape was what most people did to survive after the British were defeated in the Revolutionary War.

After the Louisiana Purchase was documented, settlers of many cultures began the settlement of the new land. Trapping animals to be sold for the value of fur was one of the main occupations. Having a set of good traps to catch wild animals was a blessing richly desired by those who did not live in town. In the late 1700's dying was what most people did when an epidemic of smallpox struck a settlement. When it did come, the survivors would move on to another place to avoid death's reach. One such survivor was named, Trapper John.

There was a small creek flowing close to their cabin he had built from logs. John had hewed the lumber from the standing timber in the lowlands of the South Louisiana swamps. He chose that location, to trap what he could from the small pickings available at that time. Always referred to as Trapper John, he was known for minding his own business and expected everyone else to live by the same rule. Existence is all he, his wife and two children ever expected from life because every generation before them had the same expectation. He liked trapping in the south because there was a broader market for different kinds of pelts from coon to beaver.

Even as secluded as they were at times, an Indian would stop by while hunting to mooch a bite of cornbread and for sure, a taste of salt bacon. As he looked back at the tragedy that struck his family one morning, he recalled his wife telling him of two Indians coming by from the Snake tribe looking for a bite of food.

When his wife complained of high fever, he knew they had infected his family with smallpox. His wife and two children passed on in two weeks. He burned the cabin and their bodies and set out for Natchez on the Mississippi River. It was not that he had a certain destination in mind, it was he needed to move away from the sorrow from his family's death. The closest settlement to his cabin was Abbeville. He went by the trading post to tell Sam Cormier he was moving on. Sam told him he would be missed.

After the visit, he headed out for Natchez on his way to Missouri. Some other trappers had told him the trapping was good on the creek south of St. Louis on the river. It wasn't that he was bound for anywhere, it was just somewhere to go. As he quietly moved through the wooded areas, he was mindful of needing food for the day. He had some salt bacon and some syrup he had traded for in Abbeville. After several days and nights of mourning his loss, it seemed like the hurt would get worse at sundown every day. The next morning, he would wake up, start over and head north.

One day, as he was easing through the timberland looking for a squirrel or two, the wind was blowing out of the northeast. He began hearing a sound which was strange to his ears. He began to think, *he was wheezing, maybe had a cold coming on.* The more he walked, the closer he came to recognizing the sound as that of a child crying. He picked up his pace even though he was in a yaupon thicket and couldn't see more than ten feet in front of himself. He knew he could find the source of the sound if he could get out of the thicket. He finally managed to find a deer trail that led to the northside of the grove. When he reached the clearing, he caught another sound fainter than it was previously.

When he reached the sound, he was correct. There lay a dead mule that was hitched to a small wagon that contained two dead people, one man and one woman. They had obviously died of smallpox. The sound he heard was from a young girl that appeared to be close to six years old. The little girl with blue eyes was sitting there on a log, as if she was waiting for Trapper John to come along.

John knew what he had to do, but he didn't want to set fire to everything with her looking at him. He took the girl back to the thicket and left her while he set fire to the wagon and its contents. When the fire was roaring because of the lard he left in the wagon, he gathered the child and headed for a creek. When he found water, he put her in it to get as much pox off her as he could while wondering what on this side of heaven he was going to do with a child. The little girl kept watching Trapper John do what he had to do to get ready to move on.

While he was bathing the smell off himself and the child, he thought of pouring some syrup in a wet rag to give the child a sugar tit to suck on, until he could find dry wood to build a fire to fry some bacon. What he was really hoping to find was a goat to give her some milk to drink. After they had settled on syrup and bacon for supper, Trapper John took off his buckskin jacket and wrapped her, as he made a pallet for her to lie on. He was close to tired, and Miss whatever was her name, was tired too, but was enjoying having been rescued by Trapper John.

The next morning, Trapper John knew he had to pick up the pace to get her to someone to take care of her. At the end of the fourth day, he could tell he was approaching Natchez, because the trail was clearer. It took until nearly sundown to reach the river. There was a ferry for the crossing but would only cross during daylight hours. Several other people gathered before dark to wait for the morning ferry. While waiting, Trapper John asks all of them if they knew of any of their kin they were expecting to meet at the ferry from Louisiana. No one responded to his inquiry.

As the sun rose the next morning, Trapper John was anxious to get medical care for the orphan girl. The ferry boat owner told Trapper John to go to the trading post to get his questions answered, and he did say there was a doctor in town. After locating the doctor's office, he told the doctor he had found the girl in the woods. John told him of his personal tragedy and he had no way to care for the child. The doctor told him the best advice he could give him was to report it to the Sheriff.

The Sheriff of Natchez, Mississippi was a caring person and he recommended he talk to some of the church house preachers. After

Trapper John had paid the doctor and fed the child, his money was almost gone. He needed traps and groceries to go on to Missouri and didn't have enough money for either one. The only hope he had was to go to the trading post owner and try to trade for traps and groceries on the credit. He hoped the trading post owner was someone who would lend a hand to his needs.

The exact opposite of all he had hoped for began to become the truth. The trading post owner reminded him of a squirrel that had crawled out of his hole backwards. There was not one hair on him that looked like it was growing in the right direction. He acted like his mama had fed him sour milk on his first birthday. He wasn't just putting up a front, he was a man that was mean to the bone, at least that's what he wanted everyone to think.

When Trapper John had finished surveying the trading post, he had located just about everything he needed, except tobacco. When the other customers had thinned out, Trapper John started trying to tell Cale Brown, the trading post owner, the trail of misery he had walked since he lost his family. Most anyone would have been shaken by the sorrow that had struck Trapper John's life. Not so with Cale, because he had become conditioned to tales filled with tears since the smallpox epidemic had begun two years before. When Trapper John saw there was not going to be any help coming from Cale Brown, he asked him how many kids he had. Trapper John could tell he had asked a question that caught Cale's interest. Cale asked, "Why do you want to know?" Trapper John revealed to him having found the girl in the woods where he also found what appeared to be her parents and a dead mule still hitched to a wagon. He told Cale he had been feeding her syrup, berries and salt bacon, but she was needing some milk. Cale asks, "Where is she?" Trapper John went outside and found her sitting where he told her to stay. He took her hand and led her to meet Cale Brown, the trader. She walked in behind Trapper John and peeked out from behind his left leg to see who it was she was going to meet. Cale had sat down in a cowhide bottom chair waiting to see a surprise. He saw her hiding behind Trapper John's leg. He didn't want to make her afraid of him by talking in his loud gruff tone. He said, "Sweetheart, are you hungry?" She said, "Yes sir!" He then asked her, "Do you want some candy?" She said, "I am hungry for bread and meat and a great big bean!" Cale got up and went to the back door of the trading post and talked to his wife, Molly.

Both returned to discuss business with Trapper John. John wanted both of them to know he had no connection with the child, other than having found her in the midst of a tragedy. He explained his loss to Mrs. Brown and the fact he had to do the only thing he knew how to do, which was trap animals and sell the fur. Mrs. Brown told the trapper she had not been able to bear children without them dying a few days after birth. He told Mrs. Brown it sounded to him like she needed some company. Mrs. Brown started trying to talk with the child by asking her to come go with her to eat some meat and some beans. The child said, "I want a big bean." Mrs. Brown took her hand as they went to the back of their house.

After they had been gone over an hour, they returned. Mrs. Brown had given her a bath which included a good head scrubbing. When Trapper John and Cale Brown saw the child, they couldn't believe she was the same person. Mrs. Brown told her husband to give Trapper John what he needed, because she wanted the child to stay with her. Trapper John said, "I never even asked her name, did she tell you her name?" Mrs. Brown told him her name is, "Mary Belle." Trapper John said, "Now, if that ain't the prettiest name I ever heard." Mrs. Brown told Cale to give Trapper John $20.00 for traveling money for the joy he had brought to their place. Trapper John said, "Mam, ya'll have already helped me more than you should have, but I am deeply indebted to you for what ya'll have done." Mrs. Brown said, "You have brought the joy to our lives that we have been waiting on, for over ten years. I needed company, and you brought it to me." Trapper John said, "I don't know anyone that has a claim on her, but I do hope she becomes the joy you have been waiting for." Mrs. Brown said, "She will be, and don't you forget to come by and check on her when you pass this way again." Trapper John said, "I can't wait to see how this turns out." When Trapper John started for the door, Mary Belle wrapped her arms around his leg to hug him goodbye. She looked up at him, as a tear ran down her cheek and said, "Thank you for helping me, I won't forget you." Trapper john squatted down and held her as they shared the memories of the loss of their loved ones. He said, "I'll be back to see you soon." Mary Belle said, "I'll be looking for you." She stood outside the trading post and watched Trapper John until he disappeared into the forest.

The sun was on its way to hide while the newly formed Brown family was deciding which bed their new member would like best. Each breath Molly breathed was a breath of new life that had come to her, not by accident, but by prayers she had prayed for years to have a child she could love with her whole heart. Through the years, she and Cale had committed themselves to working the trading post for a living. They had lost hope for a life with children, because every time they felt their hopes would be realized with the next child, the child would die. Their hearts had become broken so many times, they had become numb for one another, numb to caring for, or about anything.

Molly and Cale decided to talk to a lawyer to make certain they were doing the right thing. The attorney advised them to allow the child to live in their home for at least one year to make certain other relatives did not assert a claim to the child. He advised them they needed time to decide whether they wanted to adopt a child whose background was unknown. They took the lawyers advise and began to treat Mary Belle as their own child.

As each day passed, they became fonder of one another. The Cale Brown crusty, loud taking, uncaring, brash, know it all began to disappear before Molly and Mary Belle's eyes. He was an early riser and so was Mary Belle. They began a ritual of visiting with one another in the early mornings. He would warm Mary's milk and put a touch of coffee and sugar to make her feel big. As time passed, she learned to make biscuits, which she would cook for Cale every morning before Molly would wake up. After a while, Mary Belle and Cale became closer and closer. He asked her if she knew how old she was. Mary Belle replied, "Not exactly, but I do know my birthday is February 10th. Cale asked her if she ever had a birthday party. Mary Bell told Cale her daddy was very poor, they worked for other people and had never had a home. Cale said, "Well, you do now." Mary Bell said, "Mr. Brown what would you like for me to call you?" Cale asked her, "What would you like to call me?" She said, "Would you mind if I thought about it for a while before I answer, because I want it to be right." Cale said, "That sounds good to me."

It wasn't long before Cale, Molly and Mary Belle were working together in the trading post. They began to see Mary Belle was a very bright young lady, who had a way with people. Molly and Cale became concerned about Mary Belle's education, so they enrolled her in the Natchez school. She began making good grades and within a short while, she was being requested by the students to help them with their studies. Mary Belle was admired by all the students; the teacher suggested Mary Bell assist her in teaching the more difficult courses. Mary Bell enjoyed the math classes more than the other classes, which caused her to be the best math student in her grade. It seemed Mary Belle was going to like living with Mr. and Mrs. Brown.

After more than a year had passed, Molly decided to talk with Mary Belle about becoming their adoptive daughter. When Molly said that to Mary Belle, she began to have tears in her eyes. Molly said, "Mary Belle, I wouldn't hurt you for anything, I am sorry I mentioned it." Mary Belle said, "Oh No, I am not sad, it is because you have made me so happy!" Molly put her arms around Mary Belle's neck and gave her a big hug while she was saying, "You have made me so happy. I do not know what I would have done if you had not come to live with us." By that time, Cale had wondered, *what they were talking about.* He joined them as Molly told Cale, "Mary Belle has agreed to become our daughter." It was a hard thing for Cale to manage a smile before Mary Belle arrived, but after she had been with him every morning before daylight for more than a year, smiling seemed to come to him naturally.

Brown's Trading Post was not the only trading post in Natchez. There were two others that gave the Brown's a run for their money. Mary Belle had felt the breach between the competitors. She had a deep-seated belief in making friends out of enemies. By the time the competitors had eaten dozens of Mary Belle's now famous biscuits, it was hard to find anyone that didn't have good things to say about the Brown family.

Being in the trading business had its advantages. Mary Belle had learned from the local baker about a magic thing called, yeast. She became well acquainted with the baker who loved having Mary Belle around because when other people saw her there, they would come to talk to her and buy cookies and something called dough cakes. The baker loved Mary Belle so much, she let Mary Belle help her and eventually taught her the secret of baking the wonderful rising dough with yeast.

As time passed, Mary Belle had learned that fresh cooked pastry, cookies, dough cakes and biscuits was a drawing card for the family business. She and Molly always kept fresh cookies for the customers. It didn't take long before the news of Mary Belle's cookies, dough cakes and biscuits were known all along the River. Mary Belle continued to rise early to be with Cale to drink their coffee together. One morning, Cale asked her if she had enjoyed living on the river. Mary Belle said, "Daddy, I never knew life could be so good. I thank God for you and Molly allowing me to be your only daughter. Cale said, "Mary Belle, I need to tell you something, but it has to be a secret between you and me." Mary Belle said, "OK, what is it?" Cale said, I think we are going to have another baby." Mary Belle was very surprised. She was accustomed to being the only child, but she told her dad, "I will share you with whatever it is, girl or boy."

As the months quickly passed, Molly knew she would eventually tell Mary Belle about the baby, but she wanted to put it off as long as she could. Finally, when it became obvious that Molly was gaining weight, she told Mary Belle she was going to have a brother or sister. Mary Belle was so full of joy, because she wanted to have someone in the family for her to help care for.

When the time came for the birth, the doctor told them it was not going to be easy. As the procedure began, the doctor determined it would be a breach birth. The doctor stayed with Molly for fourteen hours. When he began to see Molly's life leave her body, he told Molly it was either her life or the baby's life. Molly chose to let the baby live. The doctor called Cale and Mary Belle to Molly's bedside. Molly took Mary Belle by the hand and told her how much she loved her. She told Mary Belle to raise the baby to be a Christian believer in Jesus Christ, like she was. Mary Belle told her of her love and she would take care of the family and raise the baby right. Cale held one hand and Mary Belle held the other, as the doctor delivered a healthy baby boy. When the delivery was completed, Molly closed her eyes for the last time.

Molly was born in a settlement south of Natchez and was well known and loved by everyone, but when Mary Belle came into her life, she became happier than she had ever been before. Molly loved her family, but because of the great sorrow, she and Cale had suffered, they had become hardened by the daily burdens of life. Mary Belle's presence in her life had caused their good spirits to come alive.

After the funeral, Cale was totally devastated. Molly was the only woman who had ever seen a worth in Cale. Without her he would have spent his life in isolation and if he had come to town, he would have been known as a rabble rouser that stayed in trouble with the law. But that precious, sweet spirit of Molly had to some extent curbed his proclivity to be totally repulsive.

Mary Belle took the baby to her room and traded for a baby bed that her daddy place by her bedside. She remembered Trapper John had told her goats milk was the best milk for new born babies. They continued their same routine of early rising and steady baking good cookies to attract new customers. The business began to really flourish. One morning, while Cale and Mary Belle were readying for the day, she asks her daddy if he had heard about the new mint that had been built in Philadelphia. Cale was not exactly one to keep up with the happenings in other places. He was focused on what was happening in his trading post, and nothing else.

Mary Belle had a knack for knowing what was important and she knew hard money was going to become more valuable than paper money. She had seen it took a whole lot more paper money to buy something than hard money, because hard money had more value.

While they were drinking their coffee one early morning, Mary Belle told her daddy, "We are going to do two things today, one of which is, we are going to name my brother. The other one is, we are not going to accept paper money anymore for payment of goods." Cale asked Mary Belle if she had a notion about what to call him. Mary Belle said, "You haven't ever asked me, and I have never told you that my family's last name was Harrison. Her daddy asked, "Are you thinking about calling him Harris?" Mary Belle said, "We will probably call him Harris, but Harry is a good name, and I loved my mama and daddy. His name will make me think of them every time I say it." Cale said, "That sounds good to me. Now about this paper money, what did you mean about switching to hard money?" Mary Belle said, "Paper money is going to buy less and less goods for what is printed on the paper. Gold and silver will never be of less value that what is stamped on the coin. There will come a day when we can buy more for half of what someone pays in paper money, if we have hard money." Cale didn't understand a word of what his God sent treasure, Mary Belle had just told him, but she said it and that made it law to him.

It seemed as if everything around their lives began to grow and blossom. Harry had reached the age of being able to hit his thumb with a hammer. One morning while the three of them were making ready for the day Harry asked, "When do I get a bed to sleep on?" Mary Belle was so committed to taking care of him and watching over him while he slept, she hadn't paid attention to him being old enough to sleep by himself. Mary Belle took him to town with her to trade for him a bed of his own. That was the first step Harry was able to take toward manhood. Mary Belle made certain Harry was going to be a Christian just like his mama, Molly. But, she did not depend on church house preaching to take the place of being home taught about Jesus.

One-day Harry asked, "Where is Jesus?" Mary Belle answered, "In your heart," Harry asked, "Why is he there?" Mary Belle said, "He stays there all the time, to keep you from doing bad. He is your conscience that hurts when you do wrong." Harry asked Mary Belle, "What is the worst wrong?" Mary Belle said, "It is the one that is easiest for us to do." Harry asked, "What is that?" She said, "Telling a lie." Mary Belle said, "Harry, the most important thing you will ever learn is to never, never tell a lie, because the truth will always be known." Mary Belle said, "You see that piece of rope hanging on that nail?" Harry said, "Sure do." Mary Belle said, "That is not new rope, is it?" Harry said, "No!" Mary Belle said, "If it was new rope, we could make more money for it, couldn't we?" Harry said, "Yes." Mary Belle said, "If you took some lye soap and washed that rope it would look new, wouldn't it?" Harry said, "Yes, and we could sell it for more money." Mary Belle said, "Harry, no matter how clean the rope is, it will always be old rope." Harry said, 'But they would never know it." Mary Belle said, "But, you would and that is what counts. God will not bless a greedy, lying man. It may look like he is blessed, but he is not. A second-hand rope will get someone hurt if they are needing a new rope. Don't ever cheat anyone and God will bless you even if you don't get paid by the man that bought the rope from you." Harry said, "Mary Belle, do you really think I'm gonna remember all of this." Mary Belle said, "You will Harry because I will never let you forget it."

They continued to work hard, do right by everyone and their trading post prospered. It would have been difficult to improve the blessings God was continuing to give them until one day while Cale was in the trading post by himself talking to a man who had come to rob him. Cale saw the pistols pointed straight at his heart and he heard the gun snap which told him the cap did not fire. He reached for the man's hand that held a knife which he plunged into Cale's heart. The robber ran back to his boat. Mary Belle ran next door to the other trading post and told the man they had been robbed. Mary Belle told him he was getting away. The man loaded his gun, stepped out on the boat dock and put a musket ball between the robber's shoulder blades. The man fell forward in his boat. Other onlookers paddled out and pulled the boat to the dock.

Mary Belle asked for someone to go to town to get the doctor. When the doctor arrived, it was too late. Cale was dead from the knife wound to his heart. There was an out pouring of grief for Cale's death, while grieving for the bleak future of two children left alone to make a way for themselves. Mary Belle was most grateful to everyone for their concern. She told each person she would be back in touch with them when she had made up her mind about what to do. She said, "However, the trading post would remain open, until I make up my mind." Mary Belle knew it was a part of being human for others to take advantage of those who were in peril. But, Cale had taught her every detail of the trading business. She learned the art of doing business her way.

Early the next morning, she was drinking coffee with Harry to get him involved in getting grown in a hurry to give her some help to keep them from going to an orphan's home. She told Harry they needed to get a guardian to keep someone from getting themselves appointed to steal their business. She also told Harry, "We need to get a lawyer to draw up some papers." She closed the trading post for a week to mourn Cale's' passing and to give the vultures time to get ready to start picking their bones clean.

She went back to the lawyer who had taken care of her adoption. She told him she would pay him a fee each month to be their guardian. She also told him she did not need for him to do anything but keep thieves from stealing their business. She was aware of at least two more who had tried to buy the business from Cale. She knew they would be back. The attorney, Ben Hammock, was most capable to provide Mary Belle and Harry the protection they needed to continue their business.

CHAPTER THIRTY-TWO

ADVENTURING

It didn't take Mary Belle but two weeks to become a Prophetess as to the town vultures pretending to be concerned about her and Harry's welfare to begin their inquiry about the status of Mary Belle and Harry's future. The first inquiries were, the ever-predictable bank president, named, Mr. Ben Hammock, who was known as the king vulture of the county. He brought Mary Belle and Harry a box of groceries with plenty of sweet treats as an opener of his Christian concern for their welfare. Mary Belle had trained Harry well to keep his mouth shut and let her do the talking when people showed concern for them.

Mary Belle let Mr. Ben Hammock do all the talking. She pretended not to understand any of his questions. She did offer him some of her cookies and dough cakes. She made him some coffee and made him feel welcome. He stayed long enough to interfere with her taking care of at least four customers. Two of them had dropped by just to get a cookie.

About one week later, the undertaker named, Jeremiah Swooper, came by to check on them. The thing Mary Belle detested about him was he was one of those double dip vultures, meaning, he didn't just wait to make money off putting someone's body in the ground, he was waiting to get all he could of what they left on top of the ground.

Mary Belle thanked God every day for Cale and Molly for not only taking her in but training her how to survive in the mass of greed in the business world. But she had to admit to herself now and then she enjoyed the games of manipulation and deceit. The two assets she and Harry had was there wasn't anything on earth they wanted except what God had given them and the other was, they appeared to be helpless children that could be taken advantage of by anyone.

Mary Belle knew how good she was at the trading game. She used her skills to accomplish two things, one, for the seller to be satisfied, two, for the buyer to be satisfied with the bargains that was agreed upon. All the fur traders preferred to take their pelts to Mary Belle over anyone else, because they could depend on her word. Mary Belle could see a bright future for the trading business up and down the big river. What she and Harry had to do was figure out how to stay out of an orphan's home and be able to keep their money. As time passed, the bank president got impatient and decided to make a run at purchasing the trading post.

He went by to talk to Mary Belle on a Monday morning. which was usually a slow day on the river. Mary Belle was courteous and respectful. She had Harry wait on customers while she did the talking. Mr. Hammock got right to the point by offering Mary Belle $1,000.00 for the trading post and their home. He told her he would sign a note to pay her $200.00 a year for five years but he needed to check her books and records first. Mary Belle told Mr. Hammock he knew she was not old enough to understand one word of what he was saying, because she was too young to know what was best for her and Harry.

She continued telling him what she knew for sure was the trading post provided them a place to stay and plenty to eat and that was all they wanted. The one good thing Mary Belle had done was not put money in any banker's bank because they would know too much of her business. Mr. Hammock told her there was a big concern in town for their welfare and all he was trying to do was make sure nobody took advantage of them. Mary Bell told him she was deeply grateful for his concern and he would be the first person she would contact if she needed help. Mr. Hammock seemed satisfied to leave the conversation at what she said, because he felt like she trusted him and that was what she wanted him to believe. She couldn't offend him because he had friends at the courthouse that could hurt her and Harry by taking their business. She made up her mind she was going to appear dumb and grateful. She knew she owned one of the best businesses in town and she didn't want to lose it. She had put Mr. Hammock in a good position by telling him he had the first chance of getting the place if she decided to sell. He couldn't tell anyone else because they would also try to buy the place. What Mary Belle needed more than anything was to come of age.

One morning, she had a thought she needed to talk to over with her lawyer. She wondered, if *there was any way to have the minority restrictions removed from her doing business*. The attorney told her there is a law that the minority capacity can be removed under certain circumstances. Mary Belle asked him if she qualified to have the restrictions removed. The attorney told her how much he admired her because of her willingness, knowledge and ability to manage a business the size of the trading post and raise a child at the same time. He told her he would try his best to get the judge to remove the restrictions.

Mary Belle told him she couldn't ask for more than that and thanked him in advance for all he had done and was doing.

The judge had the attorney file the request who was also an admirer of Mary Belle and really didn't need much of an explanation because he knew from his own personal knowledge she was a most capable young lady and was wise enough to ask for help if she needed it and knew who to ask for help.

After all the papers were signed, Mary Bell and Harry made a special trip to the courthouse with a big plate of dough cakes and cookies. To sum up the meeting, the judge told her she was the most admired young lady in Natchez, and certainly the most industrious. Mary Bell left the courthouse feeling a lot better, because she was uncertain about any one in town even knowing her, but she was glad at least one important person knew her. Harry was glad he went to town. He had never been to a town in his life. Mary Belle told him they needed to go to town more often to be reminded of how much better they have it on the river than the town people did living in town.

Mary Belle told Harry they had a decision to make soon, because the work had increased so much, they needed help. Mary Belle had been watching a young man about her age whose father had lived with a Cherokee squaw. It was very apparent he was born of that woman. The family did business with the Snake Indians who became infected with the smallpox. The boy's mother and father died of smallpox. The young man grew to be a huge man, over six feet five inches tall and as strong as a bull. Mary Belle had watched him grow up and he had always treated her with deep respect. She had noticed he was not as good a trapper as his father and his production of pelts had left him basically without adequate food. She knew he was due to come in soon and she wanted to talk to him first, because she needed protection as well as a strong back.

She was right, in about two weeks, he came in with less than half of what he needed to buy food to last for a while. Mary Belle asked him if he had time to talk about work. He told her he was very interested in a job because he was tired of the woods for a while. He told her the number of trappers numbered more than the beavers. He said, "It is time for me to learn something new." Mary Belle told him she had a place for him to stay and she was a good cook. He told her he was ready when she was. She said, "How about now?" He asked, "What do I need to do first." She said, "All the last week pelts are hanging from the big oak in the back. They need to be sorted and graded to make ready for the two buyers who will be here Tuesday. He told her he would have them ready. She said, "One more thing, I have a brother and he needs to know how to be a man. He is yours to train. I don't like sissies. Make a man out of him. Oh yeah, what is your name?" He said, "I am half Cherokee, my white name is, Sam Pollock." Mary Belle asked him if he had a gun. He told her he had his father's rifle. She said, "Teach Harry how to shoot."

Harry and Sam made a good work force as well as a good defense force. After six months had passed, the relationship between the three of them had developed into trust for one another. They were able to learn an abundance of information from up the river and from down the river. Mary Belle and Sam had begun to notice some pretend trappers and frontiersman that asked way too many questions. Some of the questions they were asking were questions relating to military matters. Sam told Mary Belle he had overheard two of them talking about an invasion of New Orleans with help coming from up river.

Mary Belle made Sam and Harry aware they needed to be very careful about answering any questions because it could be the British are coming back for another war. She told them she knew a man in Memphis, Tennessee that could put her in touch with the right people. She had a trusted friend who would take a message to her contact to get him to come for a visit. It took nearly four weeks to make all the parts to the puzzle fit, but she finally put it together. The man she knew was associated with the Tennessee militia.

A stranger came to the trading post one afternoon asking for Mary Belle. When they were in private, he told her he was from Memphis and was with the Tennessee Militia. After he proved his identity, she disclosed some of the accidental information they had gathered which seemed to her to be of great importance. She asked him if he could take a message to James O'Neal in Memphis. The stranger agreed to take the message and left for Memphis. After two weeks elapsed, a young man dressed in buck skins, looking like a trapper, came by from down river. He introduced himself as Dan O'Flaherty with the Tennessee Militia. He told her he was enlisted with the Army of the United States of America but had become attached to the Tennessee Militia under the command of Major General Andrew Jackson and he was at her service.

After she had fed him some of her cookies and was satisfied Dan was who he said he was, Mary Belle told him she and her brother, Harry, as well as Sam Pollock an employee, had begun to notice total strangers stopping by the trading post asking questions that didn't fit in any other conversation other than a military inquiry. She told him the questions required answers that only military people would know and because of all that, they became suspicious and decided to contact the authorities. Dan told her they had been hearing some rumors like the ones they were hearing. Dan asked her if she could use some help around the trading post. He explained he needed to know more about what was going on. She told Dan they could certainly use the help and she was willing to pay him and feed him as much as he could eat. Dan said, "No mam, I'm on some other payroll. My job is to gather information for the commanding officers to make a decision."

Mary Belle told Dan to make himself a job looking busy and if there was anything suspicious, she would turn it over to him. Dan got busy sorting furs and visiting with the customers when they arrived. After a two-week period, Sam recognized one of the men he had talked to previously, and he motioned for Dan to come closer to listen to what the man had to say. Dan walked close to Sam pretending to need information when the stranger asked Dan how far it was to New Orleans. Dan said, "They tell me, it is a far piece. Why do you ask?" The stranger said he was doing survey work for the government and needed to know the mileage to New Orleans.

Dan knew from the training he had received in the military, he was a spy. Dan felt he had to learn more about the spy to see if there were others learning the landscape to prepare for another war. Rumors of infiltrators and strangers to the communities were being talked by everyone in the river basin from Natchez to New Orleans.

Without telling Mary Belle, Dan had brought a partner with him to the trading post. Dan told his partner to follow the suspect to find the spy's campsite. Dan had become very suspicious there may be Loyalists in the area that was providing the cover for the spies. He told Mary Belle she had done a brave thing by reporting what she had learned timely. Mary Belle told Dan she was glad he came when he did because they had no idea how serious the discovery really was.

Dan wanted to know more about Mary Belle. She told him her entire story from the beginning with Trapper John to the present time. Dan told her his family was living with a Cherokee Indian tribe when he was born along with his twin sister named, Bridget. He told her his father was also named Dan and his family was basically a military family that enlisted to fight for freedom from the tyranny of England. The more they visited, the more they could tell their lives had been a tough road to travel. Dan was interested in how she had learned so much about so many things in the trading business. She told him her adoptive parents were the greatest blessing of her life after she lost her parents. She said, "They blessed me every day I was with them. They were wonderful people. I respected them and that is what made me want to learn." Dan was impressed with how mature Mary Belle was. He thought to himself, t*his is a very wise lady.*

There were so many surprises in Mary Belle's ways that kept everyone wanting to know more about her. She never gave way to pettiness or foolishness. She had learned from experience the presence of God in her life and how deadly serious all the matters of life truly are. She would tell others not to forget, t*his is a day God has made, let us all be glad in it.* Mary Belle had taken all the steps as they came to her even to the edge of death itself and had been delivered for which she was eternally grateful. She often thought of, *Trapper John being lost in a thicket of dense undergrowth; if he had taken but one wrong step, she would have died lost in the forest, as she looked upon the dead bodies of her smallpox ridden parents.* Gratitude had come to her heart because of the knowledge she gained by experiencing God's unending mercy and grace. Because her lessons had been learned by the harshness of reality, she intended to never squander even one minute of time on the childishness of self-pity. She knew she had been spared for a reason and she was ready to forego the falsity of pleasure to experience the reward God had planned for her life.

Dan could see the depths of her commitment because his family's experiences had been very similar to Mary Belles. As they were visiting one morning, Dan asked her if she would really like to become involved in learning all the British had planned to start another war. Mary Belle told Dan, "Up to now, all our suspicions had been guess work. I am willing to learn but we are going to need a good instructor. Dan told her he had been sent to that area by his commanding officer to learn all he could. That information made Mary Belle feel more comfortable about her new adventure. Dan asked her about Sam. She gave Dan information on his back ground and she said, "The truth is, he is our protector." Dan said, "You made a wise decision having him here. He has warrior blood in him." Mary Belle told Dan, "He is half Cherokee." Dan said, "That makes us brothers, because my Godfather was Chief Attakullakulla of the East Tennessee tribe." Mary Belle said, 'You know what Dan, all the sudden I am beginning to feel more safe." Dan said, "You are safe." Dan asked her if she was willing to become a spy for the United States of America. Mary Belle asked, "Does that mean I have to shut the trading post down?" Dan answered, "No, for goodness sake, this place provides all of us the perfect cover that will give the enemy a reason to talk more about what they are doing." Mary Belle asked Dan to tell her the first rule. Dan told her he didn't want to hurt her feelings, but the most important lesson is, to keep your mouth shut; the second rule is listen good to everything you hear. He told her most of the people who come to her place want to talk about buying and selling. But, whenever someone starts asking questions, everyone needs to be on the alert. Dan said, "You could become a good spy because no one would ever suspect someone as young and pretty as you are to be their enemy." No one had ever told Mary Belle she was pretty before. All the sudden, she started thinking about *if her hair was combed.*

Mary Belle was blessed by God with beauty, innocence and joy. Mary Belle came to Natchez as an orphan but, regardless of the sorrow, she had known she was the happiest person most people had ever known. There was something born in her that made her try her best to always make other people happy. Most people could see her walking their way and they knew when she talked to them they were going to be happy. It was just a gift. That was why Dan wanted her help because he knew she would never be suspected by the enemy.

Since Dan was her trainer, he told her she had to take an oath. Mary Belle asked, "About what?" Dan said, "You've got to tell me you agree to uphold the laws of the United States." When he said that, Mary Belle went to laughing. Dan asked her what she was laughing about because this was serious stuff. She told him that she hadn't ever broken a law and wasn't gonna start by breaking a United States government law. Dan said, "That's good enough for me." He was thinking to himself, t*hat is the first time he had ever heard her laugh. he liked it and wanted to hear it more often.*

Mary Belle had become so proud of Harry. He was becoming a man and could handle his part of the work. She didn't want any harm coming to him which is why she didn't want him knowing about her working as a spy. She made up her mind she wasn't telling anybody her business with the government.

One morning, Mary Belle and Dan were drinking coffee in the kitchen when he said, "The British are going to put people in this area that look and act like they are wanting to move here. He said, "Those are the ones we have got to watch because they will buy a place for the others to come in and stay." Mary Belle was learning more and more about being a spy as she listened to every word Dan said to her. One morning she asked Dan, "Where did you learn all this spy business?" Dan told her, "One of these days, I will tell you everything."

One morning, Dan became suspicious of a customer. He kept a close eye on him because he had come to the place in a boat from the other side of the river. The stranger had bought enough groceries to feed several people. Dan made Mary Belle aware of him being a suspect, so she began asking questions in a playful manner about him gaining too much weight. The man was attracted to her which caused him to say, "It is not just for me." Mary Belle looked across the store at Dan who was listening to his every word. Mary Belle asked, "Are you intending to take all this in one load?" The man replied, "I've got help to meet me on the other side." Dan thought to himself, t*his is something we are going to have to check out.*

It was near sundown when they put the last sack of corn meal in the boat and the wind had come up which made Dan wonder whether he would make it across the river. Dan told Mary Belle he needed to borrow Sam to help him paddle across the river. Dan borrowed Mary Belle's small boat and Sam. They were dressed and equipped to fight a war. Dan and Sam paddled up the river a good way before they began to attempt the crossing. He knew one man paddling straight across with a high wind would be blown down the river. When they landed on the other side, they pulled the boat on shore and began walking quietly to the south to see if the man had made it back across. After they had walked over 100 yards, Dan and Sam heard the faint sound of several people talking. They didn't hear any dogs barking, which told Dan he did not interrupt a hunting party. Dan and Sam eased closer until they saw a fire about two hundred yards from the river bank. They continued their approach to the point they could plainly hear the men talking. It was obvious to Dan and Sam one man was in charge and it was not a get together of friends. The leader asked, "Did anyone follow you, Sargent?" The Sargent said, "No one is going to follow me in this weather. I am lucky I made it myself, Lieutenant." Dan knew he had found a group of infiltrators, just as he suspected.

Dan's mind was trying to decide his next step. Except for the fire, it was completely dark. There was no doubt they were the enemy. He also knew they were not going anywhere because they were where they had been sent. He whispered to Sam, "*let's find our boat.*" It was nearly midnight when they made it back to the trading post. Mary Belle was still up waiting to hear some news. Dan told her, they are who we thought they were. All we must do is wait and see what develops. The more secure they feel; the more additional troops will come." Mary Belle asked, "Then what?" Dan said, "It will then be up to them as to whether they want to stay alive." Mary Belle asks, "Are you thinking about killing them?" Dan said, "Only if I am forced."

The next day, Dan sent his companion to Memphis with a message requesting orders for the next step. When the return message arrived, it stated, "When their number grows to 20, do what you have to do." The amount of food and supplies they were buying let Dan know the size of the clan. Over the next six weeks, the number increased gradually to the amount that told Dan the matter needed his attention. His command post was near New Orleans on the east side of the river. He told Mary Belle he needed to make a trip to New Orleans to get some help. In two weeks, seven strangers came to the trading post asking to speak to Mr. Dan O'Flaherty. Dan had seen them arrive and was walking toward them when they also saw him. Mary Belle suggested they do their visiting away from the trading post because she was looking for the man from across the river to buy groceries.

They moved their location to the north about 200 yards where the community had church picnics. Dan was at the kitchen the next morning to visit with Mary Belle. She had to admit she was becoming a little anxious since her world had become involved with the beginning of another war that was not in her plans. Dan assured her everything was going according to schedule and the entire matter would be resolved within a few days. Mary Belle asked Dan, "Who are these men?" Dan told her it was of the greatest importance she not know the answer to her question. Dan said, "Let me put it this way, we are men who have been trained to do what has to be done." Mary Belle trusted Dan's judgment and did not discuss it any further. Mary Belle continued to be aware of the intent of everyone who came to buy goods from her. She felt her and Harry were in good hands and she was right because within a very short span of time the annoyance the spies had brought to her life would soon be over.

Dan waited until the wind settled down to eliminate one of the risks of crossing the river with men and equipment. That particular group of Special Force soldiers were night fighters which gave them the advantage over soldiers who had been trained for conventional warfare. The crossing was made without incident. Dan had set 2:00 a.m. as the darkest part of the night for the attack.

Within twenty minutes time, the attack had ended. Their number had grown to eighteen soldiers and all of them had been eliminated. It was the type of warfare that neither side could discuss in a town meeting. Certainly, Great Britain would not admit to having combat soldiers in America. America would not admit that Great Britain had invaded America's shores again. It was a situation that was taken care of by elimination. It was time for the enemy to decide to forego the attack on America the second time.

Within a week, the atmosphere that had surrounded Mary Belle's world was back to normal without anyone questioning the outcome of the interruption. Dan had become what appeared to be a permanent fixture at the trading post. Mary Belle had to admit regardless of his military training, he was good help for her at the trading post.

Mary Belle had been at the trading post since the day Trapper John brought her across the river from Louisiana. She had no experience with boy and girl relationships. Molly and Cale had died and left her with a brother. She guessed her age was close to seventeen. She had no training about holding hands or even liking someone in a special way. It was not something she wanted to get involved with because it took her mind away from business. Her goal was to have a steamboat that traded goods from New Orleans to St. Louis, Missouri and nothing was going to interfere with that.

Mary Belle was glad they had quit taking paper money years before because hard money had become the money to have. She had studied steamboats privately and had never breathed a word about what she was going to do with her money, until one morning while she was talking to Dan. She had come to know Dan and trusted him more than anyone she had ever known. That morning as they drank coffee together, Mary Belle asked Dan what he thought about the trading business. Dan told her it was the best business you could be in, if your name was Mary Belle Harrison Brown, but if your name is Dan O'Flaherty, do not get in the trading business.

Mary Belle decided to tell Dan her plan to make a fortune. Dan was interested in hearing the plan. Mary Belle told him the way to compete in the trading post business is to have the trading post go to the trappers. That got Dan's attention. He said, "Tell me how you do that." Mary Belle said, "Look around this place, what if all you see here came floating up to your campsite instead of you having to come to Natchez to do your trading?" Dan was amazed at the plan Mary Belle had contrived. He thought to himself, s*he will put everyone else out of business that can't afford a steamboat.*

Mary Belle told Dan, "This river is the best thing we have going for us. All we need is a boat to make it useful." Dan asked, "Mary Belle, where in the world would you ever get enough money to buy a steamboat?" Mary Belle grinned and whispered in Dan's ear, *"I've almost got enough."* Dan was astonished at what she had said. Dan asked, "Mary Belle, have you ever thought about having a partner?" Mary Belle said, "It depends on who it is." Dan asked, "What about me?" Mary Belle laughed and said, "The last time I heard, they were paying soldiers 50 cents a day." Dan said, "It is a little less than that, but I have saved my money." Mary Belle said, "You are serious, aren't you?" Dan said, "The best proof of that is for you to tell me how much you need for us to be partners." Mary Belle could tell it was time for her to do some looking and some trading to find the best steamboat on the market that didn't cost too much.

CHAPTER THIRTY-THREE

STEAMBOAT MARY

Dan often inquired of Mary Belle why she enjoyed the river so much. Mary Belle began educating Dan as to the advantages of having a connection with the entire world as a gift from God. Dan had never had a thought that big in his life. Mary Belle would tease Dan about him being afraid to learn more about everything. She told Dan she wanted to know more about everything. Dan ask her, "What is it you want to know about the most?" She told Dan she had been made aware of several men working on a steam powered engine that could power a boat loaded with people over 100 miles. Dan's interest began to wonder, *if she was really on to something.*

She explained the different theories each of the inventors had tried. She told Dan the best invention is the one Robert Fulton is working on. Dan wanted to know what made his engine better than all the others. Mary Belle said, "Not only does it work, the price is affordable and guess what, he did away with the oars and replaced them with paddle wheels front and back. The reason I like his best is, if you run upon a sand bar at night, you can reverse the boat and back off the bar and keep going." Dan was amazed with Mary Belles knowledge. Mary Belle told Dan he needed to get himself focused on what he was going to do to earn a living after he got out of the military service. Mary Belle had convinced him buying a steamboat would be a good investment. Dan asked her how to contact Robert Fulton. She told Dan he was building a steamboat in Pittsburg and had planned to come down the Ohio River and end up in New Orleans. Dan thought to himself, *I need to talk to him before he makes that trip.* Dan asked, "How long would it take for you to get ready to go to Pittsburg?" Mary Belle asked, "What is the fastest way?" Dan told her the best route was the Appalachian Trail. Mary Belle told Dan she didn't know anything about that part of the country. Dan told her it was time she learned.

Dan sent a dispatch to the militia headquarters in Memphis telling them he would be unavailable for two months. He told Mary Belle to make arrangements for someone to take care of the trading post for a month. Mary Belle was in shock. She had always made a practice of being at least several thoughts ahead of whoever she was talking to, but not this time. She was being told what to do, and she was liking it. She was wondering what the difference was about Dan that made him different from all other men. She didn't ask any questions when Dan told her to take some warmer clothes for later.

In two days, they were ready. Dan made ready two pack horses and plenty supplies. From Natchez, they traveled northeast on the road his father had traveled when the war was over. Because of his connection with the Cherokee and having been named by the Chief of the Cherokee Tribe, Dan had passage over all other Indian Territories. When they reached the trail through the mountains, the territory began to become familiar to him. He saw several Cherokee hunting parties. On one occasion, he stopped to visit with one of them. When he told them in the Cherokee language he was God son to Chief Attakullakulla, known as "First Beloved Man," the braves treated him as a brother. One of the groups said, "Two Dan." Dan's eyes lit up, as he smiled pointing at himself saying, "Two Dan." The Indian had remembered the ceremony when "Two Dan" was adopted as a Cherokee. Mary Belle was in an amazed state. She could tell Dan had been other places before he arrived at Natchez. She was learning there was more to Dan than she realized. When the hunting party learned who Dan was they traveled with him for many days. As they traveled along, Dan could tell Mary Belle was becoming adjusted to being in the wilderness. She awoke each morning with a smile he had not recognized before. The Indians continued to travel as guides for several days to protect them. One morning they told him they had to return to their village. When the Indians had gone, Dan began to wonder if Mary Belle would like to learn to shoot a rifle. When he asked her, she responded, "I've been wanting to learn that all my life." Mary Belle liked the mountains. It wasn't long before Dan found an area with mountains high enough to muffle the sounds of the rifle. While Dan was teaching Mary Belle how to operate a rifle, he could tell she was a fast learner. After she had accomplished becoming a marksman, they rested the horses for the remainder of the day. They slept late the next morning because it was mid-morning before the sun came over the mountain. Mary Belle said to herself, *she had never seen anything as beautiful in her life.* Dan was anxious to get to Pittsburg to meet Robert Fulton, but he was enjoying every moment of being with Mary Belle.

Robert Fulton had put together a group of extremely talented men to work on a joint project to build and travel from Pittsburg, Pennsylvania on their specially designed newly built steamboat, "New Orleans," solid enough for a trip down the mid-western Ohio River, with stops at Wheeling, Virginia, Cincinnati, Ohio past the "Falls of

Ohio" at Louisville, Kentucky, to near Cairo, Illinois and juncture with the Mississippi River, past St. Louis and follow the "Big Muddy" as it was acquiring the nickname all the way down past Memphis, Tennessee and Natchez, Mississippi to the City of New Orleans on to the Gulf of Mexico coast. (33)

Mr. Fulton was a very hospitable man. He told Dan of having met his father when he was much younger. Dan revealed his father had passed away a few years ago. Mr. Fulton admitted, "He was my all-time hero" of the Revolution. Eventually, Mr. Fulton asked Dan if he knew anything about the steam engine. He told Mr. Fulton he did not know anything about the progress of the steam engine until Mary Belle told him. Mr. Fulton turned to Mary Belle and began speaking to her. He was surprised by the responses he was getting from a young lady with no apparent claim to any prestigious name or position. He wondered how she could possibly know all she knew about his invention and was baffled by her plan to have a steamboat trading post on the Mississippi River. He thought to himself, t*his young lady will be the beginning of the trading and river transportation business, in the new territory.*

After they had visited a while, Mr. Fulton insisted they have a meal with him. He agreed. Mr. Fulton told Dan of an occasion when he got to shake his father's hand. He told Dan, "All I can remember is, he was a giant." During the meal, Mr. Fulton began to wonder, *whether or not Dan would reveal his purpose for making such a journey.* Finally, Dan told Mr. Fulton they wanted to purchase the "New Orleans" steamboat with one condition. Mr. Fulton asked, "And that is?" Dan told him the condition would be he and Mary Belle would be allowed to make the maiden voyage with them. All Mary Belle could do was listen. She loved the art of trading, but this was way above her expertise. Dan told Mr. Fulton he was aware of the expense he and his partners had invested. He wanted them to complete the vessel with the knowledge they had a purchaser.

Mr. Fulton was overjoyed because he had been involved with many ventures that did not have a pleasant outcome. The next day, Mr. Fulton introduced Dan to his partners and they reached an agreement. Dan sent a courier to Weston Collier who sent him a check for the full amount agreed upon. Dan was certain Mary Belle knew every part of the agreement, except the final purchase price which was far in excess the amount Mary Belle had thought it would cost. Dan allowed her to think she paid the full amount of the vessel.

By the time they reached Natchez, Mississippi, Mary Belle knew enough about all the rivers, she was ready to buy two steamboats. Harry and Sam couldn't believe their eyes when they saw the giant steamboat pulling into the dock with Mary Belle standing in front waving to them.

Dan had made arrangements to travel with Mr. Fulton and his friends to New Orleans and pay their fare on a sailing ship to New York. It took two weeks for Dan to complete his business in New Orleans. Dan hired the captain and the crew to return to Natchez to dock the steamboat. When they docked the boat at the trading post, Mary Belle was there to greet them. When they had time to discuss all they had experienced, she told him how much she thanked him for taking her on the journey of her life. She concluded by telling Dan she felt like she made a good choice when she made him her partner. Mary Belle said, "Dan, I just wanted you to know, I feel like we are more than partners." Dan said, "I am sure we will be."

Harry had made up his mind to learn how to become a steamboat captain. Mary Belle told him he was going to have to learn how to cut wood first. Harry asked, "What is the wood for?" Mary Belle said, "Harry, we have to build a fire to boil water to make steam." Harry said, "I can learn to do that." Mary Belle said, "We'll see."

After a few days, they were back to looking for traitors. Dan received a message from his brother, Cathal. Cathal told him he was being transferred to the northwest to fight the Indians for attempting to make an Indian nation within the borders of the United States of America. Both of General Dan O'Flaherty's sons had always seen themselves joining in a major fight together with the overall strategy to protect one another. Circumstances seemingly were disallowing them fighting together.

Mary Belle could hardly sleep that night because she had a realized dream docked in front of her trading post. She stayed awake that night to walk the decks of her dream come true. Her very active mind was planning her first voyage. She felt a need to establish relationships with major suppliers of goods she needed to supply the customers along the banks of the Mississippi. Her plan was to set up a monthly stop at certain locations along the river. She had a reputation with most all the settlers and fur trappers for doing what she said she would do. She set up a route to meet at certain locations along the river that had a potential landing. Because of knowing most everyone, it didn't take her long to find 20 families that took the responsibility for notifying the neighbors of the landing schedule. She made a bargain to compensate them for their help by reducing the price of the supplies they needed until her next stop.

Another need she had was to find an honest, hardworking, person that could learn the trading business. Dan told her the preacher at the local church had told him of a woman named, Bessie Walker who had lost her husband because he had caught the consumption and died. She had two children named Billy Jeff and Mildred and they were old enough to work. She was left destitute by her husband's death. Mary Belle had a very soft heart for the needy, but when it came to work and responsibility, she was all business. She knew she was going to have to leave some kind of protection for the trading post, but it needed to be knowledgeable protection. She asked Dan because of him being there to search for British spies, if he could take care of the post for her. He told her the post had become a major source of information for him and he would be glad to be of help.

Children raised on the frontier in the later 1700's, were taught two things, (1) work, (2) speak when you are spoken to. When Bessie brought her two children to the trading post, Mary Belle thought to herself, *my goodness, these kids are starving.* Their clothes were what was called, overalls. There was not one inch of their clothes that had not been patched. The suspenders were made from heavy twine. Mary Belle's thoughts went, *back to her years in Abbeville, Louisiana before the smallpox killed her parents.* Mary's heart broke, as she saw their eyes that were wide open and seemingly bewildered. Mary Belle knew exactly how they felt. It reminded her when, *Trapper John brought her to the trading post for the first time.* Mary Belle got up and walked over and gave them a big hug, then asked them if they liked cookies. They looked at their mother, she nodded her approval. Mary Belle had the day's plate full of cookies on the counter, so she handed it to them. Mary Belle asked them if they wanted some fresh milk. Both nodded their approval. Mary Belle marveled at how similar their backgrounds were.

Dan was on the boat with Sam and Harry. They were all ready to build a fire in the boiler. Harry was ready to blow the boat whistle. Dan was ready to see them off on their first trip to New Orleans to stock up on merchandise. Mary Belle told them, "When we get started, stay in the middle of the river except for dodging snags." Even though Mr. Fulton had designed a sturdy bottom for the boat, she didn't want to knock a hole in it on their first trip to New Orleans.

Mary Belle was doing some thinking about, *the two children playing around the dock and maybe even falling in the river.* She went to Bessie and asked her if she would care if the children rode to New Orleans. Bessie said, "If you think it is alright, it must be, go ahead and take them." Mary Belle asked them if they were ready for a boat ride. They smiled saying, "We are ready." It would be hard for anyone to know how good their lives had become from being around Mary Belle just one day as compared with the hopelessness they had always known. Billy Jeff walked up to Harry and asked, "Whatcha want me to do?" Harry told him he didn't know much but it looked like the main job was keeping enough wood burning. Mary Belle overheard Harry getting Billy Jeff lined out and she was proud of him. It reminded her to get some wood chopping tools for them to stop and cut some more wood along the river bank. They got everything loaded and headed out on their first journey on the Big River.

Mary Belle had her eye on the ferry boat crossing the river to the south of where they were docked. Sam and Harry had built up to 220 pounds of pressure. Dan waved good bye and threw the bow and stern line to them. Mary Belle had to blow the whistle, but she knew how much Harry had planned on it. She handed him the cord; he pulled down on it and for the first time in the history of America, a steamboat whistle was heard. The boat whistle began as more of a deep bellowing sound and as the pressure on the cord lessened, the whistle became more mellow. One could almost hear the female bull frogs discussing the new sound of which, the substance of the conversation would probably have been, "Now, that's a bull frog." For sure it was different than any sound that had ever been heard before and after the Louisiana Purchase.

Mary Belle felt much better when she knew they had not collided with the ferry. The fact that the boat was moving, and no one was paddling was a new way to travel. Mary Belle's mind was always working with the flood gate of thought going wide open. In her mind, she began to see people riding on a much larger boat with as many as 100 people. When it began to get dark, Sam asked her if they should tie up for the night. Mary Belle told him to find a good tree to secure it for a while. Sam let the boilers cool down before he pulled over to tie to a tree. Sam told Harry they needed to keep some steam up with a little wood over night to give them a good start in the morning. To Mary Belle where they were, was strange country. She told Harry and Sam to get the gun ready in case they had tied up next to some outlaws. She had heard her daddy telling her mama, t*he woods were full of outlaws.* He had said that more than ten years ago. Mary Belle fixed her crew a good supper on a fire she had made on shore. It didn't take long for them to get sleepy.

Sam made sure enough wood was in the boiler to keep up a touch of steam for leaving in the morning. About 2:14 a.m., he heard a noise on the river bank and it didn't sound like an animal. Then he heard a muffled cough which he knew was human. His only question was, "How many of them were there?" Sam didn't wait to find out. He went to the back of the boat and jumped to shore. He stood up by a tree that allowed him to see between the shore line and the boat. There was enough moonlight to tell that Sam's half Cherokee culture was fixing to get serious. He began by getting on his hands and knees to make certain he didn't step on a dry limb and snap it. He crawled about half way from the stern to the bow. He could make out two men. He didn't wonder if they were up to no good, he knew they were. He began crawling more to the west to try to get behind them. He could hear their footsteps. One of the men had made his way to the boat while the other was about 30 feet behind him. When he tried to walk by Sam stood up and cut his throat before he could make a sound. He let the man slide out of his arms to the ground without a sound. Sam gently pulled the body out of the path. He waited for about 20 minutes and here came the other one to check on his partner. Sam stuck him in the throat with his knife while he used the man's hair to pull his head back. The second man was dead also. Sam went back to the boat to keep the boiler hot until day break.

The next morning, just before the sun rose, Sam told Mary Belle he didn't want to cook breakfast there because it would take too much time. All he wanted was a hand full of cookies and he was ready to go. Mary Belle knew they would reach New Orleans before dark, which kept her excited. Billy Jeff and Mildred didn't want anything but Mary Belle's cookies for breakfast. Harry was satisfied also. Mary Belle had brought some smoke sausage for lunch. She asked Sam if he thought the boiler was hot enough to boil some water. Sam told her to come look and then tell him if it was hot enough. Mary Belle put a pot near the furnace and the water was boiling in five minutes. She boiled the sausage, warmed some biscuits and gave them a sweet dough cake for dessert. Again, everyone was full and happy.

As the sun began setting, they pulled into the New Orleans harbor. There were several sailing ships tied to the dock. Mary Belle wanted a private dock because she knew they would be loading the boat for at least two days. Sam pulled into a private area which pleased Mary Belle. When they had tied the boat, she said, "Either Harry or Sam needs to stay with the boat. Sam said, "Mam, I need to go with you." Mary Bell knew Sam meant what he said. She told Harry to keep his gun handy and to remember this steamboat is the only one of its kind, which means someone will steal it, if you let them. Harry told her he would take care of it. She told the three of them to clean the deck for them to have a place to put the new merchandise.

Mary Belle had a list of supplies and she was ready to do some trading. The first place they stopped was a hardware store. She asked to speak to the storeowner, whose name was Ned Culligan. When they had gathered in Mr. Culligan's office, he asked how he could help. Mary Belle revealed her entire plan to Mr. Culligan who was wishing he had thought of her plan first. When she told him about the steamboat, she had bought, he knew Mary Belle was who and what she said she was. She told Mr. Culligan it appeared to her she would be back in New Orleans almost every thirty-five days to get more supplies. She then said, "What I am trying to do is find probably ten major merchants who can supply the goods I need at the price I intend to pay. Mr. Culligan asked, "Cash or Credit?" She said, "Hard money is all I know anything about." Is that cash or credit?" Mr. Culligan said, "It will do." Mary Belle gave him the list and asked him to bid on what it would take to buy that load of goods. He told her she didn't need to go anywhere else, all she needed to do was tell him what the price had to be. Mary Belle had already figured her profit from the list. When Mr. Culligan's price was $150.00 better than she had figured, she said, "Mr. Culligan you are right, I don't need to go anywhere else." For two days, she met with suppliers where she bargained, agreed and paid every one of them with hard money and loaded her boat with the goods.

When she returned to the boat after meeting all the major merchandise owners, she found a steamboat cleaned and ready to receive cargo. Mary Belle was thinking to herself about how, *to best teach Harry, Billy Jeff and Mildred the trading business.* She decided Harry needed to learn how to be boat captain first. She put the question of what to teach Billy Jeff and Mildred on hold. She said to herself, "*I can train anybody who is not lazy, and they are not lazy.*"

The ride back took exactly twice the amount of time it took to go to New Orleans. The boat was loaded to the hilt which was something she told herself, *would never happen again because it was too big of a risk.* Sam noticed the buzzards had started gathering where he had left the two bodies. Mary Belle asked, "Wonder what they are after?' Sam said, "Something already dead."

Dan and Bessie met the boat, tied the lines, and welcomed everyone back home. Bessie was so glad to see Billy Jeff and Mildred. They could hardly wait to tell their mother how big the earth is. Billy Jeff said, "Mama, if the earth is as big the other way as it was where we went, I'm telling you, the earth is a tremendous big place." Bessie smiled and said, "Billy Jeff, what if I told you it is bigger than that." Billy Jeff stared toward heaven and said, "Goll..eee! this is a big place."

Bessie took her two by the hand to get to where they could tell her the most exciting story of their lives. Mary Belle had the job of deciding what to leave on the boat or unload. She told them, "No matter what we do, it's going to be wrong. This first load is hard to figure out, but it will get easier as we move along and start knowing what we are doing."

After they all had made their best guess, Mary Belle told them to get some rest. She told Sam to sleep on the boat to make sure someone didn't steal anything. Dan asked Mary Belle, "Why don't you let Sam get some good rest and let me stand guard duty?" Mary Belle said, "That sounds like a whole lot better plan." Sam said, "Sure sounds like it to me." Sam was tired. He had been up three nights in a row, and she didn't know it, but he wouldn't turn her down for anything. Sam wasn't about to let anyone hurt Mary Belle's feelings about anything, but he felt better when Dan gave him some relief.

The next morning, Dan was thinking to himself, *I am sure glad we buried those spies. I thought by now someone would be looking for their location.* Dan didn't realize how right he was because as the next day began, a group of three what Dan guessed to be spies, began asking questions about some surveyors. No one remembered the men and they moved on further down the river.

The time was drawing near for Mary Belle to make her first trading trip up the river. She had to guess the amount of supplies she would need. She had sent out the word she would be on the river the first week of June. She had thought of what she believed was everything, except the crew she intended to take. Just before she was ready to leave, she was talking to Dan asking him if she had forgot anything.

Dan wanted Mary Belle to realize how vulnerable she would be up and down the river because as he said, "Everyone is going to know you have money aboard. All I am asking you to do is check the place out good before you get close enough for them to take a shot." Dan's concern for her made her feel so good. She finally said, "Well, Dan if you want me to be really safe, you can take Harry's place, but I want to ask you, "What do you think about Bessie being able to take care of the place?" Dan said, "Mary Belle, the woman is a natural born trader. Right now, she's carrying a load of grief from a dead husband but as soon as she gets reconciled to him being gone, she is going to do good." Mary Belle told Dan, "Both of those children have good sense. They are going to help take care of their mama." Mary Belle asks Dan, "Are you going with me?" Dan half smiled and said, "Let me put it this way, you are not leaving here without me, understand?" Mary Belle smiled and said, 'You're coming around pretty good, ain't cha?" You could tell I wanted you to go with me, couldn't you?" Dan said, "I had begun to wonder."

The next morning, they launched out into an adventure that was going to make history. They were met by family after family that had needs Mary Belle could handle for them. Everyone knew Mary Belle and the first thing they wanted was some of her cookies and dough bread. Toward evening was when Dan began to become leery. His thinking was, *thieves could lure them into the bank at dark, kill them, steal all they wanted and be twelve hours away from the river by day light.* He asked Mary Belle, "Let's only stop for those you know. This could get dangerous."

Right at dark, Mary Belle saw a light not far up the river. Sam and Dan were looking for any signs of trouble. Then Mary Belle heard a familiar voice that cried out, "Mary Belle it's me, Carolyn Sue Warner." Mary Belle's face lit up; she hollered back, "We will be there in a minute." Sam and Dan were on their toes looking for any sign of trouble. Dan threw the rope to Carolyn's husband and the boat came to a stop. Mary Belle had in her mind, *my goodness, what a blessing, we can stay with the Warner's tonight.*

Dan let the walkway down and as he passed her husband, Delton Warner, he whispered, *be careful!* Dan went to full alert. He turned and said, "Mary Belle, reach for the tobacco in my coat pocket before you leave the boat." Mary Belle knew Dan didn't use tobacco and Sam didn't either. When Dan got to the fire, a voice said, "Keep your hand away from your weapon and tell the others to come on and warm up." Dan said, "Ya'll hurry up, this fire is comfortable. Sam did not have a clear rifle shot from the captain's chair. He grabbed his pistol and knife and began walking down the walkway. He turned and whispered to Mary Belle, "Keep looking for the tobacco." Mary Belle knew there was something very wrong going on. Sam walked over by Dan and the same man said, "Keep your hand away from your weapon, or I will kill her." A total of three characters stepped into the light of the fire, one of which was holding Mrs. Warner with his knife at her throat. Dan assured them they had no intention of causing any trouble, but just wanted to know what it would take to just be left alone. The one who had done the talking said, "Money, and whatever else we want." Dan said, "Let me assure you, there is not anything more important than our lives, just tell us what to do." When the robber heard Dan's desperation, he turned the woman loose, at which time Sam's knife blade hit him in the throat and as he was taking his turn to die, the other two were wondering how a knife got in one of their throats while the other two was wondering how he was shot in the heart. All three dropped to the ground dead as Mrs. Warner fell to her knees as her husband ran to catch her before she fell. Mary Belle walked down the walkway with her gun wanting to kill them after they were dead. Delton Warner said, "We owe you our lives. They were going to kill us until they heard the boat coming closer." Dan said, "I am glad we came along when we did. The three men dug a grave apiece, while Carolyn Sue and Mary Belle cooked a light supper.

The next morning as Mary Belle was leaving she said, "Ya'll need a good dog if you are going to stay on the river." They all laughed as good friends had just become better friends from the tragedy that almost occurred.

CHAPTER THIRTY-FOUR

THE WAR

They continued for two more stops the next morning and then made a left turn to go south on the west side of the river. The first stop was J.W. Henry an old customer of Mary Belle's. He said, "I seen you working the other side yesterday and I knowed you was coming over here today." J.W. was half fisherman and half trapper. He asked Mary Belle if she could use some good fresh catfish. Mary Belle told him she needed thirty pounds, if he had it. J.W. told her he had a 40-pound yellow catfish he would let her have for $1.00. She agreed but told him he needed to get the hide off of it first, so she could get to cooking, because everybody was hungry. He told her he was going to start salting the fish meat down soon and needed for her to bring him 200 pounds of salt. J.W. had built up a good trade with fresh catfish, dried and salted down.

When they had completed the trip, Mary Belle had money on her mind. She needed to know if they had made any money, and if so, how much. Dan could tell the trade goods were down to 25% of what they had when they started. Mary Belle got quiet and went off to herself in the bow of the boat. After an hour, she came to get Dan to check her figuring. She had taken the inventory of what was left, subtracted that from what they started with and had more than doubled their money. She told Dan they could use half the money they had taken in to buy more goods and put their profit in a sock for a rainy day. Dan could tell from the brightness of her Irish eyes, she was happier than he had ever seen her before. Dan was so proud of her. He knew the dreams, plan, prayer and effort she had invested as well as all her money to hope something would happen that could change her life, forever.

As Dan was partaking of her grace filled moment, his mind was beginning to focus on, *the preparation necessary to fight a war.* His strategy was to keep the British contained in the Gulf of Mexico to prevent the hordes of British troops from going north up the river to meet those British who were invading from the north.

It had begun to appear the British and the United States were doing all they could to avoid the open conflict. But, it seemed no matter how sincere their efforts were, the ingredients to cause a war continued to mount. One of the ingredients was brought about because of the trade restrictions caused by the war between France and Great Britain. The second element that inflamed the Americans was the British had impressed 10,000 American merchant sailors into the Royal Navy, which was nothing more than the continued practice of slavery they had practiced with the Irish and Scotts for decades. The British policy was to force other nations to yield to their desire. The third cause was the British covertly involving themselves with the disagreement between the Indians Confederacy of the northwest tribes and the frontier expansion of the American European settlers. The forth unsettled issue was what had become known as the "Chesapeake-Leopard Affair," that occurred off the coast of Norfolk, Virginia in 1807. It was a Naval engagement between the British warship HMS Leopard, and the American frigate USS Chesapeake. Rumors were being talked about British sailors deserting from the British Navy and forming the American Navy. The real proof was going to be determined by examining the crews of the American Navy. The British warship Leopard located the American frigate Chesapeake and launched an attack and boarded the vessel looking for deserters from the Royal Navy. The Chesapeake was caught unprepared and after a short battle involving broadsides received from Leopard the Commander of the Chesapeake, surrendered his vessel to the British. The Chesapeake fired only one shot. Four crew members were removed from the American vessel and were tried for desertion. One of them was later hanged. Chesapeake was allowed to return to America to where James Barron was court martialed and suspended from command. The American interpretation of the incident was the British had committed an act of war. President Thomas Jefferson attempted a hollow bluff by talking war which ultimately became reduced to the Embargo of 1807. The fifth cause was the American interest in expanding its borders westward.

The succeeding President, James Madison sent a message to Congress for war to be declared against Great Britain in June 1812. (34) When the declaration of war against England was made, America's warriors stepped forward to again protect the shores of freedom.

The war would be fought in three theatres. First, at sea, warships and privateers of each side attacked the enemy's merchant ships, while the British blockaded the Atlantic Coast of the United States and mounted large raids in the later stages of the war. Second, land and naval battles were fought on the US-Canadian frontier. Third, large scale battles were fought in the Southern United States and Gulf Coast.

Dan and Cathal received messages from General Andrew Jackson to meet with him in Memphis, Tennessee. Upon arrival, one of the first statements the General made was, "We are going to have the opportunity of our lives to fight like your father taught us to fight and the best part is, it is against his same old enemy."

He told them he had decided to call for 50,000 volunteers to get ready for an invasion of Canada. He told Cathal to continue in his efforts against the confederacy of Indian tribes led by Chief Tecumseh which was supported by the British with weapons and ammunition. General Jackson wanted the British defeated and abolished from all financial interest in the Western Hemisphere. The British were determined to maintain as much of Canada as they could, but America was determined to protect the frontier settlers as they expanded the borders of America westward. There was not a cause for the Americans to attack Canada to annex the land. The leaders saw the defeat of the British in Canada as a method to change the British trade policies and correct the national insults that had offended the American honor. (32)

General Jackson determined the Indians to be the threat to American's expansionist desires for land in the south and northwest. He saw the defeat of the Creek Indians as a method of ending the hostility in Florida as the only way to open expansion of desired lands in Alabama and Florida. Businessmen in the south and north supported expansion as a clear cause for Americas involvement in the war, as well as to defend against the British that had been a threat to America since the sound of the last shot was fired in the American Revolutionary War. King George III wanted America returned to his toy chest for him to pour out his venom on Irish Catholic slaves and every other species of humanity he held in disrepute.

Of the available Generals to fight against the British with the tenacity and will to win, General Andrew Jackson stood alone and above every other military commander in the War of 1812. (30) He knew the British mind and had suffered their form of cruelty. General Jackson was given a command in the field against the Creek Indians who were allied with the British and who were a threat to the southern frontier. (35)

The Battle of Burnt Corn between Red Stick Creeks and US troops, occurred in the southern parts of Alabama on July 27, 1813, prompted the State of Georgia as well as the Mississippi Territory Militia to immediately take major action against Creek offensives. The Red Stick Chiefs gained power in the east along the Alabama Coosa, and Tallapoosa Rivers Upper Creek territory. The Lower Creek lived along the Chattahoochee River. Many Creeks tried to remain friendly to the United States, and some were organized by Federal Indian Agent, Benjamin Hawkins to aid the 6th Military District under General Thomas Pinckney and the state militias. The United States combined forces were large. At its peak, the Red Stick faction had 4,000 warriors, only a quarter of whom had muskets.

Before 1813, the Creek War had been largely an internal affair sparked by the ideas of Tecumseh farther north in the Mississippi Valley, but the United States was drawn into a war with the Creek Nation by the War of 1812. The Creek Nation was a trading partner of the United States actively involved with Spanish and British trade as well. The Red Sticks, as well as many southern Muskogean people like the Seminole, had a long history of alliance with the Spanish and

British Empires. This alliance helped the North American and European powers protect each other's claim to the territory in the south. On August 18, 1813, Red Stick chiefs planned an attack on Fort Mimms, north of Mobile, the only American held port in the territory of West Florida. The attack on Fort Mimms resulted in the death of 400 settlers and became an ideological rallying point for the Americans.

The Indian frontier of western Georgia was the most vulnerable but was fortified already. From November 1813 to January 1814, Georgia's militia and auxiliary Federal troops from the Creek and Cherokee Indian nation and the States of North and South Carolina organized the fortifications of defense along the Chattahoochee River and expeditions into upper Creek territory in Alabama. The army led by General John Floyd, went to the heart of the "Creek Holy Grounds" and won a major offensive against one of the largest Creek towns at Battle of Autosee, killing an estimated 200 people. In November, the militias of Mississippi with a combine 1200 troops attacked the "Econachca" encampment (Battle of Holy Ground) on the Alabama River. Tennessee raised a militia of 5,000 under General Jackson and Coke and won the battles of Tallushatchee and Talladega in November 1813. In 1814, General Jackson moved south to attack the Creek. On March 26, 1814, General Jackson and General John Coffee decisively defeated the Creek Indian force at Horseshow Bend, killing 800 of 1,000 Creeks at a cost of 49 killed and 154 wounded out of approximately 2,000 American and Cherokee forces.

The American forces moved to Fort Jackson on the Alabama River. On August 9, 1814, the Upper Creek Chiefs and Jackson's army signed the "Treaty of Fort Jackson." The most of western Georgia and part of Alabama was taken from the Creeks to pay for expenses borne by the United States. The Treaty also "demanded" that "Red Stick" insurgents cease communicating with the Spanish or British, and only trade with the United States approved agents. Once the threat of the Creek Indians was eliminated, General Jackson and Dan moved their forces to New Orleans in late 1814. The army of 1,000 regulars and 4,000 militia, pirates and other fighters as well as slaves and civilians built a fortification south of the city.

On January 8, 1815, a British force of 8,000 battle hardened troops under General Edward Pakenham attacked Jackson's defense in New Orleans. The Americans won the victory and the British suffered high casualties; 291 dead, 1,262 wounded, and 484 captured or missing. The Americans suffered 13 dead, 39 wounded and 19 missing. The victory was hailed as a great victory across the United States making Jackson a national hero and eventually propelling him to the presidency.

After the victory, General Jackson asked Dan to visit with him before he returned to duty in Natchez. The General asked Dan if there was anything he could do for him. Dan told him he had seized a steamboat from a lady in Natchez, named Mary Belle, to be used as a troop transport. and with his permission, he would like to return the boat to her. The General responded by asking, "I am assuming you have a personal interest in returning the boat to her." Dan said, "Very much so, because I am thinking of marrying her." The General said, "You can take the boat with you to Natchez." Dan asked the General what his plans were for the future. The General said, "Dan, I have had the opportunity to learn more about politics in America I ever thought I was capable of comprehending. Your father afforded me an education and a living, I would never have had any idea would be available to me, because I had no connections with anyone by birth or otherwise. During that period of education, I learned American politics has caused America to become for sale and has for the most part been purchased by wealthy industrialist in the north. The problem is, our freedom goes with the bargain. The wealthy of this nation has bought the freedom we won from the British." Dan asked, "What can we do to regain our country?"

The General responded, "We need another political party because presently there is only one party which is the party of the rich and powerful who are in the process of creating a one bank policy that will control all the money in America. That is dangerous, because one person will decide for everyone else who can borrow money and who can't." Dan asked, "What do we have to do to get started?" General Jackson told Dan his strategy was to follow the frontier and enlist people like us to join the Democrat Party. We have got to get our people interested in politics because whoever is in office, represents all of us and I can tell you the people I know in the Congress are not interested in you and me." Dan asked, "When do we get started?" General Jackson said, "Now!" Dan said, "Let me know how much money you need, and I will try to help you get America great again."

General Jackson asked about his mother. Dan told him she is doing wonderful. She has some of her grandchildren around her and that makes her very happy. I am thinking about taking the boat back to Mary Belle and then going to see her." The General said, "Don't ever miss an opportunity to see your mother. You will regret it forever. Tell Mary Belle how much we appreciate the use of her steamboat and that I will be by to visit with her someday."

Sam had waited for Dan while he was talking with the General. When Dan saw him he asked him, "Do you know where the steamboat is?" Sam said, "I think we can find it." They found it at the docks. Sam got on the boat and built a fire to heat the water for steam. Within two hours, they were on their way to Natchez. When they reached the big bend before being able to see the trading post, Dan pulled the steamboat whistle cord and he began to see people coming to the river bank to see the boat.

When they arrived at the dock, Mary Belle had never known the joy she was getting from her loved ones returning home alive. She couldn't help it, she had to shed some tears. When the walkway hit the dock, she ran to grab Dan. He held her and whispered, "I take it you missed me." Mary Belle said, "I don't know why, but I did a little bit." They laughed together because her heart was broken when they weren't together. Then Sam walked up and Mary Belle said, "My own personal Cherokee Indian, my goodness have I missed you!" Sam didn't think he could ever blush, but sure enough Mary Belle showing special affection for him almost brought him to tears. She said, "Sam, if you shed a tear it's from your daddy because Indians don't cry." Sam laughed for the first time in his life.

When they went to the trading post there were the Walkers. They loved Dan and the Walkers loved him. He asked Billy Jeff and Mildred, "How big are ya'll gonna get?" They laughed, Mary Belle went to cooking. She knew Dan, Sam and Harry were ready for a sit-down meal where someone could say, "Pass the biscuits." They were tired of military food. They wanted to eat Mary Belle's cooking. But what else they wanted was a bed of their own to sleep on. They were tired of sleeping sitting up and lying on the ground especially in the Louisiana swamp.

When they got up the next morning to drink coffee, Dan told her what the war had done to New Orleans. He told her he thought it would take some time for the supply businesses to re-open. Mary Belle asked Dan what he had in mind to do if they were not going to be spying on people. Dan said, "I am glad you asked me that." Mary Belle asked, "Why?" Dan replied, "Because I want to go see my mama, my family, my home and everything else that is in Savannah, Georgia, but, most of all I want her to meet Mary Belle." Mary Belle asked, "Why do you want her to meet a little old thing like me?" Dan thought a minute and said, "Because, I want her to meet her daughter-in-law before we get married." Mary Belle asked, "Are you sure you want to do that?" Dan looked at her and said, "I'm sure." Mary Belle said, "You know Dan, with the whole country starting over, it probably is a good time to do some family visiting." Dan said, "It's always a good time to visit your mama." Mary Belle asked Sam if he and Harry could take care of things for them for a few weeks while they visited Dan's mama. Sam told her not to worry about anything, she deserved a vacation. Mary Belle knew Bessie Walker could manage the business with Sam and Harry to do whatever she needed.

The road home was familiar to Dan because the Natchez Trace began going northeast at Natchez. The land was fertile, rich soil and was later to become known as the State of Mississippi. Mary Belle was living far beyond her expectations for herself and was enjoying every moment of the hope and joy Dan had brought to her life. Mary Belle felt secure with Dan. For the first time in her life she had found a trustworthy soul mate.

As they traveled, Dan told her all he remembered his father teaching him about the different cultures of the tribes of Indians. She was amazed how Dan had no fear of the Indians. She noticed he was on his guard when white men came upon them in the woods. She asked him the difference. He told her the Indians didn't have the same value system as white people. Indians seek food every day they are alive. White men want money and valuable things. Dan's father had eliminated many white men in his travels through America. Being Attakullakulla's God son was a gift that blessed him every day of his life. Runaway slaves were dangerous to everyone. They were usually starving and had no trust for anyone. Dan had never had the occasion of having to resolve a problem with any of them.

Dan and Mary Belle enjoyed every moment of being with one another. Mary Bell asked Dan what he thought they might end up doing. Dan told her she had really come up with the best business he had seen in his life time. He told her the shipping and transportation business was the future of America, because of the Big River. He also told her he wanted to talk with Robert Fulton again about modifications to the steamboat design. He said, "Mary Belle can you even imagine traveling four miles an hour up the river and eight miles an hour going down the river? I think the steamboat and the steam engine were made for that big river. You have access to all the water you need, free; you also have all the firewood you need, free. No business could ask for better than that combination. I have a feeling cotton is going to make us enough money to live on." Mary Belle ask him, "What does cotton have to do with steamboats?" Dan said, "Mary Belle, the south is going to grow the cotton, the north is going to wear it and we are going to haul it both ways." Mary Belle asked,

"What about my trading post?" Dan said, "Knowing you, you'll probably need four boats." Every time Mary Belle talked to Dan, she got more excited about the future.

As they entered the west side of Georgia, Mary Belle asked him for a hint about his mother. Dan said, "She is Irish." Mary Belle asked, "What is Irish?" Dan said, "That is what you are." Mary Belle asked, "How did I get to be Irish?" Dan said, "Your mother and father were Irish, so you are Irish." Dan said, "When your parents are from Ireland, you are Irish. When you are from England, you are English. When you are from Germany, you are a German." Mary Belle told Dan, "Thank you for telling me that, I didn't know." Dan said, "That is something we will work on as the questions come up." Mary Belle said, "Dan, it will probably take us at least a little time to work all the problems out, what do you think?' Dan said, "I think we are on our way to a good life with one another. We share unwavering faith in the true and living God. We also share the belief, He sent His Son to give us hope of being included with His chosen people to share with them, by our adoption, in the Holy of all Holy places called heaven. We share the belief that common sense or human reason is not the basis of the true law of man, because that approach is based on a lack of faith in God. Faith in God is the basis of all truth. Common sense and faith are as different from one another as the natural life is from the spiritual and impulsiveness is from inspiration. Nothing Jesus Christ ever said is common sense, but is a revelation sense and is complete, whereas common sense falls short. We believe and share that the natural law of God lives, moves and controls our very being and these are the fundamental beliefs that must be in effect in our lives as opposed to the worship or obedience to a monarch or a government and its laws.

Mary Belle, this is what we believe. This will be, what we will teach our children. This is, what my parents taught me. This was the light my parents saw as slaves of a demonic government and was willing to die to save their neighbors, friends and loved ones from the bloody hands of a despotic ruler. We now see their efforts have achieved a reality called, America.

At first glance, America looks like a piece of good dirt. At second glance, it looks like a good place to raise a family. At third glance, we see it as the only nation on earth where God used the hands and minds of good men to create a home for the brave in a land that is free, governed by the natural laws of God and a few folks they elect to enact laws to assist them in learning to love their neighbors as they love themselves. The net effect of all the blood that has been shed, all the effort that has been expended and all the money that it cost has produced a culture blended from every culture known to man and that one culture is now referred to as Americans. From the outside the American culture appears tough and durable but the truth is it is a very delicate balance of the elements of the best that all cultures have to offer as a heritage. That perfection must be protected at all costs. My prayer for this soon to become a great nation, is that we will avoid the temptation to become worshippers of ourselves because the worship of man's abilities is humanism, not the worship of God. But, I have faith there will always be at least one among us who will step forward to relight the eternal flame of the hunger and thirst for righteousness and freedom. If a man and a woman can join themselves to a goal such as that, I think the foundation of their relationship has a solid base, what do you think?" Mary Belle was taken by the words Dan had said, because she knew it was from his heart. She said, "Dan, take all you just said and add a touch of God's grace and we will have a good life."

They had not gone much further, when Dan recognized the road to the O'Flaherty home. The thrill of being close to his mother made him stick the spurs a little harder in the horse's flank. Mary Belle joined her heart to his excitement. He knew his mother would be in the back yard doing something. When they arrived, he didn't even slow down at the front of the house. He went to the back and there was his beautiful mother with her Irish sunbonnet to protect her tender skin ready to hold her son in her arms once again. Dan had grown so much, she told him, "I thought it was your daddy. My goodness look at you! Someone has been feeding you proper food." Dan said, "And mama, I brought that someone with me for you to meet." Mary could tell right off he had chosen from deep within the Irish culture to select a mate. Mary said, "Come here pretty girl and let me look at you." She said, "Dan, if you have been thinking about keeping on looking for a darling, my thinking is, you have found her." Mary looked at Mary Belle and asked her name. Mary Belle was so completely swallowed up in all the refinement and luxury, she could hardly speak. But, what took her breath was, Dan's mother was so real and gracious, as if none of her surroundings affected her in any manner. She finally told Mary her name. Mary said, "You are such a precious darling, come sit in the swing and tell me where you're from." While they were talking, a servant brought a tray of eats and drinks. Dan pulled up his father's favorite resting chair and just listened to the blessed harmony of the two spirits God had given to him. Mary Belle began at the beginning in the swamps of Louisiana and didn't miss a single event that brought her to be found by Trapper John who brought her to the river to the love and care of Cale and Molly Brown. Mary Belle told Mary, "It was as if God took one family and put me with another one with as much love as I could ever hope for."

Then Mary Belle thought, *it was time to share her prospective mother-in-law the other side of her serious side.* Mary Belle told her, "And then, along came this tall, quiet soldier boy dressed in a buckskin suit looking for help to find traitors and there went my peace-loving life. All the sudden, I found myself looking up in trees, under rocks, bridges, creek bottoms and everywhere else for anyone that was even thinking about hurting Americans." Mary began to smile realizing the humor Mary Belle intended. Mary had that same blend of humor to an otherwise serious manner. They talked on and on. Mary Belle's life story was so interesting Mary had reached that point she was wondering what Mary Belle was going to say next. Mary didn't want to miss a word of what she had to say. It had been a long time since she heard Irish laughter. After they finished the evening meal, it didn't take long before time to rest had caught up with them. Dan asked Mary Belle if she wanted to bathe, outside or inside the house. Mary Belle asked him if there was a tub in her room. Dan said, "Well, of course." She said, "I'll save the outside bathing for later, thank you."

The next morning, Mary looked as if she was ten years younger. Laughing was just what she had needed. They ate breakfast and went to the barn to choose a horse to ride while they surveyed the land. When they were upstairs dressing, the dogs started barking. Mary said to herself, *we don't have accidental visitors, I wonder who that is?* When she opened the shade and saw riding toward the house was another soldier coming to see her. She hurriedly finished dressing and was down stairs as quick as she could just in time to see Cathal dismounting from his horse. Mary's heart sunk. She could not believe her eyes. Both of her soldiers were home at the same time. Mary, Dan and Mary Belle rushed outside for the family to hold one another close. Cathal looked at his brother and said, "We made it!" Dan said, "We made it!" Mary said, "This is what prayer is all about!"

The family had more joy than had come to them in all their days. They knew they had done everything in their power to win the war, and they had survived as their father had done so many times. They had the cook prepare a late breakfast for Cathal. As they sat down to eat, the dogs began barking again. The cook went to the front and opened the door and she hollered, "My Lord, it is Bridget and her bunch, even the banker. They all went to the front just as the horses had stopped by the entrance to the front door. O'Flaherty's started running toward one another ready to touch the flesh of love they had so desperately longed for through the war years.

It was very obvious Bridget was enjoying her Nanny job. She had added another one for her mother to put to sleep in her rocking chair, and with another one due at any time. When they had rested, Mary suggested they walk and or ride to the burial site for their father to enjoy their home coming to be together again.

When they had gathered, Dan thanked God for placing them together as a family in the greatest country in the world known as the United States of America.

THE END

NOTES

1. Eamonn Laidir O'Flaithbertaigh from Wikipedia, The free encyclopedia, Eamonn Laidir O'Flaithbertaigh, Irish Jacobite, died 1749.

2. The Jacobite Uprising of 1745 by Emp. Barbarossa Category: Early Modern: Political History. The Jacobite Uprising of 1745 – All Empires.

3. James Oglethorpe (1696-1785) New Georgia Encyclopedia, Edwin L. Jackson, University of Georgia.

4. History of Florida - Wikipedia, The free encyclopedia.

5. Grace O'Malley, The 16th Century Pirate Queen of Ireland, Ancient Origin From Wikipedia, The free encyclopedia.

6. Brown Bess, From Wikipedia The free encyclopedia

7. Liberty! The American Revolution, Thomas Fleming.

8. Attakullakulla, Wikipedia, The free encyclopedia.

9. Liberty! The American Revolution p.146, Thomas Fleming.

10. Liberty! The American Revolution p.147,Thomas Fleming.

11. Liberty! The American Revolution p. 182, Thomas Fleming.

12. Bernardo de Galvez- Wikipedia, The free encyclopedia.

13. Oliver Pollock Unsung Hero of the American Revolution From the Historian's Corner, Clan Pollock, International.

14. Battle of Kings Mountain from Wikipedia, The free Encyclopedia.

15. Biography of American Revolutionary: Major General Nathanial Greene by Kennedy Hickman, Military History Expert.

16. The American Revolution of The Battle of Cowpens. The Glorious Cause of the American Revolution.

17. Banastre Tarleton, The most complete guide to Banastre Tarleton Facts by Russell Yost.

18. American Revolution: Battle of Guilford Courthouse occurred March 15, 1781 and was part of the Southern campaign and the American Revolution by Kennedy Hickman –Military History Expert.

19. Liberty! The American Revolution by Thomas Fleming.

20. At the Master's Feet, a daily devotional, Selections from the Best of Charles Spurgeon, November 19.

21. Irish Immigration to America. www. Emigration.info/Irish-immigration-in-America.

22. Natchez Trace – Traveled for Thousands of Year, Legends of America, Mississippi Legends, The Natchez Road.

23. Gypsies- The Columbia Electronic Encyclopedia,enclopedia2.the free dictionary.com/Gypsies.

24. The Story of the Irish Race. Seumas MacManus Chapter LIII, The Later Peril Laws p. 454,

25. The Story of the Irish Race, Seumas MacManus, chapter XLVIII, The Rising of 1641.

26. First Inauguration of George Washington, from Wikipedia, the free encyclopedia.

27. Washington's Inaugural Prayer – USA Heritage.org USA heritage, org/Washington'sprayer.html.

28. The Truth about George Washington's Presidential Inaugural Bible by Dr. Catherine Millard.

29. The first coins of the USA, by Dr. Sol Taylor, the Signal Saturday, May 19, 2007.

30. Andrew Jackson – From Wikipedia, the free encyclopedia.

31. The Death of George Washington Mt. Vernon.

32. War of 1812, Wikipedia, the free encyclopedia.

33. Robert Fulton, from Wikipedia, the free encyclopedia.

34. War of 1812, from Wikipedia, the free encyclopedia.

35. War of 1812, from Wikipedia, free encyclopedia, southern Theatre.